Praise for Shirley Kennedy

Three Wishes for Miss Winthrop

4 Stars: "Shirley Kennedy spins a tale sure to pull at the heartstrings of her readers ..."
—*Romantic Times Magazine*

"I highly recommend this enthralling tale of two lovers who meet and overcome various difficulties for themselves and loved ones."
—*AOL Romance Fiction Forum*

The Rebellious Twin

"Clarinda, Lord Robert, and the secondary characters are a delightful mixture of personalities. Enjoy."
—*Rendezvous*

"The best Regency I have read in a very long time. Excellent! Even if you like Historical Romances and NOT Regencies, this one is guaranteed to please. I cannot recommend this book highly enough. Brava!"
—*The Huntress*

"A captivating story of perseverance and dedication .... This book is absolutely fantastic and worth the read .... I had no idea how much I would fall in love with it .... a vivid and moving portrayal ...."

—Lady Victoria Kelly's *Historical Romance Book Reviews*

5 Stars: "Readers will feel they are part of the harrowing wagon train heading west.... The audience will enjoy riding along Heartbreak Trail as gold fever strikes the country."

—Harriet Klausner for *Midwest Book Review*

The Last of Lady Lansdown

The Last of Lady Lansdown

SHIRLEY KENNEDY

CAMEL PRESS

Seattle, WA

CAMEL PRESS

Camel Press
PO Box 70515
Seattle, WA 98127

For more information go to: www.Camelpress.com
www.shirleykennedy.com

Cover design by Sabrina Sun

The Last of Lady Lansdown
Copyright © 2012 by Shirley Kennedy

ISBN: 978-1-60381-818-6 (Paper)
ISBN: 978-1-60381-819-3 (eBook)

LOC Control Number: 2012932492

Printed in the United States of America

Chapter 1

Northern England 1814

To all who knew her casually, even those who knew her well, Jane Elton, Countess of Lansdown, appeared to be a most fortunate woman. Possessed of charm, wit, and a radiant beauty, she had attracted plenty of suitors during her one London season. Although she rejected them all—to the infinite distress of Amelia Hart, her mother—she eventually married the wealthy Arthur Elton, Earl of Lansdown. "A magnificent marriage!" declared Amelia. She had every reason to think so, considering that her husband's gambling led to the family's financial ruin. In the nick of time, Jane's alliance with Lord Lansdown elevated Amelia and her daughters from the brink of poverty to a life of wealth, privilege, and luxury.

That Jane did not love the earl was of little consequence. Despite the earl's lack of compassion and superior air, Amelia felt certain that her daughter would learn to love him in good time and all would be well.

Chatfield Court, Lansdown's ancestral mansion, nestled amidst the trees on a verdant hillside overlooking the River

Hulm. Early one warm June morning, Jane decided to take a stroll along the bridle path bordering the river. The stables were close by, located on the banks of the river, but since her husband had sold Beauty, her beloved horse, she took pains to avoid them. Soon she saw two horsemen approach. One she recognized as her neighbor, Lord Rennie. The other she did not know.

"How delightful to see you, Lord Rennie," she exclaimed when the two horsemen drew alongside. She meant her words. As a first son who inherited a huge estate and a bachelor besides, Rennie could easily have become one of London's arrogant dandies. To Jane's surprise, however, he never attended a London season. She suspected that his shy, retiring nature kept him home. Then, too, it might have been his appearance that made him shy. Tall and stoop-shouldered, he was nothing to look at, what with his awkward gait, large, protruding ears, and pock-marked face. Rennie was a good man, though, affable and kind. What a shame he could not find a wife.

Rennie gave her a big, open grin. "Countess! Why are you walking? I should think you'd be riding on such a lovely day as ... oh dear," Rennie said with dismay, "I forgot you cannot—"

"Quite all right," Jane hastily interrupted. Not for the world would she have dear Rennie feeling uncomfortable. "I will ride again someday. Meanwhile, I am quite content to stroll along this beautiful riverbank."

What a lie. Not a day went by that she did not eat her heart out because she couldn't ride.

Rennie swung from his horse and faced her. "You have not met my houseguest." He gestured toward his companion, still on horseback. "Come down here, Douglas."

Jane gazed up at the stranger. Age around thirty, she guessed. Tall, lean, and sinewy ... dark hair worn long and slightly disheveled. In fact, an unruly lock hung over the middle of his forehead. She judged from the careless manner in which he sat his horse and the slightly amused smile on his face that he did not much care what she thought of him, or what anybody thought of him. As she watched, he swung from his horse—with infinite grace she noticed—and joined Rennie, who said, "May I present my friend, Douglas Cartland. Douglas, meet my next door neighbor, the Countess of Lansdown."

Jane hardly heard the introduction, so startled was she by two piercing brown eyes that seemed to focus on her face while observing every part of her. He looked familiar. Did she know him from somewhere?

"Mister Cartland is my guest. He's a hydrologist."

"He's a *what*?"

"Douglas designed the canal I'm building. As for hydrology, it's the study of water as it moves on earth. For example, around four thousand B.C., the Nile was dammed to improve agricultural productivity of previously barren lands. Then we have the ancient Roman aqueducts—"

"That's enough," Cartland interrupted in a casual, jesting way. "I am sure the countess has little interest in ancient water projects."

How true. She remembered her manners and dipped a curtsy. "I am delighted to meet you, Mister Cartland. I have the feeling we have met before."

Cartland bowed, his eyes never leaving her face. "We have."

Her curiosity was aroused. "When and where did we meet?"

His answering smile held a touch of irony. "On the evening of June sixteenth, eighteen hundred nine, you were in London at Lady Morton's ball. You wore a blue satin gown and flowers in your hair ... roses, if memory serves."

"Of course, now I remember. We danced twice. First the Ecossaise, and then—"

"A Scotch reel."

Memories flooded back. She remembered dancing with this man and finding him quite beguiling. She also remembered how her mother spotted her during the second dance and could hardly wait to yank her off the dance floor. "Douglas

Cartland is not suitable," Mama hissed in Jane's ear, eyes wide with horror.

"He seems perfectly charming to me."

"You do not see him at Almack's, do you?"

"Just what is wrong with him?"

"For one thing, he's a ne'er-do-well rake of the worst order. He drinks. He gambles. He's the disgrace of the family. Besides that, he's the fifth son of Viscount Kellams. *Fifth!* There is no inheritance there, just a stipend. Practically nothing."

Jane assumed a wide-eyed expression of innocence. "Does that mean he's off the list?" She loved to plague her mother.

"Are you daft?" Mama replied in amazement. "He was never on the list!"

As expected, Jane's attempt at subtle humor went right over her mother's head. Even so, she could not resist adding, "What a catastrophe I wasted two whole dances on such a rascal."

Mama's answer was a dour, "If he asks you again, you must refuse."

Douglas Cartland had not asked her again, and by the time her next dance partner whisked her away, she had totally forgotten him. She had not thought of him since, either, except ... was there not something else about him she should be remembering? Something bad. Something very bad ... "I find it interesting that you would recall the exact day, sir, considering that was five years ago."

His smile had a strange, haunted quality she did not understand. "I have a good memory."

She waited for him to say more, but he did not. Instead, Rennie asked, "How is your sister?"

"She's fine." Poor man. She knew he was quite enamored of her younger sister, but Millicent, madly in love with Lord DeWitt, would never give poor, plain Rennie a first glance, let alone a second.

"Please do give her my regards."

"I most certainly shall." She tried to sound enthused, as if her scatterbrained sister would be thrilled to receive a greeting from their awkward neighbor.

"Please tell Miss Hart I shall come calling soon. I trust she will be at home?"

"She will be delighted."

No she won't. Poor Rennie. For the fleetest of moments her eyes met Douglas Cartland's. The glance they exchanged spoke volumes. *No chance. Poor fool, he's wasting his time.*

"My regards to your dear mother and grandmother, too." As an obvious afterthought, Rennie added, "And, of course, give my regards to the earl. I trust he is well?"

"He's in excellent health." Actually, she would not dream of conveying Rennie's regards to her husband. In the first place, Rennie was only being polite and did not give a fig for her husband's health. Nobody did. In the second, she could easily envision the cynical curl of his lordship's lip should she convey such a greeting.

For a few minutes, they chatted before the gentlemen mounted their horses and went on their way. Realizing she might be late for breakfast, Jane reversed her course and headed home. As she walked, her thoughts centered on Douglas Cartland. *What an intriguing man! How handsome, too. Now, if only she were single ...*

Her spirits sank. She was *not* single. She recalled her season in London. She had flirted outrageously, enjoying every moment. What could be more exciting than meeting, flirting with a man, always with the prospect he could be *the one*? Not that he ever was, but the fun was in the looking.

Then the fun ended and she had to marry the earl ...

As she trudged up the hill to Chatfield Court, her mind drifted to a dark place far away, a miserable, dungeon-like spot where no matter which way she turned, there was a high, blank wall. No escape. She knew when she married Lansdown she didn't love him. And now ...

Try not to think about it. I must focus on the good things in my life.

Hard as she tried, she could not think of any good things. Her mood remained gloomy.

Minutes later, in the spacious dining room of Chatfield Court, Jane sat at breakfast while family chatter ebbed and flowed around her. The endless prattle of her love-struck sister ... the pithy, if not downright crude, remarks of her impossible grandmother ... the carefully chosen words of her mother, who, as far as anyone knew, had never allowed an improper phrase to slip past her lips.

Mama glared accusingly. "Jane, you have not touched your eggs."

"Well, then, I guess I should be hung at Newgate, or at the very least transported to Australia on a convict ship."

Mama bristled. "I must say, you are out of sorts this morning. For what reason, might I ask?"

"She doesn't need a reason." Granny Harriet, always Jane's defender, snapped at the daughter she had never understood. "Lord sakes, Amelia, the woman is twenty-six years old. If she doesn't want to eat her eggs, that's her business, not yours."

Jane shoved a portion of her eggs across her plate with her fork and sighed. She should know by now that her mother, who possessed absolutely no sense of humor, would not appreciate her attempt at wit. "Sorry, Mama. I am simply not hungry this morning."

"Well, I cannot understand why." Amelia regarded her daughter with critical eyes that suddenly lit up, as if a pleasing thought occurred to her. "Unless ... You are not—?"

"No, I am not expecting." Good lord! If such an earth-shaking event should occur, she would make haste to inform the world. Mama would be ecstatic. His Lordship would be beside himself with joy, and with good reason. Elizabeth, his first wife, had been barren, a lamentable condition for which he blamed her entirely. What irony that now, after nearly a year into his second marriage, Jane, too, had yet to conceive.

Mama shook her head. "I cannot understand what is taking so long."

"Don't be a goose, Amelia." Granny Harriet slurped her tea, a habit she knew full well set her daughter's teeth on edge. How sweet she looks, Jane mused, gazing across the table at the tiny old lady wearing a lilac shawl over her frail shoulders, a lace cap perched atop her silver head. Sweet indeed, until she opened her mouth to speak. "Don't nag the child. God's blood!"

"Mother, for heaven's sake, watch your language." Aside from her husband deserting her, the greatest tragedy of Amelia Hart's life was having to endure the constant embarrassment of living with a mother like Granny Harriet, who uttered whatever uncouth remark entered her head and never gave a fig about her status in society.

"Granny has a point." Jane once again attempted to mediate the thorny relationship that always existed between her mother and grandmother. More than once she had wondered how it was possible that prickly, blunt Granny Harriet could have given birth to a slavish follower of society's rules like Mama, whose main concern in life was that she, or one of her family, might do something "unacceptable."

Mama's snobbishness notwithstanding, Jane loved her dearly. She possessed a generous heart and could not have been a better mother to Jane and Millicent. At one time she possessed a cheerful disposition, too, and was known for breaking into gales of merry laughter. Those days were nothing but a nostalgic memory since Papa had left. Now Mama had a bitter, caustic edge, which Jane coped with and totally understood.

Am I developing the same attitude?

Unhappiness seemed to accompany her everywhere she went these days, like a dark cloud constantly floating over her head. Now this latest ...

"Come to my bed chamber directly after dinner this evening."

His lips twisted into that cynical smile of his. "I shall have a special surprise for you." Her nerves tensed at the thought of what her husband might be up to now. She became even more suspicious when he ordered up the coach and left for an unexplained errand in the village. Why? His lordship hardly ever ventured into Sudberry. Running errands was beneath him. Let the footmen perform such menial tasks.

So what could be so important Lansdown had to journey to Sudberry? The question nagged. A sense of unease spread through her. Whatever it was, it could not be good.

Her sister flashed her a teasing smile from across the breakfast table. "I hear we are having company. Your favorite sister-in-law. Are you not thrilled?"

"I, for one, am not thrilled," Mama said. "Beatrice Elton puts on such airs that you would think *she* was the countess, not you, Jane."

That had set her mother off again. Jane hardly expected any other response when informed that the earl's twin brother, his wife and eldest son were about to descend upon them. Actually, Jane agreed. Beatrice Elton possessed a habit of being constantly critical, as though she had the right to order everyone around. If truth be told, Jane didn't care for her, either, but she felt no desire to encourage Mama's vitriol. "Look at it from Beatrice's point of view. It's not easy being married to a second son, especially one who's only one minute younger. It must be galling hearing me addressed as 'your ladyship' while she remains merely 'Mrs. Elton.' It truly is unfair. Have you ever thought how unjust it is that the first son gets the title, money, properties—everything—while the other sons get little or nothing?"

"Why, Jane," Granny said with mock astonishment, "are you questioning the laws of primogeniture?"

"Certainly not ... well, yes, I suppose I am."

"Beatrice Elton knew her husband's status when she married him," Millicent lightly declared.

Mama nodded. "She has only herself to blame. If she had any sense, she would have found herself a first son to marry." She directed one of her small, tight smiles toward Jane. "Like you had the good sense to do."

Granny sniffed. "Did she have a choice?"

"Let's change the subject." Jane did not wish to give Mama a chance to answer. Granny spoke the truth. Jane had had no choice. Thanks to Papa. Once again, thoughts of her father triggered a depressing wave of grief. Her beloved Papa was gone. Not dead, she fervently hoped, but gone to America where he might very well be dead. No one knew. The family had not heard a word since that terrible day nearly two years ago when he took the coward's way out and left England, a passel of bill collectors hot on his trail. Only after his ship sailed did his family discover they were destitute. Unbeknownst to them, Papa had squandered the entire family fortune gambling at his London clubs. Of them all, poor Mama suffered the most. Her sheltered, well-ordered world had collapsed irretrievably around her. The shock nearly did her in. One minute she was The Honorable Mrs. John Hart, wife of a baronet, wealthy and respected, a pillar of society with the proper friends. The next, a deserted wife, dirt poor, friends gone, left with two unmarried daughters and no dowries, having to pawn the silver and family jewels, as well as sell their beautiful country manor just to pay the debts and survive.

Mama glowered at Jane. "I do not wish to change the subject. You know you didn't have to marry Lord Lansdown. The choice was yours."

"Of course she had to marry him," Granny snapped. "Who else was going to marry her without a dowry? It's a good thing she did, Amelia. Otherwise, you would be living in some thatched-roof hovel, collecting rags in the street."

"I shall not dignify that remark with a reply." With a haughty tilt of her nose, Mama turned to Jane. "Tell me you are at least fond of the earl. Tell me you were quite willing to marry him and restore our fortune."

Jane's sister put down her fork and tossed her blonde curls. "How could she be fond of a man who is full of arrogance and never laughs?"

"Millicent!" Mama looked highly annoyed. "Need I remind you that if it had not been for the earl, you would never have had your coming-out and your season?"

Millicent's blue eyes lit. "Plus my dowry. Yes, of course, I'm grateful for that, but he's all I said, nonetheless." She stood and pushed back her chair. "The seamstress is coming this afternoon to finish the blue calico. When Lord DeWitt arrives next week, I shall look so absolutely smashing he will have no choice but to propose."

"Are you sure you love him?" Granny asked.

"Love him? Lord Dewitt is perfect in every way and I absolutely adore the man."

Granny emitted one of her skeptical grunts. "No man is perfect, missy."

"Well, Lord DeWitt is, and he's going to be mine, all mine!"

After Millicent bounced out of the room, Granny turned to Jane. "I wonder if that girl realizes the sacrifice you made."

"Does it matter? I'm just glad she's happy." Jane recalled her sister's sad plight after their father left. Her flighty heart had been set on a coming-out and season wherein she would meet and fall madly in love with her future husband, who of course would be rich, titled and incredibly handsome. Instead, after Papa fled the country, she spent her days sobbing on her bed, convinced her life was over. Not until the earl proposed to Jane, promising in his zeal to support her family, did Millicent bounce back to being her lovable, scatter-brained self. She'd had her season. Even better, she had met rich, titled, handsome Lord DeWitt, who, everyone predicted, was bound to propose when he came for his visit.

Mama cast a triumphant look at Granny. "There, you see? Jane is happy."

"Quite happy." A lie, of course, but some things were best left unsaid.

"Now all she needs is to present his lordship with an heir and her life will be complete."

"Well, I don't see that happening." Granny's voice had a sly lilt. "It's been a year. What do you say, Jane? Can Lord High-and-Mighty not get it up?"

Mama jerked as if she'd been stung by some insect. "Mother, *please*." Furtively, she looked around, as if to make sure no servant overheard such an indelicacy. "Mother, how could you?" She drew herself up into a quivering bundle of self-righteousness. "There are some matters we simply do not ever discuss."

"Maybe we should." Granny looked at Jane. "Well? Are you going to answer my question?"

"No, I am not." Jane had long since learned the best way to deal with her grandmother was to counter bluntness with bluntness. Besides, if ever there was a subject she did not want to discuss, it was her intimacies with her husband. Little did they know ... and as far as she was concerned, they would remain in ignorance.

Mama stubbornly continued, "Jane, it has been a whole year. Do you not have any idea why—?"

"No, I do not." Jane rolled her eyes toward the ceiling. "So, what are you saying? My year of grace is up and therefore you will be hounding me from now on?"

"You need not be so touchy. I am only thinking how important your producing an heir must be to the earl. How it must gall him—not having one child while his twin brother has eight."

"Of course he would like a child, but please have patience and don't keep asking."

Her words seemed to make no impression on her mama. "You do realize what would happen if his lordship dies without issue? The title would pass to that worthless twin of his." Seemingly horrified at the vision she had created, she scowled. "Dear God, that awful Beatrice would be the new Countess of Lansdown. She would get everything, and you, Jane, mark my words, would be thrown out on the streets with nothing but your jointure."

"I won't be out on the streets. I'll have my dower house."

Mama ignored her. "The rest of your poor family would be out on the streets, too. I can just see Beatrice flouncing about, Queen of the May, with her fancy title." Mama seethed with mounting rage. "Oh, I cannot bear the thought. You must give the earl an heir immediately!"

Easier said than done. Jane stifled her smile. "You are the one who always says 'Everything in its own good time.' Well, give it more time and don't look for trouble."

"Oh, indeed," Mama sniffed, "I would not be surprised if Beatrice prays every night you will go the way of the first countess."

Enough was enough. "Let's proceed to a more pleasant subject, *please*."

Granny spoke up. "I wish to go upstairs now. Jane, ring for Griggs. Tell him I want that new young footman to carry me up, the one with the shapely calves." She sneaked a conniving glance at Jane. "Do you suppose he pads them?"

"Mother, please! You are not supposed to even notice a mere servant, much less—"

"She's joking, Mama." Jane rose hastily and went to the bell pull. "I'll ring." She was grateful to Granny for distracting Mama's attention. She wished *she* could be distracted. No such luck. Ever since her husband had issued his command invitation, her ordinarily sunny mood had given way to joyless apprehension. She had grown to hate the summons to her husband's bedchamber. Worst of all was knowing that she did not have a choice.

Why did he go to Sudberry this morning? What was so important he had to go himself?

She could not imagine what it was.

Chapter 2

On the cobbled main street of the small village of Sudberry, passersby stopped to watch the shiny black coach, resplendent with the Lansdown coat of arms on its doors. It was pulled by four matched grays that brought it rumbling to a stop in front of Felton's Apothecary Shoppe. The interest of the passersby turned to ill-concealed surprise when the earl stepped from the coach. Seldom were they privileged to gaze upon His Lordship in person.

"Wait here, Thomas." Arthur Elton, Earl of Lansdown, a tall, spare man in his early fifties with a thin face and hawkish nose, stepped to the curb and cast a scowling gaze upwards at the wooden green apothecary's sign swinging above the door. A mortar and pestle were painted on the sign, circled by the Latin phrase, *Major Agit Deus*. "A God more powerful is the agent," the earl silently mouthed. From Virgil's *Aeneid*. He would lay odds that nary an oaf in this wretched village could translate the words, and that included old Felton. Well, he did not give a farthing which God was more powerful as long as he acquired what he came for.

A bell jingled as he stepped inside the shop and closed the

door. *No other customers, thank God*. Felton stood behind the counter. He was a stooped, bespectacled old man, backed by shelves lined with the Dutch blue delft jars storing his various nostrums. One was filled with water that was teeming with a disgusting collection of leeches.

"Ah, Your Lordship!" Felton's rheumy eyes lit with delight. With a bright smile, he came around the counter and gave an obsequious bow. "Again, I am honored you have graced my shop by your presence, sir. I—"

"Do you have it?" Lansdown's lips tightened. Smiling at underlings was a waste of time.

"Indeed, I do, m'lord. At last!" Felton, his smile stifled, scurried back behind the counter. He reached underneath, brought up a brown paper packet and laid it before the earl. "Just arrived this morning." Employing great care, he unfolded the paper. Within, cradled in cotton, lay a small vial filled with a black liquid.

"Here it is. Not easy to come by, if I do say. Just as you ordered—genuine Spanish Fly."

Spanish Fly. The very words caused Lansdown's heart to skip a beat. "You're sure it's genuine?"

"Indeed, yes. 'Twas shipped direct from Spain through a most reliable source." Felton held the vial up to the light. "Actually, flies have nothing to do with it. The substance comes from a powder made from the crushed dried wings of a greenish beetle found in Southern Europe called Lytta vesicatoria. It's an aphrodisiac for men as well as women. Although it's little known—"

"I'm in a hurry."

"Of course, m'lord." The apothecary hastened to rewrap the package. As he did so, he leaned forward, glanced around as if other ears might be listening and whispered, "It drives them wild." He gave a lecherous wink. "A few drops of this and she will be on her knees begging for it. Dying to please you, to do whatever you want her to do. She will—"

"Five crowns as agreed." Lansdown drew out a bag of silver coins and unceremoniously poured them on the counter. "Good day, Felton." He scooped up the package and turned to leave.

"Use it with care," Felton cried to the retreating figure. "No more than ten drops mixed with any liquid and not a drop more." He heard a near-indistinguishable grunt from the earl, who did not bother to turn his head as he opened the door. "Mind, it is a most dangerous drug, m'lord, and must be used properly, else—"

The door slammed. Felton shrugged and softly addressed the empty shop. "Else you could kill the poor girl."

At last he had his Spanish Fly. Back in the coach, Lansdown leaned back against the squabs and allowed himself a satisfied smile. The months of frustration were at an end. By God, his wife of a year, the high-and-mighty Jane, would soon receive the surprise of her life.

Arthur gazed out the coach window, taking no notice of the beauty of the lush shades of green foliage lining the road to Chatfield Court, nor the ever-changing view of the River Hulm, which resembled a ribbon of sparkling blue on this warm summer day.

I was cursed from birth. Everyone said he was the lucky one, the twin born first, the older son who inherited the title, mansion, vast estates, while James, born a minute later, was merely the second son, left with the dregs.

So was James the unlucky twin? No, by God, not with a wife who had borne him eight children! With all the delicacy of a rabbit, Beatrice popped out a baby every other year or so, all of them healthy, not a runt in the bunch. Among them, five sons. Five! Whereas he, Arthur, the honored and revered Earl of Lansdown, remained childless. No sons. Childless, by God, and not only that, forced to beam with delight at the christenings of his brother's brats while he seethed inside, his envy nearly tearing him apart. Galling!

Of course Elizabeth was entirely to blame. His utterly barren first wife tried her best, he supposed, spending countless hours in useless prayer, stuffing herself with pomegranate seeds and God-knew-what concoctions. Nothing worked, and when she finally died, some said of desperation, he felt a certain amount of regret—yes, of course, he did—but even as he stood by her freshly dug grave, he vowed his next wife would be young, beautiful and fertile. Above all else, *fertile*.

Jane had deceived him. Even he, as intelligent and perceptive as a man could be, was fooled by her beauty and surface charm. There was a time when he was so smitten he thought he could not do without her. Even married her without a dowry. She seemed perfect at first. Miss Jane Hart, daughter of a baronet, had a coming-out and a season in London where she'd been the belle of the ball and could have caught any one of the many beaux who pursued her. Only after he married her, when it was too late, had he discovered her cold witch's heart.

A year passed, but he still remembered his much-anticipated wedding night when he thought he could, with a little luck, impregnate his new bride, and thus end the humiliation he had suffered because of the fecundity of his twin brother. Instead— he still shuddered at the memory—he found he could not perform. To say he was shocked was an understatement. Never had there been the slightest hint of a problem with his first wife. True, after Elizabeth died, he had experienced a bit of difficulty with his mistresses, but they were only whores who could pleasure him in other ways, so what did it matter whether or not—he allowed a caustic laugh to escape his lips— he could rise all the way to the occasion.

A wave of smoldering anger coursed through him. All Jane's fault. How could he be expected to achieve an erection when he was bedded with an iceberg who lay there with that get-it-over-with look on her face? To be honest, at first she made some pretense of welcoming his advances, but later on, he could feel her flinch when he touched her. Now the feeling was mutual, even though just last week ... He reflected upon his partial success the week before. He surprised himself, but even so, at best his performance bordered on pitiful. So nothing had really changed. Over time, his love had turned to hate, and who could blame him?

Now he took great pleasure in finding ways to hurt her. When she needed a lady's maid, he hired Bruta, the ugliest, most odious woman he could find. Then he sold Jane's horse. He had to smile every time he recalled the stricken look on her face when he informed her Beauty was gone, sold at Tattersall's in London to someone—he could not recall whom. It was the first and last time he saw tears in her eyes.

"Why?" she asked.

"Riding a horse is not conducive to a woman's good health. Especially one in her child-bearing years, such as you. It is for your own good. You are not to ride anymore."

She said no more, although the pain in her eyes clearly showed her dismay. Served her right. She was the most frustrating woman he had ever known, and the most galling.

Well, she would soon get what she deserved. Oh, yes! He smiled and patted the pocket containing the Spanish Fly. He could hardly wait for tonight.

❧❧❧

Later in the day, Jane stood chatting with Mrs. Stanhope, the head housekeeper, in the entryway of Chatfield Court. She employed her usual tact in discussing what to the servants was indeed an unpleasant subject—the plans for the upcoming visit of James and Beatrice Elton.

Mrs. Stanhope had worked at Chatfield Court for many years. Once she confided in Jane how, while the first Countess of Lansdown was alive, the servants of Chatfield Court sent up endless prayers that she would bear a healthy child—a boy, of course. Their pious concern was based less on a genuine desire for her ladyship's happiness than the fervent hope that her persistent foul temper and shrill histrionics would disappear if only she could present his lordship with an heir. Such an event was never to be. When the countess died without issue, the servants heaved private sighs of relief.

The servants' joyful respite came to an end when the earl's twin brother and wife came to stay shortly thereafter. Their eight unruly children were mostly grown, but Beatrice Elton herself proved to be far more loathsome than the late countess on her worst day. "We always knew where we stood with her ladyship," Mrs. Stanhope confided. "She might have screamed at us, but at least she did not parade around as if she were Queen of England."

Much to the Eltons' rage and dismay, the earl remarried and packed them off to their modest home in London even before the new Countess of Lansdown arrived. What the housekeeper did not tell Jane was how the servants' delight knew no bounds when they met her. At only twenty-five, she was the very antithesis of the unstable first countess and the insufferable Mrs. Elton. Pleasant, even-tempered and kind, she undertook to run Chatfield Court with a firm but gentle hand, restoring peace and harmony to what had been a miserable, disordered household. Not to mention that she was a delight to look upon: tall and slender with rich, auburn colored hair, full, rosy lips and large, intelligent, wide-set blue eyes.

"The Eltons arrive tomorrow, Mrs. Stanhope. I trust all will be in readiness?"

"Indeed, m'lady." The plump, gray-haired housekeeper could not quite conceal a frown. "How many of the children will be coming?"

"Only Percy." Jane disliked giving Mrs. Stanhope such distressing news. Of the Eltons' eight detestable children, Percy was the standout. As a boy, he had played nasty tricks on his younger brothers and sisters, as well as the servants. Rumors abounded concerning his cruelty to small animals—

rumors that were promptly denied and quashed by his adoring parents. As an adult he had not changed. His sly ways and sarcastic comments made him impossible to like. Jane didn't care for him at all, taking pains to avoid being alone with him in the same room. "I recall your mentioning that all the Elton children were quite lively when they were small."

" 'Lively' is hardly the word, m'lady. We tried to confine them to the fourth floor, but their mother thought nothing of letting them run screaming and yelling throughout the mansion—all eight of them—and no hand lifted to discipline them, I might add." Mrs. Stanhope huffed indignantly. "During their visits, his lordship kept to his study. The first countess—if I may be frank—only added to the uproar with her constant screaming."

"Well, at least they are all grown now."

"Thank the Lord."

Just then, the sounds of dogs barking, horses neighing and footmen shouting announced the arrival of Lord Lansdown's coach rolling to a rumbling stop at the front portico.

"There are matters I must attend to." Accompanied by the jingling sound of the many keys dangling from Mrs. Stanhope's belt, she beat a hasty retreat.

Jane felt a flutter of anxiety, as she always did when about to confront her husband. She, too, would have liked to make a hasty retreat, but that would only postpone the inevitable. She stood waiting, her gaze sweeping the vast entry hall of Chatfield Court, a dark corridor dominated by a massively beamed ceiling, huge stained glass windows of Gothic design, a curved staircase and above, a galleried hall hung with sober-faced portraits of the many Earls of Lansdown. They began with the first earl, deceased in 1581, and ended with Arthur, the sixth and present earl, whom many would have liked to see dead.

Griggs, the butler, hastened to open the door. His lordship strode inside. Jane noticed he held a small package in his hand—rather unusual considering he ordinarily deigned not to carry his own purchases. That was the work of his footmen, not his exalted self.

Jane forced a smile, wondering if the surprise the earl talked about was in the package. A pretty bobble of some sort? No, not that. Since their wedding and his initial generosity, Arthur had stopped giving her any sort of gift. Besides, she still had the feeling the "surprise" would not be a pleasant one. Whatever it was, she reminded herself, this was all her own doing and she must make the best of it. After all, she had known when she married the Earl of Lansdown that she did not love him. *At least you respected him.* What she had not counted on was how, over the one year of their marriage, her respect gradually shifted to a vague distaste, spiraled down to a definite dislike, to ... did she now hate him? For a moment she closed her eyes in utter misery. With all her heart, she yearned to love her husband, but how could she love a man who constantly looked down his hawkish nose at her as if she were a lesser being? Who sold her horse and kept her in the country like a prisoner? Who gave her the world's most awful lady's maid, and, worst of all, who summoned her to his bedchamber for those unwelcome nights when she performed what Mama delicately referred to as her "wifely duties." *No! Don't even think of it.*

"Hello, my pet." The earl's small, granite eyes fastened upon her with what seemed like unusual interest.

"Your Lordship." Jane dipped a quick, near invisible curtsy. She nodded at the package in his hand. "I see you've been shopping."

He returned a smile that seemed almost a smirk. "Indeed I have. It's the little surprise I mentioned and it's just for you."

She had long since become expert at detecting the falseness in his voice. She heard it now. "How nice."

The smile faded. "I shall expect you in my bedchamber directly after our dinner guests leave." He twisted on his heel and left, his bony fingers still clutching the mysterious package.

Frozen, she stared after him. Something in his voice ...

something in the way he looked at her ... made her stomach clench.

The butler appeared. "Cook wants to know how many will be at dinner tonight."

"Let's see ... I believe the family plus seventeen guests." Arthur entertained often. Not, she suspected, because he liked people all that much; he simply liked to show off the opulence of his mansion, the quantity of his servants and, of course, the priceless Lansdown jewels, which had been in the family for generations. She had never seen the entire collection. Only on special occasions, such as when guests came for dinner, did he select a piece for her to wear.

"Thank you, Griggs." She hoped the guests would all stay late tonight. Anything to delay receiving her husband's so-called "surprise."

Chapter 3

A lone in the dim candlelight of his bedchamber, the Earl of Lansdown picked up one of two silver-rimmed wineglasses and flicked it with his fingertip. He nodded agreeably at the exquisitely clear ping! *Nothing but the best for my lovely bride.* His lip curled in a sardonic twist. The set of fine wineglasses had belonged to Elizabeth, who had only brought them out on special occasions. If ever there was a special occasion, this was it.

The earl picked up the bottle of Madeira he'd had Griggs bring up from the wine cellar. He poured the wine into the glasses, each to half full, and raised a glass. Swirling its contents, he admired the deep golden color of the Madeira and savored the faint aroma of oak teasing his nostrils.

It was time. She would be here shortly. He reached into the pocket of his brocade dressing gown and pulled out the vial. Removing the cork, he balanced the vial on the rim of one wineglass and with great care tipped it slowly. The drops fell one at a time. One ... two ... three ... four ... finally ten, each one sinking quickly into the golden depths of the wine. What did Felton say? Ten drops? *By God, if ten drops were good, then twenty would be twice as good.* He allowed ten more drops to fall into the glass, noting with satisfaction that the color of the Madeira appeared unaltered.

After he tipped the twentieth drop into the glass—adding one more for good measure—he slipped the vial back in his pocket and looked around his bedchamber to see if all was in order. Fire burning in the fireplace ... the covers folded back invitingly on his huge, elevated bed ... Ah, the jewelry box. Not even Griggs knew its location. Best return it to its hiding spot now, what with his brother and family arriving tomorrow. Not that James would steal, but he would not put anything past that greedy, conniving wife of his.

As usual, he could not resist opening the lid of the carved wooden box to admire the glittering family jewels. He fingered his special favorite, the blue heart diamond ring—originally one of the French crown jewels. He ran his finger over another favorite, a pearl and amber necklace once owned by a Russian czarina. He had allowed Jane to wear it at dinner. Not that she deserved to wear it, but how else could he display the family treasures? He closed the lid, carried the box to the fireplace, and set the box down. With both hands, he slid up one of the large stones from the hearth. Then he picked up the box and dropped it into the large, empty cavity beneath, replacing the stone. *A fine hiding place.* He was the only one who knew of it. Someday he would make other arrangements. After all, he would not live forever, but no need to worry now. He heard a discreet knock on his door. "Enter!"

She glided in, holding herself tall, lovely as always. At dinner she had looked strikingly beautiful with her upswept hair intertwined with pearls, the pearl and amber necklace around her swanlike neck and a gown of white satin displaying her magnificent breasts to perfection. Now she had changed into her tartish, red velvet dressing gown, the one he ordered specially made for her. He insisted she wear it whenever she came to his bedchamber. She had not said as much, but he knew she hated it. How she must despise him. His mouth pulled into a cynical smile. He would change her hate to panting desire before the night was over.

"Good evening, m'lord." Her voice was quiet, courteous, and oozed with innate sensuality.

He loathed the woman, absolutely loathed her. What he loathed the most was how she stood there with her head held high, shoulders squared, the hint of an inscrutable smile playing on her full red lips. Well, she did not fool him. He had to look deep but could always find the gleam of defiance buried in the depths of those turquoise blue eyes. God's blood! He had tried to tame her, but thus far nothing he did could efface that gleam. It was as if he could not reach her, as if her body might belong to him, but her soul within would remain ever aloof, unmindful of whatever small cruelty he might inflict upon her.

He would take care of that tonight.

He picked up the two glasses and offered one to her. "Come sit by the fire. This is my finest Madeira."

Glass in hand, she seated herself in a chair by the fireplace. He sat opposite and raised his glass in a toast. "To a pleasant evening."

"To a pleasant evening." Her voice held no warmth. Flames from the fireplace danced a golden reflection in her wine as she raised it to her lips. She took a long sip. "It's very good."

"It ought to be. It's from Malvasia. True liquid gold, they say. Gentle and smooth, seductive, mysterious, sensual. It's the elixir deities suckle from, not the drink mere mortals can bear." He took his first sip. "Been in my cellar for years."

"My, my," she replied without enthusiasm. "What's the occasion?"

"Drink up, my dear. You will soon find out." He watched her tilt her head back to take another sip, feeling a stirring within himself as he devoured the tantalizing sight of that slender white neck and the suggestion of those delicious, naked curves beneath her red velvet dressing gown.

Why wait? With one swift gesture, he brought his glass to his lips and gulped its contents. The wine cut a warm, smooth path down his gullet. It tasted delicious despite all those drops of Spanish Fly he had added. Better get her to his bed. He was told on good authority it worked almost instantly, *without fail*. He laughed to himself. That fool Felton thought he wanted it for his wife. What nonsense. Why waste a drop of his precious aphrodisiac on a woman?

"Come to bed, Jane. Now."

❧❧❧❧

Beneath the covers of the canopied bed, Jane lay waiting for her husband to join her. A sinking feeling overwhelmed her. What was she doing here? How could she live with this detestable man for the rest of her life? In happier times long gone, she had been Miss Jane Hart, the respected, and in all ways content, young lady who loved her life and looked forward to the future. Now she could hardly contain her growing bitterness.

Try to think of the bright side. My sacrifice was worth it. Just to see the lines of anxiety leave Mama's face. Just to see Granny Harriet content again, fortified by her nightly little nip of gin ...

He headed to the bed.

At least this whole, sad affair would not take long. No doubt the same old scene would repeat itself. He would try desperately—despite her gloomy mood, she almost had to giggle—to "get it up," as Granny said. Nearly every time he tried, he failed miserably, his precious member remaining limp and flaccid, refusing to cooperate no matter how much he grunted, turned red in the face, cursed, and worked up a sweat. To her surprise, last week he had managed a half-hard effort, but such moments were rare. The worst of it was that after exhausting himself and giving up, he inevitably blamed her. He would heap abuse upon her head, reminding her that with his first wife he had never had a problem, that if he died without issue, Jane was to blame and he would curse her for eternity.

He warned her not to tell. If she did, both she and her family would find themselves penniless on the streets. He was certainly safe on that score. Pride alone prevented her from breathing a word regarding her husband's unfortunate performance in the bed chamber.

"Take a look, my dear!"

Arthur strutted toward the bed, completely naked. She raised her head off the pillow. *Oh, my Lord.* Never had she seen such a sight. Her married friends hinted what a man with a full erection looked like, but even they declared she would really have to see for herself. *Just huge*, was all she could think.

His lordship placed his hands on his hips and tilted his pelvis forward, thus forcing his engorged member to even greater prominence. "How about this? Have you ever seen the like? It is hard as an oak branch."

"It is ... quite impressive, m'lord."

He greeted her remark with delighted laughter. "All the more to pleasure you with, my dear." He paraded toward the bed and had almost reached it when he suddenly stopped. A peculiar, sort of questioning expression crossed his face.

"Is something wrong?"

"Not a thing." He took a step toward the bed then stopped again. He threw his head back. "Ahhhhhhhhh!" came a guttural cry from deep down in his throat—a weird, downright frightening sound, one she never heard before. His face distorted. He clutched at his chest. "Ahhhhhhhhh!" Before she could even begin to grasp what was happening, he crashed to the floor.

"M'lord!" She leaped from the bed and knelt beside him. He lay on the floor, face up, eyes staring at the ceiling. Oh, God, was he dead? She placed two fingers at the side of his neck and felt for a pulse. Nothing. She recoiled and slapped her hand over her mouth. She had never seen anybody dead before, but somehow she knew for a certainty that her husband had expired.

She must get help. She grabbed the red velvet robe and slipped it on. She went to the bell pull and was about to give it a tug when she suddenly thought, what was she going to tell everyone? The earl died while about to do *that*? How undignified! How embarrassed he would be. To save his dignity she had best make up some story. They were sitting, enjoying a glass of wine when suddenly ... She glanced toward the earl.

Dear God in heaven!

It had not shrunk. His member still stood at full mast, still resembling that branch of oak. Her heart sank. How could they conceal it in the casket? She had no idea.

Griggs! She grasped the bell pull and tugged with all her might. Pray God the perfect butler would know what to do.

Chapter 4

Jane spent the next two days after her husband's death in a daze. Nothing seemed real except for her grateful awareness that never again would she be obliged to perform her odious "wifely duties." That lovely fact seemed very real, and each time she thought of it, she wanted to shout, "Hurrah!" Naturally, she did nothing of the sort, even though thoughts of all the good things resulting from the earl's demise kept popping into her head. No longer would she be obliged to endure the earl's constant belittling criticism. No longer his little cruelties, like selling her horse and forbidding her to go riding. Such a relief! *Thank you, God.* She kept her feelings to herself, though, and went about her business with a solemn, unsmiling demeanor, doing her best to act the part of the grieving widow.

Now, standing before her mirror in her bedchamber, she examined her pale face and remarked, "Absolutely not my color." The black bombazine dress trimmed with black crepe gave her a ghostlike, pallid look. "I would look bad no matter what I wore." She heaved a sigh. "Now, if I can just get through the funeral tomorrow ..."

Mama and Granny sat watching. "It doesn't matter if black is your color or not," said Mama. "Now, hurry up. Sir Archibald is coming. Beatrice wants us all to meet in the library."

Jane rolled her eyes at the thought of having to deal with the earl's long-time solicitor, a man she considered stuffy and opinionated. She pressed the back of her hand to her forehead in an overdramatic way. "Tell him I am overcome with grief and cannot attend. You and Granny go hear what he has to say."

"Jane, I do not care for your attitude. Don't think it hasn't escaped my notice you are not exactly heartbroken over the death of your husband."

"Why should she be?" Granny sat resting her chin on the top of her cane, her sharp eyes assessing her daughter. "Are you daft, Amelia? The earl was an arrogant, mean-spirited, nasty excuse for a man. Nobody liked him. Everyone is glad he's dead."

"That's not so. Some of the best families in England will be represented at the funeral tomorrow. People are coming from far and wide to pay their respects."

"Hypocrites, every last one of them," Granny replied. "Although you won't think so when you see them all dressed up in their black mourning outfits, weeping and wailing over a pompous ass who had a heart the size of a pea."

"It is not proper to disparage the dead." Mama's voice did not carry much enthusiasm, no doubt because it was hard to argue with the truth. "Oh, Jane." She heaved a troubled sigh. "Whether you loved the earl or not is beside the point. We haven't talked about it yet, but have you given a thought to our future? His lordship is not in his grave yet, and already Beatrice has summoned the solicitor. Who would have thought Chatfield Court would ever be hers? But now it will be. No doubt she wants to know how soon she can turn us out. I so loved it here, and now we will have to leave." Mama's eyes dampened. "Oh why did the earl have to die? It is so unfair!"

Jane put a comforting arm around her mother's shoulders.

"We are going to be fine. Really, I can hardly blame my dear sister-in-law. Don't forget, the Eltons moved in here after the first countess died and Beatrice pretty much ran the place. I'm sure she still thinks of Chatfield Court as her own. Now just think, after all these years she's gotten her wish. Her husband is the new earl. She's the new Lady Lansdown. I would wager she's hard pressed to keep from doing a jig on the front lawn."

"We will have nothing," Mama wailed.

"That is not true and you know it." In all the turmoil since Arthur died, Jane took solace in the thought that she and her family would be well provided for. "I will have the dower house, won't I? Plus some income? As I recall, a widow normally receives a third of the income from her husband's estate. We'll have plenty. So what is there to worry about?"

Granny sniffed.

Mama shifted her gaze away, a sure sign something wasn't right. "There might be a few things to worry about," she replied in a very small voice.

"Like what?" Jane was perplexed. "I can't remember the details of the marriage contract, but it's pretty much standard, isn't that what you told me?"

Her mother's long pause caused a flicker of apprehension to course through her veins.

"You will recall, you did not have a dowry. Thus, I had much less bargaining power over what you would receive in your jointure."

Jane squeezed her eyes shut. The flicker of apprehension was fast becoming a heart-sinking foreboding. "So tell me the worst. Out with it."

"Well, as for your jointure, you do get a dower house. I haven't seen it, but it's on the estate somewhere. Your income ... I did not want to tell you." Mama shifted her gaze toward the door, as if she would like to make a quick escape. "It won't exactly be a third of the entire estate. Instead, the earl agreed to grant you the income from his estates in Ireland."

"How much?"

"At the time of the settlement, the estates yielded six hundred to a thousand pounds a year."

How disappointing! Much less than she expected. They would have to cut corners, but still, they could manage. "With the dower house we can live quite well on that amount. That's not so bad, is it?"

"Yes, it is," Mama wailed. "What about Millicent's dowry?"

"It's not in the agreement?"

"We were desperate, remember? Lord Lansdown was the only suitor in sight who would take you without a dowry. Plus, I had a problem finding someone to represent us."

Granny wagged a finger. "I warned you not to hire that sleazy solicitor."

"She was right, I'm afraid," Mama continued. "The solicitor I hired left a lot to be desired. I'm afraid he did not do too well by us."

"I had no idea."

"You were busy with your wedding plans. Why would you concern yourself? I knew the terms were not all that good, but it never occurred to me the earl would up and die so soon. I still cannot understand. He seemed in perfect health." Mama threw Jane a puzzled gaze. "He was alone, sitting in front of the fireplace, drinking a glass of wine and suddenly fell off his chair stone dead? It just seems so ... hard to understand."

Hard to understand, all right. What a nightmare. She would never forget Griggs' cool and aloof demeanor when he arrived in response to her frantic tugging at the bell pull. What a sight she must have been, kneeling over the body, trembling, fighting hysteria. The butler had not cried out, gasped, or even lifted an eyebrow when she said, "Griggs, come quick! I think his lordship is dead."

She might have been asking for another biscuit while at tea. His face a mask, Griggs walked to the body, knelt, placed his fingers around his lordship's wrist and felt for a pulse. After a few seconds, he looked up. "He is indeed deceased, madam."

She had known in her heart her husband was dead, but just hearing the words plunged her into a state of near panic. "He was ... we were ... he was walking toward the bed. One minute he was all right and then the next he grabbed his chest and fell to the floor."

"Really?" the butler skeptically inquired. "That is hard to believe when it is obvious he died *in flagrante delicto*."

"In flagrante *what*?" She had never heard the words.

Griggs ignored her question. He arose with purpose and addressed her. "You will go to your room, madam."

"But ..."

He pointed toward the door. "Leave."

Griggs had never, ever addressed her in any but the most obsequious of tones, but he seemed to know what he was doing, and besides, whom else could she turn to? "All right." Her eyes strayed to the incredible sight of his lordship's member, still as fully erect as a sturdy stanchion in gale force winds. "What about *that*?"

"I shall take care of it." Griggs gave no flicker of emotion. "Just go."

She turned and left, desperate, sure the whole world would soon know the intimate details of her husband's demise. The stony-faced butler proved true to his word. The news soon circulated that the Earl of Lansdown had been alone, attired in his dressing gown, lying prone in front of the fireplace, his dead fingers clutching an empty wineglass. Not a word concerning the unfortunate condition of his ... *Don't think about it*.

"His sudden death does seem strange. I, too, thought he was in the best of health, but doubtless it was his heart. You never know, do you, Mama?" She took one more look at her dreary self in the mirror and squared her shoulders. "Very well, let's go downstairs."

Jane had little love for dark, gloomy Chatfield Court, but

one of the rooms she admired was its spacious library, so restful with its plush Axminster carpet, coved, arched ceiling painted with sumptuous baroque paintings, and many shelves of books lined up against the dark, wood-paneled walls. When Jane entered, she saw James and Beatrice were already seated. As usual, she felt a strange qualm at the sight of Arthur's twin brother. The physical resemblance to her late husband was unmistakable, but James's temperament was completely different from his brother's. His milquetoast demeanor sharply contrasted to Arthur's caustic, demanding, arrogant attitude. James was so quiet, in fact, that people hardly noticed him. When his wife was around, he pretty much disappeared into the woodwork, content to be an observer, generally with a glass of port in his hand, a sly, vaguely lecherous look in his eyes that Jane always found unsettling.

As always, Beatrice took the lead. "Sir Archibald will be here in a moment. We need to go over your marriage contract. There are certain arrangements that must be discussed."

Could the woman not even wait until the funeral was over? Jane sank onto a sofa, Granny and Mama beside her, and observed Beatrice with concealed distaste. One would think she was the sweetest woman in the world with her girlish voice, plump, motherly figure, pouty lips and big, innocent-looking gray eyes. She even looked good in mourning, what with her white and rosy pink complexion that contrasted well with black. *So unfair.* "What arrangements do you mean?" Jane was all innocence.

"Your move to the dower house, of course. Ah, there you are, Sir Archibald."

Horace Archibald, the earl's long-time solicitor, entered the library and seated himself behind the large mahogany desk. He was a portly, distinguished-looking gentleman with thin, white hair, whose wise old eyes peered at them through silver-framed spectacles perched on the end of his nose. Giving a courteous nod to all, he said, "You wished to know the particulars of the earl's marriage contract, Mrs. Elton?"

"Exactly. I have glanced it through and was just going over the contents with the countess."

Granny leaned over and whispered in Jane's ear, "*Glanced*, my foot. More likely she's got it memorized word for word."

"I have it here."

"I was about to tell the countess how comfortable she will be in the dower house. I believe it will be best for all if she moves soon. Naturally, I am anxious to move to Chatfield Court, and I'm sure the countess will wish to get settled in her new home. Oh, dear," Beatrice made a little moue at Jane, "or should I even call you 'the countess'?" She broke into a self-satisfied smile that made Jane seethe inside. "Of course *I* am the Countess of Lansdown now."

Sir Archibald frowned and cleared his throat. "She will retain her title, Mrs. Elton. We will simply have two countesses instead of one. We must not be too hasty. There is a most important matter to consider."

"What is that?" Beatrice hitched slightly forward toward the edge of her chair.

"It's a rather delicate matter. I don't think—"

"Please, out with it." Judging from the sharp edge to her voice, Beatrice did not take kindly to the thought there might be a dark cloud on her otherwise rosy horizon.

"Very well then." The solicitor gave a shrug of resignation. "There is always the possibility a recently-widowed young woman might be with child. So, as I am sure you are aware, Mrs. Elton, we must wait to see if such a possibility exists. If her ladyship is, and the child is a boy, then the title and the entire estate—"

"Of course I was aware of it." Bridled anger shone in Beatrice's eyes. "In Arthur's case, it is simply not possible. I see no need to wait. Arthur wasn't capable of fathering a child. He always blamed poor Elizabeth, but I knew better. He was the one at fault. There's just no way—"

"It's the custom. We must wait." He addressed Jane. "My apologies for broaching such a delicate subject."

With child? Impossible. Jane had to gather her wits about her before she answered. "I don't think—" She was about to explain why she couldn't possibly be carrying Arthur's child when she felt a sharp jab to her ankle. What on earth? She looked down and saw the source—Granny had just jabbed her with her cane. Hastily, she withdrew her foot. Granny didn't want her to protest? All right then, she could take a hint, but why? She would find out later. "How kind of you, Sir Archibald, but there's no need to apologize. Can you tell me, what is the proper time to wait?"

"Six months at the very least."

"*What?*" Beatrice's face flushed an unbecoming, mottled red.

"Actually, an heir to the estate can be born up to ten months after the father dies, so waiting ten months would be even better." He directed a mollifying smile toward Beatrice. "Of course, a doctor would be called upon to verify the ... er, ahem, condition, if such should be the case."

"So we must wait nearly a year for something that is utterly impossible?" Beatrice's voice sounded tight as a drum-head.

"I am afraid so."

If Jane had not been in such a wretched mood, she might have enjoyed the sight of Beatrice's mouth working as she vainly tried to maintain a semblance of a smile. She was fooling no one.

Mama looked relieved. "So we won't be moving right away?"

"Indeed not."

Mama looked even more relieved. "Sir Archibald, could you briefly review the terms of the marriage contract? As I recall, my daughter will receive the dower house plus the income from his lordship's estates in Ireland. Correct?"

The solicitor's pleasant expression faded. "That's true. Although, she won't be as well off as we had planned." He rifled through some papers. "The countess was to receive six hundred to a thousand pounds a year from the Irish estates. Lately, however, the estates have not been doing well. I regret to inform you she is more likely to receive three hundred pounds a year, if that."

"Are you sure?" Mama's voice sounded distressed.

"Very sure."

Mama had turned pale. "Will we have enough for Millicent's dowry?"

The solicitor shrugged. "I'm afraid not." He gave her an encouraging smile. "Let us not jump to unpleasant conclusions. Let us wait." He cast a meaningful glance at Jane. "Let's see what the future holds."

Jane felt like leaping up and proclaiming there was no way in the world she could be with child. Leery of Granny's cane, she kept her silence.

Later, when the meeting was over and everyone else had left, Sir Archibald drew Jane aside and bent his head confidentially. "A word of warning, if I may."

"Of course."

"During the next few months, you must be extremely discreet. By that I mean—"

"I know what you mean, sir. I must avoid any hint of scandal."

"Exactly." The old solicitor looked relieved to have relayed his message so easily. "Many eyes will be upon you. You must be the soul of discretion. Avoid any encounter that might be misconstrued. I would go so far as suggest you live the next few months as if you resided in a nunnery."

A nunnery? How quaint and old-fashioned. Had the circumstances warranted, she would have laughed, but she managed to maintain her solemn expression. "You are absolutely right, Sir Archibald. Never fear, I shall heed your warning."

Sir Archibald smiled solicitously. "It's only a matter of time before this will all be behind you."

A matter of time? As if she cared. After her dreadful

experience with the earl, she planned to remain single. It would be a cold day in hell before she ever did *that* with a man again.

Jane did not find a chance to speak to her grandmother until later that night when she visited the old lady's bedchamber. Granny lay propped on her eiderdown pillows, holding an open Bible and wearing a pink beribboned nightgown. A lace night cap was perched askew atop her silver-haired head.

"Come in, dearie." Granny reached for the cup and saucer sitting next to her on the nightstand. She took a long sip and gave Jane a conspiratorial grin. "What lovely tea."

"I'm sure it is." Jane had long since been in on Granny's little secret—her delicate, rose-painted china cup held not tea but a healthy slug of gin.

"I'd wager I know why you're here," Granny said.

"I'd wager you do. I want to know why you jabbed me with your cane when I was talking to Sir Archibald. I simply wanted to assure him I am not with child."

Granny peered at her over the top of her spectacles. "What makes you so sure you're not?"

"It's simply not possible."

"Why is it not possible?"

"Do you think I don't know how babies are made?"

"You've been married a year. Don't tell me—"

"This may surprise you, but I am still a virgin. Practically, anyway."

"What?" Granny's spectacles slid down her nose. "How could that be? The earl seemed a rutty old goat if ever there was one."

"Well, he wasn't so rutty. All year long, he tried, but he could not ... uh ..."

"Get it up?"

"Exactly. If you want to know the truth, it was always soft. He would try to ... you know ... but the thing would bend in the middle."

"That's strange." Granny's lips curved into a mischievous grin. "From what I hear, he certainly got his cock up the last night of his life."

Jane gasped. She sputtered. Words escaped her.

Granny jammed her spectacles back up her nose. "You were there, missy. He didn't fall off his chair. Either he fell off you or he was about to."

She finally found her tongue. "How on earth do you know?"

Granny grinned. "You think servants don't talk?"

Damnation. Did Mama know? Did Beatrice know? "I trusted Griggs. I thought he was the soul of discretion. He assured me—"

"Ha!" Sudden sympathy filled Granny's faded blue eyes. She nodded at a bedside chair. "Sit down before you fall down." Jane sank onto the chair. "You're safe. Don't worry. I hear things the fancy snobs in this house will never hear. It's true, though, isn't it? You were there."

She could never lie to her grandmother. For one thing, she would never get away with it. Actually, she felt a sudden rush of relief at the prospect of letting it all pour out. "Oh, Granny, it was all just horrible! He was parading around the room, showing off, if you know what I mean. And then—"

"Did he poke you?"

"Did he *what?*"

"You heard me. Did he get it in or not?"

"He did not get that far." She took a thoughtful pause. "At least not that time."

"So, he has poked you before?"

"Well ... last week he ... sort of."

"You mean his lordship was a stuffer?"

Struck with the absurdity of their conversation, Jane clapped her hand over her mouth and started to giggle. "You could say that, yes, he was a stuffer, but he managed to stuff it in just a little bit."

Granny raised her eyebrows. "Just a little bit and you think you're still a virgin?"

Strange, how she could talk about the most intimate things with her grandmother and remain at ease. With anyone else she would die of embarrassment. "Granny, the truth is, last week he sort of stuffed it in, as you so quaintly put it, but only the once, and then just barely. So there is no possible way—"

"Hog wash. You cannot be a little bit of a virgin. Either you are or you are not, and you definitely are not. You could have a bun in the oven right now."

"I do not believe it."

"Time will tell, missy."

Granny could not be more wrong, but she would not argue. Time would indeed tell. "At least I have gained us some time. We won't have to move tomorrow."

"That's the spirit. You *will* be happy, Jane. I can feel it in my bones."

Jane smiled wryly. "There's only one thing in the world that would make me really happy."

"What might that be?"

"If I could go to America—find Papa—start a new life."

"What?" Granny feigned surprise. "You mean you would give up all this wealth and privilege just to go live among the savages?"

"In a minute—a second. If I had the chance, I would not even have to think about it." Jane sighed. I can't do that, can I? I can't just run off. I have my obligations."

"I'm afraid so."

"If I were a man, I could."

"Well, you're not. You're a woman, and women cannot do as they please."

"Even you." Jane cast a piercing gaze at her grandmother. "Independent though you are, I would wager there have been times in your life when you could not do as you wished."

Granny got a faraway look in her eyes, as if momentarily lost in her reveries. "More than you will ever know, my dear."

Was that a tear sliding down Granny's cheek? At any rate, it was time to change the subject. "I wonder what the dower house is like. I've never seen it."

"Don't get your hopes up." Granny left it at that.

Thank God, the funeral was over. Now mourners, fresh from the cemetery, filled the house. Guests milled about wherever Jane looked. Women in elaborate black dresses, men wearing black armbands around their sleeves. The general mood had lightened considerably from the gloom of the funeral. Coming down the stairs, Jane heard animated conversations and easy laughter. Apparently, many of the mourners had managed to recover from their profound shock and grief at the tragic passing of the Earl of Lansdown.

She joined some of the guests. Soon Lord Rennie strolled up to greet her.

"My condolences, Lady Lansdown," Rennie remarked in his usual sincere fashion. He spent the next minutes desperately struggling to extol the supposed virtues of her late husband. Finally she could not stand one more minute. With a furtive shift of her eyes, she searched for a means of escape and noticed Douglas Cartland standing alone in the corner, watching her.

Rennie turned to follow her gaze. "Yes, I brought Douglas along. He knew your husband back in the old London days when he," there was an uncomfortable pause, "uh, when he lived there."

Jane turned her attention back to her neighbor. "I was surprised he remembered the exact day we met."

"Of course he would remember. June sixteenth is the very night he—"

"The night he what?" She was curious at Rennie's mid-sentence halt.

He bit his lip. "Guess I should not say. Something personal, you know. Something I don't guess Cartland would like bandied about. Is Miss Hart here?"

"Millicent?" Jane looked about, her gaze combing the crowd for a glimpse of her younger sister. "I don't see her at the moment, but she must be around somewhere." Come to think of it, she had not seen Millicent for quite a while.

"Then I shall look for her. Excuse me, Countess."

Jane watched as Rennie wandered off. Poor man. Even if he found her, it would do no good.

Jane felt someone come up beside her. "Ah, there you are, my dear aunt," said an oily male voice, "may I offer my sincere condolences?"

It was odious Percy, the Eltons' oldest son. Just the sound of his voice made her flinch inside. She wished she could run and hide, but good manners decreed otherwise. She turned to face him, noting his utterly bland appearance. Percy was of medium height, in his middle thirties, and slight of build. His thin, sandy hair and pasty, unhealthy-looking complexion attested to the decadence of his life in London. Jane never cared for his patronizing attitude, and Millicent hated his shifty-eyed, lecherous gaze. The oldest of the Eltons' five sons, he was still a bachelor. "No woman would have that slimy fop," Millicent had proclaimed.

Jane put on her polite smile. "Thank you, Percy. How kind of you, and may I express my condolences to you? I know how you must be grieving the loss of your dear uncle."

"I am desolate." His eyes raked over her boldly. "Keep in mind that I stand by to console you in your grief at any time." He leaned intimately close, his lips curving into an inviting smile. "When you feel lonely, and I am sure you will, *do* let me know, dear Aunt."

Despicable man. "I doubt I shall be feeling *lonely*, as you put it, any time soon, Percy. Now I must see to my guests." Disguising her disgust, she turned her back on her nephew and walked away. How frustrating that she could not be rid of him. No chance now, especially since his father was about to become the new Lord Lansdown.

Carrying on her duties as hostess, Jane drifted through the crowd, talking to this person and that. When would this farce be over? How long must she greet people she had never met and receive their insincere condolences? How she hated acting the part of the grieving widow, mournfully repeating again and again how she would sorely miss her dear, departed husband, a lie that became increasingly burdensome with each repetition.

Later, after she had received what seemed like the thousandth condolence, she came across Douglas Cartland, still in the same corner, alone, with that same curious smile on his face. She stopped in front of him, searching for something to say. "Ah, Mister Cartland, have you partaken of the refreshments? If you will look in the dining room—"

"I am not interested in refreshments, and I don't think you're especially interested in whether or not I *partake*, as you put it, of your punch and tarts and whatever else you're feeding your guests."

Struck dumb by his rude reply, she made herself busy by snapping open her black lace mourning fan. Fluttering it beneath her chin, she inquired, "So what *do* you think I'm interested in?"

An easy smile played at the corners of his mouth, which brought out two dimples in his cheeks she hadn't noticed before. "Countess, I have been watching you. The only thing you are interested in right now is quitting this charade so you can set aside your ludicrous façade of the grieving widow and act yourself."

What? She abruptly stopped waving her fan and stared at him. "Sir, that comment was most inappropriate." *Oh no!* She sounded exactly like her mother. Even so, what an outrageous thing for him to say. "I think you should apologize."

With mock solemnity, he bowed slightly. "Then I abjectly apologize, madam."

He didn't mean it. She could see his eyes were still openly amused. "Talk about a weak apology!"

"Ah, but I can see now I have made a terrible mistake. There must have been two Earls of Lansdown. Unfortunately, I, in my abysmal ignorance, was thinking of the Lansdown who was so obnoxious that even his dog detested him. Of course, your husband is the *other* Lord Lansdown, the one who was kind and generous to all, who loved children and animals, who spent his life thinking of ways to help others. My, my, you must be devastated, Countess. If this were India, I should wager you would be hastening to throw yourself onto one of those burning pyres, as wives do over there, so profound is their grief. You would be—"

"Stop!" She brought her fan to her face, this time to hide her laughter. With a struggle she composed her expression to its former solemnity. "Please. My mother would faint from shock if she saw me enjoying myself."

"My apologies." He grew serious. "I knew the earl from my London days. Every now and then I would run into him at the gambling tables in the London clubs. He had a reputation for ... well, I must not speak ill of the dead. Isn't that what they say?"

"That is what my mother would say. What did he do? Cheat at cards?"

"Among other things." He stood regarding her a moment, his eyes raking admiringly over her black clad figure. "What a pity a beautiful woman like you must wear mourning for a year in honor of a man you could not possibly have cared for. How could our society entertain such hypocrisy?"

She shrugged. "An excellent question for which I have no answer. That is simply the way it is."

"Ah, yes." Lightness returned to his voice. "We must never flaunt society's rules. How is your horse?"

His abrupt change of subject left her speechless. "My ... horse?"

"Beauty, your horse. You told me about her when we danced at Lady Morton's ball."

"I'm surprised you remember."

Here came that sad smile again. "It was an unforgettable night in many ways."

"I don't have Beauty anymore." Anguish filled her heart, as it always did when she thought about her horse. "My husband sold her at Tattersall's. I don't ride anymore."

"Would you like to ride?"

Like to ride? Her heart leaped at the thought that no longer would his lordship be able to dictate every nuance of her life. Beauty was gone forever, but now she could ride as much as she pleased. What a joyous thought! "Oh, yes, I shall be riding."

"I know of some fine trails along the river. You and I will go riding someday soon."

She started to say yes, but Sir Archibald's advice came to mind. *Many eyes will be upon you. You must be the soul of discretion.* "Thank you for the invitation. However, it suddenly occurs to me I am not supposed to ride while in mourning."

For a moment she thought he would utter a curse. "Of course. Again, my apologies for suggesting you have any fun in your life for the foreseeable future." He bowed slightly. "Goodbye, Countess. I shall leave you to your grief."

She watched as he moved away, then he suddenly turned and came back. "One more question."

"Yes?"

"What did they do with it?"

"With what?"

"With his lordship's ... shall we say, problem? Did they strap it down? Cut it off perhaps?"

His meaning came clear. "You are impossible! You truly are a scoundrel, just as they said. How did you know?"

He laughed and began to back away. "I will see you at the river."

"No you will not."

"Yes, I will," He disappeared into the crowd.

Later, when Jane went upstairs, she found her sister in her bedchamber, flung face-down on her bed.

"Millicent, whatever is wrong? Why haven't you come downstairs?"

"My life is over," came Millicent's muffled words. "I shall never be happy again."

Jane sat on the side of the bed. "What on earth are you talking about?"

"Read the letter on my bed table. You'll see."

Uh-oh. Jane picked up the letter. As she read it, her heart sank.

Dear Miss Hart,

My condolences on the loss of your dear brother-in-law.

Due to a sudden change of plans, I deeply regret I cannot come to see you next week. As I shall be extremely busy these next few weeks, I fear I cannot see clear to rescheduling my visit any time in the foreseeable future.

Sincerely,
—*DeWitt*

Filled with a sudden fury, Jane could hardly speak. "How dare he!"

Millicent turned on her back, revealing red eyes and cheeks wet with tears. "He seemed so smitten. Those little gifts ... those hints of his undying love. I thought surely ..." Smothering a sob, she turned over and buried her face in the pillow again.

Jane placed a comforting hand on her shoulder. "I am so sorry," she whispered. "I'm sure he did love you, but I can see his parents had a hand in this. They must have realized the earl's death means a change in my status, and therefore yours. No doubt they suspected you would no longer have a dowry, or a reduced one at best."

Millicent wasn't listening. "I have lost everything."

Feeling utterly helpless, Jane patted her sister's shoulder. "Don't worry. Everything will be all right."

"Will it?" Millicent's words were choked with despair.

When Jane left her sister's bedchamber, she was sick at heart. How could she feel otherwise when their lives had changed completely?

Everything most definitely would not be all right.

Chapter 5

By the next day, the guests had left. All, that is, except James and Beatrice. "They're not really guests," Jane replied to her mother's complaint. "You know very well Chatfield Court will soon be theirs."

"That horrible woman!" Mama's face grew red. "Haven't you noticed how Beatrice is already parading around the house as if she owns it? She has even begun to order the servants around, and that's not right. *You* are still the countess."

At times Mama truly tried Jane's patience. She had to remind herself that her mother meant well, that her concerns were not for herself but for her family. "We all hate the thought of leaving Chatfield Court, but we must learn to accept the inevitable. I already have, and it doesn't bother me a bit."

That evening, upon entering the dining room, Jane realized that—contrary to what she had told her mother—she had not entirely accepted the inevitable. She was headed toward her usual place at the foot of the table when, with a sickening jolt, she discovered her sister-in-law sitting in her chair. In Arthur's chair at the head of the table sat James, the supposed new Earl of Lansdown, looking decidedly uncomfortable. No doubt Beatrice insisted he assume his rightful place.

"Well? Are you going to do something?" Mama asked in an infuriated whisper.

"I don't need the aggravation," Jane whispered back. "Let them sit there. What difference does it make?"

"Jane, my dear," Beatrice cried out, the soul of cordiality. "I hope you do not mind the new seating arrangement. We shall all have to get accustomed to it, will we not?"

"Of course," Jane said through gritted teeth. After all, what did it matter where she sat? Her new chair along the side was just as comfortable. The food was the same, and so was the company. Still, whenever she looked at Beatrice, she felt an urge to yank the chair out from underneath the greedy woman and dump her haughty derriere upon the floor. To make matters worse, her mother glared daggers at her from across the table. *Do something!* her eyes said. Even Granny sent her a questioning look.

The soup plates had not been cleared away before Beatrice began a cutting commentary on the reception following the funeral. "I noticed that despicable Douglas Cartland was there."

Jane's ears perked up. "Why is he despicable?"

"You mean you don't know?"

"No."

"Well!" Beatrice put her fork down, eager to tell. "It happened in London about five years ago. In the early hours of the morning, Cartland was racing his phaeton down St. James' Street, deep in his cups, the story goes. He rounded a corner at top speed and struck a little girl in the middle of the street. She was only an orange girl, an orphan, from what I understand, but even so, two of the wheels ran right over her and ... well, as you can imagine, it was all quite dreadful. She died right there in the street. After it happened, he disappeared. Good riddance, I say. What person of quality would have anything to do with him? He's a despicable man, a totally depraved individual."

From the head of the table, James inquired in his quiet voice, "Then why was he here at Arthur's funeral, my dear?"

"We could hardly turn him out." Beatrice gave a disdainful sniff. "He is the guest of Lord Rennie. Some business about building a canal."

"Is that so?" James' eyes brightened. "'Pon my word, canals are a great investment these days. For years Rennie has talked about building one that would run from the River Hulm to the River Clearsy. Not an easy task, what with having to dig tunnels and build the locks and all." He frowned in puzzlement. "I wonder how a rake like Cartland got involved with canal building."

"I'm sure I don't know." Beatrice addressed Jane. "Speaking of the River Hulm, did you know your dower house sits on its banks? There's the most gorgeous view ... but I'm sure you have seen it by now."

"No I have not." Jane's mind drifted to the painful memory of her first days at Chatfield Court. She had so looked forward to riding Beauty all over the vast estate—a consolation of sorts for having entered a loveless marriage with a man she didn't even like. Before she could take even one ride, Arthur sold her horse, nearly breaking her heart. After that, he had kept her virtually a prisoner, hardly allowing her out of the house.

So no, dear Beatrice, I have not seen my dower house.

"You must see it soon. The old dowager countess lived there for many years. In the end, she was quite mad, you know. I understand she collected all kinds of art work which is still there. You are going to love it, just love it!

Looking across the table, Jane caught the look of

apprehension that clouded her mother's face. No wonder. If that queen of hypocrites, Beatrice Elton, said they were going to love it, then the opposite must be true.

Later that night, after Bruta helped Jane into her night clothes and put her clothing away, she inquired in her usual sullen fashion, "You want anything else?"

"Thank you, that will be all." Just as she felt every night, Jane was more than happy when her lady's maid departed. Back when she was single, before Papa ran away and left the family destitute, she had Celeste, who was French and a perfect lady's maid in every respect. Jane wanted to rehire Celeste after she married. Instead, Arthur gave her Bruta. Heavyset, with a lantern jaw and small, close-set eyes, Bruta didn't walk so much as she plodded, didn't talk so much as she muttered in some kind of a foreign accent that Jane could not place. "She never smiles, and she looks as if she disapproves of everything we do," Millicent had once said of her.

"She's awfully good at fixing hair," Jane had countered.

"Even so, how can you stand her?"

"I don't have a choice." Even worse, Bruta once worked for Beatrice. Jane suspected Bruta served as a spy as well as a lady's maid and reported to Beatrice everything she did.

All that is over. Jane's spirits lifted. She could soon get rid of the sullen woman. What a delightful thought.

Shortly after Bruta left, Mama came by. The tightness around her mouth told Jane she was still upset. "Beatrice is taking over the house. Can't you do something?"

Poor Mama. She had yet to face the facts. "Chatfield Court truly will be hers. Soon. Much as we don't like the idea, we must get accustomed to it."

Mama threw a hand up in despair. "There's no chance you might be—?"

"None. Well ... almost none."

"When will you know?"

"I know now."

Mama frowned in exasperation. "You know what I mean."

"A week and a half or thereabouts."

"You will let me know when it happens? *If* it happens."

"It will happen all right. I suppose the whole world is dying to know. Perhaps I should raise a red flag on the rooftop when the big event occurs."

Mama looked askance, just as Jane knew she would. "You need not be flip. A red flag will not be necessary. Just tell me, and in the meantime, while we're waiting, I can only hope you will heed Sir Archibald's words of warning."

"You mean about being discreet?" Mama nodded. "Of course, I shall be discreet. What else? Do you honestly think I would take up with another man after ...?" She decided not to finish her sentence. Mama didn't need to know the sordid details of her marriage to the earl. She wouldn't want to know. "Suffice to say, you needn't worry. Men are out of my life. Forever, as far as I'm concerned."

Mama regarded her strangely. "I would not have thought so the other night when you were talking to Douglas Cartland."

"Whatever do you mean?"

"I saw the two of you laughing. You seemed quite enchanted with that scoundrel."

"I was simply being polite to a guest."

Mama drew herself up. "You should not have anything to do with Douglas Cartland, unless, of course, you wish to disgrace the whole family."

"In case you haven't noticed, I'm a grown woman now. I make my own decisions. However, you needn't worry. I was most certainly not enchanted with the likes of Douglas Cartland."

"This is all your father's fault. I only wish John could see us now—poverty stricken, with barely a roof over our heads. Oh, why did he leave us? What did I do to deserve such a fate?"

There she went again. No doubt to her dying day, Mama

would grieve for her beloved husband. Why had he run off to America? Even though he lost all their money, they could have worked something out. Why had they not heard from him? He could be dead. If he was, he could be buried in some unmarked grave in the wilderness and his loving family would never know.

I will find him. If I can sail to America, I will find Papa, I know it.

Jane's heart ached for her mother, but she knew better than to argue, or even try to answer the questions that had no answers. Instead, all she could offer was comfort over what had to be the worst, most heartbreaking experience Amelia Hart had ever suffered in her otherwise sheltered life.

"Tomorrow I want to see your dower house."

"So do I." Jane gave her mother an encouraging smile. "We shall see if our new home is as wonderful as Beatrice claims."

Mama left her room.

Situated on a bend in the river, not far from Chatfield Court, the two-story dower house built of faded gray stone appeared quite habitable from a distance. The closer they came, however, the worse it looked. A tangled, overgrown garden surrounded the house. *It can easily be salvaged*. Jane was in an optimistic mood as she, Mama and Granny traveled up the cobblestone walk to the front door. Gardeners could clear the undergrowth, trim the roses and honeysuckle vines that choked the yard and cut back the branches of the tall elm trees.

As directed by Mrs. Stanhope, Jane searched under a mulberry bush until she found a jar that held the door key. Her heart sank when she turned the key and they stepped into the entry hall. Immediately they were struck by a blast of musty air.

"Horrible!" Mama put her hand over her nose. "We shall all suffocate."

"I believe Mrs. Stanhope mentioned the place needs airing."

An understatement if ever there was one.

They crossed the small entry hall and stepped into the drawing room. "Dear Lord!" Mama exclaimed.

Jane had never seen so much clutter in her life. A true deluge of bad taste. Gilded, overstuffed sofas, an untold number of mirrors and pictures with elaborate frames, black lacquered cabinets, statues, every sort of gewgaw imaginable ...

"Weren't the birds outside enough?" Granny rested on her cane and gazed with amusement at the large assortment of stuffed birds, each under its own glass dome.

"With a bit of cleaning and sorting out, it will be fine." Jane fought to keep a note of optimism in her voice.

Mama sniffed in disgust. "A *bit* of sorting out? We shall need a lot more than that. This place is a wreck, and you know it."

Jane silently agreed. A closer look brought even more small calamities to light—pieces of the fleur-de-lis moldings had fallen and littered the floor, ugly water stains marred the pale lilac walls. Heaven only knew what else was wrong.

Mama, who tended toward the dramatic at times, pressed a forearm against a faded lilac wall, leaned her forehead against it and wailed, "This is horrible! We cannot live like this." She turned and faced Jane with imploring eyes. "You *must* be expecting. You *must*."

Jane didn't have the heart to smile at her mother's desperate words, laughable though they were. Nor could she bring herself to point out yet again the utter impossibility that she might be carrying the earl's heir. She patted her mother's arm. "We shall cope. As for me expecting, we will just have to wait and see, won't we?"

When they returned to Chatfield Court, Jane found Griggs waiting for her in the entry hall. The usually stony-faced butler had an unusual gleam in his eye.

"What is it, Griggs?"

"Timothy, the stableman, was here." Jane detected repressed

excitement in his voice. "He requests your presence at the stables."

She had not visited the stables for ages, not since ... "Do you know why he wants me?"

"It's best if Timothy explains."

"Very well, then." Mildly curious, she left the house by the back entrance and headed down the path that led to the stables. *Always a pleasant walk*. She would never tire of the sight of Chatfield Court, a gem among country homes, dark and gloomy though it was. It sat atop a low-slung hill, its ancient stone walls and English Gothic chimneys nestled amidst tall oak and elm trees. A vast expanse of beautifully manicured lawn edged by rhododendrons, camellias and magnolias stretched from the rear portico, down a gentle slope, to the banks of the River Hulm. On both sides, thick growths of woods spread in either direction, all of them his lordship's special preserve where only he could hunt. Out of sight beyond the woods and higher up stood Lancaster Hall, Lord Rennie's estate.

The path led Jane to the stables, built close to the river around a bend and hidden from the house. Timothy O'Leary stood in the cobblestone courtyard in front.

"Hello, Timothy. How are you this fine day?" Jane meant her greeting sincerely. A sturdy Irishman somewhere in his sixties, the head stableman had a pleasant way about him, as well as a deep love of the horses he cared for.

He removed his battered hat and smiled. "'Fine, Your Ladyship. It's been a while since you visited the stables. Since Beauty left, I believe."

The thought of her lost horse brought a sudden lump to her throat. Swallowing with some difficulty, she replied, "Yes, it has been a while. Griggs said you wanted to see me?"

"Yes, ma'am." Timothy inclined his head toward the low-roofed wooden building that housed the estate's horses. "There's something for you inside."

"What?"

The stableman grinned. "You had best go in and see for yourself."

Jane stepped inside and paused, adjusting her eyes to the dim light. She drew in a deep breath, savoring the old, familiar odors of hay, alfalfa and fresh manure that brought back memories of happier times. Oh, what a beautiful smell! Only a true lover of horses could love such a smell. She started walking down the aisle between the stalls. Most were empty, the plow horses and the earl's stallion and carriage horses having been turned out to pasture. Farther along the walkway, she saw a horse's head poking out of the furthermost stall. Then she heard a whinny.

That whinny ... something about it ... Her hand flew to her heart. "Beauty?"

The answering whinny told her what she needed to know. With a glad cry, she picked up her skirts, ran the remaining distance to the stall and gazed for a joyous moment at the noble brown head, a perfect white star on its brow. She was looking into the soft brown eyes of her beloved horse. "I can't believe you're back!" She threw open the half door, flung her arms around Beauty's neck and buried her face in her silken crest. The horse whinnied in response, causing tears to well in her eyes. She was wiping them away when Timothy appeared.

"She's in good shape, mum. She's been over at Lord Gamfield's stables on the other side of the village. From the looks of her, she's been well-treated. Lord Gamfield has the best pasture around."

Jane patted Beauty's sleek, well-groomed flank. "I can see that, but I thought ..." The shocking truth dawned. Arthur told her he took Beauty to London and sold her at Tattersall's. That liar! She had assumed she would never see her horse again. All those tears shed! "She has been not five miles from here the whole time?"

"It would seem so, mum."

She bit back angry words and remembered her manners. "How can I ever thank you? Surely money was involved and I will happily pay you—"

"Oh, no, mum. 'Twas not me what brought her back."

"Then who?"

"'Twas that guest of Lord Rennie's. He brought Beauty back this morning and sent me up to the house to fetch you."

Could it be? "Do you recall his name?" She held her breath.

"Mister Douglas Cartland, I believe he said his name was. He's the one who is building the canal for Lord Rennie."

"How could he possibly have known where Beauty was?"

From behind came a familiar male voice. "Simple. Rennie told me. Seems he was with the earl when he made the sale to Gamfield."

She looked over her shoulder. *Him.* Simply dressed in a white shirt open at the throat and dark breeches, he stood behind her, a crooked grin on his deeply bronzed face. "Well. Did I get it right? I would hate to think I brought the wrong horse back."

"Yes, you did." She withdrew her arms from around Beauty's neck and whirled around, resisting the wild impulse to fling her arms around Douglas Cartland instead. "It's Beauty, all right. I am overwhelmed, sir. I cannot thank you enough for bringing her back." A horrible thought struck her. "She's not just borrowed, is she? Tell me you don't have to return her to Lord Gamfield."

His hearty laugh instantly relieved her mind. "She's here to stay. Let's take her outside, shall we?"

"Of course." Nothing would give her more pleasure than to see her beloved horse in the sunlight, in all her glory. Jane noted Beauty wore the same leather-tooled harness she'd bought for her years earlier, back in the days when she thought her happiness would go on forever. She clipped a lead to the harness and led her horse outside, Cartland close behind. In the courtyard, she checked Beauty over, growing more pleased by the minute as she noted the horse's hooves were well cared for, her mane and tail free of dust and dirt. She picked up a brush and began stroking Beauty's shining flanks. "You don't know how much I worried about her, how I imagined all sorts of horrible ways she could have been mistreated. How can I thank you?"

Cartland stood watching her, a glow of satisfaction in his deep brown eyes. "No need to thank me. It was my pleasure."

She cocked her head. "You hardly know me. I can't understand why you would go out of your way to do such a great kindness."

An ironic smile played on his lips. "Neither can I. A moment of madness, perhaps?"

"At least allow me to reimburse you."

He shook his head. "If you must pay me back, come riding with me. Have you ridden the trail by the river? It's quite spectacular."

"I would love to." Her heart lifted at the thought of riding Beauty again. She called to Timothy, "Do you still have my saddle?"

"Yes, mum." The stableman beamed. He disappeared inside.

"I took the river trail once but didn't get far. It will be so lovely to—" Oh, *no!* What was she thinking of? Beatrice's words came back to her. *Despicable ... a depraved individual* ... Sir Archibald's words followed. *You must be the soul of discretion.*

She should not even be talking to Douglas Cartland, let alone riding with him.

She bit her lip and lowered her eyes. "I cannot." How to explain? She could easily think of a dozen white lies, but instinct told her not to lie to this man.

A flash of humor crossed his face. "Ah, but, of course, you cannot ride with me, especially now. No doubt Sir Archibald has warned you of the perils involved in so much as speaking to a man during your ... shall we say, period of waiting? Aside from all that, your reputation would be in tatters. You could never hold your head up again. Mama might be so horrified she'd go into a decline. All because you chose to ride along the river with that scoundrel, Douglas Cartland."

Despite his sarcasm, she felt relieved she didn't have to lie. "I'm glad you understand."

"I understand all right." His shrewd eyes drilled into her. "I feel sorry for you."

She bristled. "I may be recently widowed, but I am in no way an object of pity."

"That's where you're wrong." He crossed his arms and assessed her with a critical squint. "You, my dear countess, represent everything that's wrong with our society."

"That's a rather grandiose statement. Would you care to explain?"

"Gladly. You have been born into a society that keeps its women virtual slaves."

"Are you daft?"

"Let me count the ways." He brought up his fingers and began to count. "One. You were forced into a marriage with a heartless sod who hadn't the faintest notion how to treat a woman."

"I suppose you do?"

"Yes, I do, but that's beside the point. Two." He ticked off another finger. "Look at you, all dressed in dreary black on a lovely summer day. You wouldn't dare wear anything else, would you? All to mourn a man who treated you badly, an old letch you never loved in the first place. You would never admit it, even to yourself, but you're glad he is gone."

Now he had definitely gone too far. "How dare you, sir? I refuse to listen to more of your outrageous remarks. I will have you know—"

"Don't bother." He paused, then shook his head as if genuinely concerned. "Don't you ever get tired of living a lie? Doing what you're told to do and not what you want to do?"

"We must all do our duty." After the words left her mouth,

she silently cringed, aware of how priggish they sounded.

"Duty be damned." He ticked another finger. "Three. You would like to ride along the river with me, but you won't because Mama, sister-in-law Beatrice, and a whole slew of self-righteous ladies of the *Ton* would not approve. Therefore, you must forego all pleasure in your life and do as they say."

The whole time he'd been talking, she knew she should turn her back and walk away. First, of course, she should thank him again for bringing Beauty back and insist upon reimbursing him for whatever he paid Lord Gamfield. Then she should inform him his remarks were unacceptable and she would never again engage in conversation with a man so vile.

She opened her mouth to speak but could not get the words out. She had to admit that he was absolutely correct in every respect. She had been forced to marry the earl. She was *not* sorry he was dead. She hated wearing black, and most of all, she very much wanted to take Beauty for a ride along the river with Douglas Cartland. Why, she didn't know, because Beatrice was right. The man was despicable, a totally depraved individual.

Timothy emerged from the stables carrying a blanket and her hand-tooled lady's saddle, a treasured gift from Papa long ago. Before she could say a word, he walked to Beauty, set down the saddle and laid the blanket over the horse's back. He picked up the saddle and with one easy motion slung it over the blanket.

"Never mind. I am not going riding after all."

"That's too bad, mum." Timothy's broad Irish face reflected his disappointment. He reached for the saddle.

"No!" The word escaped her mouth before she could stop it. Why couldn't she go riding with whomever she pleased? Just once. No one would see them on the secluded river trail. "Leave the saddle. I have changed my mind."

"What is this?" Cartland's eyes squinted in mock surprise. "A change of heart?"

She lifted her chin. "Not that I was in the least bit influenced by," she held up her hands and ticked off an exaggerated one-two-three with her fingers, "your so-called *persuasive* arguments, of which there is absolutely no truth, by the way. I simply changed my mind, that's all."

"Then let's go riding, shall we?"

"How wonderful to have Beauty back again!" Jane called to Douglas Cartland who rode beside her on his own horse, Thunder, a beautiful thoroughbred with a shiny black coat. "I love this trail." There could not be a more beautiful spot on earth than the riding path that followed the lazy current of the River Hulm upstream. At times they rode not more than a few feet away from the blue ribbon of water. Other times the path cut away and led them through dense woods where pine and poplars grew, where green moss and lichen made a soft, silent carpet on the forest floor. Time and again Jane reached for Beauty's withers and stroked her long, silken hair. In return, Beauty would give a nod and a snort, as if she knew her beloved mistress was riding her again. At times Jane and Cartland brought their horses to a gallop. She would laugh from sheer joy, every care forgotten as she tore up the path, her beloved horse beneath her, the sun in her face, her loose auburn hair streaming behind her in the breeze.

After they had ridden for at least an hour, they came to a shady forest glade that overlooked the river. Such a beautiful spot.

Douglas called, "Here's where we stop. Are you hungry?"

"Starving." She wondered what he meant. There was no food around here. They were in the middle of nowhere.

He swung off his horse and came to assist her. "I don't know how you women put up with these ridiculous side saddles." She was about to inform him that she could easily dismount by herself, but before she could, he gripped her waist and swung her down. Other than that one dance years ago, it was the very first time he touched her. She laughed to herself, amused that such an irrelevant fact should enter her head. Perhaps it had to do with her liking the feel of his strong hands and sure grip around her waist.

"Tie your horse. We will sit under that tree over there." He pointed to a large oak that grew on a grassy knoll overlooking the river.

She tethered Beauty to the sturdy branch of a small pine tree and stood waiting while Douglas reached into his saddle bags. He pulled out a small blanket, which he proceeded to spread under the tree. He gave an exaggerated bow and broad sweep of his arm. "Do have a seat, Your Ladyship." Amused, she settled herself upon the blanket and watched while he returned to his horse and pulled a large packet from his saddle bag. He brought it back and set it in the middle of the blanket. Pulling out items one by one, he announced, "We have bread, cheese, fruit and chicken, all prepared by Rennie's cook, Mrs. Groton, who happens to be one of the best cooks in the world. And," he held up a sterling silver hip flask "a bit of brandy to keep us warm in case a storm should strike."

"It's July."

"This is England. You never know." With a flourish he unfolded two linen napkins and placed one in front of her. "The table is set. Let's eat."

Famished, she dug in, soon concluding that she had dined on many a fancy meal in her life but nothing as good as this simple picnic by the river.

"Mmm, it all tastes wonderful. The chicken, everything." She popped a bit of cheese into her mouth.

Sitting across from her, he uncapped the flask and poured brandy into a small sterling silver cup. "Wash it down with this."

She accepted the cup and gazed at it uncertainly. "Brandy in the middle of the afternoon? Mama would be scandalized. I'm not sure I—"

"If ever there was someone who could use a bit of fortification, it's you. Drink up. It won't kill you. In fact, it will doubtless do you some good."

She didn't feel like arguing. She brought the cup to her lips and took a generous sip. Umm ... the fiery liquid slid down her throat, leaving behind a delicious trail of warmth and comfort. She took another sip, which felt even better than the first. "It's good, although I mustn't make a habit of it."

"I doubt you will end up a drunken doxy lying in some gutter," he said with some amusement.

"How very kind of you to say."

After the meal, she leaned back against the oak tree, totally content. "I'm reminded of when I was a little girl and my father used to take us on picnics. It was such a happy time."

Looking as contented as she, Douglas stretched his lean body full out and propped himself up on one elbow. *Even at rest, he looks powerful.* Her gaze locked upon the rich outline of his strong shoulders straining against the fabric of his open shirt. "Tell me about your father."

His request opened a floodgate of memories. While the birds chirped, the lazy river flowed by and a warm, gentle breeze ruffled her hair, she recalled her childhood. "My sister and I had a governess, but even so, our parents spent a lot of time with us, not like other parents you hear about who hardly know their children exist." She paused and smiled. "Papa gave me a pony when I was six, then Beauty when I was twelve. My mother and sister didn't care to ride, but Papa and I used to ride together all the time—every trail on our estate and then some. What fun we had! That's why I'm so reminded of him today ... all the good times." A sudden heaviness settled in her chest. "The good times don't last, do they?"

"What happened?"

"My father started spending more and more time at his clubs in London. Boodles, mostly. Mama was aware of his gambling, of course, but little did she dream he was throwing every last penny away. After he fled to America, she ... well, she has never been the same."

Douglas nodded in sympathy. "I have seen more than one man gamble himself to utter ruin at the faro tables." He gave a self-deprecating grimace. "I almost did it myself."

"What stopped you?"

After a long pause, he sat up and leveled a gaze at her, unspoken pain alive in his eyes. "What stopped me? A little girl dying in my arms stopped me."

Of course, the accident. Her hand flew to her mouth. "How thoughtless of me to ask. I am sorry I reminded you."

"Don't be." He gave her a rueful smile. "A day doesn't go by that I'm not reminded. I provided enough scandal to the wagging tongues of the *Ton* to last for years. What they don't know is my life changed forever on that day."

"Were you arrested?"

"Of course not. I was a man of rank and privilege, beyond reproach," his voice resonated with bitterness and self-derision, "whereas she was only an orange girl and orphaned besides, obviously a lesser being." He paused and took a shaky breath, as if touched by some deep emotion. "I left London immediately. No great loss to the *Ton* since I was labeled as a worthless reprobate anyway," he raised a cynical eyebrow, "which actually, I was. Since then, I haven't held a card in my hand." He raised the silver flask high. "I've rarely tasted spirits until today."

She pulled back in feigned concern. "Good heavens. Have I driven you to drink?"

"No. My drinking days are done except for special occasions such as this."

"So where did you go when you left London?"

"After the accident, I knew I had to get away, to escape the memory of what I did. So I went north and found work on a canal."

"Was it interesting? Did you get to steer the boats?"

He burst into hearty laughter. "No, I did not 'steer the boats' as you put it. I was a tow man. Believe me, there's nothing lower on this earth. I dredged channels, cut weeds, drove mules and horses, fed them and cleaned up after them. You could say I was a horse myself at times, helping to haul the narrow boats along the tow path when the horse power wasn't enough."

"How awful."

"No, it wasn't. Hard work is good medicine. It makes you forget. In the process, I not only learned about canals, I learned I could build canals. If fact, I'm rather good at it. You have to know how to take a level, dig a channel, remove tree roots, dispose of tons of earth, mix underwater cement, create locks and a hundred other things. So that's what I'm doing now for Lord Rennie." He gazed at his outstretched hands, roughened with calluses. "These are not the hands of a gentleman, which pleases me to no end. I shall never be a so-called *gentleman* again."

Didn't all men aspire to be gentlemen? She had never met a man like Douglas Cartland before and she was not sure how to answer. "That is most interesting, Mister Cartland." She sat with one leg neatly folded beneath her. The other, stretched straight out, she kept carefully covered with her long, black skirt. Now she noticed the hem of her skirt had crept up, enough to reveal her black kid shoe and a bit above. With care, she reached to tug it down again.

Watching her, he suddenly smiled. "Perish the thought I should see too much of your lovely ankle."

She willed herself not to blush. "I was just—"

"Just what?" With the swiftness of a snake, his arm shot out and grabbed her foot. With one swift tug, he pulled her shoe off and cradled her foot in his hand. "Trying not to awake my base desires? You know how men are." He gave a devilish grin. "Who knows? One more glimpse of your ankle and I might not have been able to contain myself. You could have been ravished on the spot."

Despite herself, she started to laugh. "You are outrageous." She tugged at her foot, which he still held tightly. "Unhand me."

"Don't you mean, *unfoot* me?"

She laughed harder. "Just give me my foot back."

"Not just yet. Hmmm ..." He directed his attention to her foot, holding the heel in one hand and lightly tracing his fingers over the top with the other. "Do you realize, my dear countess, you may have the most beautiful foot in all of England? Small ... slender ... beautifully arched." He shook his head in regret. "What a pity it's enclosed in ugly black." He gazed up at her. "What is the latest fashion in mourning these days? Are you all in black? Dress, shoes, stockings ... does that also include your drawers?"

She should be outraged, appalled, but she wasn't. In fact, she could not suppress a giggle. If he thought she would act like a squeamish schoolgirl, he was mistaken. She grew serious and shot a cool gaze at him. "You, sir, are no gentleman."

"Did I not just finish telling you that?" He cupped her foot with both hands, obviously in no hurry to let go. "Lean back and close your eyes."

"I shall do no such thing."

"Yes, you will. Foot massage is an excellent way to relax. You need to have your eyes closed."

She closed her eyes.

He began rubbing her foot slowly, the warmth of his hands penetrating through her stocking. A delicious, tingling feeling spread along the sole of her foot from her toes to the back of her heel. The more he rubbed, the better it felt. His fingers slid to her toes where he began massaging. *Umm ... that felt good.* She leaned her head back against the tree trunk, thinking she really ought to tell him to stop, and she would ... in just a little while. *So good. Too good.* His fingers moved again. This time his thumbs massaged in a tantalizing circling motion over her arch. "How does that feel?"

She opened her eyes. "Not bad." Perhaps it was the warmth of the sun on her face, or maybe the brandy spreading its magical comfort throughout her insides. Whatever it was, she had never felt so relaxed in her life or so utterly powerless. He continued the massage. *Do not let him get above your ankle,* a little voice inside her warned. If his hands slid higher, what would she do? She didn't know. All she knew was, nothing had ever felt so good. She closed her eyes again, wondering what she would do if his hands roamed higher. Surely they would. He was a man, wasn't he? She would stop him when the time came but right now ...

It took her a moment to realize his hands had dropped away. Her eyelids flew open. He was looking at her, his eyes sharp and assessing, as if he knew exactly what she'd been thinking. "That's enough for one day." He reached for her shoe. "I'll do the other foot next time."

"No, you will not." What on earth had she been thinking? She, who had just vowed her independence, who had decided never again to bow to the dominance of any man on earth. Not only that, she could guess what Sir Archibald would say. "There will not be a next time." She grabbed the shoe from his hand and slipped it on. Standing quickly, she busily brushed at her skirt. "I must get back. I've been gone much too long."

In silence, they cleared up the remains of the picnic, storing them back in Douglas' saddle bag. She untied Beauty and led her back to the path.

"Need a leg up?"

Without thinking, she responded, "I can do it myself." How could she? She had no mounting block. If she were dressed in something light, she could possibly gather her strength and sling herself over the horse, but her bombazine mourning gown was anything but light. "All right then, I need help."

Keeping a very straight face, he bent and laced his fingers

together. She placed her foot in his clasp, her hand on his shoulder. "Ready."

"Up you go, Your Ladyship," he said in a teasing tone. She seated herself firmly in her saddle. "I shall be gone a couple of days, but when I come back, we shall go riding again."

From atop Beauty, she gazed down at him. She liked what she saw: his compelling brown eyes so full of life, the set of his chin that suggested a stubborn streak, the humorous lines around his mouth. She liked his massive, self-confident presence, too. In fact, what about him was there not to like?

Plenty. Whatever attraction she might feel for Douglas Cartland must end right here. "I cannot go riding with you, ever again. In fact, because of certain circumstances, I should not be riding at all."

"You mean, in case you're carrying the earl's child." His reply was so matter-of-fact it took a moment for his shocking words to sink in.

"Ladies do not discuss those matters."

"Unfortunately, they don't—not in this shallow, artificial society," he countered with a gleam in his eye. "What a shame pregnancy and birth are not to be discussed except behind closed doors. They are both in truth natural events, more to be celebrated than censored."

She could see his point but had no wish to argue. "Be that as it may, I won't be riding for a while, not with you or anyone else." Wanting to move away, she flicked the reins, but he held fast to Beauty's harness.

"How do you feel? Do you want the child?"

Strangely, no one had asked her that question before. She should remain silent, yet she wished to answer because she sensed his genuine concern. "There are many reasons why my family would rejoice if I had a child. We could continue to live in Chatfield Court. Millicent could have her dowry ... all sorts of good things. Whereas, if I am not with child, our lives will be rather bleak. On the other hand," she pondered, biting her lips, "do I wish to carry the offspring of a man I despised? No, I do not. Now, let go of the harness."

He complied, and she flicked the reins again. Beauty leaped away, carrying her back down the trail in a satisfying, soothing gallop.

Chapter 6

When Jane returned to Chatfield Court, she hoped no one, especially her mother, would discover that she had gone riding. Mama would be appalled that she took any sort of risk while possibly expecting. Jane made her way quietly through the entry hall to the drawing room. Poking her head inside, she found Granny alone, furiously stitching on a piece of embroidery. How very peculiar. Granny loathed needlework. "A waste of time," she had said many times, scoffing at the ladies who slaved over their needles.

"Granny, are you upset about something?"

"No." The old lady stabbed her needle into the cloth as if it were a rapier. She held it up for Jane to see. "It's a sampler. I started this stupid thing when I was twelve. High time I finished it." She took another vicious stab.

"What's wrong?" Jane asked softly.

Her grandmother slammed the sampler in her lap. "If you must know, she has taken away my medicine."

"Who has taken away what?"

"My gin!"

"Who took it?"

"Beatrice." Granny practically spat the name out. "She told Griggs not to bring me my medicine anymore and she took what I had out of my room. 'It's not good for you,' she said. I informed her I was eighty years old and if I did not know what was good for me by now I never would. She would not listen."

Jane saw tears in her grandmother's eyes. The heartrending sight made her realize how much she loved this crotchety old woman who had given her nothing but love, loyalty and good advice over the years. "I shall see about this immediately."

"You know it's for my health, Jane. How dare that woman take it away?"

How dare she indeed? For whatever reason. "I shall be right back." Jane hurried from the room, infuriated, not sure what she was going to do but determined to do something. In the entry hall, she encountered the butler. "Griggs, wait up. I want to talk to you."

"Yes, madam?" The butler's expression remained neutral, as usual.

She sucked in her breath, trying to calm herself. "I believe you told my grandmother you would no longer bring her evening ... uh, medicine?"

"On orders from the new countess, ma'am."

Fury almost choked her, but she tried to remain calm. "She is not the new countess yet, Griggs."

For once, a look of confusion crossed the imperturbable butler's face. "The situation seems unclear."

Perceiving she had the upper hand, Jane asked sternly, "So it was Mrs. Elton who forbade you to take Granny her medicine?"

"Yes, Your Ladyship."

"She should not have done that. Be advised, I am still in charge here. You take orders from me, not Mrs. Elton."

"Yes, Your Ladyship." The butler's face clouded. "If I may be permitted to say so, Mrs. Elton is not an easy person to deal with. When she finds out—"

"She won't. How would it be if you brought the medicine to

me, instead? Then I shall take it to my grandmother."

Griggs smiled in relief. "I believe that can be arranged."

"Fine, then. Starting tonight." She started to turn away, but Griggs was not done.

"Perhaps I should mention also ... in case you did not know."

What next? "Do continue."

"Mrs. Elton is planning a small dinner party for tomorrow evening. Nothing elaborate, of course, what with the house being in mourning. Just a few guests. She's calling it a commemorative dinner for the earl."

She knew her surprise must show on her face, but she could not fool Griggs anyway. "Who is invited?"

"Sir Archibald and his wife. Also some of the neighborhood gentry including Lord Rennie and that guest who's staying with him. Douglas Cartland, I believe his name is, the one who's building the canal." Griggs bent forward confidentially. "Mrs. Elton did not want him, but Lord Rennie said he would not come if Cartland was not invited."

"I see. Is there anything else you wish to tell me?"

"As a matter of fact ..." There was a peculiar look on the butler's face.

Dear Lord, what now? "Go ahead, Griggs. Out with it."

"She has been in your bedchamber twice today. Measuring, I believe, for new drapes and—how shall I put it?—assessing the furnishings as if, possibly, she might wish to move in, and soon."

"Thank you, Griggs. I trust that is all?"

"That's all, Your Ladyship."

The butler left her in the entry hall, numb with rage and shock. But what else should she have expected? Of course, Beatrice would want to move into her lovely bedchamber. Other than his lordship's, it was the best in the house, large and spacious with a gorgeous view of the river. Beatrice would naturally want to establish herself as the gracious hostess of Chatfield Court.

I will not let it bother me.

Easier said than done.

After she calmed herself, Jane returned to the drawing room. Granny gave a satisfied grunt when informed she would still get her gin. When Jane related her entire conversation with Griggs, Granny frowned in disapproval. "You didn't talk directly to Beatrice?"

"No. I thought it would be better—"

"That woman should be put in her place."

"You're absolutely right." Jane felt ashamed of herself. "I didn't want to confront Beatrice because, in the end, what good would it do? She'll soon have everything she wants, so why create a scene?"

"Are you like your mealy-mouthed mother—too afraid to speak up for yourself?"

"Of course not. That's not it at all ..." Jane proceeded to defend herself, but she knew in her heart Granny was right. She should have gone directly to Beatrice and had it out. Was she a coward? Or was it just that she had too many other battles to fight right now?

Now content, Granny threw down her embroidery. "I hear you went to the stables. You were gone a long time."

"I was out, uh, getting some air."

Granny let out a cackle. "Douglas Cartland bought Beauty back from Lord Gamfield. The two of you went riding along the river trail."

Jane sank in defeat into the cushions of the sofa. "How did you know?"

"The servants, how do you think? You can't keep a secret around here, not with fifty pairs of ears listening." Granny's eyes shifted to a chambermaid, busy polishing the andirons in the fireplace. "See what I mean? No doubt the girl has heard every word. Don't worry, no one is about to tell your mother. That includes me."

"Please don't! You know how upset Mama gets. She would

certainly not want me to ride while there's any chance I might be expecting. Which, of course, I am not." A surge of rebellion arose within her. "I hate this! Why should I have to please my mother? Why must I be nice to Beatrice? Why can't I have some privacy without the whole world watching for when I next come 'round?"

"That's not the way life is," Granny answered quietly.

"I don't have to like it, do I?" Protests were useless. She tried to calm herself. "Why can't we just go live in my dower house as I would like us to?"

"We'll see about that, missy. You needn't worry. Amelia doesn't know a thing. You're right. She would throw a fit if she knew you went riding. You don't need the aggravation. I suggest you don't do it again, not until you can raise that red flag over the roof."

"I hate to be treated like a delicate flower, but I've already decided I won't ride. It shouldn't take long, anyway. Only another week or so, and meantime, I shall visit Beauty every day. I just won't ride her." She broke into a joyous smile. "Oh, Granny, it's so good to have Beauty back!"

Granny gave her a piercing glare. "Thanks to Douglas Cartland. He must have paid good money for that horse. Did you pay him back?"

"He wouldn't let me."

"Do you want to be beholden to him?"

"After all I went through with the earl, I don't want to be beholden to any man."

"That's what you say now, but you'll change your mind."

"No I will not." No man was ever going to order her around, ever again. That wasn't all. No man was ever going to touch her again. Unless ... She felt a tingle, remembering the way Cartland's hand had caressed her foot. No! That was over. She would not let him touch her again.

"I rather like Douglas Cartland," Granny said.

Had Granny read her mind? "I didn't know you knew him."

"I met him at the funeral. He actually talked to me like I was a person instead of a worthless old lady who had lost her wits. That's more than I can say for all those chitty-faced dandies who looked past me like I was already dead."

Jane burst into laughter. "Granny, how could anyone ignore you?"

"Cartland didn't. That's why I like the man."

"He has a terrible reputation."

"That's another thing wrong with our society. You need to judge for yourself, not go by what others think."

First Douglas, now Granny. This was the second time today the society in which she lived had been insulted. Maybe they were right. She would give it more thought later, when she had time. "I told you what I think. In another week or two, when I know I'm not with child, I shall be perfectly content to live in my little dower house by the river. I certainly won't want to wait months and months like Sir Archibald said. That's ridiculous. Let Beatrice have Chatfield Court. I'll be content in the dower house with you, Mama and Millicent, as long as they want to stay. And Beauty, of course. No one else, ever."

The door burst open. Beatrice entered the drawing room. She nodded briefly, her perennial smile more forced than ever. She seated herself stiffly, regarding Jane with humorless eyes. "Well, any news yet?"

She could mean only one thing. "Nothing has happened. But it's early, and I'm sure in another week—"

Her sister-in-law's lips thinned with displeasure. "This is so ridiculous. There is no way in the world Arthur could have left an heir, yet we must go through all this rigmarole. The laws should be changed."

Why argue? "I suppose you're right."

Beatrice nailed her with an icy stare. "Where are the Lansdown jewels?"

"I have no idea." How annoying. Beatrice had already asked her twice.

"When did you see them last?"

Resentment welled within her. Her sister-in-law so obviously suspected her of taking the jewels and concealing them. "I already told you. I wore the pearl and amber necklace at dinner the night Arthur died. He often wanted me to wear the jewels, as you very well know. He always brought them to me, or had Griggs deliver them. I never knew where he kept them. I didn't want to know."

"I see." Beatrice's voice was laced with sarcasm. "Then I shall just have to keep looking, won't I? I *will* find them." She arose abruptly and left, closing the door behind her with a heavy hand.

Jane turned to Granny. "I would give them to her in a minute if I knew where they were."

"I suggest you do no such thing." Granny gave a firm bob of her lace-capped head. "She's not the Countess of Lansdown yet. Who knows what might happen?"

Later, after Granny had left and Jane was about to vacate the drawing room, the chambermaid she had noticed earlier called, "May I have a word, your ladyship?"

"Of course. Your name is Meg, isn't it?" She vaguely recalled Mrs. Stanhope mentioning Meg was one of the few servants who did not live in. She came from a farm on the other side of the river and walked to work every day.

The girl got up from her knees, the polishing rag still clutched in her hand. Even in her lace cap and starched white apron, she looked like what she was—a sturdy farm girl with strong arms and shoulders, rosy cheeks and a pleasant, round face. "Yes, ma'am, my name is Meg." She approached with hesitation, as if she expected to be chastised at any moment. Well she might. Griggs and Mrs. Stanhope, both stern disciplinarians, insisted none of the staff should ever speak directly to their superiors unless addressed first.

Jane smiled, hoping to put the girl at ease. "Do speak up. I won't bite."

"Well, Your Ladyship, I couldn't help hearing your conversation and I just wanted ..." She stopped and cleared her throat.

Would she ask a favor? Make a complaint? "Do go on, Meg."

"I just wanted to tell you how glad I am you got your horse back."

After Meg's words sank in, Jane returned an appreciative smile. "Why, how very kind of you."

Meg nodded eagerly. "It's just that I remember when his lordship ... when Beauty got sold. I felt so sad for you. We all did."

Jane was reminded once again that with servants around, nothing in her life was sacred. "I felt sad, too. Now it's wonderful to have her back."

"I have a horse, too."

A servant girl with a horse? Unheard of. "How nice. Do you ride?"

"Yes, I do. That is, when he isn't working in the fields, I do."

"So he's a plow horse?"

"Oh, no! Jupiter's much more than a plow horse. He's the fastest of steeds—a Pegasus without wings—you should see him when he gallops. He fairly flies."

Meg intrigued her. Never had she heard a maid so poetic, and with such imagination. "Do you ever ride the river trail?"

"Me and my family live on the other side of the river. I don't take the river trail because Jupiter don't like to cross that wooden bridge."

Jane nodded. "Beauty's exactly the same. She acts up every time her hoofs hit wood. She just hates that noise. I have to coax her across."

"Horses can be so skittish, and another thing Jupiter does—"

"Meg! What are you doing?" Mrs. Stanhope's sharp voice resonated throughout the room.

Meg cringed. "Sorry, ma'am, I was just ... just ..."

"I was giving her some instructions, Mrs. Stanhope." Jane assumed her lofty countess voice, the one she hardly ever used. "I was most concerned the andirons weren't ... uh, shiny enough, so I was telling Meg she must give them a bit of extra polish."

"Very well, madam." The housekeeper made no attempt to hide the skeptical look in her eyes. She knew very well Jane didn't give a fig how shiny the andirons were, but what could she say?

"You may get back to your polishing." Jane maintained her lofty tone. She turned to the housekeeper. "Thank you, Mrs. Stanhope. Keep up the good work." She swept from the room with as much dignity as she could muster.

What an extraordinary chambermaid. She had enjoyed talking to the girl. In fact, there was a moment there when she'd forgotten she was a countess and Meg the humble servant. It seemed more as if they were two young women who loved horses, chatting together.

The reality was quite different, of course. They lived in different worlds, and that was too bad. She liked Meg very much. She would have enjoyed having the servant girl as a friend.

Chapter 7

Jane visited the stables in the early morning for the next three days. Despite her vow not to do anything but visit Beauty, she could not resist and took her for a short ride each time. At that hour, who would see her? Even if her mother found out, she was prepared to take a stand. After all, she was the countess and certainly not under Mama's thumb.

Because everyone else still lay abed, she refused to wear her ugly mourning clothes. Bruta bristled with disapproval. "You must wear the black, madam. You are in mourning."

"I don't care. Who's going to see me except Timothy and the horses?"

Thank goodness she had saved her colorful riding habits. No ugly black until later in the morning. She wasn't all that proud of herself. If she really had the courage, she would cease wearing black altogether. What a furor she would create. Would she ever have the nerve to flaunt society's rules to such an extent? It was fun just to envision the look on Mama's face should she appear at dinner in her bright pink satin.

The fourth morning after Beauty came home, Jane strolled down the path to the stables wearing her favorite habit—a blue, close-fitting jacket worn over a cambric shirt, a blue riding hat decorated with two high-standing feathers and a matching riding skirt, extra full, long enough to completely cover her shoes when she sat sidesaddle. She carried a riding crop, too, knowing she looked extra elegant when Timothy gave her a boost and she settled into the sidesaddle. The minute she did, she felt better. The problems that had plagued her of late slipped away like drops of quicksilver. On even the shortest of rides through the peaceful countryside, a feeling of well-being overtook her. She forgot about horrible Beatrice, Mama's stress over a nonexistent baby, poor, heartbroken Millicent, the missing jewels, the future state of her finances—which, if what Sir Archibald said was true, was about to change disastrously.

Over the past few days, she had ridden over parts of the estate she had never seen before. Today, though, she chose the familiar river trail. It really was the best and had a long, straight stretch where she could let her horse full out. She walked Beauty to the trail, gave her a nudge, and off they went at a gallop. Instantly, her mind cleared of all the hassles and frustrations. She could concentrate on the trail, the horse ... and Douglas Cartland. What was the matter with her? Since the day he caressed her foot, she could not stop thinking about him. He was totally unsuitable. Everyone thought so, and she thought so, too. She should never see him again. The problem was, ever since they went riding, the image of his laughing face danced in her head, and she could not get rid of it. No matter. If she met him on the trail, she would give him a polite hello then be on her way.

She saw a speck of something in the distance. As she drew closer, she saw it was a horse and rider. Closer still, her heart jumped. Speak of the devil. Douglas Cartland.

They drew parallel and reined their horses. "Good morning, Countess." Like last time, he was dressed informally in a white shirt open at the neck, breeches and Hessian boots. He scanned her critically and beamed approval. "No mourning today? What happened? Don't tell me they brought the old boy back to life."

"You are absolutely blasphemous." She was not the least perturbed. Now was the time to bid him good day and move on, but she couldn't. She smoothed her blue velvet skirt, grateful that she looked her best. "You were right about the black. It is so unbecoming. I cannot bear to wear it unless I absolutely must. I do apologize. I can see how properly shocked you are that I've broken the rules."

"Shocked, indeed." With a careless laugh, he circled his horse around hers so they faced the same direction. "Let's ride together, shall we? We'll go back to where we had our picnic." He touched one of his saddle bags. "I trust you haven't eaten. Mrs. Groton has fixed us a marvelous breakfast of Bolognese sausage, hard-boiled eggs, bread, cheese, and a bit of Russian caviar and brandy to wash it down."

She wanted to ask why he was so sure he would meet her on the trail but thought better of it. "Actually, I haven't had my breakfast yet, so, yes, I accept your offer. If you think I'm going to drink brandy at this hour of the morning, you are sadly mistaken."

The brandy slid down her throat like velvet. Her stomach full, Jane leaned back against the big oak tree, just as satisfied and comfortable as before. Once again she found herself under the spell of that scoundrel, Douglas Cartland. He had been gone a few days to oversee the work on Lord Rennie's canal, his return having been delayed by many problems.

"Forgive me, but I cannot see what is so difficult about building a canal. Isn't it simply a matter of digging a ditch? Why do we need canals in the first place? England is full of rivers."

He might have laughed at what she sensed was a foolish question, but instead he grew serious. "Not many of the rivers are navigable, whereas canals are built to haul all manner of goods, from coal to cabbage, as well as people. There are profits to be made, which is why Rennie hired me to engineer his Berkferd Canal. It runs only fifteen miles, between the Rivers Clearsy and Hulm, but it requires twenty locks and a tunnel, not a small engineering feat, I assure you."

"What is a lock?"

"Let's take a look." Cartland picked up a stick and drew a line in the dirt, then another line beside it. "Let's say these are two rivers, twenty miles apart. England is not a flat country. There are hills in-between, so what do you think the chances are the two rivers would be at exactly the same elevation?"

"I hadn't thought of it, but practically none."

"Exactly. One is bound to be higher than the other. That's where the locks come in. Picture long boxes." He continued scratching diagrams with the stick. "The boat sails into the box and a gate shuts behind it. Then the box is filled with water. The ship rises with the water until it gets to the top, then sails out the other end to a new, higher level. Reverse that, of course, the other way."

While Cartland talked, Jane perceived an entirely new side of him. Up to now, she had not seen much depth, just his amusing, slightly cynical side. Now she saw a man whose eyes glowed with enthusiasm while he earnestly described his work. Obviously, he loved what he did with a passion. Odd, really. A true gentleman wasn't supposed to work. But then, as he had said earlier, he was no gentleman.

The thought occurred to her, too, that no man had ever talked to her this way before. Most of the men she knew treated her like she did not have a brain in her head and would not have the least interest in anything as complex as the construction of a canal.

Aside from all that, she enjoyed watching him. She liked the way that lock of his dark, curly hair fell over his forehead, and how, with his body stretched out as it was now, she could see every well-muscled inch of him. Most of all, she liked his face—his determined jaw, generous mouth, and those brown eyes usually sparkling with amusement.

He looked up from his diagram. "Stop me if I'm boring you. Get me on the subject of water and I'll go on for hours."

"You're positively not boring me." She looked out over the river, so shallow one could walk across. "I see what you mean. A boat could never navigate the River Hulm."

"Not at this time of year, but you never know. There have been some bad floods in the Midlands when there's too much rain. Water flows off the moors and into the rivers, sometimes becoming a raging torrent. Actually, you have a disaster waiting to happen right here." He pointed up the river toward the north, where mountains loomed in the distance. "Do you see that steep, narrow canyon? I would hate to think what would happen to the village of Sudberry and all that's between should torrential rains pile up in that canyon. You would get a wall of water that could—" He caught himself, as if not wanting to worry her with predictions of gloom. "I've said enough. The chances of such a disaster occurring are remote, but it happened once before, back in the fourteenth century."

She listened, fascinated. "So you think it could happen again?"

"Yes."

She gazed out at the River Hulm, a narrow stream not more than thirty feet across, its sluggish current hardly moving. Cows grazed peacefully in the pasture on the other side. In the distance lay the plowed fields and thatched cottage where Meg Twimby lived. "I certainly hope you're wrong."

"Uh-oh." His mood swiftly changed. A twinkle gleamed in his eye.

"What's wrong?"

"Do I actually see a foot?"

She looked down. Drat! Up to now, she had sat with both legs tucked primly beneath her billowing riding skirt. Distracted by their fascinating conversation, she had allowed her booted right foot, along with part of an ankle, to poke out. Quickly she drew it beneath her. "It was all your talk about floods that made me careless."

"Lord help us." He cast a disgusted look at the sky. "Do you remember what I told you last time we were here?"

Every word. "I cannot recall."

"If memory serves, I massaged your very lovely left foot. I said next time I would do the same for the right."

"So you did. I just remembered."

"Of course, you *just remembered*." His gaze raked boldly over her, finally dropping to the hem of her skirt. "Stick that right foot out. If there's anything I can't stand it's a namby-pamby woman who is stuck on her own false modesty. There's nothing sacred about feet, no matter what Mama taught you."

Without giving the matter another thought, she held her right foot out. What harm would it do? He spoke the truth. Besides all that, she wanted to.

He leaned across the blanket and lifted her foot, encased in its half boot. "Let's get this off." Slowly, very slowly, he gripped her ankle with one hand and slid her boot off with the other. He cupped her foot in his hands, one underneath, the other resting lightly on the top. "White silk stockings this time," he murmured, as if to himself, and began rubbing her foot gently with his upper hand. "Relax. Even a countess deserves a foot rub now and then." He cocked an eyebrow. "Have you ever had one? From the earl perhaps?"

"Surely you jest." She giggled.

"I thought not." For a time, he bent to his task, concentrating on rubbing her foot, the touch of his fingers sending a warming tingle through her. "You did not like being married to the earl."

"It was horrible. I hated it. I shall never have another husband."

"Why?"

"Because I don't want to do *that*, ever again."

He pondered a moment. "When you say *that*, I take it you

mean the sexual act that takes place between a man and a woman?"

"Well, yes." She felt a rush of blood to her face.

He looked up. "You're blushing. That's what this stupid society does to you women. Makes a perfectly normal activity into something shameful, unmentionable." He stopped rubbing her foot and looked her square in the eye. "Sex can be a beautiful thing, you know."

Sex. He had actually said that forbidden word aloud! But somehow she no longer felt uncomfortable. Perhaps because he spoke so honestly, his remark seemed commonplace, as if he were talking about the weather, not intending to shock her at all. "I suppose it *can* be a beautiful thing, but not in this case." She was proud she managed to sound nonchalant. "I want nothing to do with it, ever again. Instead, I plan to devote myself to riding Beauty, decorating my dower house and planting lovely flowers in my garden ... that sort of thing. I shall be quite content, thank you, without a man in my life."

"What a lofty plan. Quite admirable, but for a woman as attractive as you, it won't work."

"Why not?"

"The men won't leave you alone. Not with that voluptuous figure and that come-hither look, which is there whether you want it to be or not. Then there's that marvelous hair and the way your whole face lights up when you laugh." He sat back, his gaze sweeping over her. "You're quite fetching, you know."

"No, I don't know."

"Your naivety is part of your charm."

"I am *not* naïve. I cannot imagine why you would think so."

He laughed softly. "I'll tell you something you don't know. The reason you don't know is no one will tell you, fearing such an unseemly disclosure will shock your so-called delicate sensibilities."

"Really? What?" So intriguing. She could hardly wait to hear.

"Have you ever heard of Spanish Fly?"

Spanish Fly. Hearing the words brought an instant sense of something sinful, forbidden, to be spoken of in whispers. "I've heard of it, just vaguely."

"You do know what an aphrodisiac is?"

"Of course." Actually, she wasn't sure, aside from knowing it was not to be discussed in polite society.

"Spanish Fly is a powerful aphrodisiac, used for both men and women to enhance their sexual desire, and in a man's case to ... shall we say, provide the assistance he needs. Your husband used it the night he died."

For a moment his words didn't sink in. When they did, she gasped. "You mean he, he—?"

"A small vial of Spanish Fly was found in the pocket of his dressing gown. Obviously, he took it to enhance his performance. Obviously, it worked. I can only guess, but I suspect his inability to satisfy you must have been driving him wild. I'm sure part of his motivation must have had to do with his wish to produce an heir, but I would wager a lot of his motivation had to do with his wanting to make mad, passionate love to his beautiful countess."

"How do you know all this?"

"The servants, of course. Griggs is the one who found the vial. He told your housekeeper, Mrs. Stanhope, who couldn't wait to pass on such a delicious tidbit to her good friend, Mrs. Shelton, who's Rennie's housekeeper. Mrs. Shelton told Rennie's valet, who passed it on to Rennie, who passed it on to me."

She shook her head with annoyance. "It's not fair. The servants know everything."

"Of course they do. By the way, the consensus of opinion is, some of that Spanish Fly was meant for you. If not that night, then probably the next. The earl, being the complete bastard he was, wanted it for himself first. Half of it was gone, so obviously he took too much, *way* too much, and that's what killed him. Spanish Fly is a deadly drug that should be used with extreme caution. Consider yourself fortunate he didn't slip a few drops into your wine." He smiled with amusement. "For more than one reason."

The very thought that some of the aphrodisiac was meant for her caused her to slap her hand to her mouth. It remained there while she gazed at him with increasing horror. "I'm shocked ... I never dreamed ..." Realization struck. "So that's why—"

"That's why the old boy's flagpole was raised to full mast when he 'departed this mortal coil,' as Shakespeare wrote."

She opened her mouth to say, "That's not respectful," but an image of the earl and his flagpole flashed through her mind and laughter bubbled out instead. She couldn't help it. He started laughing, too. Suddenly, with a movement so swift she was hardly aware of it, he was sitting directly in front of her, his laughter stilled. "You must have been driving him mad. I can only imagine how desperate he was to make love to you and frustrated that he could not. Am I right?"

"I suppose." His openness had opened the door to a flood of memories. "He tried so hard and got so angry when he couldn't, you know. It was horrible. He screamed and cursed at me. He ... well, *enough*. He's gone now. They say you shouldn't speak ill of the dead."

Douglas nodded with understanding, as if he knew she would prefer to change the subject. In a sudden move, he reached up and pulled off her blue riding hat. "I've seen enough of that silly hat." He held it up and tweaked one of the high-standing feathers. "If I let go, do you suppose it will fly off on its own?"

Again, she had to laugh, all bad memories forgotten. "It *is* a bit silly, isn't it? It's the height of fashion, I can assure you."

"So much for fashion." He dropped the hat next to her discarded boot. Moving closer, he ran his hands up her arms to her shoulders and gripped them tight. His nearness bothered her so much that she gulped and became aware that she was breathing hard.

She found her voice. "You're a long way from my foot."

"Really?" Suddenly his lips were on hers, surprisingly gentle. So surprised was she, she stiffened and didn't respond. He lifted his lips and murmured, "You *will* kiss me back, Countess." His arms encircled her, one hand in the small of her back. She could feel his uneven breathing on her cheek. "Let's try that again," he said softly into her ear. He pressed his lips to hers again, at first caressing her mouth more than kissing it. The feel of it made her go all soft inside, and instead of pulling away, which propriety demanded, all she wanted was to melt into him. She pressed back, surrendering herself to the warmth of their kiss until he lifted his lips from her mouth and murmured an "Umm" in her ear, then a shaky, "Ah, Countess."

She slipped her hands behind his neck and murmured an answering, "Umm," before eagerly locking her lips to his again. Such a delicious sensation, as if she were floating in a dreamy intimacy with this man whom she found deucedly attractive, despite herself. She hardly noticed when with one swift, sure movement he lowered her to the blanket so that she lay prone on her back, looking up at him.

"Why am I doing this?" she murmured.

"Because you like it." His lips skidded over her chin and down her neck where his tongue found the hollow of her throat. There it halted and swirled in tantalizing circles, sending a warm wave of delicious feeling clear to her toes.

"Sir Archibald would not approve of this." She spoke without the least bit of conviction.

"Sir Archibald would be scandalized." His voice was husky. His hand had lain against her side. Now, slowly, it slid up her side and over her breast, where it stopped and rested. The pleasure from its warmth radiated through her jacket and cambric shirt clear to her flesh. He bent to kiss her again. While he sprinkled kisses liberally on her cheeks and nose, she felt his fingers making their way beneath her jacket, then slowly pulling aside first her shirt, then the soft batiste chemise she wore underneath. His fingers found the top of her breast and started rubbing with a feather touch against her bare skin. She really ought to stop him, but it felt too good. Then one finger slid from the top of her breast to her nipple and pulled it gently. An indescribably warm feeling flowed through her as he kept pulling, over and over again and her nipple grew hard beneath his hand.

"I want to see you," he whispered. She lay beneath him, powerless to move, while he spread open her jacket and shirt. With both hands he slid her chemise down over her breasts so they lay completely exposed. "Beautiful." His brown eyes were murky with desire, his breathing hard. He bent his head and sucked on her nipple. She gasped with shock and pleasure. Then he placed his warm, wet mouth on her breast and slowly ran his tongue over and over again across her erect nipple. She gripped his shoulders, hearing a low groan coming from her own throat, the feeling so intensely delectable she forgot time and place, forgot everything except a driving need that made her want to spread her legs so he could do what he wished with her.

Still busy at her breast, he reached for her hand and guided it to his manhood. She clasped it through the cloth. How amazingly hard it was, about to burst from his breeches. She couldn't help but ask, "Spanish Fly?"

"Good God!" Choking with laughter, he raised his head. "When the right time comes, you will find I have no need of Spanish Fly."

A mooing sound came from across the river. Jane turned her head and saw a row of cows standing behind the wooden fence, all gazing in their direction. A cow at the end of the row mooed loudly, raised her nose high and gave her a look that seemed to say, *bad countess*. "What am I doing?" The mood was broken. Bad enough the cows could see her, but what if somebody came along? She would die. She pulled up her chemise and moved to a sitting position. "Apparently we've been entertaining the cows."

He sat up, too. "We shall find a more secluded spot next time."

Pulling shut her shirt and jacket, she rose unsteadily to her feet, her riding habit disheveled, one boot off, her hat lying on the ground. *Good God.* What had she been doing? She, the esteemed Countess of Lansdown, rutting around in full view of every cow in the area. "There won't be a next time, Douglas Cartland." She bent to retrieve her hat and started to lose her balance.

He caught her arm and steadied her while she recovered. "So you don't want to see me again?"

"Never would be too soon."

"No more picnics? No more riding?"

"I'm going home." She marched over to where Beauty was tethered to a mulberry bush.

He followed her. "You need a leg up."

She wanted to refuse but knew better. She could never manage by herself. "Very well." After she untied Beauty, she lifted her foot so Douglas could cradle his hands and give her a boost. Instead, he clasped her waist. Standing intimately close, he lifted her like a feather into the saddle. From her waist he trailed his hands down her hips, along her thighs and down her skirt. He looked up at her, his mocking smile back in place. "You haven't seen the last of me."

"Yes, I have."

He looked down to where her skirt was slightly hiked up so her boots were exposed and clicked his tongue. "What a scandalous display." He jerked her skirt down, carefully adjusting it to cover her boots. "That's better. Gracious me, what would people say?"

"Oh, you are impossible." She nudged Beauty and rode away, riding crop in hand. She should have given him a good whack with it, she thought as she rode back along the river trail.

When she reached the stables, she hastily dismounted and

instructed Timothy to rub Beauty down. Ordinarily, she liked to do it herself, but time was flying and she was later than usual. Hastening up the path to the mansion, she hoped no one was around. If ever there was a time she wanted to slip into the house unobserved, this was it. She needed to compose herself, as well as get back into her mourning clothes.

No such luck. When she slipped into the entryway, she encountered Griggs, who appeared to be waiting for her. "Your family awaits you in the drawing room, m'lady."

Drat and damnation. She looked down at herself. A big grass stain decorated her skirt. God only knew what her hair looked like or if her hat was on straight. "Tell them I shall be there as soon as I go up and change."

She started toward the staircase but Griggs spoke again. "Your mother said it was most urgent. She wanted to see you the instant you arrived home."

Had she and Douglas been seen? No, that was impossible. No one but the cows could possibly have seen them in their isolated picnic spot and yet ... A dreadful image filled her mind: Sir Archibald peering at them through the bushes, shocked and horrified, his glasses about to fall off his nose. Oh, God no! Her stomach clenched tight. *Why* had she done such a stupid thing as to allow Douglas Cartland such liberties? She wanted to run to her room and hide, but, of course, it was too late. Nothing to do but face whatever fate held in store for her and make the best of it. "Thank you, Griggs. I shall go right in." She removed her hat, ran a hand over her hair and went to find out what her mother considered so urgent.

Chapter 8

Jane stepped into the drawing room, finding her mother, sister and grandmother engaged in excited chatter. "Hello, everyone."

"Jane!" her mother called when she spied her, "do come sit down. You will never guess what has happened."

No word about her not being in mourning? No looks of condemnation because someone had seen her with Cartland? She seated herself, completely mystified. "What has happened?"

Mama held up a letter. "This just arrived from America. It's from your father."

When the words sank in, Jane's heart swelled with relief. "So he's alive?" A lump had formed in her throat.

"Read for yourself." Her mother handed her the letter.

My Dear Amelia,

How can I begin to apologize for my weakness and cowardly actions? How can I begin to tell you how much I have missed you and the girls since I left those two long years ago? I can only say I still love you dearly.

Not a minute has gone by that I have not missed you and wanted you all by my side.

I have done well here in this young country, where opportunities abound. After a short apprenticeship with a shoemaker, I opened my own shop in New York City, with living quarters above. If you will forgive a bit of immodesty, I have prospered. I am doing so well, in fact, that I can now afford to send for you and the girls, provided they have not married, of course. I cannot promise you the life of luxury we once had, but if my love, caring and devotion still mean anything to you, then you will be rich and doubly blessed for the rest of your life.

Know I love you dearly, my dear wife, and Jane and Millicent, too. I yearn to see you again and will never cease striving to make up for the harm I have done.

I have sent a draft for £50 to our bank to cover the cost of passage for the three of you.

Longing to see you again ...

Your devoted husband,
—*John Hart*

Jane dropped the letter to her lap, tears welling in her eyes. "Papa is safe! What wonderful news." She leaped up and gave her mother a hug. "I'm so happy for you. I knew in my heart he hadn't truly deserted you."

Millicent clapped her hands in delight. "Isn't it wonderful? Imagine, he owns his own shop and is prospering."

Even Granny had to smile. "I suppose that rascal isn't all bad. At least he's finally done the right thing."

Jane sat down again, her thoughts scattered. "This is so sudden. I can't even think. But ... America! Why not? I cannot imagine how wonderful it would be to see Papa again and live in a land where everything is new. Mama, you must be so excited and thrilled at the thought you'll soon see Papa again."

Her mother tossed her head. "Are you daft? Do you honestly think I would set even one foot on one of those leaky boats and go live in a land full of savages and uncouth colonists?"

Jane was taken aback. "They're not colonists anymore, Mama. We lost the war, remember? Now they're Americans. But I don't understand. Papa broke your heart when he left. I thought you would be overjoyed to hear from him. I thought you would want to be with him."

"I'm glad he's not dead, if that is what you mean." Mama's expression softened, but only for moment. "Did you know they have no titles in America? How, I ask you, is one supposed to know who is important and who is not?" She thought a moment. "Who would know you are a countess?"

"In America they wouldn't care if I was a countess. I wouldn't care, either. I just want to see Papa again."

"So do I." Millicent's eyes glowed with excitement. "They say America is the land of opportunity. I could find myself a rich young man there."

"I'll come, too," said Granny, "if these old bones can survive the Atlantic."

"I am not going," Mama said firmly.

"Why?" Jane was astonished. She would have guessed her mother would want to sail on the next ship across the Atlantic.

"How could John think I would actually want to be a shoemaker's wife living over some shabby shop? Besides, this is no time to even consider leaving England. Have you forgotten what we're waiting for? I'm pinning all my hopes on your coming through for us, Jane. Chatfield Court is our home, not Beatrice's. The very thought of her taking over galls me no end. Besides, Millicent must have her dowry and marry a proper Englishman."

"She would not need a dowry in America. Mama, please reconsider?"

Granny cackled. "You won't change Amelia's mind. As far as she's concerned, the world is England and England is the world. There's nothing beyond, and you won't convince her otherwise."

"Your grandmother is absolutely right." Mama regarded Jane, and after a long moment, a look of enlightenment came over her face, followed by a frown of disapproval. "Why are you wearing that blue riding habit when you're in mourning?"

Jane's heart sank. How could her mother even think of such a minor matter at a time like this? "Because I don't have a black one." That was as good an answer as any, and besides, at this point, she didn't care. She had just learned her father was alive—a wonderful surprise. She also realized how deeply her mother had been affected by Papa's leaving. She remembered Mama as she used to be: generous, always laughing, always a stickler for the rules yet willing to try something new. That woman was gone forever. Her spirit was broken that terrible day she learned her husband deserted her. She would never be the same.

The only way I can help her is to have a baby. A matter that was now in the hands of God.

❧❧❧❧

Douglas Cartland sat at the table in the elegant dining room of Chatfield Court, doing his best to avoid the inane conversation presided over by that Elton woman. Judging from the grandness of her attitude, you would think she was already crowned and anointed the new Countess of Lansdown. At the moment, she and several ladies present were engaged in a heated debate over whether or not a girl should wear more than seven feathers in her headdress when presented to court. Before that, Sir Archibald, the Elton's insufferably boring solicitor, had pontificated for what seemed like hours on the superior importance of London banks as compared to smaller banks in the provinces. Douglas tried not to yawn, allowing his bored gaze to examine the twenty guests seated around the table. At the head sat James, the dull, insipid next Earl of Lansdown. Maybe. To James' right sat Millicent, a pretty creature, to be sure, but lacking her sister's wit, depth and compassion. To be fair, who could compare to Jane? Rennie sat next to Millicent. He'd been falling all over himself the entire evening trying to get her attention, but the shallow wench hardly knew he existed.

Percy Elton sat next to Millicent. Douglas could not recall when he had met anyone more loathsome. Sly and shifty-eyed, the man's greatest interest in life appeared to be ogling the ladies. Douglas could only imagine how much the countess must want to be rid of him.

Rennie insisted Douglas come with him. He had to admit it didn't take much persuasion. Not that he liked spending his evening gorging himself and enduring silly prattle. He had come because of *her*. He looked directly across the table. There she sat, properly solemn-faced, properly attired in black. Earlier there was some mention about a letter from her father in America. Very good news, it seemed. She seemed subdued even then, but now she'd grown even more quiet and was most definitely avoiding his gaze. Even so, all evening he was hard-put not to look at her. Stare, actually. Since their intimacy of yesterday, he thought of little else. That had to stop. He could not, *would* not, allow himself to become involved with a woman. He knew when he killed little Sarah he could never live the pleasurable life of an ordinary man. What he did that awful night was so despicable, so utterly beyond redemption, he could never allow himself the joys of marriage, children, a happy family life. Work was his salvation. He would build canals until he grew tired of it, if he ever did. If so, he would join the Navy and sail the oceans wide until, if God agreed, he would be swept overboard by a giant wave in a violent storm, a fitting end, indeed, for the drunken fool who had taken the life of a little girl. Oh, God, that awful woman was addressing him. "Beg pardon, madam, what did you say?"

Beatrice Elton returned a cold lift of her eyebrow. "I *said*,

Mister Cartland, I have heard you are building a canal for Lord Rennie."

"That is correct." He did not want to discuss his canals with this bird-brained woman who could not care less.

Jane spoke up, practically the first time all evening she had opened her mouth except to eat. "Mister Cartland is an expert on water. In fact, he thinks we might have a terrible flood." She sent him a dazzling smile. "Is that not right, Mister Cartland?"

Curse the woman. She had said that just to rile him. "It could happen." He hoped for a quick change of subject, but no, Beatrice Elton regarded him with a skeptical eye.

"Our silly little river?" She laughed and everyone joined in, even Rennie, who he thought was his friend.

He ignored the laughter. "Given the right conditions, that silly little river could change into a raging torrent in a matter of hours."

From the head of the table, James Elton, who ordinarily sat silent, addressed his wife. "He's right, my dear. Local history records a horrific flood of the River Hulm a few centuries ago. As the story goes, the third earl and his wife were compelled to run to higher ground, the water lapping at their heels." He paused and frowned. "Or was it the fourth earl?"

Beatrice waved a dismissive hand. "What does it matter? It all happened a long time ago and has no relation to our modern times." She addressed Jane. "Considering that your dower house sits by the river, we would not want a flood, now would we?"

"No, indeed not, Beatrice." Jane smiled pleasantly, as if touched by her sister-in-law's concern. Douglas easily perceived the wariness that lay beneath the smile. Well it should. Beatrice Elton wanted to be a countess so bad she could taste it, and she was dying to get Jane out of the house. He wondered what the woman would do if Jane really *was* carrying the earl's heir. If she was, she better beware. He would not put anything past that Elton woman.

Rennie spoke up. "Don't forget I live on higher ground." He cast sheep's eyes at Millicent. "If it floods, Miss Hart, I shall come and rescue you."

Rennie, you poor sod, she doesn't even like you.

Millicent fluttered her long lashes. "How kind of you, Lord Rennie. In case the flood comes, I shall feel quite safe, remembering your offer."

She was making fun of his friend, but what could he do? If Rennie wanted to make a fool of himself, who was he to stop him? A shame, though. Rennie was obviously in love. A girl as shallow as Millicent would never be able to appreciate the warm and generous heart that lay behind his poor friend's pock-marked face and awkward demeanor.

Douglas heaved a silent sigh. The night had just begun. Next, brandy with the gentlemen, then the inevitable cards with the ladies, and he'd probably get stuck with that insufferable woman who fancied herself the countess. When all he really wanted to do was maneuver Jane into a dark corner. *Stupid, stupid.* What was he thinking? He would never marry, so where would this lead? All he knew was, he had to get her alone, hold her in his arms again. That was all that mattered, and he didn't care to look beyond.

❧❧❧❧

"This is all because of Beatrice," said Mama, "and I'm still not sure we're doing the proper thing."

After dinner, in the drawing room, Jane sat at one of the Whist tables; the foursome consisted of herself, Granny, Douglas and her mother, who held a deck of cards in hand and went on to inquire, "If we're in mourning, is it proper to play cards?"

Granny was Douglas' partner. "Who cares? Just deal." She loved playing Whist, especially when a bit of a wager was involved.

"Don't worry, Mama. After all, according to Beatrice this

was a memorial dinner for his lordship. I'm sure he would have wanted us to enjoy ourselves." Douglas sat on Jane's right. She looked to him for confirmation. "Do you not agree, Mister Cartland?"

"Absolutely We owe it to Lord Lansdown to carry on. We all know what a heart of gold he had. He would be devastated if he saw his loved ones sitting around mourning, denying themselves any fun."

"Well, if you put it that way, I suppose he wouldn't mind." Mama started dealing the cards.

Jane exchanged an amused glance with Douglas. His subtle humor might fly right over Mama's head, but it was one of the things she liked about him. He seemed to understand what she was thinking, too. In fact, the more she knew him, the more she found common ground. Then, of course, there was yesterday ... She looked at his hands. They were not the soft, white hands of a gentleman. Instead, they were tanned, strong and looked so very capable. This evening they held cards. Yesterday they were on her breasts ... Her flesh tingled. A pleasurable tug warmed the pit of her stomach, just thinking about how she had lain beneath him, breasts exposed, so caught up in a passion she had never felt before.

And very much wanted to feel again.

"Pay attention, Jane. It's your turn."

"Of course, Mother." She threw down a card, hardly caring if it trumped or not. Damn him. She had better come to her senses, and fast. She needed to remind herself she wasn't going to see him again, and with good reason.

All evening long she was acutely aware of Douglas' presence. She kept telling herself there would be no chance of seeing him alone, which was most certainly for the best. Later, though, when the card playing ended and some of the guests left, she encountered him alone outside the drawing room. Her pulse began to race.

"Where can we talk?" he asked.

She knew she ought to tell him they had nothing to discuss, but the intensity in his voice made her give up any thought of saying so, and she led him into the dark, empty library.

The minute she closed the doors and turned to face him, her heart started pounding in her chest. No way could she control it. She could barely make out the features of his face in the darkened room, lit only by weak moonlight streaming through an open window. "What is there to say?" She hoped he couldn't hear the shakiness in her voice.

He reached out and caught her hand in his. "You have been avoiding me all evening."

"I told you—"

"I know what you told me. Stop talking." His arms encircled her in a swift motion that locked her tight against him. He bent her back and, with stunning urgency, crushed his mouth to hers. With nary a thought of resistance, she wrapped her arms around his neck and savored the moment, feeling sweet currents of desire course through her body. Soon his tongue pushed her lips aside to explore her mouth. It slid across the inside of her lips, touched her tongue, explored all the recesses of her mouth. She never had a man's tongue in her mouth before and would never have guessed how pleasurable it would be, how the feel of him inside her would be ... She pushed closer against him, feeling his strong muscles, wanting more, until at last, as if both could endure no more, they broke apart.

They stared at each other, gasping for air. There was something wrong with her legs. They were all wobbly and her knees felt weak. "We must stop," she gasped. "I simply can't ... not when they think I might be carrying the heir ... Sir Archibald ... this just isn't the time ..."

He stepped back, crossed his arms and regarded her. She couldn't see his face too well but sensed his skepticism. "How long will this ridiculous wait go on?"

"What a tactful way to put it."

"When?"

"Tomorrow is the day."

"Tomorrow," he repeated thoughtfully. "The world awaits, your ladyship."

She heard the distant sound of voices, most likely more guests departing. "This is insanity. I must go, and I don't want to see you anymore."

He stepped to the door and opened it wide. Peering through, she caught a glimpse of something or someone she couldn't make out, much like a shadow moving swiftly away. She could almost swear someone had been at the door listening, but why even mention it? Whoever it was would be gone now. Probably Percy. She wouldn't put anything past her shifty-eyed nephew.

"After you, Countess." Douglas waved her through. "I shall be gone a few days. I hope by the time I return your problems will all be resolved."

When she awoke the next morning, her first thought was, this is the day! A quick check told her not yet. The day was young. She was always right on time. In fact, she could count on coming 'round like the monthly arrival of the full moon.

Thoughts of Douglas Cartland filled her mind. How could she *not* think about him, not feel the aching need to be with him? She needed to clear her head. A good ride on Beauty was the answer. She could enjoy the brisk air of the early morning, and besides, maybe a bit of jogging in the saddle would bring on her monthly. She had another reason, too, for wanting to get away. Sometimes it seemed the dark, stone walls of Chatfield Court were closing in on her. It was such a dark place, and cold, too, even in summer. Beatrice's constant, bothersome presence didn't help. In fact, Jane didn't much care to see her mother this morning, either, not after her remarks about her father and America yesterday.

She dressed in her riding habit and slipped out of the mansion. Soon she had saddled Beauty and was ready to go. Which way? She left the courtyard. She decided she would try something new today—the other side of the river. At least she would not have to worry about making skittish Beauty cross the wooden bridge. The animal could easily walk across the River Hulm, which was now so shallow she would hardly get her hooves wet.

Jane crossed the river and found a good trail on the other side. Keeping Beauty trotting at a brisk pace, she passed the pasture where the very same cows who had regarded Douglas and her with so much curiosity grazed. "Hello, girls." She gave a merry little wave as she passed by. A good thing those cows couldn't talk. She was amused at her little joke. A field of corn lay beyond the pasture. Halfway past it, she saw two figures in the field picking ears of corn from the tall stalks and sticking them into gunny sacks. One was a boy of twelve or so, and the other was Meg, her chambermaid. Jane reined Beauty to a stop, raised her arm and waved. "Hello, Meg Twimby!"

Meg dropped her sack of corn and walked over to where Jane sat on her horse. She wiped a damp brow with her arm. "'Pon my word, if it isn't the countess! I see you crossed the river."

"Just trying something new." Jane patted Beauty's withers. "This is my horse, Beauty."

"Oh, I've seen her in the stables, ma'am, and a fine horse she is." Meg pointed at a nearby birch tree. "Do you have a moment? Come, let's sit in the shade for a while. Picking corn is hard work. I need a rest." Her forehead creased in a sudden frown. "I hope it's all right. I mean, you being the countess and all, and me a chambermaid."

"Don't be silly. I need a rest, too." Not true, of course, but she instinctively liked this girl and wished to share a visit. Besides, did she really want to be a snob like her mother?

Jane slid off Beauty and tethered her to a tree. She and Meg settled in the shade beneath. Sitting cross-legged, shielding her eyes from the sun, Jane pointed at the young boy still picking corn. "Is that your brother?"

"That's Jonathan, who's twelve."

"Do you have any other brothers?"

Meg's broad face lit at the mention of her family. ""My older brother, Jeremy, is twenty-two. I have another brother, Matthew, who's home taking care of our little sister, Molly. She's two, and our little darling."

"Your mother and father?"

"My mum is gone now, died two years ago when Molly was born. Then there's my dad. He's not in good health right now, but he'll get better soon. We're your tenants, as I guess you know."

Jane had only a vague idea of her husband's holdings. He never discussed them with her, nor ever said a word about his tenants or what rents he received. "I must confess to abysmal ignorance on the subject."

"Well, m'lady, your family owns the land. We rent three hundred acres and grow mostly corn and some beans. We graze cows, sheep and one very ornery goat. My family's been paying rent to the many Earls of Lansdown for generations. It's just a shame that—"

Meg's abrupt pause made her ask, "What is a shame?"

"Nothing. I misspoke."

"So you work on your farm as well as at Chatfield Court?"

"Oh, yes, your ladyship. Since my mother is gone, I do all the cooking and cleaning, and I help my brothers with the other chores, too, seeing as my dad is so poorly." She made a dismissive gesture. "But I'm talking about myself too much. It's your turn."

Jane chuckled. "Don't you already know about me? Hasn't just about every intimate detail of my life been bandied about below the stairs?"

"Almost, I suppose." Meg's eyes twinkled. "We know, for instance, you are waiting to see if you have a bun in the oven."

Jane threw her head back and laughed aloud. "I might have known. Nothing is sacred."

"Oh, madam, I have gone too far. Please excuse—"

"Nonsense. Don't apologize. I don't object to your honesty, I welcome it. As to your question, today is supposed to be the day, but it hasn't happened yet."

"Do you want the baby?"

The question startled her. Except for Douglas, no one else had ever thought to ask. In fact, if anyone else asked such a question, she would have considered it rude. But she sensed that Meg, like Douglas, asked out of genuine concern, not mere curiosity. "That's a difficult question to answer. My mother would be dancing in the streets if I were to produce a male heir. As for me, in the remote possibility I'm carrying the earl's child, it will be much anticipated and loved, but the truth is, I don't want it, and for more reasons than one."

Meg smiled sympathetically. "Too bad we women don't have more say in the matter."

"Ah, how very, very true."

They continued talking, Jane enjoying every minute she spent with this warm and friendly farm girl. She might be plain-faced, but her depth of understanding exceeded that of most of the giddy girls Jane had known in her London days. At last Meg asked, "Can you come and see our house? It won't take long. You can meet Jupiter and I'll give you a glass of buttermilk."

Jane readily agreed. Leading Beauty, she followed Meg to the yard of a rather wretched-looking cottage. Meg led Beauty to a makeshift shelter—it could hardly be called a stable—built against the side wall of the cottage, and tethered her next to one of the saddest looking horses Jane had ever seen. The creature had to be well beyond thirty years of age, with a shaggy mane, big belly and an extreme swayback. "Is this Jupiter?"

Meg's eyes brightened. "I hoped you would get a chance to meet him. Is he not handsome?" She proudly patted Jupiter on his rump. "If I had my way, he would never pull another plough again. Just take me riding."

Jane frantically searched her mind for something honest but complimentary to say. "I'm glad I finally got the chance to meet Jupiter. One thing I've noticed about him—he has the most friendly eyes. Bright, happy eyes, as if he's enjoying his life."

Apparently she had given the right reply because Meg beamed with pleasure. "Come inside and I will give you that buttermilk."

How horrible. Jane gingerly picked her way across a muddy yard surrounded by a stone fence. Aside from a few chickens running loose, the yard contained nothing except the dried-up remnants of what was once a garden. Following Meg, she stooped to get through the low doorway and stepped into a dim room with a floor of rough stones and a huge stone fireplace. The only light filtered down from two small, high windows. The furniture consisted of a few rickety wooden chairs and a table—bare except for a tin dinner service. Straw mattresses lined the walls. *This is where they sleep?* She was appalled.

A little girl of around two with chubby cheeks and blond curly hair tottered to meet Meg, arms outstretched. Meg scooped her up. "This is our darling Molly." She nodded toward a slender boy of around seven. "This is Matthew, whose help I could not do without." She pointed to one of the straw mattresses where a man lay with his eyes closed. He was so thin and emaciated Jane hadn't even noticed him. "I want you to meet my father, Edwin Twimby. "Father, this is the Countess of Lansdown herself, come to see us."

Edwin Twimby's eyes fluttered open. He tried to speak but the effort was too great and he shut his eyes again.

Matthew squatted down beside him, his pale little face tight with worry. "He's feeling poorly today."

"Oh, dear," said Meg, "I'm afraid this isn't one of his better days."

Jane said, "Perhaps I should come back—"

"Mercy, no." Meg pulled a chair back from the table. "Do sit down, your ladyship, and I will get you that buttermilk."

Jane sat at the table, feeling awkward, uncomfortable and very much aware the living conditions here were not as wonderful as her chambermaid would have her think. After Meg brought the buttermilk, she seated herself, cuddling little Molly on her lap. Jane nodded at the sick man. "If you don't mind my asking, what does the doctor say?"

"The doctor came but once, ma'am. He said Father had a cancer in his stomach and there was nothing we could do except give him laudanum to ease the pain. That's what I've been doing, but lately the pain is getting worse. He needs more and more laudanum."

Matthew still squatted on the floor beside his father. "The laudanum is just about gone, Meg. You said we didn't have money for more."

"Shush, Matthew." Meg turned to Jane. "My goodness, I don't mean to inflict our problems upon you. We'll find a way. I'm sure."

Sensing Meg's embarrassment, Jane searched for a change in subject. "You mentioned you had another brother, Jeremy. Does he live here, too?"

"Not anymore."

"My brother got transported," said Matthew.

"Matthew!" Meg squeezed her eyes shut. "It's hard to keep things private when you've got a little brother who blabbers all the time."

"Jeremy shot a partridge." Matthew seemed oblivious to his sister's annoyance and eager to tell. "The sheriff caught him, and the earl had him transported to Australia for seven years."

"Just for shooting a partridge?" Jane asked.

"Matthew's right, I'm afraid. Jeremy trespassed in the earl's forest. Of course, the earl holds all the sporting rights, so my brother clearly broke the law."

Jane shook her head in disbelief. "Even so, the punishment seems excessive."

The irrepressible Matthew spoke again. "The crops weren't good that year, and we were hungry. That's why Jeremy did it, just to get us some food. I miss him a lot."

"I'm sure you do, Matthew." Jane was sick at heart. "I cannot speak for my late husband, but it appears to me it was wrong of him to do such a thing."

"Don't feel bad. You're not responsible, and what's done is done." Meg's face brightened. "We get along quite well. I intend to start the garden again. We've got eggs from the chickens and milk and butter from the cows. I do miss Jeremy, though. When our father got sick, he took over and kept the farm running. Now that he's gone, and Mother's gone too, it's up to me, and some days," her shoulders slumped, "I find it hard to keep going." She straightened and hugged the little girl in her lap. "Well, listen to me! I should be counting my blessings instead of dumping all my problems upon a fine lady like you."

"How do you manage? I mean, how can you work at Chatfield Court and then keep all this going, too?"

"Mrs. Stanhope has been more than kind. I get there at five in the morning to light the fires, take up the breakfasts, empty the slops and such. Then she lets me go back home. That's when I cook breakfast and see to little Molly here, and see that the boys get to their chores. Later in the day, I go back to the manor to haul bath water up the stairs and the like. It keeps me busy, but I manage."

Jane noticed Meg's red, roughened hands. "You even work in the fields."

"That, too." Meg gave Jane an understanding smile, as if she knew exactly what her visitor must be thinking. She proudly raised her chin. "Don't be shocked and don't feel sorry for me. God decides our place in this world, and I know mine."

"Of course." Jane understood that Meg had her pride and was asking for neither help nor sympathy. She picked up her glass of buttermilk and took a sip. "Mmm, delicious. I suspect it's very, very fresh."

"Just churned this morning." Meg was clearly glad to move on to another subject.

They chatted for a while, Jane thoroughly enjoying herself and knowing she had found a new friend. "Come back soon," Meg called when she left.

"I will." Jane recalled the earl had taken laudanum from time to time. Surely there must be some left. She suspected Granny used it, too. Of course, no one had the indelicacy to mention that laudanum was another name for tincture of opium, especially when the crafty old lady claimed she used it for medicinal purposes only, for her shakes and ague. At any rate, Jane resolved to find some laudanum and give it to Meg tomorrow. That was the least she could do to help relieve her poor father's suffering.

Chapter 9

When Jane returned home, she intended to go straight to her bedchamber to bathe and change to her mourning clothes. Instead, her mother met her in the entry hall wearing a grim expression.

"Jane, you must come into the drawing room at once. You will never guess what that woman has done."

Uh-oh. She had to mean Beatrice. Jane followed her mother into the drawing room wondering what dastardly deed her sister-in-law had committed now.

After Mama shut the drawing room doors, she turned to face her daughter. "I am very upset."

"What has she done?"

"Beatrice ordered Griggs to move her husband's things into the earl's bedchamber. How dare she! James is not even the earl yet."

Was that all? Jane was not nearly as upset as her mother. "It's not all that bad. After all, the room has been empty since Arthur died. Let James have it. Besides, you know very well he will be the new earl, so in reality what difference does it make if he moves in early?"

"What difference? Beatrice Elton is taking over the whole household now, this minute. I am horrified."

Jane placed a soothing hand on her mother's shoulder. "I can understand your concern, but really, we must get accustomed to our new station in life. Try to look at the bright side. When we move to the dower house, we'll be away from Beatrice. Won't that be wonderful? Then we won't give a fig what goes on in this drafty old place."

"That's not all." Unmoved by Jane's attempt to placate, Mama shook her head regretfully. "I wish it were but it's not."

"There's something else?"

"There most assuredly is. Brace yourself. That woman has moved herself into your bedchamber. The servants just finished carrying everything you own to that smaller room at the end of the hall. So now what do you say?" Mama glared accusingly. "Do you still think we must just become accustomed to it?"

Jane stared at her mother. When she found her voice, she sputtered for a moment before finally managing to gasp, "She ... took ... my ... bedchamber?"

"Go up and see for yourself."

"I will in a minute, but first I need to sit down." Numb with shock, Jane sank to one of the sofas. As her wits returned, she tried to think what to do. "I really don't want a confrontation with Beatrice, but on the other hand—"

"On the other hand, where will it end? How long before Millicent and I are turned out of our rooms, relegated to the servants' quarters? I wouldn't put it past her. What about your grandmother? What will Beatrice do to a poor old lady who cannot defend herself? Throw her out in the snow?"

Jane refrained from mentioning that this was summer and there wasn't any snow. Her mother had a point, though. Where would it end? To what lengths would Beatrice go? She arose from the sofa. "Enough is enough. I shall go right upstairs and talk to her."

Mama frowned. "What about your mourning clothes? You

really should change from that blue riding habit and—"

"The devil with what I'm wearing. Right now I don't care and neither should you."

Sheer, unadulterated anger carried Jane up the grand staircase and down the wide gallery to what had been her bedchamber. She knocked firmly on the door. "Beatrice? I'm coming in." She swung the door wide, entered and found Beatrice sitting at her dressing table. Bruta stood behind her, dressing her hair.

"What are you doing here?" Jane inquired of her lady's maid.

Bruta glared. "I was summoned by Mrs. Elton, madam."

"Oh, dear," Beatrice said in her sweet, high-pitched, voice. She had yet to take her eyes off her image in the mirror. "I didn't think you would mind, my dear. Bruta is such a gem when it comes to fixing hair. I thought we could at least share her until you leave. Then, of course, you realize she'll be staying on with me, since, after all, the earl paid her salary and the new earl will do the same. You know, what with my new social obligations, I shall need a lady's maid full-time." Beatrice took up a comb and touched it to one of the little sausage curls that encircled her forehead. "Make this one a little tighter, Bruta." Her eyes were still fastened on the mirror. "Is there anything else, Jane?"

Much as she wished to be rid of Bruta, Jane found Beatrice's theft of the woman absolutely galling. She allowed a swell of anger to pass. "Leave us, Bruta."

For once the surly lady's maid looked slightly taken aback. "But Mrs. Elton—"

"I said leave and I mean right now."

Bruta left without another word. Beatrice dropped her comb and swiveled her head to look at Jane. "Must you sound so harsh?"

Good. She had gotten Beatrice's full attention. "I want you to listen carefully to what I have to say."

The older woman turned in her chair to face her. "Well, my goodness—"

"Forget about 'my goodness.'" Jane vowed to keep her voice

well under control. She would not sound angry, outraged or wounded. She would simply talk in as straightforward a manner as possible and give her sister-in-law the facts. "You have just taken over my bedchamber without any warning. Instead you took possession while I was out riding. That is sneaky and despicable."

Beatrice's gray eyes opened wide, regarding her with innocent incredulity. She opened her pouty lips. "I—"

"Don't interrupt. I shall let you get away with it this time. In fact, I'll even not protest your moving James into the earl's chambers when you know very well he doesn't belong there yet." The words flowed from her mouth as smoothly as she hoped they would. What a pleasure to let them out. She put her hands on her hips. "But that is all, Beatrice. Do you understand? Until James is officially the heir, and thus entitled to call himself the Earl of Lansdown, you will do nothing more to usurp my authority. My mother, sister and grandmother will remain where they are. Don't even think of switching their rooms. Do you understand?"

"Well, mercy me, of course." Beatrice's look of innocence was positively angelic. "I was only trying to do what was convenient for everyone."

"I do not find it 'convenient' to have my room taken away. Furthermore, find your own lady's maid. I shall not be sharing Bruta." There. She'd had her say. She dropped her hands from her hips and prepared to leave. "Have I made myself clear?"

"I hate to see you so upset." Despite the sweet smile she maintained, Beatrice's eyes hardened and filled with dislike.

Jane's first impulse was to reply that she was not in the least upset, but she caught herself. That would sound defensive— just as Beatrice intended. Instead, she sternly warned, "Don't forget what I told you," and turned to leave.

"Any news yet? Wasn't today the day?"

"Go to blazes."

"God bless you, dear," Beatrice called as Jane shut the door behind her.

God's blood, what an awful woman!

Jane marched along the gallery to her new room, head held high. She felt good. She had accomplished what she set out to do. Beatrice would make no further aggressive moves until all was settled. On the other hand ...

To what lengths would her sister-in-law go to become the next Countess of Lansdown? A chill swept over her. If she really was carrying the earl's heir, she had better watch out.

Her new room wasn't so bad. The furnishings were not quite as elegant, but adequate enough, and she still had a lovely view of the river. She would make do and not complain. After all, this was only temporary until ...

She checked again. *Nothing.* Surely tomorrow.

Later in the day, Millicent came to see Jane's new bedchamber. After looking around, she perched herself on the bed. "It's not so bad. Is there any news? I don't suppose—?"

"Not yet. You will be one of the first to know."

Millicent heaved a sigh. "Would you mind so very much if you were?"

Jane sniffed with mild amusement. "If I were, the family's problems would be solved, wouldn't they?"

"Mine would be, and Mama's, too. I don't want you to be unhappy. It seems that so much depends on whether or not you're expecting. I can see your feelings are mixed."

"More than mixed, I'm afraid. I feel trapped. It appears I'm damned if I am and damned if I am not."

"I know how you feel, but it's just so important to me. I don't sleep well anymore. I lie awake in my bed for half the night thinking, what if I don't have a dowry? How can I find a suitable husband without one? What if I end up a wrinkled old ape leader, everyone looking down on me because I couldn't find a husband? Can you imagine a more horrible fate?"

Millicent's pretty little face appeared strained and pale. *I didn't even notice. So wrapped up with my own problems.* Jane smiled reassuringly. "A beautiful young woman like you is sure to find a suitable husband. I don't care what your dowry is. Even if you don't find a husband, it's not the end of the world."

"Easy for you to say. You've never had the need of a husband like I do." Millicent smiled. "I was so astounded when you refused a second season. When you said you would rather stay home and ride Beauty than put up with all those vain London fops another minute."

"I meant it, too."

Millicent gave a sly glance. "I know someone who likes you very much."

"Who might that be?" As if she didn't know.

"Douglas Cartland. He couldn't keep his eyes off you at dinner last night. I would swear he's fallen in love with you. I suspect you like him, too."

"I do like him, but don't count on him for husband material. I sense he's not interested in marrying."

"Uh-oh, there goes another one." Millicent gestured with her finger, crossing a name off an imaginary list.

Jane smiled. "Speaking of eligible bachelors, why have you not considered Lord Rennie? He couldn't keep his eyes off *you* last night."

"Oh, *him*." Millicent tossed her bouncy blond curls. "He's nice enough, I suppose, but not the kind of man I could ever fall in love with. I want a man who's handsome and dashing, who will sweep me off my feet. I do not want a man with a pocked face, big ears and a namby-pamby manner."

"Don't forget, there's always America."

"I've changed my mind." Millicent made a face. "At first, when I heard Papa's letter, it seemed like a wonderful idea. I could see Papa again, make a fresh start. But underneath I'm just like Mama. I don't want to set foot on one of those leaky boats, either, and sail into the unknown. No, I would be much better off staying right here where everything is familiar. Besides, I've heard those Americans are quite boorish. Give me a proper Englishman every time."

The next morning the rain prevented Jane from riding, leaving only one important chore for her to do—obtain the laudanum for Meg's ailing father. She knew exactly where to find it: at the back of a drawer in a table beside Arthur's bed. She planned to simply walk into the earl's bedchamber and take it, but now that James had moved in, she wondered what she should do. Ask Griggs? No, she didn't trust the butler. Ask James? The man was such a weakling he would probably run to Beatrice to find out what to say.

Or simply walk in and take the laudanum? Why not? After all, she was still the countess. First, she better make sure James was occupied elsewhere. She slipped downstairs, peeked into the library and spied her brother-in-law pouring himself a glass of port. The clock had not struck ten yet, but knowing James and his proclivity for drink, she was not surprised. She hastened back up, sped along the gallery to what was now his bedchamber and walked in. A weird feeling gripped her as she looked around. She had not set foot in this room since the night Arthur died. Her gaze fell upon the spot where he'd made the horrible noise and crashed to the floor ... *Don't think about it.* She went to a mahogany table by the bed and pulled open the drawer. Had someone already taken the laudanum? She fumbled toward the back and, thank goodness, found the nearly-full bottle where it lay almost hidden. She pulled it out and quickly shut the drawer. As she did so, her gaze wandered to the spot where her late husband had lain ...

"What are you doing in my bedchamber?"

Her heart nearly jumped from her chest. Clutching the bottle she spun around. Oh, dear God, Arthur stood in the doorway, *back from the dead.* She froze in horror. Seconds passed before she realized her dead husband wasn't standing there. It was his brother. She pressed her hand to her heart. "James, you frightened me."

"Do tell." James stepped inside and closed the heavy oak door behind him. "Were you looking for me?"

Uh-oh. He started to move toward her, wearing one of those sly, lecherous smiles she absolutely loathed. "I did not come to see you." She held up the bottle. "I have need of this medicine that belonged to Arthur."

She moved toward the door, but he caught her arm. "Don't be shy, sweetheart. Admit you came to see me. Admit you've been dying to get me alone."

Don't *panic*. Keep your wits about you and don't bother arguing with such insanity. "Let go of me," she said in a low, calm voice.

He drew closer. So close she could see the insolent lust in his eyes and smell his sour, wine-laden breath. "You and I have wanted each other for a long time," he whispered hoarsely, and began trailing his fingers down the sides of her face. "You have needs. I know you do. Arthur could never satisfy you, but wait 'til you see what I have for you."

She tried to break from his grasp but he held her fast. "I said, let me go, James."

"You little tiger! How I admire your spirit. It needs taming, though." His hand trailed to the stiff, black bombazine bodice of her dress and pressed against her breast. Before she could react, he bent her back over his arm and crushed his thin, moist lips to hers. She nearly gagged and tried to fight against him, but he held her so firmly she could hardly move. Finally, he raised his lips, gasping for air, panting hard. Still holding her close, he whispered in her ear, "You won't have to leave when I am the earl. You can stay right here. I shall make you my mistress. You can have your bedchamber back. Don't worry. I shall move Beatrice to the end of the hall." Before she could utter a protest, he smothered her mouth with another long, revolting kiss. As he did so, he clasped her hand in an iron-like grip and forced it down to his pants. "Do you feel that, my sweet? More than Arthur ever had, eh?" He pressed her hand into his bulge.

Dear God. She had to get away. *Must get away.* With a strength she didn't know she possessed, she pulled her hand from his grasp. He reached for her, but she took a step back and gasped, "Get away from me, you lecherous old man!"

A silly grin came over his face, making her realize he was drunker than she thought. "Don't be that way, you little tease." He reached down and started to unbutton his pants. "I've got something to show you. Just wait 'til you see ..."

No! She could not imagine anything in this world she wanted to see less than James' cock. She gave him an outraged shove. With a curse, he stumbled backward, nearly falling to the floor. Grabbing her chance, she bolted for the door, got through it and fled down the gallery. The first room she passed was her former bedchamber. The next, her mother's. She darted inside, closed the door quickly and turned the key in the lock. Gasping for breath, she pressed her back against the door. She felt something in her hand and held it up. To her amazement, she still clutched the bottle of laudanum.

"I am not the least surprised," said Mama. She and Granny were drinking tea at a small table by the window when Jane burst in. "You have only to look at James to see the lechery."

"I've always hated the way he looked at me." Jane sat perched on the side of the bed. Her mother had given her a strong cup of tea, and she felt much calmer.

Granny asked, "Did he actually say he would move Beatrice to the end of the hall?"

Jane nodded.

A rare smile appeared on her mother's face. "It would almost be worth it, just to see Beatrice's expression when he told her. I'd wager they would have to drag her down the hallway, kicking and screaming."

The three of them shared a hearty laugh. Jane felt better, grateful to her family for helping her see the humor of it all. When the laughter died, she asked half jokingly, "What did I do to deserve this? Beatrice wants me gone, the sooner the better. James wants to bed me. So does Percy. I swear, that sneaky prig has been following me around the house."

"Like father, like son," Granny commented.

"What can I do? They live here. I feel so trapped, as if I don't have any choice and must simply wait like a docile child for whatever fate awaits."

"I say, throw them out," Granny exclaimed. "James isn't the earl yet and maybe he won't be. Don't forget you're not entirely without choices. You could move to your dower house right now if you're sure you're not expecting." She cocked an inquiring eyebrow. "Anything new?"

"I am two days late, but that doesn't mean a thing."

"Hmm, we'll see about that, won't we? Another choice you have," Granny flicked a quick glance at her daughter, "is you could go to America and be with your father." Her words caused Mama to practically spill her tea, but Granny went right on. "Don't say a word, Amelia. The child has a right to do whatever she likes. You should be more than willing to pay for her passage out of that money John sent you."

Mama found her voice. "That is outrageous and preposterous, Mother. Jane would never dream of doing such a thing, would you, dear?"

Jane brought up an instant vision of sailing for America and escaping not only this dreary place but also the Eltons, as well as the inevitable question, *have you come 'round yet?* What a wonderful thought, but right now a near impossible dream. Her mother didn't understand and never would. "I must say, it's tempting."

Granny's expression turned crafty. "You have another choice."

"I do?" She couldn't imagine what.

"Marry Douglas Cartland."

Mama gasped and set down her tea cup. "Why on earth would she do such a thing? She hardly knows the man."

"She knows him better than you think." Granny cast Jane a knowing look. "Douglas isn't rich, but he isn't poor, either. He's the fifth son of a viscount, so that makes him eligible in your eyes, doesn't it, Amelia? The biggest reason of all—Jane likes him. Isn't that so, missy?"

"It doesn't matter whether I like him or not." Jane shrugged. "I sense he's not a marrying man."

"Pshaw!" Granny tittered and had to set her own cup down. "What man is? It's your job to change his mind."

"I have more important matters on my mind right now." Jane was pleased by the way her words came out, so cool and offhand. Truth was, she'd spent a lot more time thinking of Douglas Cartland than she had ever cared to admit, even to herself. She told him she didn't want to see him again, but her words didn't erase him from her thoughts. The problem was, that soft kiss he gave her played again and again in her memory, and the rough kiss, too, and his hands on her breasts, and his mouth ... Each time she remembered their moments together, she got a hot ache in her throat. Her knees went weak and sometimes she even had to sit down. Oh, yes, she thought of Douglas Cartland ... To what purpose? Now was not the time, nor would it ever be.

She heaved a sigh and slid off the bed, ready to face the day again. "Thanks, Granny, but the only choice I have right now is to wait for nature to take its course. Oh, I shall be so glad when I come 'round!"

She found Meg alone in the dining room, polishing the silver. "I have something for you." She held up the bottle. "It's laudanum. Didn't you say your father's supply is almost gone? Well, this belonged to the earl, who obviously won't be needing it anymore. Please take it."

Tears sprang to Meg's eyes. "He is in such pain ... oh, thank you, your ladyship. You don't know what this means." She took the bottle and slipped it into her apron pocket. "I hope you didn't go to too much trouble."

Jane gave her a reassuring smile. "Don't worry, Meg, it was no trouble at all."

Chapter 10

Heavy rain fell the next day, the next, and the next. The leaden skies matched Jane's mood, ever darker as each day passed with still no sign. She often sat alone by her window watching the dreary rain, yearning to ride Beauty along the trails she'd grown to love. Her mind drifted off, imagining how she would accidentally meet Douglas Cartland on one of the trails. They would ride together and stop at that secluded spot by the river. They would talk. He would make her laugh with his quick wit. He would massage her feet again, and kiss her again and then ... The thought of his searching tongue in her mouth, his hands sliding over her breasts would send a hot shiver of desire running through her.

Stop. You can't see him anymore. A great sadness overwhelmed her. She must do her duty. Other people could have what they wanted. Never her.

She tried to keep busy, grateful for her duties as mistress of the house. At least James and Beatrice gave her no further trouble. James ignored her, shifting his gaze away rather than look her in the eye. As for Beatrice, she was the soul of politeness since their confrontation. She didn't fool Jane for a moment. In fact, breakfast was a tension-filled affair, with Beatrice hardly able to control her agitation. And every day it became worse.

Jane slid into her place at the table.

"Good morning, Jane. How are you this morning?" Translate that to *Have you come 'round yet?*

"Just fine." Translate that to *No, not yet.*

An awkward silence would fall around the table. Everyone—Granny, Mama, Millicent, Percy, even James if he happened to be present and sober—could sense Beatrice's disappointment from the way her eyes hardened, her lips twitched, her smile became increasingly more phony as she tried to hold it in place. So far, she'd managed to counter with some politely inane remark such as, *I do believe we will receive more rain today,* but it was obvious she had to choke the words out. As the days went by, everyone wondered how much more time would elapse before she erupted.

The inevitable finally happened at breakfast on the tenth day Jane was late. Upon hearing Jane's *Just fine,* the frustrated woman's face flushed bright red and she threw her fork down. "I am sick and tired of your saying 'Just fine.' Do you know what I think?"

In the dead silence that fell over the table, Jane replied in a quiet voice, "No, Beatrice, I do not know what you think, so why don't you tell me?"

Beatrice slammed her fist on the table, so hard the plates jumped, the silverware rattled and everyone bounced in their chairs. "I think you're lying. You've come 'round and you're not telling anyone."

Everyone gasped. Mama's eyes went wide. "How dare you accuse my daughter of such a thing!"

"Beatrice Elton, you are daft," Granny said. "My granddaughter doesn't tell lies and well you know it."

Even Millicent spoke up. "Don't you talk that way to my sister!"

"Don't be a damn fool," James called to his wife from the head of the table. "Arthur could not have fathered so much as a gnat, so don't fret. It's bound to happen."

"I don't have to stand for this!" Pale and shaken, Beatrice arose from her seat and threw her serviette on the table. "You had better come 'round soon." She stalked from the room.

They ate the rest of the meal in dismal silence until James and Percy left and Granny spoke again. "That is one angry woman. If I were you, I would be very, very careful."

"Thank you for the warning, but really, aside from making life unpleasant for us, what could Beatrice possibly do?"

∽∾∾∾∾

"God's blood! I can't tie this thing. I had better borrow your valet."

Douglas Cartland jerked the cravat from his neck and frowned at his image in the full-length mirror in Lord Rennie's dressing room. Rennie, slouching comfortably in a nearby chair, his boots stretched in front of him, eyed his friend with amusement. "You never could tie a cravat. Frederick! Come help Mister Cartland."

The impeccable Frederick, Rennie's stoic German valet, appeared and took the cravat from Douglas' fingers. "Which style would you like, sir? The Oriental? The Mail-Coach? Perhaps the—?"

"Just tie the damn thing."

"Testy, testy," commented Rennie.

Douglas tipped his head back while Frederick worked on his cravat. "Who wouldn't be testy after what you just told me?"

"I suppose." Rennie scrutinized his friend's elegant attire. "Except for Lansdown's funeral, I haven't seen you this dressed up since the old days in London."

"You don't have to be Beau Brummel to haul a long boat along a tow path." Douglas sniffed ironically. "If I don't pass Griggs' inspection, he likely won't let me in, and I must see the countess immediately. What that Elton woman is planning is monstrous."

A clap of thunder rattled the room, accompanied by the sound of pounding rain. "You can't go out in this. At least wait until the storm passes."

"The devil I will."

"You could send her a note."

"Her very life could be in danger and you think I should send a note?"

"Oops, sorry, old man." Rennie appeared properly chastised. "You said you weren't going to see the countess again."

"I've changed my mind. It was kind of you to offer the loan of your carriage."

"Of course. Thank God you're not planning on riding Thunder to Chatfield Court in this god-awful weather."

"Thanks. I appreciate your concern."

"Don't flatter yourself. I wasn't concerned for you, I was concerned for your horse."

Douglas caught the amused smile that flickered across Frederick's face, quickly replaced by his usual expression of aloofness. He wished he, too, could be amused by Rennie's jest, but his worry over the countess had robbed him of his humor. "You're sure about this? You heard correctly?"

"Of course I'm sure." Rennie grew serious. "I don't wish to belabor the point, but it strikes me you're going to a lot of trouble for a woman you claim to have no interest in."

"As you very well know, I shall never marry. However, I have a great admiration for the Countess of Lansdown. She's a woman of great virtue and outstanding character. She—"

"Spare me." Rennie raised a protesting hand. "Whom do you think you're trying to fool? I've seen the way you look at her. That gleam in your eye is sheer lust." Rennie made kissing noises with his mouth. "Ah, those firm, high-perched breasts! Those rounded hips! Ah, how I'd like to wallow between those long, lithe thighs." He rolled his eyes toward the ceiling.

"Don't give me that blather about her virtue and outstanding character."

Douglas answered with an unintelligible grunt. What could he say? How could he argue with the truth? "Suffice to say, the countess needs to be warned immediately and I intend to do just that."

"Tell her she can always come here to Lancaster Hall. She would be safe here. She can stay as long as she likes."

"I'll keep that in mind." The valet finished the cravat and stepped away. Douglas took a quick glance in the mirror. "Thank you, Frederick. It looks splendid." He had no idea whether his cravat looked splendid or not. It didn't matter. A flash of apprehension coursed through him. He must get to Chatfield Court as quickly as possible.

He was almost at the door when Rennie called, "Wait up!"

Douglas turned to see his friend rise from his chair, duck his head and shuffle his feet. "When you're at Chatfield Court could you ... uh ... uh ..."

The transformation was amazing. In less than a second, Rennie changed from his confident, witty self into Rennie the insecure, lovelorn, practically drooling idiot. All because of that bird-witted sister of Jane's. "You want me to ask after Millicent, do you not?"

"Well, yes, if you could." Rennie's expression reminded Douglas of an eager puppy. "Tell her I said 'hello' and I'll come to call ... as soon as I get the nerve. No, don't tell her that. Just say I send her my regards. No, don't say anything. Just ... find out how she's faring in this inclement weather. What I mean to say is—"

"Rennie, for God's sake, just leave it to me, all right? I'll say the right thing. If at all possible, I shall bring you a report on the state of Miss Millicent Hart's health. Will that be satisfactory?" Watching Rennie's grateful nod, he remained straight-faced. His friend's aching, unrequited love for Millicent Hart was no laughing matter.

Turning on his heel, he hurried downstairs and out to the covered portico where Rennie's carriage awaited him. He scrambled in quickly and took up the reins.

Must hurry. No time to lose.

❧❧❧❧

Late in the afternoon, Jane was sitting in her room, watching the rain from her window, when there was a knock on her door. When she opened it, Griggs informed her, "You have a visitor, m'lady."

"Who?" She could not imagine anyone coming to visit in weather like this.

"Mister Douglas Cartland. I put him in the drawing room."

Douglas. Her heart gave a little leap. "Thank you, Griggs. Tell him I shall be down directly."

She hurried to the mirror. Dear Lord, what a depressing sight. She had not realized till now, but she'd lost a bit of weight and the black bombazine made her look almost skinny. Not only that, she had dark circles under her eyes and her skin looked sickly pale. At least her hair looked presentable. Bruta had swept her auburn curls to a loose knot atop her head and fastened it with a comb decorated with black onyx. Black, nothing but black. How she hated it, especially considering she wore mourning for a man she hardly thought of anymore.

What on earth did Douglas want? Why was he here, especially when she'd told him she would not see him again? She took a final peek in the mirror and pinched a bit of color into her pallid cheeks. Telling herself she must not appear too eager, she left her bedchamber and descended the staircase at a slow, dignified pace, as if she didn't give a fig that the man who kept her from her sleep at night awaited her below.

She stepped into the drawing room. He was looking out the window, hands behind his back, appearing deeply absorbed in examining the rain-sodden landscape. He turned when he heard her. "Your ladyship." He did not smile and gave her a formal bow.

"Mister Cartland." She curtsied and shut the door behind her. My, how handsome he looked! All dressed up for a change, in a short frock coat with brass buttons, a light brown waistcoat and matching breeches, top boots and a perfectly tied cravat. Kid gloves and a polished beaver top hat rested on a nearby table. "How elegant you look. I see you've put your valet to work for a change."

He sniffed with amusement. "I don't have a valet. I borrowed Rennie's. Sit down. I want to talk to you."

He seemed so solemn, not at all like his usual irreverent self. Mystified, she seated herself upon one of two facing elegant birch sofas, and he seated himself across. He still had not smiled, and she could see he was in no mood for light humor. "How is your canal?"

"Wet." He flicked a disgusted glance toward the rain out the window. "Very wet. All work is stopped until this hellish storm passes." His eyes drilled into her. "How are you?"

"Very well, thanks."

"I do not want platitudes. I want to know if you've come 'round yet."

What a question! How rude. No gentleman would ever think of asking such a question, or lady either, for that matter. She felt the blood rushing to her cheeks. "How impertinent! How—"

"You women ... I swear to God. Just answer the question and don't go all feminine on me. Stop blushing. Although, I must say, you need some color in those pale cheeks of yours."

Despite his rhetoric, she detected an underlying current of concern in his voice. She could not imagine what, but he must have a good reason for asking, so she wouldn't be coy. "No, I have not. In fact, I am ten days late, which, if you must know, worries me sick."

"I see." He remained silent, his face expressionless, except for a troubled glint in his eye.

"What on earth is the problem?"

He abruptly switched sofas, sat next to her and took her hand. "Have you ever heard of oil of pennyroyal?"

"No."

"It's what they call an abortifacient."

"A what?" She had never heard the word.

"An abortifacient is a solution used to end a pregnancy. It can be dangerous if not used correctly."

She began to feel a tightness in her stomach. "Why are you telling me this?"

"Your sister-in-law is desperate. She does not want you bringing the next Earl of Lansdown into the world. If what I hear is correct, and I believe it is, she has recently obtained a vial of oil of pennyroyal. Indications are she plans to use it on you."

Jane sat silent until his words sank in. When they did, a soft gasp escaped her lips. "Are you sure?"

"Very sure."

"How do you know?"

"Beatrice made the mistake of enlisting the help of that lady's maid of yours."

"Bruta?"

"Yes, Bruta, who, you will recall, used to work for Beatrice and apparently is still loyal. From what I understand, she's the one who actually procured the oil of pennyroyal. Unfortunately for Beatrice, Bruta has a dalliance going with one of the footmen at Lancaster Hall."

"Bruta?" Jane was amazed. She could not picture her ugly, dumpy lady's maid cavorting in bed with anyone. "You must be mistaken."

"We all have our moments," Douglas equitably replied, "even less-than-attractive lady's maids. At any rate, Bruta mentioned Beatrice's request for the oil of pennyroyal to the footman, who told Rennie's valet, Frederick. He told Rennie, who obviously passed the information on to me." He frowned with concern. "I wanted to tell you immediately."

So Granny was right about Beatrice being a threat. But perhaps she was using the oil of pennyroyal for something else. "Tell me, what exactly does it do?"

"A light extraction makes a pennyroyal tea, which is supposed to settle the stomach. A heavier dose causes severe cramps. If you actually were expecting, you would lose the baby. Aside from all that, if not diluted correctly, oil of pennyroyal is a lethal poison. The wrong dose could easily kill you."

"Dear God," she whispered, "like the Spanish Fly killed Arthur." She rose and walked to the window. For a time, she stared out at the rain, attempting to pull her jumbled thoughts together. "The funny thing is, I don't want the earl's baby, either. Beatrice and I think alike on that score. But for her to ... I find it hard to believe. No one could be that vile, not even Beatrice."

Douglas came and stood close behind her. "She hasn't done it yet, Jane. Perhaps you're right and she's using it to settle her stomach, but the circumstances reek with suspicion." His hands encircled her upper arms. The strength of his grip gave her an instant feeling of calm and security, as if a warm blanket had been wrapped around her. She liked his using her first name, too, as if he recognized the intimacy that existed between them. His closeness ... his simple touch ... made her almost forget her sister-in-law. She fought the urge to lean back against him.

"You should not stay here," he said softly in her ear. "God only knows what that woman will do. Come to Lancaster Hall. Rennie wants you to come. You can stay as long as you like."

His words brought her back to reality. She turned to face him, shaking her head. "I cannot come now. Better to wait and see what she does. This is probably all a mistake. Besides, how can I leave my family behind? Beatrice would have them moved to the servants' quarters in the blink of an eye. I certainly can't leave my sister to the charms of Percy, as well as James. Do you know what a lecherous old man he is?"

"No, tell me."

She related her disgusting encounter with James and how he offered to take her as his mistress and move Beatrice down the hall.

They both laughed at the thought, but Douglas quickly grew serious again. "If you won't come, is it possible you can find a way to get the Eltons to leave? After all, he's not the earl yet, is he? You are still the countess."

"Granny said I should throw them out." She thought a moment. "I wonder what Sir Archibald would say. After all, he's in charge of the estate."

"Go see him. It's worth a try. While you're there, you can ask him why he's raised the rents on all the tenants."

"He what?" Her voice rose in surprise.

"You heard me. I see the Twimbys from time to time. They were barely getting by as it was, but this new rent increase may cause them to lose their farm."

"I had no idea." She recalled how grim Meg looked when last she saw her. Now she knew why. "I'll see what I can do." She had no idea what good she could accomplish, but she meant what she said.

"Keep in mind you're in danger every second you stay here. Constantly be on guard, and if you're given a beverage that has the smell of mint, for God's sake, don't drink it."

"All right, I shall do as you say." She would hold to her promise, of course, but she still thought Douglas had to be wrong. "You went to a great deal of trouble to see me and I'm very grateful."

He bowed slightly. "My pleasure, your ladyship."

His sudden formality felt like a slap in the face. "Oh, for heaven's sake, why so formal all of a sudden?"

"Because for a moment I almost forgot we were not going to

see each other anymore. Let's just say I've come to my senses, and a good thing, too. You and I both know this is neither the time nor the place for anything more between us."

She gazed into his dark, compelling eyes, and couldn't resist. "I have missed you, Douglas."

"*You* have missed *me*?" His mouth twisted wryly. "Well, I have missed you, Countess. How much, you have no idea. Did you think I forgot?"

Suddenly his arms encircled her, pulling her close, and his mouth crushed against hers with a hunger that caused her heart to pound. She had no sooner wrapped her arms around his neck, wanting more, much more, when he broke away. He looked down at her, hunger in his eyes, and said in a ragged breath, "No, we won't do this."

Far be it from her to beg! She instantly decided she would match his determination with her own. "You're right. We must not see each other again. Besides, what would be the purpose? You're not a marrying man, are you?"

"No." He walked to the table to fetch his hat and cane. "I'll leave you now. Watch yourself every moment." He started to turn, then caught himself as if just remembering something. "How is your sister?"

She cocked her head. "I didn't realize you were concerned about Millicent's health, or could it possibly be it's really Lord Rennie who wants a report on her well-being?"

"You know the answer to that."

"Tell your friend my sister is in good health, although," she sighed regretfully, "Rennie hasn't a chance. He may be rich and titled, but if I may be brutally frank, not nearly handsome enough for Millicent. I heartily wish my sister's standard of values could be otherwise, but ..." She made a little moue and shrugged.

"I understand. It's her loss, you know. No finer man than my friend Rennie ever lived."

He turned and was gone. She watched after him, her knees so weak she was forced to clutch the back of one of the satin birch sofas for support.

The next morning, Jane dragged from her bed cloaked in a shroud of gloomy thoughts. Eleven days late ... the rain would never stop ... Beatrice might poison her ...

For a while, she gazed pensively out the window, wishing she had someone to talk to, but she chose to keep her worries to herself. Why share Douglas' warning with her family when it probably wasn't true? He could well be wrong. In fact, he had to be wrong. No one, not even Beatrice, could plan something so horrible.

Bruta helped her dress, insisting she wear a black, high-necked muslin that was no less ugly and depressing than the bombazine. She went downstairs, hoping she could eat a quick breakfast and leave before Beatrice arrived. No such luck. When she walked into the dining room, there sat Granny, Millicent, and Beatrice, who, despite her black gown, seemed especially bright and energetic this morning, her plump cheeks rosy, her chirpy little ringlets bobbing on her forehead. "Jane!" she bubbled. "How are you this morning?"

"I am just fine." She walked to the carved mahogany sideboard where an array of breakfast dishes awaited, each kept warm in a silver chafing dish. She picked up a crested china plate and helped herself to a spoonful of eggs and a piece of toast. Griggs, who ordinarily supervised the breakfast, was not in sight. "Where is the butler?"

"I have sent him off to the wine cellar," Beatrice replied. "We need to do an inventory and he might as well get off to an early start."

Granny remarked, "You should have waited 'til we ate."

Mama entered the dining room. "Didn't you think we would need him at breakfast? Must we now serve ourselves?"

"It won't hurt just this once." Beatrice's eyelashes fluttered like an innocent debutante's.

Jane agreed with her mother. Couldn't Beatrice have waited until breakfast was done? No matter. She brought her plate to the table and set it down, intending to return to the sideboard for her tea, but Beatrice quickly arose from the table and gestured at Jane. "Sit down, dear. I will get your tea, since I'm getting some for myself."

"Why thank you." Jane stretched her lips into a smile. She hoped it looked genuine because Douglas' warning began screaming in her head. No, it could not be happening. It just couldn't. Since when had her selfish sister-in-law ever offered to bring her anything in the dining room? What had happened to Griggs?

Beatrice went to the sideboard. Jane stared at her back, assuming Beatrice was pouring tea from the gilt, lily-of-the-valley teapot that sat at one end of the sideboard. One thing for certain, her sister-in-law was taking an extra long time. Finally, she turned and approached the table carrying two cups and saucers. She set one in front of Jane. "There you are, my sweet." She set the other cup down at her place and slipped into her chair. She gazed around the table. "My, my, do you suppose it will ever stop raining?"

Amidst desultory comments on the weather, Jane sat frozen, her gaze fixed on the china cup and saucer in front of her. How pretty it looked, painted with rosebuds and dainty purple violets. How all-of-a-sudden deadly it looked, too. How could she know for certain? She remembered Douglas' words: *if you're given a beverage that has the smell of mint, for God's sake, don't drink it.*

She reached for the cup. Pinching the delicate handle between two fingers, she raised it halfway to her mouth, bent her head and sniffed. *Dear Lord.* The unmistakable smell of mint assaulted her nostrils. She set the cup down. Now what should she do? She pictured picking up the cup and hurling its contents into the stone fireplace behind her. Amidst a collective gasp of astonishment throughout the room, she would point an accusing finger at Beatrice and exclaim, "You tried to poison me!"

No, that would not work. Beatrice would deny it, of course, and aside from actually drinking the contents, how could she prove it?

"Is something the matter, Jane?" asked her mother. "Why are you just sitting there staring at your tea?"

"Nothing's the matter." She had better decide what to do, and fast. If she were her mother, she would pretend everything was fine. She would make a show of not liking the tea as an excuse for not drinking it. Anything to avoid a scene and disturb the tranquility of the household.

I am not my mother. Her thoughts came together. *I am absolutely not my mother!* She stood abruptly. Grasping the cup firmly, she stepped to the stone fireplace and hurled the tea into the flames.

"My goodness, Jane." Mama stared at her. "What are you doing?"

"Just getting rid of this poisoned tea." Jane directed a contemptuous gaze at Beatrice. "It seems my dear sister-in-law has loaded it with oil of pennyroyal."

"Bloody hell," Granny exclaimed.

For once, Mama did not try to correct her. Instead, her mouth dropped open and she stared at Jane in amazement. "What is oil of pennyroyal?"

"It's an abortifacient. That means if I had drunk it, I would have lost the baby. That is, *if* I were carrying a baby, which I highly doubt. I don't care how many days late I am." She turned to Beatrice. "How desperate can you get?"

"Now see here!" cried James from the head of the table. "You cannot accuse my wife like that."

A babble of voices filled the room. James still bellowing, Mama and Granny both talking at once, while Millicent, close to tears, kept repeating, "Oh, Jane!"

It seemed the whole table was in an uproar, everyone talking at once. The only two people who remained calm were Percy, who sat smirking, and Beatrice, who sat listening with—hard to believe it—a little smile playing on her lips.

The chatter died down. "Poor, dear Jane." Beatrice shook her head with pity. "It's obvious you have not recovered from Arthur's death. Your hysterics are perfectly natural, simply a manifestation of your deep grief. I do forgive you." As if nothing had happened, she speared a piece of sausage with her fork. "I suggest you go lie down. You need to calm yourself."

Jane still stood before the fireplace. Despite everything, she felt a satisfaction, call it a sense of fulfillment, for having stood up to her sister-in-law. "You can act as blasé as you please, but I know whereof I speak. You recently acquired some oil of pennyroyal, and I know you just sneaked it into my tea. I could smell it."

"Really?" Beatrice raised an eyebrow. "That would be hard to prove, don't you think?"

Jane directed a steady gaze at her sister-in-law. "You and I know the truth of it, don't we? Just don't try it again." She caught sight of her poor mother's face, pale and tight with concern over what to her must seem one of those *horrible scenes*. Millicent still had tears in her eyes. Percy sat with a smirk on his face, as if enjoying all the discord. Only Granny had returned to her meal, casually buttering her toast as if nothing unusual had occurred.

Jane forced a smile. "Well now, enough has been said on the subject and we're not going to let it ruin our breakfast, are we, Beatrice?" Without waiting for an answer, she continued, "I am not going to go to my room and lie down. Instead, I shall eat my breakfast and have some tea, but this time I shall fix it myself." She headed for the sideboard. "Granny, have you ever seen such a rain in all your life?"

For the next few minutes her grandmother regaled everyone at the table with childhood memories of Bonnie Prince Charlie and the Battle of Culloden, which took place in Scotland in 1746. Exactly what that had to do with rain, Jane didn't know, but it didn't matter. By the time Granny finished, the tension that had gripped the table had ebbed. The color had returned to Mama's face, and she was happy again. Everything was right again in her tight little world.

For the rest of the day, Jane hid her distress with a smile, carefully masking the heaviness she felt in her chest. Later that evening, she went to her grandmother's room, not only to bid her goodnight but to unburden her heart. As usual, she found Granny propped up in bed, spectacles low on her nose, reading her Bible. After seating herself by the bed, Jane frowned. "Should I have accused Beatrice like that?"

Granny peered over the rim of her glasses. "Of course you should have. I was proud of you for speaking up. If it had been your hen-hearted mother, she would have kept her mouth shut."

"What should I do now?"

Granny snickered. "I think you should be very, very careful." She grew serious. "I told you to throw the Eltons out."

"How can I do that? They would not go."

"Then make them go. Get that solicitor of Arthur's, Sir What's-his-name—"

"Sir Archibald."

"Yes, whatever his name is. He's in charge of the estate, is he not? Go see him. Tell him what occurred. If the man has a lick of sense, he'll see it would be best all around if the Eltons leave until all is settled."

Jane heaved a sigh. "When will it be settled? I cannot believe I'm eleven days late, but I am, and I'm starting to worry."

"Whether or not you're carrying a child is in God's hands." Granny cocked her head and regarded her with wise, old eyes. "You can do something about Beatrice, and I suggest you had better. That woman would sell her soul to become the countess.

I wouldn't put anything beyond her. That includes murder."

"Someone else told me I should go see Sir Archibald."

"You mean Douglas Cartland."

Jane nodded. Of course, Granny would know. "If anyone has the power to boot out the Eltons, it is Sir Archibald."

"Then go see him, soon as you can. Be careful. He's kindly enough, but like most solicitors, he's a popinjay with a poor opinion of women. It wouldn't surprise me if he's already in cahoots with James. If I were to wager, I would say you'll get nowhere, but it's worth a try."

"Then I shall go," Jane looked toward the window, "soon as the rain stops."

"That reminds me." Granny laid down her Bible and frowned. "You're not going to like this."

"You mean there's more bad news?"

"One of the maids, who shall remain nameless, informed me that Percy Elton has been following you about. He has even sneaked into your bedchamber. She caught him red-handed, going through your things."

"The devil!"

Her grandmother smiled at Jane's use of profanity, knowing she would never use it elsewhere. "Percy Elton is the worst of a bad lot."

"I've heard he leads a life of debauchery in London. I heartily wish he would go back there and leave me alone."

"I fear things could get even worse. All eight Elton children could descend upon Chatfield Court, along with their spouses and unruly brats. From what I hear, the servants are already alarmed."

"Then we must get rid of them, Granny. We absolutely must!" Jane looked out the window and silently cursed the rain. Her heart hardened with resolve. The Eltons had to go.

Chapter 11

Next day the rain stopped. For two days thereafter, the roads remained muddy and impassable. Not until the third day was Jane able to order the coach brought around so she could travel to the town of Sheffield where Sir Archibald maintained an office.

She dressed carefully, pleasing Bruta no end by agreeing to wear full mourning regalia: black bombazine gown, long crepe hood, black gloves, black silk bonnet, black shammy leather shoes. For an extra touch, she carried a black crepe fan. When she viewed her totally mournful self in the mirror, she made a face. No matter. She would look the part of the grieving widow if it killed her.

During the long coach ride, she reminded herself that Sir Archibald did not approve of forward women. She must act as helpless and feminine as possible. Also, she must curb her tongue and say nothing derogatory about the Eltons. She had sense enough to realize that any accusations she made, even though true, would only make herself look bad. Besides, she had no proof of their shocking behavior, and they would surely deny everything.

When she wasn't reminding herself what to say, her thoughts invariably drifted to Douglas Cartland. Over and over she relived their kiss in the drawing room, each time wondering if lust alone was what drove him to sweep her into his arms, so urgently, so hungrily. Of course, his actions were driven by lust, and only lust. Men were like that. Besides, had he not said he would never marry? She was a fool to think he really cared. Even if he did, what could she do? Countless times she commanded herself to stop thinking about him, but she could not.

Stop wanting to be in his arms. Was she obsessed? Love sick? No, a grieving widow was not supposed to be love sick. Besides, she did not *love* Douglas Cartland. At least, she didn't think she did.

"My dear Countess, how delightful to see you." The ever-courteous Sir Archibald bowed her into his office, offered her tea and gestured her to a comfortable seat across from his desk. After initiating a brief discussion concerning the inclement weather, he settled back in his chair and crossed his hands over his ample stomach. "How are you feeling?"

She knew what he was asking. "Nothing has changed since your visit. Certain matters are still unsettled."

He gave her a knowing nod. "To what do I owe this visit?"

"It's a delicate matter, Sir Archibald." She remembered to speak softly, lower her eyes and sigh. "A troubling matter."

"Do go on."

She explained her mission. All was not well. No one to blame, but a certain tension had developed in the household ... Much as she loved her dear brother—and sister-in-law, and, of course, their fine son, Percy—she felt they would be more comfortable in their London townhouse until such time as the estate was settled ...

Sir Archibald listened intently, his expression unreadable. At first she had no idea if anything she said made an impression, but as she talked on, and he hadn't communicated one sympathetic sound or gesture, her spirits fell. When she reached the end of her appeal, she sat back, awaiting his answer with more than a little unease.

For a long moment, the solicitor sat in deep thought, tapping two fingers to his lips. "I appreciate your concerns, Countess. I realize the loss of your dear husband has caused you to be ... shall we say, overly distraught? Small problems can loom large at such a time, and though I understand your distress, I am sure it can all be worked out. You have my deepest sympathy, of course, but as for asking the Eltons to leave, my answer must be no."

"I beg you to reconsider." She struggled to maintain an even, conciliatory tone. "There are things you don't know, things—"

"I have heard quite enough." The ring of cordiality had somewhat receded from Sir Archibald's voice. "I have made my decision."

"You don't understand." Desperate, she bent forward and gripped the edge of the desk with her black-gloved hands, forgetting her chosen role as the pitiful grieving widow. "I cannot go on this way. The Eltons have made my life miserable. I want them gone. James is not the earl yet. Have you not the authority to order them to leave Chatfield Court?"

"Of course I have the authority. However, I chose not to grant your request, which, forgive me, I find to be most unreasonable."

Desperation drove her on. "Then can you at least release the dower house to me? I shall move tomorrow. I shall—"

"Impossible. As executor of the earl's estate, I must abide not only by the law but my conscience." The solicitor gave her a condescending smile. "With all due respect, my dear Countess, I feel your youth and inexperience have led you to a misunderstanding of the facts. You would be well advised to submit yourself to the care and guidance of the Eltons. Finer people I have never met, and frankly, I find your diatribe against them to be most unreasonable."

She sank back in her chair. "Then you will not—?"

"Definitely not. The Eltons are at Chatfield Court to stay, either forever, or, depending upon certain matters with which you are well acquainted, for at least another few months." Sir Archibald made a show of finding some papers on his desk and shuffling them about. "Was there anything else, your ladyship?"

Feeling so utterly defeated she could hardly talk, she wanted to give him a quick "No nothing else" and flee the office. But she'd come with another matter to discuss, and discuss it she would. She raised her chin. "I have also come to discuss the tenants' rents. I understand they have recently been increased, and—"

The solicitor abruptly raised his hand. "You needn't go on. The fact is, your late husband arranged to raise the rents directly before his unfortunate demise. Now I, in consultation with his brother, am making sure his wishes are carried out."

"But Sir Archibald, the increase is so unfair. Some of the tenants—"

"Now, now, you should not concern yourself with such matters." He smiled indulgently. "James Elton and I know what is best. My advice is, go home, take up your embroidery—or water colors, or whatever it is you ladies love to do—and leave the running of the estate to your brother-in-law and me."

"I see." Hopeless. What more could she say? Sir Archibald would laugh in her face and consider her utterly demented if she told him Beatrice had slipped oil of pennyroyal into her tea, or that sly, sneaky Percy was following her around, or that James assaulted her and asked her to be his mistress. It was clear she could throw herself to the floor, kick her heels and start to scream, and he would not deviate one iota from his rigid system of belief.

Tears of frustration filled her eyes, but she held them back. She reminded herself that this man held her future in his hands. Above all else, she had better be nice or he could ruin her.

Arising from her chair, she choked back angry words. "Thank you for your advice, sir. I shall give careful consideration to what you have said."

She swept from the office, her head held high.

She spent the first part of the journey home mired in misery. Halfway there, she envisioned the expression on Douglas Cartland's face should he see her at this moment, slumped in a corner of her coach, dabbing at her tears with her black-bordered handkerchief, the perfect picture of defeat and self pity. Despite her depression, she had to laugh. He would probably suggest that in the mood she was in, she might as well throw herself on that burning pyre in India. Thinking of Douglas made her feel better. Things could be worse, and tears would get her nowhere. She would have to cope with the undeniable fact that the Eltons would be living at Chatfield Court for some time to come, whether she liked it or not.

She might as well make the best of it because there was nothing she could do.

She reached home to find dinner over and everyone gathered in the drawing room. She would put in a quick appearance before she went upstairs. Lord knew, she wasn't hungry and couldn't have eaten anything anyway. When she entered the drawing room, Beatrice was the first to greet her. "Hello, my sweet, did you have a good journey? How is Sir Archibald?"

Jane concealed her surprise. She had not told anyone except Granny where she was going, but she might have known her snoopy sister-in-law would find out. "Sir Archibald is fine." Damned if she would give one more bit of information than she had to.

Percy stepped forward. "Ah, your ladyship, I trust your journey went well." His eyes snaked over her body, undressing her as they went. "You're looking lovely as always."

Like father, like son. She managed a brief but polite, "Thank you." *What a disgusting man. What a liar.* Lovely? In her dreary mourning clothes, she must look a bedraggled mess from her journey.

"You should have let me know, Countess. I would have been happy to accompany you. Keep in mind that I, too, love to ride. Weather permitting, we must explore those beautiful riding trails together."

She would rather throw herself in the Thames in the middle of winter than go riding with Percy. "Mmm. You must excuse me. I am dreadfully fatigued from my journey and must go upstairs."

"Of course, my dear," said Beatrice. "You go right ahead."

Jane left the drawing room thinking she had made a successful escape, but she wasn't that fortunate. She had reached the foot of the staircase when she heard Beatrice's voice behind her. "Wait, Jane. I want a word with you alone."

She turned reluctantly. "Yes? What did you wish to say?"

Beatrice's perennial smile disappeared. "I want to know why you went to see Sir Archibald."

The nerve! "It's a private matter."

"I am sick and tired of your tricks."

"I have no tricks. I am just—"

"Where are the jewels? Did you think I would forget? You've taken them, I know you have." The last vestige of Beatrice's mask of cheerfulness and amiability had dropped away. This was a new Beatrice, her face distorted by a snarling rage.

"I have no idea where the jewels are, and furthermore—"

"You are going to regret this!" Clenching her fists, the older woman pushed her red-flushed face into Jane's. "I *will* be the countess! James *will* be the earl!"

"Calm yourself." Jane borrowed Sir Archibald's galling words. "You are overwrought. I will talk to you in the morning." She started up the stairs, but before she reached the second step, Beatrice grabbed her arm and she had to turn.

"Don't push me too far, Jane. I'm warning you."

She jerked her arm away. "Warning me of what?"

Beatrice's blazing eyes drilled into her. "This is *my* home, not yours, you scheming little tart, and you will never, ever take Chatfield Court away from me, do you understand? I don't care what I have to do to get you out of here."

Stay calm. Not easy, considering the crazy way her heart was pumping. "You have made yourself quite clear," she managed to reply in a reasonable voice. "However, I choose not to answer while you are in such a rage. Anything else?"

"You heard me!" Her sister-in-law quivered with fury. She was so upset that for the first time Jane could almost feel a touch of sympathy for the poor, distraught woman.

In a voice both soft and disarming, Jane asked, "Beatrice, why are you saying these things? I know assuming the title is important to you, yet you seem so unyielding, so intent on becoming a countess that when you indicate you will go to any lengths to get what you want, I believe you, and, frankly, find it rather frightening."

Her appeasing words caused her sister-in-law to halt her tirade. Jane was surprised to see tears spring to her eyes. "You have no idea what my life has been like," Beatrice replied in a less belligerent tone. "I am only the daughter of a knight, and a poor one at that. No title, of course. I was simply addressed as 'Miss.' When I married James, the son of an earl, I thought I was stepping up in the world, but what good has it done me? As a second son, James is only 'The Honorable,' and I am only addressed as 'Mrs.' Have you any idea how galling that is? Can you imagine how hard I have worked to maintain my position in society when there is only a 'Mrs.' in front of my name and most of my friends are 'Lady This' and 'Lady That'? They love to lord it over me. It is simply unbearable."

"I do sympathize, of course, but after all, it's only a title. Why should you care that much? You're still the same person, title or no."

"I do care!" Beatrice fairly shrieked. "You don't understand the humiliation I felt when you, a little chit from nowhere, usurped my position in this household. So unfair. After Elizabeth died, I was the one who took over running this household, and I did a fine job of it, too. Then you came along, and all because that idiot, Arthur, lusted after you. All of a sudden *you* were the countess, and I was *nothing, nobody*, turned out like a vagrant from Chatfield Court and forced to move back to London." Beatrice's lips twisted into a cynical smile. "So, yes, Jane, I do care that much. I want that title, I deserve that title, and I intend to have it. No one, including you, is going to stop me."

Hearing the vitriol spill from Beatrice's mouth, Jane decided any more discussion would be futile. She squared her shoulders. "Threats will get you nowhere. Be aware that if you try to harm me in any way, you won't get away with it. Am I clear?"

Beatrice glared at her with hate-filled eyes. "You heard what I said. I meant every word."

"I meant every word as well." Nothing more could be said. Jane turned and ascended the staircase, knees trembling. She very much wanted to grip the railing for support, but feeling Beatrice's eyes piercing her back, she resisted, keeping her head high and her gait steady. Only when she reached the safety of her bedchamber and shut the door did she whisper, "Oh dear God." Clearly Beatrice meant what she said. There could be no doubt her very life was in danger.

Douglas. If only she could see him right now. How she longed to confide in him, tell him of this awful mess. She had told him she didn't want to see him anymore, but he had come to see her, hadn't he? Then why couldn't she go see him?

Well, she knew the answer to that.

Just then her grandmother knocked on her door and came hobbling in. "Granny, it is past your bedtime."

"The devil it is." Clutching her cane, Granny gingerly lowered herself into a chair. "I came to see if you were all right."

"Not really." Jane perched on her bed and described her terrible day, beginning with how Beatrice threatened her, ending with Sir Archibald's treating her like a child. "I felt utterly humiliated."

"Hogwash." Granny thumped her cane for emphasis. "Use your head. Don't ever be ruled by your feelings. What do you plan to do?"

Jane spread her hands. "What can I do?"

"You can stop feeling sorry for yourself."

Leave it to Granny to bring her to her senses. "You're right. I'm in a mess and I need to think clearly."

"That's better, missy. So, what do you want to do?"

Without thinking, she blurted, "I want to see Douglas Cartland again. He's the one who warned me about Beatrice."

"Then see him."

Her grandmother's practical reply moved her to laughter. "Easier said than done. I cannot order up the coach and present myself at his door." She slid from her bed and started pacing. "Besides, I cannot because," she felt the faint blush creep over her cheeks, "I have a lot of reasons."

"Ah, so that's how it is," Granny said softly.

"That's how it is." She sank down on the bed again. "I haven't forgotten Sir Archibald reminding me about 'the appearance of propriety,' but when I'm with Douglas, propriety seems to fly right out the window."

"Anything else?" Granny asked.

"Yes, I'm afraid so." Frowning, she glanced down at her black mourning gown. "I'm supposed to be the grieving widow. This is the worst possible time for me to even think about another man."

Granny issued one of her skeptical sniffs.

"I know, but if Mama could read some of the disgraceful thoughts that run through my mind, she would be horrified."

"When will you stop worrying about what your mother thinks?"

"Truly I don't, Granny, but I myself worry about what I'm thinking. I find myself daydreaming about Douglas Cartland all the time. I know I shouldn't—"

"Dear girl, if we ever lose our dreams, then we are lost."

"You don't know what I'm dreaming."

"Yes, I do." Her grandmother sat for a while, looking into space with a faraway look in her eyes, as if she had just drifted off to another time, another place. "His name was Daniel Barnes," she said in a soft, wistful voice.

"Someone you loved? You've never mentioned him."

"This is the first time I've spoken his name in sixty years."

"You didn't marry him."

Granny sighed. "No, I married your grandfather, a fine, upstanding man if ever there was one. Honest, dependable, and dull as a post."

"Really?" Jane could barely remember Grandfather Charles, who had died many years ago.

"Ah, but Daniel ..." Granny's eyes suddenly sparkled. "He was tall and strong, legs like tree trunks, mischief in his eyes. He was serving in the militia at the time. I was dazzled by his uniform—all those shiny, brass buttons which, of course, made him twice as handsome. Ah, love! I wanted him the moment I laid eyes on him. I was mad for him. I wanted him so badly I broke all the rules."

"You mean you—?"

"Of course I did. I lived on a farm and Daniel and I used to sneak off to the barn." Granny snickered. "My mother once asked me how I got hay in my hair. If she only knew!"

"Why didn't you marry him?

"He was only a private, and my parents didn't approve. Even so, I would have run off and married him anyway, but before I could, his regiment was sent to America. I never heard from him again and married Charles shortly after."

"How sad."

"Yes, it was sad, but I've never regretted one moment I spent with Daniel, even though ..."

Jane waited, but her grandmother remained silent. "Even though what?"

Granny set her chin in a stubborn line. "Some secrets are best kept forever."

What could she mean? Something clicked in her mind. "Granny, when you married Grandfather Charles was it because you wanted to or because—?"

"Because I had to?" Granny sat silent for a long moment, then her lips quivered in amusement. "Can you imagine what your prim and proper mother would do if she found out she was conceived in a barn with the goats and chickens looking on?"

At first Jane stared, tongue-tied, at her grandmother. Finally she gasped. "You mean my mother is—?"

"Daniel's child. My love child. Charles never knew. Nobody ever knew but me."

Jane clapped her hand to her mouth. "You mean my mother isn't ...? The devil! Oh, Granny, that is hilarious." She threw back her head and burst into a great peal of laughter. Granny joined in, and the two of them laughed until they had to wipe tears away.

When they were calm again, Granny warned, "You must never tell."

"You know me better than that."

"I never regretted it, not one single time. Over the years I've kept my fond memories." A sly smile crossed Grandma Harriet's face. "I've never forgotten those times I spent in the barn with Daniel, rolling in the hay, all sweaty and panting, feeling such passion that never again ... oh, what that man could do to me." Granny closed her eyes. When she opened them, her faraway expression had disappeared. "Ah, well, nothing stays the same in this life, but I'm telling you one thing, Jane. When you're eighty years old, and feeble, and walk with a cane, you will regret you didn't go after what you really wanted in this world."

"So you think I should see Douglas?"

Granny shrugged. "That's for you to decide." She struggled to stand. "Cursed legs. Give me a hand."

Jane slid from the bed and pulled Granny to her feet. "I'll be thinking about what you said."

"See that you do, or you'll end up with nothing to remember except what a proper lady you were and how you always obeyed the rules."

The minute her grandmother left, Jane made up her mind. She would see Douglas tomorrow, and nothing would stand in her way. As for Beatrice, how could she deal with someone who hated her and wished her harm?

She didn't know. Perhaps Douglas could help.

Jane awoke the next morning to another disappointment. Fifteen days and still nothing. Even so, she could not bring herself to believe she could possibly be carrying Arthur's child. Besides, today she had only one thought in mind. She was going to see Douglas, provided he had not gone off to tend to his canal. How? She could hear Mama now. *No lady ever, ever would dream of visiting an unmarried man. I do not care what the circumstances.*

Much as she might want to flout the rules, she could never bring herself to commit such a basic breach of etiquette. Then how to arrange a rendezvous? Of course, the answer was plain. She would send him a note and ask him to meet her ... where? Under the tree by the river? The cows would love it, but the spot was too open. Better yet, they could meet at the dower house, which nestled nearly hidden among the tall elm and poplar trees. She sat at her writing table, selected a piece of note paper and picked up her pen. What to write?

Dear Douglas, I am desperate to see you ...

True but she wasn't about to wear her heart on her sleeve.

Dear Douglas, my life is in danger and I need your help...

Also true, but much too dramatic.

Dear Douglas, I am dying for the warmth of your kiss ...

Truest of all, she thought with a giggle, but no.

My Dear Mr. Cartland,

If it is not inconvenient, could you meet me at the dower house at two this afternoon?

With utmost kind regards,
—*Jane Lansdown*

Perfect. She affixed her seal on the note and summoned a footman. "Take this to Mister Douglas Cartland at Lancaster Hall. If he's not there, come tell me. If he's there, wait for his reply."

The answer came within an hour.

My Dear Countess,

Yes.

—*Cartland*

His reply could not have been more brief, but even so, an undercurrent of excitement coursed through her veins at the thought that she would see him again. What to wear? Absolutely not black. Ignoring Bruta's look of reproach, she donned her blue riding habit. Bruta drew her hair into curls piled high atop her head. When finished, she held up the matching hat with the high-standing feathers. "Do not forget the hat, madam."

"Not today." She laughed to herself, remembering Douglas' joke about her hat flying away. But why should Douglas Cartland decree what she should wear? Why shouldn't she wear the hat if she wanted to? "I've changed my mind, Bruta. Bring it here."

Carrying her riding crop and a carrot for Beauty, Jane slipped out of the house and walked down the slope to the field next to the stables where Timothy daily turned out the horses. She found her horse grazing contentedly, and when she called, Beauty came running and nuzzled her nose up against Jane's shoulder. "I've missed you," she said, running an affectionate hand down Beauty's nose. She fed her the carrot. "If only the rains will stay away, I shall ride you every day."

She led Beauty to the stables and saddled her, declining Timothy's help. "I love doing this." When she was done, the stableman gave her a boost, and off she went, wanting to put Beauty into a gallop but refraining in favor of keeping a dignified pace.

When she arrived at the dower house, her heart leapt at the sight of Thunder tethered to one of the oak trees. Then she saw Douglas lounging on the steps, his long legs stretched before him. He waved a lazy hand. "Good afternoon, your ladyship."

"Good afternoon." She slid from the saddle and tethered Beauty next to Thunder. Must not appear too eager. Keeping a dignified pace, she took her time walking to the portico where he stood waiting, her note held conspicuously in his hand. He unfolded it with a flourish and peered at its contents.

"I am confounded by this message. It says you actually *wish* to see me."

"That is correct," she answered with an expression of complete unconcern.

"Hmm, I find that rather strange. If memory serves, at our last meeting, I received the distinct impression I was never to darken your door again."

"That's true, Mister Cartland, but circumstances change." She was proud of herself for maintaining an icy exterior, not easy when the very sight of him set her pulse racing. She searched for the jar under the mulberry bush, pulled out the key and stepped toward the door. "Shall we go in?"

"By all means."

After they stepped inside and she'd shut the door, he looked around the small entryway, then peered into the drawing room. "It's small for a dower house."

"It might be small, but I would rather live here a hundred times over than keep on in that drafty old mansion with the Eltons."

"Are you all right?"

"For the moment. Beatrice tried it, you know."

"Used the oil of pennyroyal?"

"Oh, indeed." Jane described in detail her harrowing close call. "Thanks to you, I didn't drink a drop, and I'm most grateful. I wanted to let you know."

He didn't bother with a thank you. Instead, a worried expression crossed his face. "You're still not safe."

"I'm aware of that, but what can I do?" She described her conversation with Sir Archibald.

"You must come immediately to Lancaster Hall," Douglas answered without hesitation. "Your family, too."

"I cannot. I know my mother wouldn't come. Neither would Granny. Tongues would wag if I came alone. Besides, I won't give Beatrice the satisfaction of knowing she's driven me out of the house."

"That's foolish."

"I know, but I do have my pride."

"That you do, Countess." Douglas gave an exasperated sigh. "Now tell me, was there anything else?"

"No."

Yes, there's something else. I was desperate to see you again. I want your arms around me. I want your kiss. I want the feel of you ...

"You mean you lured me to your dower house only for this? I am crushed."

She felt a blush creeping over her cheeks. "There might be other reasons."

He looked at her hat. "Good grief! I see it's flown back. You really must put it in a cage."

She started to laugh, and he laughed, too. Their laughter broke the constraints between them, and she suddenly felt relaxed, if not downright emboldened. Reaching up, she removed a jeweled pin and pulled off her hat. "To be perfectly clear, I did not lure you to the dower house solely to tell you the latest news concerning Beatrice." She flung the hat to a far corner and looked him square in the eye. "I came to the dower house because I wanted to see you again." There. How bold was that? She had just broken countless rules for proper female behavior and didn't care one whit.

Her response caused him to draw in an abrupt, deep breath, as if he'd received a shock. He gripped her arms in a vice-like hold and peered at her intently, a smoldering gleam in his eyes. "I would have stayed away, but you've done it now, Countess." Pulling her close, he took her mouth with savage intensity. With eager abandon, she flung her arms around his neck and pressed her body close to his, all the way down, so she could feel every hard inch of him, especially *there*, where his hardness pressed against her. He moved his hands to her hips and slid them upwards, causing her flesh to burn with desire wherever he touched. His hands reached her breasts. Despite three layers of clothing, the delicious sensation of his thumbs brushing across her nipples made desire surge through her veins.

He pulled his mouth away and began to shower her with tiny, fluttery kisses, above each eyebrow, down her nose to the tip, on to her chin, down to the hollow of her neck, where he planted a particularly tantalizing kiss. Raising his head again to graze her earlobe with his mouth, he asked in a heated breath, "Where's the nearest bed?"

Even in the haze of passion that enveloped her, she knew if ever there was a time when she should back away and say, *No bed, no more kisses, remember Sir Archibald*, this was it. With her heart thumping erratically and her breasts tingling from his mere touch, she was powerless to push him away. "Through there." She nodded toward the dining room. The kitchen and servants' quarters, where she intended to take him, lay beyond.

"Then let's go before I ... Let's go."

He scooped her into his arms as if she were a feather and carried her through the dining room and kitchen. When he reached the maid's room, he gently eased her down so that she sat on the edge of the narrow bed. "You're overdressed." He slipped off her jacket and pulled the cambric shirt over her head, causing the two combs that held her hair in place to loosen. "Not laced?" He viewed her soft batiste chemise.

"I hate corsets."

"Then all the less work for me." He pulled the chemise over her head, leaving her breasts fully exposed. "Beautiful." His breath came hard. "You are beautiful." She thought her own breath would stop as he guided her down to the pillow. Bruta's carefully constructed coiffure had fallen completely apart. With her long auburn hair cascading over her shoulders, she gazed up at him, her mind flashing back to that magical time by the river when she lay beneath him, just like this, her breasts fully exposed to the warm sun and to this man whom, she realized now, she had no power to resist. He pulled off his jacket and shirt and flung them to the floor. Then, propped up on an elbow beside her, he began kissing her again, letting his fingers brush lightly over her breasts, tracing each curve with a gentle touch. Occasionally he allowed a finger to brush across her nipples, sending exquisite currents of desire running through her. *Please stay there*, she silently cried each time his fingers found her nipples, but he always moved on, only to return and stay longer each time. At last he raised his head. "I am not going to stop, you know." His words caused a spurt of hungry passion to spiral through her, and when she felt his lips suddenly cover one of her erect nipples, she gasped and dug her fingers into his back. He raised his lips. "It's good?"

"Oh, very good," she whispered, "please do more."

His lips went to her nipple again, and now she felt his tongue tenderly playing over the exquisitely sensitive tip. Suddenly the rough part of his tongue dragged across it. Then he sucked hard, the very sound of sucking causing her to bite her lips so she wouldn't scream out. He sucked again, and again, then started on the other nipple. Meanwhile his hand found the hem of her skirt and slid up her leg, between her thighs, to the damp spot where the exquisite sweetness of his sucking had caused her to ache with fiery desire. His fingers barely touched her there, but the feeling was so intense she heard herself whimpering and had to consciously refrain from digging her fingernails into his back. "You're ready."

"Yes, oh, yes."

In a twinkling, he unbuttoned her waistband and pulled off her skirt and chemise beneath so that she lay completely naked beneath him. In another twinkling, he pulled off his boots and the rest of his clothes and lay beside her. "Feel." He picked up her hand and guided it to his erect cock. "Big enough?"

She gripped his throbbing member and raised her head to look. It was huge. "I believe it will be quite adequate," she managed to quip despite her driving urge to feel him inside her. She gripped it firmly, thrilled to be holding the most intimate part of Douglas Cartland in her hand.

"It's time." He spread her legs apart and knelt between them. Sliding his hands beneath her, he cupped her hips and lifted her toward him. Holding her in place, he slid a slight way inside her. "I won't go quickly."

"Please don't," she gasped, feeling how very big he was, wondering how he could get all that inside. "I'm not supposed to be a virgin but I pretty much am."

"Pretty much?" He slipped a bit farther in. "Did his lordship get this far?"

"Just about there. I do believe ... oh yes!" The feel of his male flesh inside her sent another warm pulse through her body.

He slid in farther still. "Then we will put a definite end to your virginal status, my dear Lady Lansdown."

She squirmed beneath him and gripped his shoulders tight. "Please do."

Strong and decisive, he plunged all the way inside her and began a series of strokes that sent her nerve endings singing with pleasure. Each time he stroked her, she raised her hips to meet him, warm skin to warm skin. Together they fell into a perfect harmony of pleasure. She breathed in deep drafts as each stroke brought her closer to a peak of pleasure, until finally, waves of ecstasy throbbed through her and she heard herself sob his name, her entire body shaking as the blinding magnificence of her orgasm claimed her.

"Done?"

"Oh, yes."

He drove one more time inside her. A wild rhythm overtook him and he pounded deep and hard until he threw back his head and cried out, his features rigid with a wrenching climax. With a satisfied moan, he collapsed on top of her, then rolled off so that they lay in each other's arms for a time, completely spent, in a kind of satiated languor. Never had she felt so content, so completely happy with Douglas Cartland lying by her side. Eventually he raised himself on one elbow. Twisting one of her auburn strands around his finger, he remarked, "We must do this again."

"Yes, we must, but not now. I must get back."

He gazed down at her, warm affection in his eyes. "I have never in my life met a woman like you. This is just the beginning."

Before she could answer, the distant neigh of one of the horses brought her back to earth again. She gazed about the small, bare room, furnished with only a bed, small scratched dresser and wooden chair. What had she done? What was she doing here? "I must go." She slid from the bed and began to collect her clothes, thinking with irony how she would love to see the look on Bruta's face at the sight of parts of the wardrobe she kept so meticulously neat scattered carelessly about the floor.

Douglas, still stretched on the bed, watched her every move. "You *must* come to Lancaster Hall."

"I can't, I told you that." What with all the giddy excitement of her tryst with Douglas, she had totally forgotten Beatrice, along with every other problem in her life. Now all her troubles came tumbling back, heavy on her mind.

Douglas swung from the bed and started to dress. He sent her a look of concern. "I shall worry about you."

"I'll be fine." She continued to collect her clothes. When she was dressed again, she sat on the side of the bed, tugging at errant strands of her hair that hung about her shoulders. "My hair is a mess. Bruta's sure to notice, and you know she'll go running straight to Beatrice."

"Then Bruta mustn't know." Douglas retrieved two tortoise shell combs that had fallen to the floor. "Where do these go?"

She took the combs and stood in front of the small cracked mirror. Collecting the errant strands, she fastened them in place atop her head. "Does it look all right?" She suspected her hair still looked pretty much a mess.

Douglas stepped behind her, picked up a strand she had missed and fastened it in place. "Bruta will either think you ruined your coiffure because you had a roll in the hay or," he planted a warm kiss on the nape of her neck, "because you were galloping on Beauty, wind in your hair and all that."

"Of course." Her heart swelled with feeling as she turned to face him. She had known he was someone special from the very beginning. Now she saw with crystal clear understanding how kind he was, how caring and compassionate—all the things a woman could ever want in a man. Not only that, he was a marvelous lover. Except for the inadequate earl, she had no one to compare him to, but somehow she knew that no man in the world could send her to the peaks of exquisite pleasure the way Douglas Cartland had just now. She would love to make love to him again, but other matters pressed. Now was hardly the time.

"You must be careful. Get away from Beatrice as soon as you can. That woman means to harm you. Unless you're extremely cautious, she will."

Chapter 12

Returning to Chatfield Court, Jane felt as if she were floating on a gossamer cloud in a world far away. Making love with Douglas had opened a new world of pleasure, delight, and wild passion, all of which she had never known in all twenty-six years of what she now considered a bland, boring life. One thing was certain: after today, she would never be the same. Even so, despite her newfound euphoria, a touch of unease nagged at a corner of her mind. What if someone had peeked through the window of the maid's room and seen them? She pictured Sir Archibald greeting her at the door with, "Aha! I know what you've been up to, you wicked woman, you strumpet!"

Fortunately no such event occurred, and when she walked into the empty entry hall, she found a late-afternoon stillness lay over the mansion, as if all occupants were napping, or otherwise engaged in their own pursuits, and no one knew or cared that she had just made wild, passionate love with Douglas Cartland. Her sanity returned. She realized quite probably no one except Bruta even realized she'd been gone. She was starting up the main staircase when her mother appeared.

"Jane, I want a word with you."

Uh-oh. Her mother's tone signaled that something wasn't right. "Let's go into the drawing room."

They entered the drawing room, shut the doors, and settled on the two opposing sofas. "What is the matter?" Jane inquired. "You look so worried."

"You know how I have always felt about Beatrice Elton."

"I am well aware you don't think she should be promoted to sainthood."

"No, I do not." Amelia gave no answering smile. Instead, she seemed subdued, not her usual talkative self at all. "I never liked her, what with her slyness and her nasty ways. Now my feelings go beyond that. I believe she is downright evil."

"Beatrice?" Jane asked in feigned surprise. "That paragon of virtue? I am shocked."

Mama fumbled with her lace handkerchief, a look of distress crossing her face. "Don't joke."

Jane set her expression into more solemn lines. "How did you reach the conclusion she is evil?"

"By the way she keeps asking and asking if you have ... you know, come 'round. Well, Jane, you know I am a very polite person. Up to now I've always given her a polite answer, but now she's getting worse."

"In what way?"

"She has become like someone demented. When I tell her I don't know, she pretends to be nice, but I can see her teeth clench. Then this morning ..." Mama rolled her eyes in agitation.

"Do go on. I need to know."

"This morning she asked again. It was just too much, the way she pushed me, and I finally said, 'I wish you would stop bothering me. Whatever happens will happen.' Well, she could not contain herself and this look of sheer hatred came over her face. 'I *shall* be the Countess of Lansdown,' she said, in the coldest way imaginable. I get chills, just thinking about it."

Mama pressed her handkerchief to her tight, grim mouth. "I didn't believe you before, when you claimed she slipped that oil of pennyroyal into your tea. Well, I believe you now, and I'm terribly worried. She's crazy and means to harm you."

Jane put on a reassuring smile. "What you've told me is no surprise. Don't worry. I am well aware of how Beatrice feels and am being extra careful. Besides, if worse comes to worst, I have been invited for a visit at Lancaster Hall. You're invited, too. We all are. I don't intend to go, though. I won't give Beatrice the satisfaction of knowing she's driven me out of the house."

Mama nodded her head in agreement. "I, too, shall stay right here. I wish you would reconsider, though. If you're gone, then I won't have to worry about what Beatrice might do to you." At last she smiled. "I want you and the baby to be safe."

Jane shot a "No!" at her mother before she even thought. She had to take a moment to calm down, then shook her head decisively. "I am quite aware of the indications, but I still refuse to believe I'm with child."

"All right, dear, have it your own way, but you are terribly, terribly late." Amelia made a little moue. "Ironic, is it not? I want this baby as much as Beatrice does not."

"Yes, ironic. Either way, someone is going to be extremely happy and someone is going to be extremely upset."

Mama beamed. "Happy? I shall be ecstatic, not only for my sake, but I shall rejoice when that woman gets what she deserves. Meanwhile, I want nothing to do with her. I shall take my meals in my room from now on."

"You will do no such thing. We shall not let Beatrice keep us from our own dining room. Tonight we will go downstairs and act as if nothing happened."

Jane expected further argument, but instead, Mama nodded. "Very well, if you say so."

"I say so, much as I also prefer to stay in my room, not only to avoid my sister-in-law but also to keep away from Percy and those revolting, lecherous looks he gives me."

Just amazing. Jane sat at her place in the dining room, glancing around the table. If a stranger had been invited to dinner, he would judge from the friendly, animated conversation that this was one big, happy family spending another congenial evening together. She continued to be amazed at Beatrice, who, acting the gracious hostess from the bottom of the table, helped keep the chatter going with a continual smile and occasional merry peal of laughter. To Jane's relief, Percy was not in his usual place. "Indisposed," according to Beatrice. Well, whatever the reason, it was fine with Jane.

While the servants cleared the soup bowls away, Beatrice addressed Jane. "Did you enjoy your ride today?

Caught off guard, Jane nearly dropped her fork. *How did you know I was riding? Do you also know where I went and what I did?* Another horrible vision popped into her head: this time it was Beatrice peeking through the window of the maid's room at the dower house, her eyes widening with shock as she spied Jane entwined naked on the bed with Douglas Cartland. The very thought made her want to run from the room and hide. Instead, she gathered her wits. "I enjoyed my ride immensely. The fresh air was quite invigorating."

Fortunately Beatrice did not pursue the subject. Obviously, she was simply asking in order to be polite.

After they had consumed the main course of salmon, chicken pie, and roast pheasant and were awaiting dessert, Beatrice unexpectedly arose from the table. "Is that rain I hear?" With her usual tiny, affected steps, she minced to the large, leaded glass window overlooking the sloping lawn that led to the river. She pulled back the heavy drape and peered into the darkness. "I was wrong about the rain, but ... oh, gracious!" Her hand flew to her heart. "Whatever is that glow in the sky? Is it a fire? I do believe it is coming from the stables."

Stables ... fire ... Beauty! Jane leapt up, pushing her chair back so hard it tipped over. She rushed to the window. Over Beatrice's shoulder she saw a red glow in the darkness. It indeed seemed to come from the area of the stables. "Dear Lord, my horse!" She spun around and ran from the dining room, faintly hearing her mother calling, "Now, Jane, I really don't think you should ..."

She lost the rest of Mama's sentence as she dashed across the entry hall, flung open the door that led to the path to the river, and raced outside without closing it behind her. For a brief moment, she paused and looked toward the stables, hidden from view by the bend in the river. The red glow in the sky grew larger, intensified. She picked up the hem of her skirt and started to run, her laced silk slippers pounding on the rough flagstones. Was Beauty in the stables? Of course she was. Timothy always brought the horses in at night. Perhaps he had led all the animals to safety by now, but Beauty's stall was the last in the row. He might rescue the other horses first, that is, if he was there and had been able to rescue any at all. *Oh, dear God.* She ran faster.

Halfway to the stables, she saw a slender lick of flames leap toward the sky. The thought that her beautiful horse could burn to death caused her to cry an anguished, "Beauty, oh, no!" Her lungs burned, her heart pounded, but she ran faster still, skirt held high, her feet fairly flying over the path.

She rounded the bend of the river and gasped in horror at the sight that lay before her. There stood the stables, fully engulfed in flames. Through heavy, dark smoke pouring from the entrance, she saw three figures emerge—a man, a boy, and a horse with a blanket over its head. She recognized Timothy and young Hugh, the stable boy. Was that Beauty they were leading? With the last of her strength she sped down the path, stumbled into the courtyard and stood gasping for breath in front of Timothy. Instantly she saw the horse he was leading wasn't hers. Over the crackling of flames and the whinnies of frightened horses, she shouted, "Where is Beauty?"

Rivulets of tears from his reddened eyes ran down Timothy's black-sooted face. "You can't go in, ma'am," he called in a desperate voice hoarse from smoke. "The roof's about to go."

"Is she still inside?"

"Can't stop now, ma'am." He turned to Hugh, who started back inside. "No, boy, don't go back. Too dangerous. You've done what you can."

She grabbed Timothy's arm. "Beauty is still inside? You must tell me!"

"Yes, ma'am, but I don't think we can get to her. I can save one more ..." He turned away, yelling at Hugh, "Hurry, get this horse out of here. I'll go in one more time."

A shower of burning embers fell from the sky, one landing on Jane's shoulder. She knocked it away, but not before the excruciating pain reminded her of what Beauty must be suffering at this very moment. Just then she heard a horse's desperate neigh and knew it was Beauty. She looked toward the entrance but could see nothing inside except a black cloud of smoke and an ominous red glow. As she watched, Timothy ran back inside, a wet towel pressed to his face. Could she, too, run into the flames? She heard Beauty again, an anguished, frightened neigh that tore at her heart and removed all doubt in her mind. If Timothy could do it, so could she ... or die in the attempt.

She grabbed a towel already soaked with water and a blanket from the pile outside the door. Pressing the towel to her face, she took a deep breath and plunged inside. A fiery hell enveloped her. The roar of the flames, burning embers swirling around her, black smoke ... If she breathed it in, it would surely choke her. Worst of all, the heat was scorching her skin to the point it was nearly unbearable, but bear it she would.

Timothy stumbled by, leading the last of the matched grays. "Get out, ma'am. You can't get Beauty. The roof is about to collapse. For God's sake, get out!"

No. She would not let Beauty die in such a horrible way. Pressing the wet towel tighter to her face, still holding the deep breath she took outside, she started down the passageway lined with stalls. The heavy smoke nearly blinded her. She started to feel for the floor-to-ceiling posts that marked each stall. *Must hurry, hurry.* The smoke was so thick she could barely creep along. She would not turn back, though. Beauty's desperate whinnies filled her ears, along with a hard, heavy pounding that came from the horse's continually rearing up, striking her hooves against the wall. Her hand found the first post, then the second. At the third, she could hold her breath no longer. She remembered what Papa once told her: in case of fire, crawl, stay close to the ground. She dropped to her knees and bent as low as she could. Removing the wet towel from her face, she drew in a deep breath and immediately started choking. Gasping for breath, she willed herself to continue on and began to crawl along the rough-planked floor, still choking, her eyes smarting, tears streaming down her cheeks.

She felt her way past the third post until finally finding the last stall, Beauty's stall. Taking another choking breath, she rose to her feet. She felt for the latch and opened the door to the stall. Inside, Beauty, wild with pain and fright, emitted wild, frantic neighs while rising on her hind legs, her front legs like lethal weapons as they cut through the heated air. *Avoid those hooves. No time to lose.*

Jane caught the horse between lunges and grabbed her harness. Clutching it tight, she hung on with all her strength. "Beauty, be calm." She knew full well the frightened animal was beyond obeying her commands. Just hearing her voice might help, though. She threw the blanket over Beauty's eyes, just as Timothy had done. No time to attach the lead. Hanging on to the harness, she gave Beauty a smart rap on the rump and tugged her toward the door. "Come on, girl, let's go!" The horse began to follow, then balked. The blanket had slipped from Beauty's terror-filled eyes. She backed into the stall and reared up again, wildly flailing her hooves.

Jane dodged just in time. She thought of how she could use three hands right now—one to hold the blanket, one for the harness, one to hold the wet towel over her nose and mouth.

She only had two hands so something had to go. She took another deep, searing hot breath and dropped the wet towel. Choking, almost completely blinded by tears now, she held the blanket firmly in place over Beauty's eyes and managed to lead her from the stall. Thank God, Beauty came willingly this time. Could she make it? By now the heat was nearly unendurable. Halfway down the passageway, she thought she could not go on. Her lungs burned. Her eyes stung and watered so much she could not see a thing. Worse, she was beginning to feel dizzy and lightheaded, on the verge of collapse. She *must* save Beauty. Gathering the last of her strength, she pushed on. *Come on, old girl, just a few more steps for the both of us.*

At last! She burst out the door and let go of the harness. After an excited whinny, Beauty raced away. Behind her, she heard a loud crash. The roof must be falling. She must move farther away. No use. Her legs wouldn't carry her. Amidst a whirlwind of burning embers, she sagged to the ground. The last she saw before blackness enveloped her was little tendrils of flames licking at the hem of her skirt. The last she felt was two strong arms catching her as she fell.

"Wake up, Jane, wake up!" Douglas' voice. Where was she? What happened? Jane slowly returned to consciousness, gradually aware that she lay on the ground. Both Douglas and Rennie were bending over her.

"She's lucky she's not burned." Rennie's voice. Jane opened her eyes and tried to speak but instead started to cough. Not a polite little cough but a wrenching, wheezing hack from deep in her lungs that brought up a black substance that, again and again, she had to spit on the ground. She wanted to stop but could not.

"I had better hold her up." Douglas' voice. She felt her upper body lifted and strong arms wrapping around her. Vaguely she was aware of Douglas kneeling behind her, pressing her tight against his chest for support. She needed him. Each hacking cough wracked an agonizing path through her body, draining her down to her last bit of strength, but he continued to hold her fast and whisper encouragement as she convulsively hacked, coughed and spit the black substance from her lungs.

"Yes, cough it all out, my brave girl. You must expel it all from your lungs." Occasionally, she felt the gentle touch of fine linen on her face. It had to be Douglas wiping her mouth with his handkerchief. What a fright she must look, but right now she didn't care. "You'll be fine, my darling," she heard him whisper, his voice choked with emotion.

Her coughing had begun to subside by the time she became aware that her mother and sister were kneeling beside her, too, both pleading to know if she was all right.

"She'll be fine." Douglas' voice was so reassuring.

She heard Rennie add, "She took in a lot of smoke, Lady Hart. It's a miracle she's not burned. Look at her skirt."

She heard her sister exclaim, "Oh, no, look how it burned. Are you sure she'll be all right?"

Still in Douglas' arms, Jane forced her eyelids open. Both Mama and Millicent looked down on her with furrowed brows. "I'm fine," she gasped in a broken, cracked voice. "Beauty ... is she all right?"

In a reassuring voice, Rennie replied, "Don't worry about a thing, Countess. Timothy has taken her and the other horses up to my stables where they will remain as long as you like. Your horse has a burn on her back, nothing too serious. She's going to be fine, thanks to you."

Douglas said, "You have the bravest of daughters, Lady Hart. Not many women—or men, either—would risk their lives to rescue an animal, but Jane did, and you should be very proud. Jane, are you all right now?"

"I'm fine but I can't stop coughing."

Douglas addressed her mother. "We had better get her home and call the doctor."

She passed the next few hours in an exhausted blur, only vaguely aware of Douglas and Rennie carrying her to Chatfield Court and up to her bed. She remembered the doctor, summoned from the village, who treated her hacking cough by applying camphor liniment to her chest. He assured her the cough would disappear "kindly and speedily" in only a few days. "It could have been far worse."

He gave her a spoonful of laudanum "for her nerves." She fell asleep soon after, her heart full of gratitude. Beauty had survived, and so had the other horses. What more could she ask for? She cast only one fleeting thought as to how the stables caught fire.

Chapter 13

The next morning Jane awoke so groggy from the laudanum that seconds passed before she could engage her senses and comprehend why her lungs hurt and her throat felt so incredibly raw.

Something else happened yesterday ...

She snuggled under the covers, her heart swelling with feeling at the thought of Douglas Cartland and the delicious, utterly heavenly way he made her feel on that narrow bed in the tiny maid's room.

Her sister came bustling in, interrupting her reverie. "How do you feel this morning?"

"Better. I guess I'm going to live," Jane answered in a croaking voice. "The devil! I sound horrible."

"Just awful. You should not get up today."

Jane swung from her bed. "Right now I'm anxious to visit Beauty. I want to see with my own eyes she's all right."

"Then you have a busy day ahead. I'll call Bruta. By the way, she's mad as blazes."

"Please don't tell me why. I'll find out soon enough."

Minutes after Jane arose, Bruta, wearing her fiercest scowl, fairly exploded into the bedchamber, the black bombazine draped over her arm. "Just look!" Clenching her jaw with disapproval, she spread the damaged gown on the bed.

Jane took one look and croaked an "Uh-oh." Her gown reeked of smoke. Holes of various sizes, caused by hot embers, dotted the fabric. Flames had destroyed a large, jagged portion of the hem. She felt a shiver of dread just looking at the remains of her mourning gown. It reminded her that last night she could have burned to death. What a close call she'd had!

It seemed Bruta's concerns lay elsewhere. The lady's maid glared at her with reproachful eyes. "Your best gown is ruined, m'lady, utterly beyond repair."

Jane turned up her nose. "I am desolate. Oh, what a pity. Now find me something to wear."

"The doctor said you are not to get up today."

"Well, I'm up, I want to dress and I need your help."

"You really should not, madam."

For the barest of moments Jane thought she detected a look of concern deep in Bruta's eyes. No, it couldn't be. Her lady's maid took her orders from Beatrice and didn't care if Jane lived or died. "Just get me something to wear."

Muttering to herself, Bruta plodded to the wardrobe and pulled out the dull black muslin, which, if anything, was more ugly than the bombazine. "You'll have to wear this."

"Really?" Rebellion was mounting within her. How utterly stupid to wear mourning clothes for a man she didn't mourn. Why should she? Because society's rules told her to? Well, she was tired of society's ridiculous rules, tired of obeying, tired of suppressing her own desires for the sake of ... what? Everyone's approval? The trouble was, she'd had a giddy taste of freedom. Last night she had nearly died. What if she had? What would it have mattered then whether or not she chose to wear the dull black muslin? *Not one whit.* Life was too precious to waste doing things she did not want to do.

Perhaps, if she continued throwing caution to the wind, she

could keep on seeing Douglas, too. That thought made her want to dance a little jig across the room, but the stony gaze of her lady's maid brought an end to that idea. Even so, her new euphoria remained. "Put that ugly thing away. Bring out the green batiste."

Bruta's eyes bugged out and her jaw dropped—a satisfying sight if ever there was one. "Madam, you cannot. What will people say?"

"I don't give a fig what people say. Bring me the batiste and don't say another word."

Except for Amelia, both families were at the table when Jane entered the dining room for breakfast. To her surprise, everyone, even James, gave her a heroine's welcome. After the congratulations died down, a somber atmosphere ruled the table with everyone, from James on down, discussing the shocking events of last night. Speculation ran high on how the fire started. Various theories were proposed. Beatrice wondered if Timothy might have started the fire with his pipe, but no one had ever seen him smoke. Percy speculated that lightning might have sparked the fire, yet there was none in the sky last night. No one could supply a reasonable answer, yet all agreed, thank the Lord, that a horrible tragedy had been averted.

Beatrice assumed her façade of cheerful innocence. "How are you, my dear?" she chirped to Jane. "Weren't you supposed to stay in bed today? My, my, what a dreadful ordeal! I'm happy to see you're all right this morning." She eyed Jane's green gown. "My goodness, not in mourning? Well, of course, the gown you wore must have burnt in the fire. I'm sure Bruta will see to it you soon have another one."

Jane resisted the urge to inform her sister-in-law that she did not plan to wear mourning ever again. Now was not the time, though—not when her throat hurt so much she could hardly speak.

"How is your horse?" Beatrice inquired.

"I don't know yet," Jane croaked in reply. "Beauty is at Lord Rennie's. I want to go see her as soon as possible."

"All the horses but mine are up at Lord Rennie's stables," Percy said, raising an eyebrow in his lecherous way. "My horses were not in the stables last night. They were in the field, so they're still quite close. My carriage is at your disposal, Countess."

She returned her prettiest smile. "Why, thank you, Percy." She would rather die a million horrible deaths than ride in a carriage with Percy. "If I need a ride, I shall certainly keep you in mind."

Fortunately, she did not. Directly after breakfast, Lord Rennie arrived, pulling up front in his curricle. Griggs showed him into the drawing room where Jane was chatting with Millicent. When he entered, Rennie forgot to make his bow but instead rushed to take Jane's hands in his large ones. "Are you all right, Countess?" Concern was written on his plain, honest face.

"I am fine." Her voice cracked. "Do sit down."

"Confound it, Countess, you sound terrible."

"I just want to know if Beauty is all right."

"She's doing fine. In fact, as we speak, both Timothy and Cartland are taking care of the horses. None of them suffered a serious burn. I came to see if I could take you back up to my stables. I knew you would like to see for yourself."

Her heart lifted. "I would be ever so grateful."

Rennie looked toward Millicent. Although at least thirty years old, he looked like a lovesick schoolboy. "You are welcome to come along, Miss Hart."

To Jane's surprise, her sister nodded. "I would love to come, Lord Rennie. I, too, am concerned about the horses."

When they climbed into Rennie's carriage, Jane had to laugh. Whereas Rennie helped her in with the standard amount of courtesy, he handed Millicent to her seat with the utmost care, as if she were a fragile flower whose petals might blow away in the slightest breeze. *No wonder he finds her attractive.* After spying Jane in her green batiste, Millicent exclaimed, "If you can do it, I can!" She had rushed to her bedchamber with lightning speed and changed out of her mourning gown. "I wouldn't have to wear it much longer anyhow." Sister-in-laws were only required to wear black for three months. Now, dressed in a yellow sprigged muslin that complemented her fair skin and delicate features, she really did resemble a beautiful, fragile flower.

"I hope you will be kind to Rennie," Jane whispered while Rennie, perched on the curricle's high seat behind, drove them up the hill. "He's positively lovelorn."

Millicent giggled. "I shall be kind," she whispered, "but you know how I feel. Rennie is most definitely not my knight in shining armor."

Poor Rennie, Jane thought, and not for the first time.

Upon reaching Rennie's stables, located above Lancaster Hall, Jane slid from the curricle and hastened to talk to Timothy, who stood in front of the stables attending the horses rescued from the fire. "Are they all right?"

"Right as rain." Timothy patted a horse's flank. "Not a one badly burned, m'lady.

"I shudder to think what would have happened to the horses had we not got them out."

Timothy cast his gaze upward. "Through the grace of God we *did* get them out, and in the nick of time."

"Have you any idea how the fire started? I suppose it was an accident."

Anger flashed through Timothy's eyes. "That fire was set deliberate. 'Twas no accident. I saw the man who set it, and so did Hugh."

She was barely able to control a gasp of surprise. "It was not an accident? Then who was it? You must tell me."

"I'll tell you what I know, ma'am, and you can draw your own conclusions."

"Do go on."

"Hugh spied him first, m'lady, right after we saw the glow of the fire. He was sneakin' up the path, away from the stables."

"A man? You recognized him?"

"Now, I'm not positive. It was dark. But I believe it was Percy Elton who I've known since he was a little tyke. The whole family used to live here, you know." He nodded his head decisively. "I'm almost positive 'twas him. We found the remains of an oil lamp in the ruins. That's what he used to set the fire. No mistake. All he had to do was toss it onto the bales of hay piled by the door."

Percy Elton set the blaze? Her insides went cold. Never would she have believed the fire was started deliberately. Why would he set such a fire? She had no idea, but at the moment she had best remain calm and learn all she could. "Did you see anyone else?"

"No one except Master Percy."

"I'm at a loss for words, Timothy, but never fear, I shall look into the matter."

"You certainly should, if you don't mind my saying so." An uncharacteristic look of outrage crossed the stableman's face. "All our horses could have been killed. Whoever did such a terrible thing should be caught and punished."

"I absolutely agree, and I shall do my best to make sure they are. Meanwhile, let's keep this to ourselves, shall we?"

"Of course, m'lady."

"Where is Beauty?"

"Inside. Mister Cartland is taking care of her."

"Thank you, Timothy. Jane hastened inside, where she found Beauty in her new stall and Douglas brushing her sleek coat.

He looked up and smiled at her over the top of her horse. "Countess. I thought you would still be in bed today."

"You were wrong," she replied in her hoarse, cracking voice.

"You sound terrible."

"So I've been told." She ran her hand down Beauty's nose. "She's all right then?"

"Right as rain, as Timothy would say. There's just the one spot near her tail where she got burnt, but I've put salve on it. Don't worry, it should heal fast."

"Thank God." She pressed her cheek against Beauty's nose.

Douglas asked, "Has Timothy told you how he thinks the fire started?"

"Yes, he thinks it was Percy, and I'm stunned. I don't even want to think about it right now."

"You had better think about it. Sure as I'm standing here, Beatrice Elton is behind the setting of that fire."

She took a quick, sharp breath. "I find that hard to believe. Why would she do such a thing?"

Douglas threw the currying brush in the corner with more force than necessary and circled around Beauty to confront her. "How else could that fire have started? Face the truth, Jane. Beatrice wants to hurt you. I doubt she knew what to expect when she told Percy to set the stables on fire. Either she was hoping you would die in an attempt to rescue Beauty or, at the very least, she hoped the shock would cause you to lose your baby."

She bristled. "I am *not*—"

"You have not come 'round yet, so you don't know what you are." Douglas seized her shoulders in a move so swift she drew in her breath. "The world can be an ugly place, Countess. Don't be an ostrich and stick your head in the ground. I don't want to see you hurt."

"It's ... just so hard to believe that anyone could do such a horrible thing."

"If what Timothy says is true—and I have no reason to doubt him—your life is in more danger than ever."

Seeing the concern in his eyes, she realized her desire to avoid the truth was not going to work and she must explain. "But it's more of the same, Douglas. Timothy is fairly certain the man he saw set the fire was Percy Elton, but he's not positive. So how can I prove he did it? And how can I prove Beatrice put him up to it? You know I cannot."

He bit his lip with frustration. "Then come stay with Rennie."

"You know I can't do that, either, but I promise I'll be careful." She was becoming aware of his strong hands on her shoulders and how very close he was. She did not want to argue anymore. "Douglas, please." She lifted her hand and ran the back of it lightly down his cheek. Immediately his expression changed from anger and frustration to surprise to ... ah, there it was, that enchanting mixture of excitement and desire.

"Ah, Countess," he whispered in her hair. "I am mad to see you again."

Her body ached for his touch. "I know. I, too ..."

"This evening after dinner. Come to the dower house again."

"I will be there," she whispered back as they heard voices and hastily broke apart. "I shouldn't."

"Of course you shouldn't, but you will be there."

When Jane stepped outside the stables, she was quickly distracted by what she saw. Rennie was showing his beloved horse, Major, to Millicent. "He is a beauty. I trained him myself. Do you ride, Miss Hart? I was just thinking ..."

Say you do, Millicent. Say you will go riding with him. Nothing in the world would give her more pleasure than to see her sister fall in love with Rennie. Moneywise, she would be set for life. Not only that, she would never find a kinder, more generous man, nor a man who could love her more than Rennie. If only she would open her eyes.

"I don't ride. I fear my sister is the horse lover in the family." Millicent looked toward Jane. "We should be getting back soon. I have a million things to do today."

Ah, well. Jane put the lovely dream aside. She had learned long ago that not every wish came true.

Later that day, Amelia summoned her daughter to the

dining room where she sat at the table, drinking tea. When Jane entered, Amelia was taken aback. "Why are you dressed like that? Where is your mourning gown?"

"I am not concerned about my state of dress right now," she croaked.

To her surprise, Mama switched the subject. "I want to hear what really happened last night." Her voice hardened. "I'll wager Beatrice had a hand in this. How did the fire start?"

Of course, Mama wasn't going to let it go. With a resigned sigh, Jane sank in the chair across from her. "I was coming to that. Here's what Timothy told me ..." She went on to describe how both the stableman and his helper saw Percy Elton running from the fire. "It's more than a little suspicious. In fact, Douglas Cartland thinks Beatrice is behind it, but I'm not sure—"

"She did it. I know she did." Startled, Jane watched her mother leap to her feet and start an angry pacing. In the middle of the room, Mama stopped and raised clenched fists in the air. "Oh, what an evil woman!"

"We cannot prove she set the fire," Jane responded, shocked at her mother's near hysterical accusation. "Are you forgetting she was with us in the dining room the whole time?"

"She didn't actually set it. Obviously she sent Percy to do her dirty work." Mama's eyes lit up, as if she had just had a revelation. "Was he at dinner last night? No. That's because he was down at the stables, setting them ablaze."

"Mama, will you please sit down?" Concerned, Jane arose, took her mother's arm and led her back to her chair. Except when Papa left, she had never seen her mother so upset.

"Can't you see it?" Mama's voice rose to a near-hysterical pitch. "You are sixteen days late, am I not right?" Jane nodded. "You have never been that late or even close before." Jane had to nod again. "Then it is obvious to me you have conceived a child. I don't care what you say. The events of last night could easily have caused you to lose that child. If you had, it would be all," Mama was shouting now, "that horrible woman's fault. She wanted to make you so upset you would miscarry, and she nearly succeeded, did she not? She is a scheming, evil woman." Amelia emphasized her words by striking her fist on the table. Her action caused the saucer to jump and the cup to overturn, sending a small rivulet of tea running over the linen cloth. Jane grabbed a serviette and quickly mopped it up while she searched for the right words to say. How awful, seeing her mother, always in control of herself, so terribly distraught. With good reason. Hadn't Beatrice tried to cause her to miscarry with the oil of pennyroyal?

"Mama, please calm down. You don't have to explain further. I see what you mean. Douglas Cartland said the exact same thing. Beatrice could very well be responsible for setting the fire. But, just as with the oil of pennyroyal, how can we prove it? If I accuse her of setting the fire, she will suggest I haven't recovered from Arthur's death and my hysterics are perfectly natural. So what can we possibly do about it now?"

Mama shook her head but remained silent. She could give no helpful answer.

That night no one raised any questions when Jane announced she was not feeling well. She would take dinner in her room and go straight to bed thereafter. Strange how she felt no guilt at telling such a lie. At best, it was a harmless lie made necessary because her burning desire to see Douglas far overshadowed all the moral teachings she had learned as a girl. Perhaps tomorrow she would dwell upon her shortcomings. Not tonight.

She waited until darkness fell, slipped from the house and followed the path to the river and on to the dower house, reflecting how easy it was to slip away.

Douglas was waiting for her. Her pulse quickening, she stepped into the mad countess' cluttered drawing room,

Douglas close behind. She sniffed the air. "It smells better in here, doesn't it? I told Mrs. Stanhope to send a maid to dust and air the place out."

Actually, she could not care less whether the musty smell was gone or the furniture dusted. She turned to face Douglas, her heart jolting and her pulse pounding. Since the moment she agreed to come to the dower house, she knew her fate was sealed. She was going to make love with Douglas again.

"It smells much better." He obviously didn't care, either. His eyes never left her face. The perennial look of amusement in his eyes had been replaced by some indefinable emotion she had never seen before. Before she could reply, he pulled her close and swung her into the circle of his arms. "I worried about you," he whispered, his breath hot against her ear. "I couldn't wait to get back to you."

His admission struck a vibrant chord within her. He cared. She wasn't just another female he wished to bed. She wrapped her arms around his neck. "I thought about you. I missed you ..." Any further words were stilled by the hunger of his kisses, on her nose, her mouth, sliding down to the hollow of her throat, then back to her mouth again. She eagerly responded, nothing on her mind except her hot desire for Douglas Cartland.

After a long, searing kiss, he raised his head. "Not the maid's room again. We need a bigger bed."

"Upstairs." She took his hand and led him toward the staircase. "Did you know the old countess haunts the place?"

Douglas grinned. "Then her ghost had better cover its eyes."

Laughing, they stumbled up the stairs and into the dowager countess' bedchamber. Like the drawing room, it was filled with the old lady's disorganized jumble of useless items. A huge, four-poster bed underneath a pink satin canopy stood amidst the clutter. A pink satin bedspread and pink pillow shams matched the canopy.

"My God, it's pink enough," Douglas declared. "And big enough," he added, a devilish gleam in his eye. His hands went to the top button of her jacket. "You have too many clothes on." He started down, unbuttoning as he went.

She giggled. "So do you." She undid the top buttons of his white linen shirt, revealing his muscled chest and a patch of crisp, dark hair. "Hmm." She ran her fingers through it. "You have a very handsome chest, Mister Cartland. Very masculine. Very—"

"How I want you," he whispered, his whole body trembling in response to her touch. "I am going to strip you bare." She stood quietly, a delightful shiver of wanting running through her body as he slid off her jacket and the chemise beneath. His eyes glowed with admiration as he regarded her full, rosy-tipped breasts, now completely exposed. "Beautiful ... beautiful," he said with a ragged breath. "Halfway there." He gave each of her nipples a fleeting kiss as he bent to his task and loosened her skirt and the drawers beneath.

Soon she was stepping away from her skirt and drawers, trembling slightly at the thrill of standing naked before him. There was something else that needed doing. She reached up and removed the four combs Bruta used to fasten her upswept coiffeur so that her hair came tumbling down in loose waves around her shoulders. "Is this better?"

"Much." His voice was thick with passion. He scooped her up, carried her to the bed and laid her gently on the pink cover. "One moment and I'll join you." She watched, utterly fascinated as he stripped off his coat and shirt, then pulled off his breeches, revealing as he did so an erection that rivaled the earl's at his finest moment.

When he lay beside her, she wrapped her arms around his neck, pulling his hard body against her. "I am indeed impressed."

"Umm, you should be." He devoured her with his mouth, his tongue exploring, touching its tip to hers, massaging it gently. At the same time, his fingers roamed over her body. Light as feathers, they glided from her cheeks, down her neck, down her chest to where they lingered over her breasts. At first, their touch was so gentle she could hardly feel their swirling motion around each nipple. Nevertheless each subtle stroke caused a swell of excitement within her. His fingers moved away. "Don't leave yet. More, please."

"Of course, Countess." Cupping both her breasts in his hands, he pushed them up into tight, white mounds, bent his head and gave each nipple a hard suck that sent such a smoldering flame through her that she cried out, "Oh, dear God, Douglas, do that again and I shall float away."

He gave each nipple another quick suck that made her gasp. Then he raised his head. "Float away? We can't have that. Wait right here." He slid off the bed.

She lay waiting, curious as to what he was doing. She could hear him opening drawers, rummaging through the old countess' things as if he was looking for something. "Aha!"

He returned to the bed carrying something in his hand. Upon closer look, she saw it was a pair of black silk stockings with a wide band of lace around the top. "Douglas, what on earth ...?"

He sat beside her on the bed. "We can't have you floating off the bed, now can we? It appears we can put the crazy countess' stockings to good use. Now give me your hand."

Without protest, she held out her right hand and watched while he wrapped one end of a stocking around her wrist and made an expert knot. "You're fast at knots," she murmured.

"But slow at other things." He looped the other end of the stocking over a bed post and tied another swift knot. "When you work on canals, you're good at tying knots. Now give me the left."

Caught up in the moment, she did not protest while he tied up her left hand, too. "It would appear I am completely at your mercy," she whispered in a husky voice. She closed her eyes, picturing how she must look stretched out completely naked on the hot pink cover, outstretched arms tied with their silken bonds. The image served as an aphrodisiac thrumming through her veins, shoving all sensible thought to the very back of her brain. In fact, she wasn't thinking at all. *More, more!* her body cried. She would die if he didn't put his hands on her again.

"Keep those eyes closed," he commanded. "It's high time someone drove you wild."

She obediently kept her eyes closed and soon felt a delicious fluttering of his tongue on her eyelids, Next, his mouth traveled over the tip of her nose to her cheeks; then, like a whisper, it lingered with surprising gentleness on her mouth before skidding to her earlobe. There, after his lips teased it gently, he nibbled at the earlobe until the delicious sensation made her quiver. "Oh, Douglas, that ... feels ... so ... good."

"We're only getting started." He moved farther down. She gave a little gasp as his thumbs brushed her nipples again, first lightly, then with more pressure, each touch sending a hot cascade of passion to that spot between her legs that was beginning to throb with growing, demanding desire.

"Umm, that's marvelously good." She quivered beneath the strokes of his thumbs.

"It gets better." His hands remained on her nipples, teasing them relentlessly, while he moved down her body, his mouth lingering at her navel, which he swirled with his tongue. Never had she imagined such feelings were possible. Tied up, completely in his power, her head spinning with need ... all she could think of was that throbbing place between her legs that was now so demanding she would die if he didn't get there soon.

Then he did. His hands glided from her breasts and down over her taut abdomen, where they gripped her thighs and thrust her legs apart. Swiftly they slid around, cupped her bottom and raised her up. "Now, I'm going to kiss the best part of you, Countess."

She felt his tongue *there*, at that little nub that was the seat of her passion. With a cry of surprise she arched upward, out of control, wanting more, *more*, and she would die if he stopped now. He did not stop. He licked. He nuzzled, causing sensations so utterly pleasurable she was pulling hard on her bonds, biting her lip so she would not scream.

Just when she thought she could stand no more, he raised his head. "Now, darling, are you ready?"

"Oh, yes!"

The gentleness ceased. She felt the solid roughness of his tongue over her throbbing clitoris once ... twice ... "Oh god!" she screamed as her climax ripped through her, tearing an animal cry from her throat.

When it was done, she was gasping. He whispered, "Was it good? Now my turn," and untied her bonds. Quickly, he entered her. She clasped his shoulders, and in what seemed no more than seconds, he, too, was gasping with pleasure. He collapsed beside her, his arms holding her tight. Time stood still while their lingering passion subsided. She had no idea how long they lay entwined, their arms around each other, until she remembered her obligations at last and reluctantly whispered, "I must go."

Soon she wriggled out of his arms and began to dress.

"I'll be leaving for Rennie's canal early tomorrow. I will be gone for at least two weeks."

She slipped her chemise over her head. "I would like to see this canal of yours sometime."

"Why don't you?" He swung his legs from the bed and sat up. Even now she could hardly tear her eyes from his powerful, beautifully proportioned body. "In a couple of days Rennie is leaving for the canal in that fancy coach of his. Why don't you go along? He would love to have you. Millicent and your mother, too." He grinned. "Obviously, you are in dire need of a chaperone."

Feigning outrage, she threw a shoe at him, then ended up back on the bed, where they laughingly wrestled for a time before good sense again prevailed.

"I would love to come see your canal, but some other time. Right now, I have too much on my mind, and that includes getting home before anyone gets suspicious I've been gone so long."

Not that she was particularly worried, but the thought crossed her mind what a terrible catastrophe it would be if anyone should discover what she'd been up to in the dower house on the mad countess' pink bed.

Chapter 14

When Jane awoke the next morning, her first thought was that surely she would come 'round today. The stress of the fire, plus last night's wild lovemaking with Douglas would surely cause her body to take the hint and deliver her from this day-to-day agony of waiting. She checked. No such luck.

Later after breakfast, she had just returned to her bedchamber when a knocking on the door announced the arrival of Griggs, who handed her a small package wrapped in brown paper and tied with string. "For you, m'lady."

She accepted it with thanks and sat on the bed to open it. What could it be? It was such a small package, extremely light, the string carelessly tied. It was the kind of package a man might have wrapped. Perhaps Douglas? Of course. She would wager he had sent her a little gift. Smiling to herself, she tugged at the string, unfolded the paper ...

What on earth?

A pair of stockings lay inside. Frowning with curiosity, she held them up. They were black, with a wide band of black lace around the top ... *The crazy countess' stockings.*

A soft gasp of horror escaped her.

Who had sent them? It could not be Douglas. He would never do such a crass, crude thing.

Someone knows.

If not Douglas, then who?

Spying a small note, she dropped the stockings and hastily unfolded it.

My Dear Countess,

Are you curious? Come to the library now.

—*A friend*

Jane let go of the note as if it were a hot ember burning her fingers. Growing sicker by the second, she watched it flutter to the floor. Somebody knew! Somebody saw her on the bed with Douglas Cartland, naked, legs spread, wrists tied to the bed posts, screaming with pleasure ... Oh, the very thought was unbearable. What should she do? Given a choice, she would crawl into bed and pull the covers over her head. What would happen if she chose not to face whoever was waiting in the library? Would this person tell all?

A wave of despair surged through her, but she fought back. She knew she must go to the library, whether she wanted to or not, and find out who it was and what exactly they knew and—her heart sank—what they wanted.

With leaden steps, she left her bedchamber and started down the stairs. As she did so, an image of Mary, Queen of Scots, popped into her head: those last moments of the poor Queen's life when she bravely and calmly marched into the Great Hall of Fotheringhay Castle to have her head cut off.

I, too, shall be brave and face whatever it is I have to face.

Chin held high, Jane continued on to the library. She found the door closed. When she knocked, she heard a sing-songy voice call, "Come in, dear Countess."

That voice. She might have known.

Stepping inside, she found Percy Elton seated behind the large mahogany desk, regarding her with cold, contemptuous eyes. "Come, sit. I trust you received my little package?"

She seated herself across the desk from Percy, her humiliation so acute she could hardly speak. "Where did you get those stockings?"

His smile mocked her. "Now, now, my sweet, everything in its own good time."

Ordinarily her nephew's blatant disrespect would have aroused her instant rage, but now all she could do was muster a weak, "Get to the point."

"Get to the point?" With maddening slowness, Percy leaned back in his chair. With feigned contemplation, he brought the tips of his fingers together and tapped them lightly. "What's to be done with you? Bad enough, you spread your legs for Cartland, but the bondage? Shocking!" He shook his head and pursed his lips in disapproval. "Naughty, naughty, Countess. Gracious me, what will everybody say?"

She gripped the arms of the chair. Before she could stop herself, she blurted, "You saw?"

"But of course. You put on quite a show. I must confess, watching you rutting on the bed with Cartland aroused my own excitement. I even thought of joining you, but then, considerate fellow that I am, I would not have wanted to disturb your little tryst. You were so enjoying yourself."

She felt sick inside, to the point that she was afraid she might throw up, but she gathered her strength, drew her shoulders back, and gave him a withering stare. "You followed me? How utterly despicable."

Percy shrugged. "Yes, I've been following you, and I must say, in the process I have been most entertained. You may as well save your words of condemnation. I care not one wit what you think of me."

"Go to the devil!" She rose to leave, determined to save whatever self-respect she had left.

"Sit down, Countess, I'm not finished yet."

What did he want? She had better find out. She sat back down. "Then say what you have to say, but bear in mind I won't listen to more of your insults."

"Oh, really?" Percy tapped his fingers together again, in his maddeningly casual way. "Then let's talk about your mother, shall we? What do you suppose she will say when she hears every sordid detail of your ... shall we say, 'encounter' with Cartland?"

"You wouldn't—"

"I would indeed, and not only your mother. Your grandmother wouldn't give a groat, of course, but I can only imagine how my own mother will receive the news. What a delicious tidbit to share with her friends."

The thought of Beatrice finding out stunned and sickened her even further. "What a swine you are."

"Possibly, but that's not the point, now, is it?"

She grasped at straws. "Who would believe you? It would be your word against mine."

"Silly girl, did you think I was alone? I shall not reveal who else was privy to the delicious spectacle you put on, but if I were you, I would not risk assuming no one saw you but me."

In complete frustration, she flung up her hands. "Then what do you want?"

"You."

She would not pretend she didn't understand. "What you are saying is, if I don't submit to your advances, you will—"

"I shall feel it is my duty to report your disgraceful behavior to your family, my family, as well as Sir Archibald, who surely will question whose child you are carrying when he hears such distressing news." Percy's mouth took on an unpleasant twist. "Think about it, Countess. Since I am the soul of generosity, I shall not demand an instant reply. Mull over your options. I must remind you, though, that I mean what I say."

Yes, he does. Too shocked to speak, she stared across the desk at the man who was about to ruin her life. She had always found him repulsive, with his weak chin, pasty complexion, and nearly lashless eyes; now, the very thought of his taking possession of her was more than she could bear. "I ... I shall think about it." Without another word, she arose from her chair and started for the door.

"Come to my bedchamber when you decide, Countess. Bring those black stockings with you. I fancy we shall have a jolly good time when I tie you up again."

She rushed blindly through the doorway and slammed the door behind her. Holding her skirt high, she raced up the stairs. She passed a gawking servant along the way, but it didn't matter. Nothing mattered. When she reached her bedchamber, she flung herself on the bed, nauseous, gasping for breath. She lay on her back and stared at the ceiling. If she didn't move a muscle, perhaps her stomach would not rebel.

Without question, Percy Elton's proposal had brought her to the most terrible crisis of her life. This was worse than her husband's sudden demise, worse than nearly burning to death in the fire at the stables. If she did not do what Percy asked, she, as well as her family, would be totally disgraced. If she did as he asked ... A shudder ran through her, summoning up the image of slimy Percy having his way with her, running his soft, flaccid hands over every inch of her body as she lay there, submissive.

She let out a moan, closed her eyes and let the tears roll down her cheeks. Could anyone help? Douglas perhaps? She would be too ashamed to ask. Besides, she must face the fact that Douglas Cartland was not obligated in any way. She had willingly—in fact, eagerly—entered into their intimate relationship. She had demanded nothing and received nothing in return. That's the way it would remain. No, definitely she would not go to Douglas. In fact, after this latest, if she never saw him again, it would be none too soon. Never, *never*, would she make love with Douglas again.

The trouble was, whatever she decided, no matter which way she went, she was doomed.

"Are you all right, child?" Granny's voice.

Jane had no idea how long she lay on the bed in her miserable stupor. Perhaps she had even slept for a while. She opened her eyes to see her grandmother standing over her. "I'm all right. I was just taking a nap." She swung her legs over the side of the bed and sat up.

Granny eyed her skeptically. "I heard you were upset."

Of course, the gawking servant on the stairs must have spread the word. "I was a little upset." Her grandmother's gaze was skeptical. "All right, a *lot* upset, but I am not going to tell you why."

"You don't have to tell me why. Just tell me you're going to do something about whatever it is and not lie like a lump on the bed and cry."

Jane pushed back her hair, which had to be in disarray. "There are times when your fate is sealed and there's nothing you can do."

"Fiddle-faddle. There's always something you can do." Granny sank into a chair and thumped her cane. "Is that little worm, Percy, involved in this?"

"Yes."

"How about Douglas Cartland?"

Why did Granny have to be so maddeningly perceptive? "Douglas, too."

"Then why are you not asking Douglas for help?"

"Because Douglas Cartland is not obligated to me in any way."

"He's part of the problem, isn't he?"

"Yes, but he's just a friend. I have not heard any proposal of marriage coming from his lips, nor do I expect to hear one. Besides all that, I have no wish to see the man ever, ever again."

"You're not thinking clearly. Now listen to me." Granny thumped her cane, harder this time. "Leave marriage and your personal feelings out of this. You're in trouble. Use your head. You need help, and from what I can see, the only person in the world who can help you is Douglas Cartland."

Jane dabbed at her eyes. "I have my pride."

"Your pride isn't worth a farthing at a time like this."

"He's gone. He went back to work on Rennie's canal."

"Then go after him."

"I cannot and I will not. Didn't I tell you I never want to see him again?"

"Nonsense. He can help."

"You do not know what happened."

"I can pretty much guess. Look at it this way. As women, we are supposed to let the men lead the way and follow like docile sheep. You and I don't fit the mold because we have an independent streak most women don't have. Unfortunately, I include my own daughter in that category, but," Granny gave a regretful sigh, "that's another story."

Jane nodded. "You're so right, Granny. I want to do things my way. I want to solve my problems and not rely on a man."

"That's all very well and good, but there are times when we must let a man take the lead." Granny's faded blue eyes drilled into Jane's. "This is one of those times. From what I gather, this is a man's business. Go to Douglas. Tell him. I guarantee he'll take matters into his own hands, as well he should."

Granny's words made sense. So much so that Jane suspected her crafty grandmother knew more than she was letting on. She slid off the bed, a small glimmer of hope arising within her. "Douglas said Lord Rennie will soon be visiting the canal. I could ride with him."

"Good for you," Granny said with a spirited thump of her cane.

"I shall need a chaperone. Would you come with me?"

"These old bones don't take well to a jostling ride in a coach.

Amelia won't go. She does not want to venture beyond her tight little world. In fact, you had better not even tell her where you're going, or she will scream to high heaven that you're jeopardizing your baby. At the least, she will demand you take Bruta along." Jane opened her mouth to protest about the baby, but Granny continued, "Don't bother to argue. Just take Millicent and go. Not that your silly sister would be much of a chaperone, but she might enjoy the trip. I know Lord Rennie would like to have her."

"I'll do it." Could there possibly be a way out of her hopeless situation? She might be grasping at straws, and she most definitely did not want to see Douglas again, but she would give it a try.

When Rennie heard Jane wanted to accompany him on his journey to his canal, he expressed his delight, especially when he learned Millicent would come, too. "We shall stay at the Blue Bull Inn, where Cartland stays. It's quite close to the canal. Good food. Music. Each evening a rousing good time is had by all."

Having a rousing good time was the farthest thing from Jane's mind. Still, all things considered, she was grateful for Millicent's presence on the coach ride. Her sister provided a welcome diversion, acting her most bubbly self, chattering nonstop. In her gloom, Jane occasionally blocked out her sister's flighty conversation, choosing instead to stare out the window at the passing landscape. Not Rennie, though. Millicent's smitten suitor sat on the seat across from his adored one, wearing a look of rapt attention, drinking in her charm, beauty, and—only to his own ears—brilliant wit.

"Jane, you are awfully quiet," Millicent remarked when they were halfway there.

"I'm fine. Just a bit tired." She might appear calm on the outside, but little did they know how her mind was churning, alternating between hope and despair. How she dreaded facing

Douglas, having to reveal Percy's sordid scheme then beg for help. More than once, she thought of asking Rennie to turn the coach around and return home. Or, perhaps more practical, when they reached the canal, she could pretend nothing was wrong, that she had just come for a pleasant visit. Such a deception would not work, though. Douglas, perceptive man that he was, would sense her dark mood immediately. So she had no choice. The very possibility of Beatrice hearing every lurid detail of her encounter with Douglas drove her on. Finally, after five long hours had passed, Rennie pointed out the window. "There it is. We've reached the canal. See? That's one of the locks."

At last she would see Douglas' canal. Eagerly Jane looked out the window and spied a blue ribbon of water, not more than thirty feet across. A long, narrow boat sat in the water, which ended at an enormous wood-and-iron door. She saw three men pushing against the door, straining to open it. One of them was Douglas.

Rennie pointed again. "They're about to open the lock. Once the boat is in, they will close the door and then use a winch to open the paddles. In turn, the paddles will send fifty thousand or so gallons of water into the basin. The boat will float to the top, and then they will open the door at the other end to let the boat out. It can be exhausting. Good thing Douglas is in good shape."

Good shape? Jane's heart jolted at the sight of him. The day was warm, and he had stripped off his shirt, as had the other two men. What a magnificent body he had. Those broad shoulders and slim hips—that chest rippling with muscles— that patch of silky hair on his chest that only recently she'd delighted in running her fingers through. He was not aware of their presence yet. As she watched, he gave instructions to the other two men in a voice that rang with authority. Everything about him was masculine and commanding. Simply the way he stood there, so very sure of himself, made her want him, made her realize her decision to end their affair was prompted by her shocked reaction to Percy's revelation. Because in truth…

I am in love with Douglas Cartland.

Thanks to Douglas, she had discovered the strong passion within her, undiscovered for all these years. She had been so blinded by their love-making that she had not stopped to examine her true feelings. Her timing could not be worse. She could not possibly think of love while facing complete disgrace at the hands of Percy Elton. Not only that, more time had passed and she had not come 'round. Though she still could not believe she was expecting, she had to admit it was a distinct possibility.

Rennie helped Jane and Millicent alight from the coach, then yelled down at Douglas, "Get your shirt on, Cartland! There are ladies present."

Douglas looked up to where the coach stood on the road. A smile spread over his face when he saw them standing there. When his eyes met Jane's, they took on a special glow and she knew he was as thrilled as she. "Be right with you!"

She watched as he pulled on his shirt and quickly buttoned it. With agile strides he came up the bank, shook Rennie's hand and bowed to her and Millicent. "What a marvelous surprise." His eyes lingered on Jane.

Rennie slapped his friend on the back. "Just a quick visit, old boy, but I wanted to show the ladies this marvelous canal you've built."

They chatted for a while. Douglas proudly gave them a detailed description of how the locks were built. Briefly they wandered along the bank, but Jane was never alone with Douglas longer than to whisper, "I have something to tell you. Something urgent."

"Come to my room after dinner," he murmured back.

She could say no more without being overheard and could only hope Douglas would not misconstrue her words. At the moment, making love was the furthest thing from her mind. In fact, considering her current desperate situation, she doubted she would ever want to make love again.

Even in her despairing mood, Jane managed to enjoy the rollicking evening at the Blue Bull Inn. The food was not as good as Rennie claimed, consisting of leg of mutton roasted to a cinder, a huge joint of boiled beef, potatoes that were hot outside and hard within, bread, cheese, and some gritty cabbage. No one seemed to care. The crowded, open-timbered dining room rocked with laughter, the babble of voices, and lively music from a fiddle and harp. Spirits, including hot spiced ale, flowed freely; patrons frequently burst into song, sometimes ribald ballads to which Jane, and all at her table, raised their tankards and enthusiastically sang along.

She sat across from Douglas. Although she tried not to, she occasionally allowed her eyes to meet his, and she could not prevent the sparks of passion that passed between them. Too bad it all had to end. Too bad she would soon face complete disgrace and have to go into hiding for the rest of her life.

Only much later, after they had all retired, was Jane able to slip from the room she shared with Millicent after her sister fell asleep. Dressed in her nightgown and blue silk robe, she slipped down the hallway and knocked lightly on Douglas' door. He immediately opened it and she slipped inside.

"Darling," he murmured and tried to take her into his arms.

She pushed him away. "I'm not here for that."

His expression of ardor immediately changed to one of controlled curiosity. He backed away and indicated a chair next to the bed. "Then sit down and tell me why you are here."

After seating herself, she began without preamble, "It's Percy ..." and proceeded to relate in detail her nephew's threats and demands. Douglas sat on the bed and listened carefully, his eyes never leaving her face. "So there you have it. Percy must have followed me to the dower house. He must have seen everything, Douglas, *everything*!" She felt a blush creep over her cheeks. "When I opened that package and saw the stockings, I wanted to—"

"Hush!" He slid off the bed and knelt in front of her. His roughened hands enveloped hers. "You should not have had to go through such a humiliating experience."

She could not prevent the tears that sprang to her eyes. "It's just ... just all so horrible. He made me feel like a whore."

"You're not a whore." He touched her cheek with the back of his hand. "What we did was what people do when they love ... when they are fond of each other. It gave me great joy to give you pleasure, so how could that be wrong? What I, myself, felt with you was ..." He sighed and looked away. When he looked back, the softness in his eyes had disappeared. "You are not to concern yourself further, do you understand?"

"How can I not?"

"Say no more." Douglas pulled her to her feet and held her close. "You are not to feel one iota of shame or guilt. You must not feel bad about anything we did."

"What if my family finds out? And Beatrice! I would die if she knew."

"She's not going to know." Douglas softly kissed her forehead, then her cheek. "Whatever we did shall remain between the two of us. Nobody's business but ours." Gently he tipped up her chin with his fingers and gazed directly into her eyes. "Understood?"

"What do you plan to do?"

"I shall handle it. That's all you need to know."

She gulped back her tears and nodded. "You are sure?"

"Positive."

"Then I trust you. I believe you." She had just placed her reputation, her entire future, in the hands of Douglas Cartland. She had no idea what he planned to do, yet already she felt as if a huge weight had been lifted from her shoulders.

"I shall accompany you to your room," said Douglas.

"All right," she replied, grateful he understood that she was in no mood to make love.

❧❧❧❧

When Rennie awoke the next morning, he found a note under his door.

Rennie,

I have left on urgent business. I shall be back later today.

—*Cartland*

Strange. What could Douglas be up to? When he arrived for breakfast in the dining room, he found Jane and Millicent already there. After joining them at their table, he unfolded the note and read it aloud, frowning in puzzlement. "Douglas never said a word to me. I have no idea where he's gone, or why."

To his surprise, the countess spoke up. "I believe I know where he's gone. Let's just say it's something personal. Don't worry, he will be back."

Something in her voice made him refrain from asking anything further. Truth be told, he sensed something was amiss with the countess from the moment she got into his coach yesterday. She had been distant, not her usual amiable self at all. In fact, she seemed almost distraught, as if something was terribly wrong. Well, he would not pry and would try to cheer her up as best he could. Of course, Millicent, too. "Ladies, shall we go for a walk after breakfast? There is a beautiful walkway by the river I would be delighted to show you."

The countess shook her head. "Thank you, but I have a headache. I believe I shall go to my room and rest."

"Of course." He turned to Millicent, his pulse suddenly racing. How beautiful she looked this morning, wearing a bright blue gown that brought out the blue of her eyes. Golden curls peeked out from beneath the matching bonnet tied with a big bow—a most fetching sight indeed. "Uh, then Miss Hart, I wonder if you would care to ... uh ..."

"Accompany you?" She smiled, an action that not only brought out two adorable dimples in her cheeks, but also caused his heart to nearly turn over in his chest. "I should be glad to, Lord Rennie. I have been dying to see the river."

"Splendid!"

The Blue Bull Inn overlooked the banks of the River Clearsy, one of the rivers connected to the canal. Soon Rennie and Millicent were strolling along its shallow banks on a pathway lined with languid eucalyptus trees and dense river ferns. Along the way, they noted a variety of birds—cranes and the occasional heron hunting for fish among the reeds. "This is indeed a beautiful walk, Lord Rennie. I am so glad you brought me here."

Ever since they'd left the inn, Rennie's mind had churned with a variety of emotions. At long last he was alone with Millicent! He knew she didn't really like him, not *that* way, and yet ... should he seize this opportunity and ask for her hand? She would likely say no, thus sending him into the dark pit of rejection. But what if she said yes? Perhaps she could see he loved her so much that, given time, some of his love was bound to rub off and she would love him in return. Besides, he'd been told he was an excellent catch. Maybe he was, considering he could offer her great wealth, a title, and a huge estate. And of course he would not require a dowry.

Besides all that, she was the only woman in the world he loved or could ever love ...

By God, it was worth a try.

They stopped to watch a flock of herons rise slowly to the sky. He took her elbow and turned her toward him. His heart pounding, he began, "I have something to say to you, Miss Hart."

She fluttered her long eyelashes at him. "Really, Lord Rennie?"

He took the plunge, a feeling that must be similar to diving off one of those high cliffs at Dover. How to say it? Words spun madly in his brain. "I have a certain fondness for you, Miss Hart." No! That was not what he meant to say. "What I mean is, I am madly in love with you and I want you to marry me. That is, I am asking for your hand in marriage. That is—"

"Why, Lord Rennie, I had no idea!" With a merry laugh she placed her tiny hand on his arm, as if to prevent him from further embarrassing himself. "You must know how very fond I am of you, but marriage?" His heart began to sink, "While I am deeply honored by your proposal, I fear I cannot accept, although you know how much I value your friendship."

Oh, no! She was giving him the standard let-him-down-easy speech, the one every well-brought-up young lady memorized, to be used for occasions like this when some poor sod had to be rejected.

"You are such a dear man. So very amusing, and so very kind ... why, sometimes I think of you as a big, friendly puppy dog without a mean bone in your body."

A big friendly puppy dog? Rennie shriveled inside. He felt an urge to throw himself into the River Clearsy and sink to the bottom, never be seen again. Of course, he would do no such thing. He must not let her know her words had cut him deeply. Kind soul that she was, she would be greatly distressed if she knew, and he could not have that. "Say no more, Miss Hart, I quite understand. Rest assured I shall not bring up the subject again." Rennie fixed a smile on his face and offered his arm. "Shall we stroll back? I fancy we should be leaving for home before long."

❧❧❧❧

On the ride back from the canal, Jane's spirits seesawed between high and low. One minute she was positive Douglas could do nothing to prevent Percy from destroying her life and she was doomed. The next, she would remember Douglas' utter confidence when he told her, "You are not to concern yourself further, do you understand?"

She believed him, and yet, how could she not concern herself? Percy's threats hung like the blade of a guillotine over her head, and by the time Rennie's coach rumbled up the driveway to Chatfield Court, she felt empty and drained. There was no way out; she was sure of it.

"Oh, look!" Millicent was looking out the coach window. "Isn't that Percy's carriage under the portico? It looks as if he's going somewhere."

Jane looked out and saw a footman strapping a piece of luggage to the back of Percy Elton's high flyer phaeton. Percy sat in the driver's seat, reins and whip in hand. "Hurry up!" she heard him yell. Obviously he was anxious to depart.

Lord Rennie's coach pulled up behind the phaeton. As it did so, Rennie, always friendly and gracious, poked his head out the window. "Ho, there, Elton! Going somewhere?"

Percy turned in his seat and glared back. Jane saw he was hatless, cravat askew, his upper lip appearing twice its normal size. What on earth had happened? Her usually impeccably dressed nephew looked as if he had been in some sort of a fight. A wild look gleamed in his eyes. "No time to talk!" He turned back, raised his whip in a near-frantic gesture and lashed it above the backs of his two horses. The carriage started off so quickly that the footman strapping the luggage was compelled to leap back, barely escaping the rear wheel.

"How strange," Rennie remarked as he helped his two passengers from the coach. "The man seems in a bit of a pet."

Once inside, Jane was greeted by Griggs, who handed her a note sealed with a splotch of red wax embedded with an "E." The straight-faced butler explained, "From Mister Elton, madam. It appears he was in too much of a hurry to deliver it himself."

Jane was hard-put to keep from snatching the note out of Griggs' hand and rushing to her bedchamber to read it in private. As it was, she wasted no time in getting to her room, closing the door, and ripping open the note.

Countess,

The matter we discussed has been settled and will never be brought up again. My apologies for any inconvenience you may have suffered.

—*Elton*

Douglas did it! Never had she felt so relieved, so blissfully happy. How did he manage? She must find out.

The servants knew everything. She would talk to Meg.

She found her chambermaid on her knees in the drawing room, scooping ashes from the fireplace. After a greeting, she asked, "Meg, do you happen to know if anyone came visiting today?"

"Indeed I do, ma'am." Meg sat back on her haunches, the trace of a grin on her face. "Mister Cartland came calling on Mister Elton. They had a conversation right here in the drawing room. It was," Meg bit her lip, as if searching for the right word, "most interesting. I didn't hear it myself, but afterwards the sound of a scuffle was heard. Others—I shall not say who—were listening at the door."

"A scuffle?"

"Oh, yes, ma'am. They were quite loud, and there was a bit of banging about and the like. Apparently, Mister Elton got the worst of it. It's said when he left the drawing room, he was pale and shaking and had a big swollen lip. But that's not all."

"There's more?"

"The person at the door just happened to have overheard some of the conversation," Meg went on. "It was quite ... quite

..." she put her hand over her mouth to smother a giggle.

"Quite *what*, Meg?" Jane was dying to hear.

"I hardly dare say."

"You can tell me anything and I shall not be shocked."

"Well, then," Meg calmed herself, took a gulp of air and carried on, "it seems Mister Cartland was telling Mister Elton what he was going to do if Mister Elton didn't stop doing whatever it was he was doing. We don't know what that was, madam, but it must have been something really bad."

That is not the half of it. "Do go on. What did Mister Cartland say he was going to do?"

"Well, the person who was listening didn't catch all of it, but among other things, it seems Mister Cartland was going to cut off certain ... I guess you could say, masculine parts of Mister Elton's anatomy. He said he was going to," Meg started giggling again, "it was something about stuffing the parts he cut off into Mister Elton's mouth."

Jane tried to keep a straight face. "How very boorish, so terribly unrefined." She burst into laughter and couldn't stop. Meg joined her. They laughed until tears streamed down their cheeks and they had to stop to wipe them away.

"Thank you, Meg," Jane finally said. "I appreciate our telling me this, more than you will ever know."

Her heart full of gratitude, she hurried to her room, sat at her writing desk and penned a quick note to Douglas.

My Dear Mister Cartland,

My heartfelt thanks for your handling of the matter we recently discussed. All is well now, thanks to you. I shall look forward to seeing you upon your return from the Berkferd Canal.

With utmost kind regards,
—*Jane Lansdown*

She folded the note, sealed it with a glob of blue sealing wax, and impressed it with her elaborate "L." Lovingly, she pressed it to her heart. If sent by Royal Mail Coach, it would be in Douglas' hands by tomorrow.

Her next stop was Granny's bedchamber, where she relayed the happy news. "I am ecstatic, Granny. Douglas did it! I absolutely adore the man."

"That is all very well and good," came Granny's sharp reply, "but don't forget, your troubles aren't over yet."

"I have not come 'round yet, if that's what you mean."

"How many days now?"

Jane sighed deeply. "It's getting on toward a month."

"Hmm ... that is very, very late, even for one who is so absolutely positive she is not with child."

"I still do not believe it."

"Isn't it time to face reality?"

Jane's high spirits slowly plummeted. "I was feeling so happy about Douglas Cartland, knowing I've fallen in love with him. I even dared to think he might feel the same and we could have a future together. But now? Why is it that every time I think my troubles are over, I'm forced to realize they are not?"

"That's the way life is, I'm afraid." Granny nodded wisely. "I told you once before, whether or not you're carrying a child is in God's hands."

"Well, I wish God would take pity for once and make me come 'round."

That night, Jane went to bed with a sad heart. If she was expecting, and it looked like she was, Douglas would have no part in her life. She would be the Dowager Countess, mother of the new earl, and expected to act accordingly.

No more Douglas.

No more happiness.

Her life stretched before her like a dark abyss.

Chapter 15

When she awoke the next morning, she gradually became aware of something unusual. Slowly she realized her lower abdomen felt heavy, the way it always did before her monthly. Her breasts were sore. Could it be? With bated breath, she slid from her bed. With careful fingers, she explored, and when she brought them up …

Dear God in heaven, I have my monthly.

She hastened to the washstand. While she washed, the impact of her discovery hit her full force. She would not be presenting the world with the next Earl of Lansdown after all! Beatrice would be thrilled. Mama would be crushed. As for herself, a vast relief flooded through her. She felt like pinching herself to make sure she wasn't in the midst of a wonderful dream. Douglas. Could she have him now? Why not? What could possibly stand in the way?

Soon after, her sister and grandmother came to take her down for breakfast. Jane drew them both into her room. "Wait 'til you hear, I've come 'round! I am not carrying the next

Earl of Lansdown!" She did a little jig in her billowing white nightgown.

Granny beamed. "What good news! I wonder what brought it on."

Jane hadn't even thought. Whatever brought it on, she was joyous. "We will never know what brought it on, and I really don't care." She looked at her sister. "What do you think, Millicent? I hope you're happy for me, too."

Millicent managed a reluctant smile. "That's wonderful news. I knew you didn't want the earl's child, but, of course," her face fell, "Mama will be devastated."

"I know."

Granny shrugged. "She will get over it."

"Poor Mama has exhausted herself with worry lately," Millicent said. "Among other things, she was upset when we went to the canal without telling her where we were going."

"I should have told her," Jane said, "but you know she would not have approved."

"Of course, I understand," Millicent continued. "It's just ... well, it's a shame after all she's been through, and now this. She was so hoping we could all continue to live at Chatfield Court. It's going to be so galling, knowing Beatrice will get everything she wants and we will be living like paupers in that tiny house."

"It's not so tiny, and we shall not be paupers," Granny scoffed.

Millicent shook her head in dismay. "You know what I mean. Jane, I don't envy you having to tell her."

"Neither do I, but it must be done."

Later that morning, Jane joined her mother in the dining room. Amelia Hart, dressed in black with a simple white lace cap perched atop her gray head, sat at the table sipping her morning cup of tea. "I have something to tell you," Jane said.

"Is it something good or something bad?"

"It depends on how you look at it. I have my monthly."

"Oh, no!" The color drained from Mama's face. Blindly, she set her cup down, nearly missing the saucer. "Are you sure?"

"Very sure."

"I am astounded. I was so certain ... what could have brought it on?"

"Who's to say? What matters is, I am definitely not with child, so I think the sooner we move to the dower house, the better."

"Beatrice did it," Mama snapped.

"I really don't think so. Why would you say that?"

"Because she's the one who caused the stables to burn."

How irrational. Jane spoke in her most calming voice. "The stables burned days ago. Although I understand your concern, I really don't think Beatrice had anything to do with my coming 'round."

Mama opened her mouth to reply but, though her mouth worked, she could not get the words out. Instead, she covered her face, bent her head to the table, and broke into wracking sobs.

Her heart wrenching in sympathy, Jane reached across the table and took her mother's hand. "Please stop. I cannot bear to see you cry." She gripped Mama's hand until finally the sobbing ceased and she raised her head.

"I might as well be dead," Mama said, tears glistening on her cheeks.

While Jane searched for comforting words, she was struck by how much her mother's appearance had changed since Papa left. Her once-abundant mane of chestnut hair had thinned and gone gray, her once rosy cheeks were now pale and gaunt, and her eyes no longer sparkled with the joy of life. *Shame on me for not noticing. I was too caught up with my own problems.* "Mama, please don't talk that way. I know how you suffered when Papa left. If there were anything I could do, *anything* that would make you happy, you know I would do it, but what choice do I have? We must leave this place and go to the dower house whether we like it or not."

Amelia took up a serviette and dabbed at her eyes. "I'm

sorry. I should not burden you with all my woes. It's just ... I don't have much to live for anymore." With a weak smile she continued, "I shall get over it. In the meantime, I assure you I'm not going to kill myself, even though all I see in my future is bleakness and despair." She dabbed at her eyes again and said in a firmer voice, "Unless ... There *is* something you can do."

"Anything."

Mama's lips twisted in a wry smile. "Perhaps you had better wait until you hear what I'm about to ask."

"Just tell me."

"I want you to remain silent and not tell anyone you got your monthly."

Moments passed before her mother's astounding request sunk in. "That is impossible. How can I kept it a secret? *Why* should I keep it a secret?"

Mama sat straight again, some of her confidence restored. "I shall be very honest."

"Please do."

"You know how I feel about Beatrice."

"It's how we both feel."

"You know how galling it is for me, watching her take over the household and have her own way. I could not believe she poisoned your tea, but she did. Then the fire at the stables. You could have been killed, thanks to Beatrice and her boundless greed."

"That is exactly how I feel, too, but what does that have to do with—?"

"I am coming to that." The older woman paused a moment before she took a deep breath. "You are having an affair with Douglas Cartland."

Jane gasped, utterly shocked by her mother's words. "Why do you think that?"

"The night of the fire I saw you two together." Mama leveled a knowing gaze. "You can't fool me, my dear daughter. If only you could have seen the two of you like I did. I saw the love and concern in Douglas' eyes. The way he was holding you, touching you. It was as if you didn't have an inch of skin with which he was not familiar. You were so very comfortable in his embrace, as if you'd been there before. His feelings were obvious and so were yours. I am just glad Beatrice wasn't there or she'd have seen it, too, and would instantly have known." Mama's piercing gaze drilled into her. "It is quite obvious you've been intimate with the man."

Words of denial raced to Jane's lips, but she couldn't say them. Why lie? If ever there was a time for honesty, this was it. "If you must know, it has only happened the once, well twice. I am not ashamed of it, and I really don't know why I should tell you."

"So I was right." For a time Mama remained silent, as if in deep thought. "I know it's risky. It might be impossible to pull off, but I do believe it is most certainly worth a try."

"*What* is worth a try?"

"Use your head. *Think*. What did Sir Archibald say? That ten months would have to go by before it was an absolutely proven fact you are not with child? Well, then ...?" Mama fell silent and sat waiting, obviously expecting an enlightened answer.

"I still don't understand."

Mama pursed her lips in annoyance. "Such a delicate subject, but you force me to lay out all the details."

"Just tell me straight out."

"Straight out then. You have just delivered the devastating news that you got your monthly. We shall, however, keep your news to ourselves. By that, I mean that absolutely *no one* must know other than the two of us. Cartland will be gone two weeks?" Jane nodded. "Perfect. When he returns, you and he will resume your ... for the sake of propriety, I shall call it *friendship*. If good fortune shines upon us, you will soon be in a family way, and, of course, give birth to a boy who will be the next Earl of Lansdown."

Jane's jaw dropped open. "That's ... that's ..." At first she could find no words to express her shock. "I cannot believe you would even suggest such a thing. It's obscene. It's insane."

Mama shrugged. "One does what one has to do."

"We would never get away with it."

"*Au contraire*. Sir Archibald might be suspicious, but there's a real chance we can fool him. I know you're shocked." Mama spoke in a voice so casual she might have been discussing which guests to invite for dinner. "But there's a real chance this plan will work. If it does, we can stay right here in Chatfield Court where we belong, with every advantage that's due us. Millicent will have an ample dowry. As for Beatrice, just think! Would you not love to see the look on her face the day she must pack her bags and leave this place forever? That's how I feel, Jane, as should you. Don't forget, you nearly died in a fire Beatrice is responsible for, and don't tell me otherwise."

Jane shook her head in amazement. "What astounds me the most is how my very proper mother, who always obeys the rules, could even suggest such an outlandish scheme."

"Out of sheer desperation, I assure you."

Had her mother lost her senses? This could not be real. Soon she would wake up and discover she had just had a horrible dream. "All right, I do understand, but what you suggest simply isn't feasible. In the first place, you know very well nothing is sacred around here. What with Bruta constantly snooping around, I would not be surprised if she's already found out I've come 'round and rushed to tell Beatrice."

Mama appeared unfazed. "I am well aware my plan might not work, but if you have any love for your family at all, you'll at least agree to try."

"Do you realize what you're asking?"

"Of course I do, but ..." Once more, Amelia's eyes filled with tears. "Everything in my life has gone wrong. This is my only chance for an even halfway decent life. Yours, too, and, of course, Millicent's."

"Have you forgotten Papa's letter? Could we not go to

America and forget all this?"

"I would never be happy in America. I admit I'm a creature of habit. I don't want anything to change and that is that." Mama folded her hands in her lap, sat back and waited for an answer. "So what's it to be? Will you give it a try?"

"It won't work. Granny and Millicent already know. I told them a while ago."

"They can keep a secret. After all, they're on our side."

"If you must know, there's another reason, too." Jane hated revealing the most intimate details of her life. "I have fallen in love with Douglas. Possibly I want to marry him. What would happen if I agree to your plan?"

"I don't see—"

"Well, I see. I would be deceiving him, absolutely making a dupe of him. If he found out, I would never see him again."

Mama cocked her head. "Has he asked you to marry him?"

"Well, no."

A look of triumph flashed through Mama's eyes. "Then how can you be sure he will ask? I know you don't want me interfering in your private life, but it seems to me he's simply taking advantage and has no intention of ... shall we say, making an honest woman of you."

Could Mama be right? In the euphoria of her newfound love for Douglas, she had not even considered he might not propose. "To be honest, I am not sure what Douglas intends."

"If he does not propose, then so much the better," her mother equably replied. "That way, he won't be involved since he won't care one way or the other that you're with child."

"If I were to take up with Douglas, it's absurd to think I would immediately conceive a child."

"I know it's absurd, but it's possible. If it doesn't happen, what have you lost?"

Jane knew full well how she ought to reply to such outrageous logic, and yet, just looking into her mother's strained, careworn face made her wonder how she could say no. But how could she say yes? "I need time to think."

"Of course."

"I'm not saying I'll do it, but I agree not to say anything, at least for a little while."

"You can handle Bruta?"

"I can't answer that. If by chance she doesn't already know, I'll do my best to keep it secret."

"See that you do, darling. I'm depending on you to do the right thing."

Although she did her best to conceal it, Jane left her mother's bedchamber in a high state of agitation. She suspected Mama had temporarily taken leave of her senses, a condition no doubt caused not only because she nearly lost her daughter in the fire but because the one thing she feared the most had finally happened. No wonder she was upset. She was about to lose her home once again, as well as her precious standing in society. Jane understood her mother's feelings perfectly well, but her request was shocking, nonetheless.

When Jane entered her bedchamber, she discovered Bruta tidying up. Did she know? "I'm going to rest a while, Bruta, so that will be all."

"Very well, m'lady." The sullen lady's maid looked her square in the eye and said in an offhand voice, "I see you've come 'round."

Uh-oh. There went her secret. Mama's plan would never succeed now. Unless ... "Bruta, have you told anyone?"

"No, madam."

Jane stood tall, tilted her chin and looked down her nose in the imperious pose she hardly ever used. "Then I prefer that you do not. Do I make myself clear?"

"Yes, madam."

Jane wondered if she was getting through to her stony-faced lady's maid. "You are not to tell anyone, and I mean *anyone*. Do you understand?"

"Of course, madam."

Bruta left shortly thereafter, leaving Jane to wonder if she would really keep her mouth shut or go running to Beatrice to give her the welcome news. Well, she would soon find out. Meantime, she would keep her promise and not tell, at least for the moment. Surely, when Mama gathered her wits about her, she would realize such a farfetched scheme would never work.

Two days later, Griggs brought her a letter. "This just arrived, m'lady." Seeing it was from Douglas, Jane hastened to her bedchamber to open it. Could there be a proposal in the letter? Had he declared his love? Eagerly she ripped it open.

My Dear Countess,

> Thank you for your kind words. I am extremely happy your problem has been resolved.
>
> Upon my return in two weeks, I shall call upon you to express in person my admiration for your strength and courage. I shall also be saying my goodbyes since I shall soon be setting sail for America.

—*Cartland*

Jane sank to her bed, totally numb and deflated. What a fool she was to expect a declaration of undying love. What insanity to think he might even propose.

You idiot, what did you expect?

In all their times together, neither the word "love" nor "marriage" had been mentioned once. In fact, had not Douglas clearly stated he would never marry? Foolishly, she had ignored his words, choosing to wrap herself in infatuation's rosy glow. Now, in the cold light of a new day, she saw their so-called romance was nothing more than a mere dalliance, prompted by lust, not love.

She crumpled the letter and tossed it into the fireplace,

where it quickly vanished in the flames.

Douglas Cartland could also go to blazes.

That evening, when she entered the dining room for dinner, she was surprised to find only her own family at the table. Beatrice and James were absent.

"Where are the Eltons?" she asked Griggs.

"Gone to London, m'lady. Rather suddenly, I must say." The butler gave her a bland smile. "Perhaps it has something to do with Mister Percy Elton's hasty departure."

"Did they say when they would be back?"

"No, they did not. However, I got the impression they would not be gone long."

How interesting that Beatrice had not said a word about traveling plans. Could it be that she had somehow discovered Percy's recent "problem"?

She doubted Bruta was in any way responsible. To her surprise, Bruta appeared to have kept her secret.

Well, whatever the reason, Jane felt vastly relieved she would not have to deal with the terrible Eltons for the next few days.

Late that night the rains began again. During the next several days, storm after storm rolled over the landscape, dumping more water on the already-soaked ground than anyone had seen in years. Jane spent the week thoroughly enjoying the absence of the Eltons, yet her mother's outrageous request weighed down on her, as oppressive as the weather.

Finally she arose one morning to see that the skies had cleared. What a happy sight! At last she could get out of the house and visit Beauty again.

When she arrived at Lord Rennie's stables, she found Rennie himself in the courtyard grooming both her horse and his. "Beauty's doing fine." He pointed to the burn near her tail. "We have kept the salve on it, and it's nearly healed."

"Do you suppose I could ride her?" She wore her blue riding

habit just in case.

"I don't see why not. I'll get you a saddle. If you don't mind, I'll ride with you."

They chose the path by the river, Jane on Beauty and Rennie riding his prize horse, Major. "I cannot believe it's the same river," Jane remarked. The last time she rode this trail, the River Hulm was nothing more than a shallow stream that Beauty could cross and hardly get her hooves wet. Now the river ran fast, deep, and near the top of its banks. She would not dare ride across it today.

"How is your sister?" Rennie inquired as they rode along. "It's too bad she couldn't come."

Damnation. She knew sooner or later he would ask about Millicent. "My sister is in good health, Lord Rennie. Thank you for asking. She's just awfully bored because of all the rain and not being able to get out." She hoped he would now have the good sense to change the subject.

They rode in silence until Rennie spoke again. "You know I'm deucedly fond of her," he said in an earnest voice. "Even though—"

"Even though what?"

For a long moment, Rennie remained silent. "I proposed, you know. She turned me down."

"She did?" Jane was genuinely surprised. "She never said a word."

"Perhaps she thought it wasn't worth mentioning," Rennie replied in a pensive voice. "I know she meant well and did her best to be kind, but she likened me to a friendly puppy dog. That rather hurt my feelings."

How awful. How could Millicent make such a cutting remark? Jane really didn't want to cause this kind, compassionate man any grief, but the time had come for honesty. "I know she admires you greatly, but anything beyond that—"

"I am desperate, Countess, sick with love for her. I know I'm not a romantic figure, but do you think there's any possibility she could ever like me in a special way?"

"I do believe she likes you as a friend, Lord Rennie." This was painful. "I, personally, see in you a man who is mature, compassionate, dependable, and ... oh, my, you have so many excellent qualities it's impossible to name them all. It would seem, though, that Millicent prefers a ... sort of dashing, handsome, devil-may-care type of man, the kind who could sweep her off her feet and carry her off to his cave, if you understand my meaning."

Rennie laughed wryly. "Oh, I understand full well, Countess. I know I'm far from handsome, nor could I ever claim to be dashing or devil-may-care, but ... may I speak honestly?"

"Please do."

"If she could ever find it in her heart to consider a man who loves her dearly, who would lay down his life to protect her, then perhaps I would have a chance."

"I do understand. I'm so sorry. If I could wave a magic wand over my sister's head, I would do so and make her fall instantly, madly in love with you, and that's because I, for one, am of the opinion she could search the kingdom wide and never find a better man than you. But the problem is—"

"The problem is, she doesn't love me." Rennie sighed. "Well, don't be sorry. We have no control over matters of the heart. If Millicent doesn't care for me, there's nothing you, nor I, nor anyone can do to change her mind. Let's stop a moment." They reined in their horses and sat looking at the swollen river. A log came floating by, twisting and turning in the swift, black current. "I don't like the looks of this. The river is nearly overflowing its banks."

"It's far from the tranquil River Hulm," Jane replied with a worried note in her voice.

Rennie pointed across the torrent toward the Twimby's farm. "If the river overflows, the banks will break on the other side first. That farm will be right in its path."

Jane realized she hadn't seen Meg for several days. Was she

all right? She decided that after she and Rennie finished their ride, she would pay a visit across the river.

When they continued on, Rennie spoke not another word about Millicent, for which Jane was most grateful. On the way back, when they came to the wooden bridge, Jane bid him goodbye. As expected, at sight of the bridge, Beauty performed her usual nervous dance, but with some urging from Jane, the edgy horse finally condescended to trot over the wooden boards.

Arriving at the farm house, Jane observed that it looked even more dismal than when she saw it the first time. The few chickens, even scragglier than before, wandered around a yard full of thick mud. Jonathan, the twelve-year-old, was halfheartedly shoveling muck from the lean-to stable on the side.

"Your ladyship!" Meg exclaimed when she opened the door. Little Molly peeked out from behind her skirts. "I am honored. Do come in."

Meg looks thinner. Jane bent low and stepped across the threshold. When her eyes adjusted to the dark interior, she saw Edwin Twimby's empty bed. "Your father?"

"My dad died two days ago." Meg's voice caught as she spoke.

"I am so sorry."

"Thank you, but he was in such pain those last days, even the laudanum wasn't working anymore. He ..." Tears welled in Meg's eyes. "We must carry on. Sorry, but I can't offer you any buttermilk today. The cow's gone dry."

Jane's heart filled with sympathy for this poor family that had just lost its one remaining parent. "Water will do just fine." Her eyes strayed to a straw mattress in the corner where Matthew, the seven-year-old, lay pale and drawn, his eyes closed.

"He's sick, I'm afraid," said Meg. "It's the flu. I've been giving him barley water for the fever."

Jane knew better than to ask if Matthew had seen the doctor. Of course, he had not. The Twimbys could not afford such a luxury.

They sat at the old wooden table, little Molly in Meg's lap, and fell into a comfortable conversation, like old friends. "Do you think the rain has stopped for good?" Meg asked with a worried frown. "I've lived here all my life and I've never seen that river so high. If it overflows its banks, I don't know what we can do, except run for the hills."

"If the water starts to rise, you must come to Chatfield Court at once. You would be safe there. It's higher up."

Meg broke into a wide, open smile. "That will be the day! I can just see the look on Mrs. Elton's face if the four of us show up on your doorstep along with ten chickens, one goat, and Jupiter. Let alone the cows!"

"You needn't worry. Don't forget, I am still the countess."

"That reminds me, is there anything new?" Meg inquired, clearly asking in a delicate way if Jane had finally come 'round.

"Nothing new." Jane hated to lie, and she wouldn't if not for Mama. She quickly switched to another subject and went on to describe in detail the terrible fire at the stables. Meg listened breathlessly to her gripping account of how she rescued Beauty. At the end, Meg asked if she knew how the fire had started. "We're not sure," Jane told her. She longed to speak the truth—that Beatrice and Percy were responsible—but she knew it was best, at least for the moment, to keep her silence.

Later, Meg described her father's passing. "It truly was a blessing when God took him home."

Jane listened intently, her heart full of sympathy. "Will you be all right?"

"I ... am not sure. At least we had a good crop this year, but, of course, with the higher rent—" Meg bit her lip. "Sorry. You have enough problems without me adding mine."

"Don't be sorry. I tried to do something about the rents

but I fear it's out of my hands." Each time Jane recalled her humiliating visit with Sir Archibald, she felt sick inside. She wished she could wipe it from her memory.

"Now that you're here, your ladyship, there is something I ..." Meg shifted little Molly on her lap.

"You want to tell me something?"

Meg nodded decisively, as if she'd just made up her mind. "Yes, I do. It's about Mrs. Elton. I don't mean to tattle, but I think you should know—"

"If it's about Mrs. Elton, then I definitely should know. Do go on."

"Before Percy left for London, he and his mother practically tore the mansion apart looking for the Lansdown jewels."

"Really?" Jane frowned in puzzlement. "How could they do such a thing when I'm usually there and so is my family?"

"She's very sly, that one." Meg made a face that revealed her dislike. "When she was sure you were not around, she and Percy dug into closets, looked under the beds, scoured the mansion for every possible place you could have hidden the jewels. I don't think she found them, though."

"I know she thinks I took them."

"She does, but I know you did not, m'lady."

Jane smiled softly. "How can you be so sure?"

"I know you, and I know you're a woman of honor and integrity, and you would never do such a thing."

If only you knew. No, she had not stolen the jewels, but she had yet to denounce Mama's sordid scheme, and that most certainly made her *not* a woman of honor. "I appreciate your telling me about Mrs. Elton. Actually nothing would please me more than if she found the jewels."

"Maybe that's why she went down to London. Maybe she found them and wanted to sell them."

"Perhaps. I don't know what I can do about it right now, but I'm sure all will be resolved, and soon."

Why had she just made such a ridiculous statement? She had no idea what was going to happen. She just had a feeling that whatever it was, it would not be good.

Chapter 16

As Jane rode back to Rennie's stables, Meg's words, *I know you're a woman of honor*, kept sounding in her head. What kind of honor would she have if she agreed to Mama's scheme? Well, she knew the answer to that, and it was *none*. On the other hand ... She loved her mother dearly and knew her heart would be broken if she didn't at least try to go along with the lie.

Dear Lord, what am I going to do?

Riding Beauty at a walk, she passed the spot by the river where she and Douglas had stopped for their picnic ... and other things. She got a tingling in the pit of her stomach just thinking about how he kissed her, unbuttoned her shirt, pulled aside her chemise, stretched her out in the sunshine before God and the cows. Desire coursed through her body. Despite everything, she still wanted him, wanted a man who said he would never marry, a man who had made it clear he would soon be off to America, alone. Well, she would have nothing more to do with him. As soon as she arrived home, she would inform her mother that no way in the world could she be a party to such a vile, immoral scheme. Furthermore, as soon as the Eltons returned, she would give them the news they were waiting for.

Something soft brushed her cheek. A raindrop? She held out her palm. Just what they didn't need—more rain.

❦❦❦❦

"Douglas!" Rennie, busy at his desk in the library at Lancaster House, looked up in surprise. "Back so soon? I thought you would be gone another week or so."

Douglas Cartland, weary after a long journey by horseback, settled himself in one of Rennie's fine Louis XV gilt chairs and thrust his mud-splattered boots toward the welcoming flames in the marble fireplace. "Your canal is nearly complete, if that's what you're thinking of. We finished the tunnel. We're almost done with the last set of locks. By the way, we used cast iron—much better than stone."

"From the looks of you, you could do with some port." Rennie poured two glasses from a crystal decanter and gave one to his friend. He settled into the matching gilt chair on the other side of the fireplace. "So why did you return early? Surely it wasn't to tell me you used cast iron instead of stone?"

Douglas contemplated his glass of port. "Have you noticed it's raining again? It started not long before I arrived."

"So? What has the rain got to do with your return?"

"I haven't seen this amount of rain for years. If you must know, it makes me uneasy."

"We have had rainy seasons before."

"Not like this," Douglas said. "Never like this."

"So what do you think will happen?" With a smile Rennie continued, "Will we all be drowned, do you think? Would you recommend I build an ark?"

His smile soon faded. Douglas, usually quick to respond to his friend's sharp wit, remained straight-faced, his brow furrowed. "It has happened before."

"Ah, yes. I seem to recall some legend about how the River

Hulm flooded its banks and caused a bit of damage a few centuries ago."

"More than a 'bit of damage,' as you so casually put it. Back in the fourteenth century, a wall of water twenty feet high swept through this valley. It destroyed the village of Sudberry and everything else in its path."

"A piddling river like the Hulm? I had no idea. How is that possible?"

"As you know, the River Hulm flows through a steep, narrow canyon upstream from here." Douglas motioned his head to the north. "The flood no doubt started in that narrow canyon. I can only make an educated guess, but I would wager conditions weren't much different than they are today. A narrow gorge, steep walls, little foliage, a sudden cloudburst that dumps ten to twenty inches of rain, and suddenly you have a wall of water crashing down the canyon to the valley below."

"'Pon my word! We would all have to run for the hills."

"Not you, Rennie. Lancaster Hall is high enough up the slope that I doubt the waters would reach you, but—"

"Chatfield Court?" Rennie asked, unsmiling. "It's closer to the river."

Douglas nodded grimly. "Chatfield Court would be directly in its path, as would all the little farms along the river clear to Sudberry."

"What about Sudberry?"

"What do you think would happen if a wall of water filled with trees, boulders, and God-knows-what came crashing down upon the town?"

"Good God." Rennie sat silent, properly impressed, no doubt conjuring up a ghastly vision of the horror that would ensue should such a disaster occur. "Do you really think it could happen again?"

"Who can say? I only know that this constant rain has thoroughly soaked the ground. One more good rainstorm and the water will have no place to go except ..." Douglas shrugged.

"What can we do?"

"Pray the rain stops."

"Oh, I shall."

"To be more specific, better pray a cloudburst doesn't open up over that canyon to the north."

Rennie took a sip of port. After a long moment of silence, he said, "Surely that's not the only reason for your early return. Aside from your fears about a flood that might or might not occur, what else?"

Douglas gazed toward the window and sighed. "That's all."

"No it's not. It's the countess, isn't it? You couldn't stay away from her."

"Why would you think so?"

"Your attraction to her is as plain as the nose on your face. Don't forget, I was there the night of the fire. I noted your behavior. A tender scene, if ever there was one. The way you held her in your arms—as if you'd just made love, not just carried her away from the fire."

Douglas opened his mouth to protest, then changed his mind. "Damn you, Rennie, you're too perceptive for your own good."

"Aha! I thought so."

"Have you ever been in love?"

"You know the answer to that."

Of course, Millicent. He should have remembered. "What is love? I don't even know. What I do know is, I cannot get her off my mind. She's ruining my sleep. So here I am, and why? What good will come of it?"

Rennie made a dismissive gesture with his hand. "She *is* a widow, after all. Why don't you marry the woman and be done with it?"

"Not possible," Douglas said with a firm shake of his head. "I just wrote her a letter saying I would soon be leaving for America, which, really, is the best solution for the both of us."

"I'm baffled. Why would you do that?"

"For one thing, her life is in turmoil. Her entire family is at sixes and sevens over whether or not she's carrying the next Earl of Lansdown."

"That's only temporary. You need more port." Rennie refilled his friend's wineglass. "So why else can't you marry the beautiful countess?"

"I shall never marry. I told you that."

"Yes, you did, but I've never understood exactly why."

"I killed a little girl, that's why." The words had just slipped out. Always a private man, Douglas never revealed his intimate thoughts. But the combined seductive forces of the port, the cozy warmth of Rennie's library and the ear of a trusted friend loosened his tongue.

Rennie set his wineglass down. "Are you referring to that accident in London a few years back?"

"I am."

"That was four, maybe five years ago, was it not?"

"It was five years, forty-seven days, and approximately twelve hours since I, in my inexcusable drunken state, ran over and killed an innocent little orange girl who had the bad luck to be in my path."

Rennie shook his head in disbelief. "All that time has gone by and you're still dwelling on it? Of course, it was a most tragic affair, but still—"

"If you're going to say she was only an orange girl, pray don't," Douglas cut in. "The events of that terrible night have never left me. I attended a ball, gambled and drank at White's half the night, then left totally foxed. But what did I care? I was so cock-sure—the London dandy who fancied himself a cut above the common man. With nary a care, I raced my phaeton down St. James' Street. I rounded a corner much too fast and all of a sudden there she was, in the middle of the street. Before I could stop, my horse struck her and threw her under the wheels ..."

Douglas shut his eyes, attempting to blot out the heartrending image. "Not a day, an hour, goes by that I don't remember how I knelt in the street after I hit her, the oranges from her basket scattered about. I held her broken body in my arms, shouting for help. She was conscious, looking up at me with eyes wide with fright. Then a trickle of blood ran out the corner of her mouth. She lived long enough to speak to me. Do you know what she said?"

"What did she say?" Rennie asked gently.

"She said, 'I am sorry, sir.' *She* was apologizing to *me*. 'I am sorry, sir' " His voice caught. Feeling the old, familiar welling in his throat, Douglas set down his wineglass, hastened to the window and stood for a time looking out at the rain. When he regained control, he returned to the fireplace where Rennie sat patiently waiting. "They told me her name was Sarah. I never knew her last name. Nobody did. I would have given her family everything I had, but they said she was an orphan. No one even knew where she lived. She was all alone, you see. Not more than eight years old and all alone in the world."

Rennie's eyes brimmed in sympathy. "How terrible. I can only begin to imagine what you've gone through. But Douglas, that was five years ago."

"It was yesterday."

"I see." Rennie refilled his wineglass and took a long sip before he spoke again. "I still don't understand why you say you will never marry."

"I vowed I would not. An innocent little girl lay dead on the street because of my carelessness. Don't you understand? How can I marry? Have children? Lead any kind of a happy life when ..." Damn, he was about to choke up again.

"Well, of course, I can easily see how you felt at the time. That's when you gave up your lodgings, as I recall."

Douglas nodded. "Never set foot in White's again, nor shall I ever."

"You left London."

"I never told you, Rennie, but I traveled north to work as a laborer on the Stratford Canal." Douglas smiled wryly. "If ever you want to forget your troubles, get a job pulling a narrow boat along the tow path. Work all day in the boiling hot sun with nothing but horses and mules for company."

"I shall make a note of it," Rennie answered agreeably. "Forgive me for saying so, but guilty though you may feel, surely you cannot forever deny yourself life's pleasures. Be a martyr if you wish, but you will never bring little Sarah back."

"It's my penance. I took a vow. I can never break it, can't you see?"

Rennie leaned back and thoughtfully fit his fingers together. "What I see is a soul in torment. You hide it well. I had no idea. If only I could say something, do anything to make you realize—"

"Don't waste your breath, dear friend. There's nothing to be said."

"What about Lady Lansdown?"

"I shall see her one more time to say goodbye. Then I shall be off to America."

"So there's no chance that you and the countess—?"

"None whatsoever. Call me a fool, and I know I am, but nothing on this earth could make me break my vow."

∿∿∿∿

The next afternoon, Jane was chatting with her grandmother in the old lady's bedchamber when Griggs knocked and entered.

"You have a visitor in the drawing room, m'lady. Mister Douglas Cartland."

Jane's pulse quickened as it always did when she heard Douglas' name. Her first impulse was to tell Griggs she would be right down, but second, wiser considerations told her otherwise. What good would come of seeing him again? She had vowed to end their relationship, and end it she would, right now. "Tell Mister Courtland I cannot see him. I am ... uh, indisposed."

"Yes, madam."

Griggs had no sooner closed the door than Granny inquired, "Are you daft? I thought—"

"You thought wrong." Jane noted Granny's look of puzzlement. "I have chosen not to continue my friendship with Douglas Cartland."

"Why in blazes not?"

"Because, for one thing, he's going to America. For another, I do not wish to be made a fool of. He made it clear he will never marry, so what can I expect? Do I want to become his mistress? I think not."

Granny applauded. "That's the spirit! But you still want him, don't you?"

"Yes, I want him," Jane replied with a grim nod. "But I'm not going to see him again. There's no point. Besides, there are other reasons for my decision."

"You mean that bird-brained scheme of Amelia's?"

"You know about that?"

"Your mother tells me everything sooner or later." Granny clucked her tongue in disapproval. "How could I have given birth to such a ninny? Don't tell me you even considered carrying out such a plan."

"I wasn't going to," Jane answered quickly. "I decided I'm done with this charade. I plan to inform the Eltons I am not with child as soon as they return from London. Mama won't like it, but she will just have to adjust."

Granny nodded her approval. "A wise decision, missy."

"I think so, too."

For the rest of the day, Jane wandered about the mansion. She couldn't eat. She couldn't read. She didn't care to talk to anyone. She kept telling herself she had made the right decision, yet her heart ached at the thought she'd sent Douglas away. She spent part of the time looking out the window of her bedchamber.

The dreary rain falling from leaden skies matched her mood. She wished it would stop, even briefly, so she could visit Beauty and perhaps have time for a ride. If she did, might she possibly see Douglas on the trail?

She laughed at her foolishness. She had made the right decision. Why, then, could she not keep Douglas Cartland out of her mind?

When the weather broke the next day, Jane quickly donned her blue riding habit and hastened to Rennie's stables. She found Beauty pawing the ground, impatient for a ride. She saddled the horse herself and headed out. One look at the gray, overcast skies told her that her ride might be a short one.

She had put Beauty up to a canter along the river trail when she heard the sound of a horse's hoofs. Without turning to look, she knew who was there.

She slowed her horse's pace as Douglas rode up beside her. "Good afternoon, Countess. A fine day for a ride, is it not?"

She chose not to look at him. Instead, she sniffed and tilted her nose in the air. "It's going to pour down rain any moment and you call this a fine day?"

He chuckled. "I cannot tell you how deeply concerned I was yesterday when I learned you were indisposed. Please, I beg you, tell me you have recovered from what must have been a devastating illness."

Finally she turned her head and gave him her most scathing glance. "I didn't care to see you again. Obviously, you could not take the hint."

"I need to talk to you." He wasn't chuckling now.

"We're talking."

"You know what I mean."

"I hope you're not suggesting another rendezvous under the oak tree? Because the ground is too wet."

"The dower house."

"Ha! You know what happened last time."

"I mean it, Jane. There are things that need to be said that I can't say from the back of a horse."

"I'm sure Thunder and Beauty are unshockable."

"I won't beg. It's either yes or no, and if it's no, then farewell forever. I wish you good fortune wherever you go."

Obviously, he meant what he said. She enjoyed their banter and was satisfied she'd shown him she was not some mealy-mouthed female he could intimidate. Yes, indeed, she would most certainly stick by her decision never to see him again, only ... *Farewell forever?* Her spirits sank at the thought. How could she bear never to see him again?

You must be strong. Bid him a firm farewell and ride off. That will show him.

She reined in her horse. Douglas did the same. She faced him. "If we go to the dower house, it will be to talk and nothing more. Is that understood?"

"Of course, Countess. Shall we proceed?"

Ah, those hips!

As he guided his horse behind Jane's, Douglas reflected how, in reality, his head and heart were in conflict. He had suggested that they meet at the dower house only because he needed a proper setting in which to say goodbye. In the kindest, most gentle terms, he would explain why they must sever their relationship. He was simply not a marrying man. No need to dwell on the details. In the event she cried, he would refrain from laying a hand on her. Instead, he would loan her his handkerchief and utter whatever words of sympathy were required. After she regained control of herself, they would part on good terms, friends forever.

His lusty heart defied his logic. He caught himself examining the totally captivating bottom of the Countess of Lansdale as she perched in her saddle ahead of him. His fingers itched to trace those luscious curves, beginning at her slender waist, flaring out over the swell of her hips, across her leg to that soft, warm triangle hidden beneath her skirt, and from there ...

Uh-oh, he was getting an erection. Not in his plans. What kind of a lowlife bastard was he? With a swift shake of his head, he put his mind to his farewell speech to the Countess. Or tried to. But, by the time they reached the dower house, Douglas, the logical man, had let all logic fly to the wind.

She stood in the entry hall of the dower house, hands on hips, head tipped to one side. "So what did you have to say that you could not say from the back of a horse?"

What indeed? "You talk too much." He pulled her silly hat from her head, tossed it aside, and pulled her into his arms. He ran his hand through her hair and tugged her mouth to his in a long, unrelenting kiss. Would she struggle? Fight to free herself? *Au contraire.* In no time, her tongue darted into his mouth, the tip of it finding his own tongue, and she thrust herself against him, pressing her hips against what was now a huge bulge in his pants.

She lifted her lips from his. "I vowed I would not do this."

He ran a trail of kisses to her ear and sucked on her delicate, white ear lobe. "I don't know why not. You like it, don't you?"

"Too much." With a low moan, she stuck her teasing tongue back in his mouth again and pressed her hips harder against his cock. Uh-oh. He would explode if she didn't stop. Better back away fast, or he would embarrass himself right here in the front hall.

"Time to go upstairs." He pulled away.

She glanced to the top of the stairs. "I'm not sure. You know what happened last time."

"I would not worry about Percy."

She started to laugh. "Did you really threaten to cut off his balls?"

His state of arousal was such he could hardly think straight, but he managed a grin. "Percy ran back to London with his tail between his legs. I doubt he'll be lurking outside the door."

"He told me someone else was with him."

"A lie. Percy indulged in his vile snooping all by his despicable self." He took her hand. "Come on, there are things I want to do to you."

Eagerly she took his hand. "Let's go."

They left a trail of discarded clothing up the stairway and into the bedchamber. By the time they lay down on the mad countess' pink satin bed, they were completely naked, their arms entwined around each other.

"Lie there while I explore." He began a slow journey down her body, kissing her lips, nibbling at her neck. When he reached her breasts, he stopped and took his time, sucking each pink nipple in turn until each grew marble hard. By now she was whimpering and crying out with little moans of delight, which brought him pleasure, too. He resumed his journey, planting kisses down her taut belly, swirling his tongue around her navel, then farther down still until he reached her silky triangle. He stopped, raised his head. "Are you ready?"

She spread her legs and gazed at him with half-closed eyes that made her look as if she were drugged with pleasure. "Oh, so ready."

"Let me see." He traced his fingers slowly through the triangle of silken hair, then slid a finger into the hot, wet spot between her legs. "Umm, so *very* ready."

"What about you?" She surprised him by sliding her legs closed and propping herself up on one elbow. "Mercy me, it's very big." She gazed down at his throbbing member, which by now was at full mast.

"Bigger than the earl's when he took the Spanish Fly?"

"Hmm, let me see."

Silently he watched as her delicate little hand traced a tingling path down his chest, his stomach, then farther down until it reached his cock. When she wrapped her fingers around it and squeezed, the feeling was so intense he let out an "Oh, God," and fell back on the pillow.

She was leaning close over his cock now, examining it closely. "Yes, it's absolutely bigger than the earl's ever even thought of being."

"Cocks don't think, they feel."

"They do?" She sounded all innocent. "Then do you think it feels this?" With a feather touch, she moved her hand up and down his throbbing shaft, causing his stomach to clench. He so desperately wanted to plunge himself inside her.

"Or this?" Grasping him firmly in one hand, she lightly brushed the fingers of her other hand across that pinnacle of all pleasure, the tip of his cock.

"You're killing me."

"Can you think of a better way to die?" She cast him a wicked little grin. "I think what it really needs is to be kissed. Do you mind?"

"If you feel you must," he replied. The understatement of the century, perhaps since the beginning of time.

He lay still, his eyes drinking in the entrancing sight of Jane's nude form bending over him, her hair loosened from its combs, falling forward in disarray around those full, white breasts that swung enticingly. When the tip of her tongue touched the side of his cock, a state of near euphoria enveloped him. She ran the roughness of her tongue up his shaft, and he had to grit his teeth from crying out. In an agony of anticipation, he waited until her slow journey up his cock ended with her lips sliding down over the tip. Then she suckled, sending him soaring toward an explosion of ecstasy.

Wait. Not yet. He could stand only so much. He reached down, entwined his fingers in her hair and pulled her head away. "Not yet. I want inside you."

❧❧❧❧

"Oh, yes." Gladly, joyfully, she let him spread her legs apart.

When he rolled atop her and entered, her pleasure increased inch by inch as his cock drove inside her. Then he began a slow, deliberate stroking, and she raised her hips to meet each stroke in a flesh against flesh tempo that bound their bodies together. All at once, his hands tightly gripped her shoulders. In one swift move, he rolled them over so suddenly she found he was on the bottom and she on top. "What happened?" she gasped.

He grinned up at her. "Change of pace. You're in charge."

At first she didn't quite know what to do, but soon she discovered the delight of controlling every move. Riding his cock at her chosen pace gave rise to increasing bursts of joyous sensations. Beyond that ...

What she was feeling was much more than plain sexual pleasure. All her life she had overheard the dirty sexual innuendoes, the tittering little jokes exchanged behind fans that had led her to believe sex was all about lust and nothing more. Now, with Douglas deep inside her, she felt not only the physical joy of their coupling but the deep fulfillment of achieving the ultimate closeness to the man she loved. Yes, *loved*. She *loved* Douglas Cartland. She wanted to tell him.

Her hair falling loosely around her face and shoulders, she looked down into his brown eyes brimming with tenderness. "Douglas, I—"

"My darling. God, how good." He raised his hips and gave a shove that caused a golden explosion within her. Her breath caught in a long, surrendering moan before she hurtled past the point of no return and erupted into an awesome, shuddering ecstasy. At the same time, so did he.

For a long while they lay together on the pink satin cover, exhausted, happy, totally satisfied. Finally, when they got up to dress, he asked in a casual way, "By the way, did you ever come 'round?"

She stopped halfway through pulling her stocking on. "As a matter of fact, it's come and gone. No little Lord Lansdown is on the way, and so ..." She made a sweeping gesture around the cluttered room and said with a touch of irony, "Just think, all this will soon be mine."

"Look at the bright side. You will have the freedom to do as you please."

"Indeed I shall." She waited. Why was he not ecstatic? Here was the perfect moment for him to speak up, declare his love for her, propose marriage or at least suggest they had a future together.

He pulled on his breeches and said in an off-hand tone, "Your sister-in-law must be beside herself with delight."

"Beatrice doesn't know yet."

He appeared not to hear. "Actually your dower house isn't all that bad. Give it a good airing ... clear out all the crazy countess' junk ... You'll be proud you live here."

No declaration of love. No marriage proposal. The remnants of her glow of happiness dimmed and disappeared, replaced by humiliation and a deep, numbing hurt. What a fool she was. Now she felt like a whore. It was a wonder he hadn't offered to pay for her services.

He buttoned his breeches, a task to which he was giving his undivided attention, as if nothing mattered more, including her. Anger filled her heart just watching him. She wanted to hurt him, and even more, wanted to save her pride and show how little she cared. She blurted the first thing that came to her head. "You would never guess what my mother planned."

"What?" He didn't bother to look up.

She moved to the old countess' dressing table and sat upon the pink upholstered bench. "My mother knows about us," she said brightly. With great casualness, she examined herself in the mirror, picked up a comb and began to fix her hair. "She wanted us to ... well, carry on."

"What do you mean?"

"Can't you guess?" She laughed gaily, determined to save her pride if nothing else. "She was hoping you could ... oh, how can I put this delicately?" Another gay laugh. "To put it bluntly, she was hoping you could get me with child. A son, of course, whom I could pass off as the new little earl."

He stopped buttoning, raised his head and stared. Oh, yes, she definitely had his attention. She continued, "A rather amusing idea, don't you think? Still, not a bad plan when you consider—"

"What do you take me for, some sort of stud?" His words came out hard, edged with anger.

"Do calm yourself, Douglas," she replied in a silky voice. "Why should you care, one way or another? This is simply a dalliance, is it not? Nothing to get upset about." She stood to face him.

"A dalliance?" Like a shot, he strode across the room and gripped her shoulders, his brown eyes blazing. "You consider this just a dalliance?"

"Yes, I do, and why not? I hear no words of love coming from your mouth, no talk of marriage, so really, why should you concern yourself with consequences?"

He gripped her arms tighter and said in a voice deep with intensity, "You want words of love? Then yes, Countess, I love you. I have never in my life met a woman like you and I absolutely adore you. You wreck my sleep each night because I stay awake thinking about you. As for marriage, I cannot." His face twisted with anguish as he thrust her away.

"I don't understand you."

"There is no need for you to understand." He drew a deep breath, seeming to will himself back to normalcy. "Your mother's scheme is monstrous. I'm more than a little surprised you would stoop so low as to be part of it."

"You misunderstand. I—"

"I understand well enough." The temperature in the room had turned frosty. "It's best I go. I've said enough."

"Go then." She was not about to beg him to stay, nor would she demean herself further by trying to explain why she would never have agreed to her mother's scheme.

He finished buttoning his shirt, sat on the bed and pulled on his boots. At the door he turned and said, "Goodbye, Countess. If you're looking for a stud, kindly look elsewhere. I will not be available."

He left before she could even open her mouth to answer. In a sick daze, she listened to his heavy footsteps pounding down the stairs, followed by a decisive slam of the front door.

With a heavy heart, she rode Beauty home. It was over. She had lost him. Why had she been so stupid as to reveal her mother's ridiculous scheme? And why, after being fool enough to tell Douglas, had she let her pride get in the way of explaining why she would never have been part of it? But then, why should she care what he thought? He was a cad who had used her and would have continued to do so had she not put an end to their affair.

One thing she knew for certain: Douglas was right. Mama's scheme was indeed monstrous. She would have no part of it. She hoped the Eltons returned soon so she could tell them the truth and get the whole sordid scheme off her mind.

It was not going to be easy. She didn't know which ordeal she dreaded more—watching Beatrice salivate with delight over becoming the new countess or watching her poor mother fall apart when she learned she must leave Chatfield Court forever.

When she arrived home, Griggs met her in the entry hall. "Mr. and Mrs. Elton have returned, madam, and Percy. I thought you would want to know."

"Thank you, Griggs." So they were back. She would tell them at dinner tonight. Better warn her mother first.

She joined Mama in the drawing room where she sat working her embroidery. "I have something to tell you."

Amelia Hart looked up from her stitching. "You've been riding? I hope with Douglas Cartland."

"Yes, with Douglas."

Mama smiled. "Ah, so you're seeing him. That means—"

"That means no such thing. It is over."

Amelia dropped her embroidery to her lap. "What do you mean, it is over?"

"I mean I want nothing to do with your plan." Seeing her mother's shocked expression, Jane sat beside her on the sofa and took her hand. "I know you meant well, but I simply cannot go through with such deception." She smiled gently. "We'll be fine, Mama. We just need to get on with our lives. I couldn't have asked for a better mother than you. I promise I will do my best to give you a good life and make you happy."

Tears sprang to Amelia's eyes. She groped for her handkerchief. "You were my last hope."

"There's always America. Don't forget, Papa wants you to come."

"Never!"

No sense arguing. Mama would never change. There was nothing more to say. What a terrible day, and it wasn't over yet. Tonight she must watch Beatrice Elton gloat over what to her would be the happiest news in the world.

That night, as expected, the Eltons appeared at the dinner table. They brought a subdued Percy with them. He sat quietly at his place, carefully avoiding eye contact with Jane. James remained his usual sly, unpleasant self. Beatrice, all smiles, chatted endlessly about their delightful visit to London, including every boring detail of how her fabulous children were doing fabulously well.

The right moment for Jane's revelation came halfway through dinner during a rare lull in the conversation. As offhand as she could manage, she remarked, "By the way, Beatrice, you will be happy to learn I am not with child."

Beatrice's eyes widened with surprise. She was struck speechless but not for long. "You are sure, my dear?"

"Positive. We shall be moving to the dower house shortly."

Jane allowed herself a wry smile. "Whether Sir Archibald approves or not."

Mama startled them all by swiftly rising from her chair and hurling her serviette on the table. "Excuse me. I am not well," she declared, her mouth tight and grim. She quickly left the room, followed by Millicent, who looked close to tears.

"Poor Amelia," Beatrice said with a satisfied smile. "Poor Millicent. Well, they will just have to get used to their new station in life, now won't they?"

Jane fought the urge to wrap her hands around her sister-in-law's chubby neck and strangle her. Instead, with slow dignity, she, too, arose from the table. "You need not concern yourself further about either me or my family."

Beatrice dropped her smile. "All I'm concerned about now is finding the Lansdown jewels."

Not again, Jane thought with disgust. Would the woman never quit? "I don't have them. This is the last time I'm going to tell you that."

"I don't believe you." Beatrice nearly spat the words out. "I give you fair warning, Jane. If you don't give up the jewels, I shall accuse you of theft."

"Do what you please, but it won't do you any good." She turned on her heels and left the dining room, her heart hammering. Upstairs, she was almost to her bedchamber when Meg Twimby approached, a polishing cloth in her hand. "May I have a word with you, madam?"

Jane stopped and smiled. "Meg, how are you? How is your family?"

"As well as can be expected, m'lady, although Matthew is still sick and don't seem to get better. Of course we're all a bit worried about the river. I have never seen it so high."

"Nor have I. We can but hope for the best." A silly question popped into her head. No doubt Meg would not know the answer, but it wouldn't hurt to ask. "Do you remember what you told me about the Eltons tearing the house apart searching for the Lansdown jewels?" Meg nodded. "Well, I don't suppose you would have any idea where they might be?"

Meg looked carefully around, bent toward Jane's ear and whispered, "That's what I wanted to talk to you about, your ladyship. I know exactly where they are."

Chapter 17

"The jewels are in the earl's bedchamber," Meg whispered. "I will show you where."

"My word! Are you sure?"

"Positive."

Jane recovered from her astonishment. "Wait here. We don't want Mister Elton surprising us. I'll make sure he's elsewhere." She hurried down the stairs and took a quick peek into the dining room, where she saw glassy-eyed James lingering over his port. Obviously deep in his cups, he did not look as if he would be moving any time soon. She raced back upstairs. Together she and Meg entered the earl's bedchamber. Meg went the fireplace and knelt on the hearth. "They're here, madam. I found his lordship's hiding place by accident this morning while I was cleaning out the ashes. I saw a crack and ..." With both hands, she slid up one of the large stones from the hearth, revealing a large wooden box beneath. She pulled it out and opened the carved lid. Inside, a dazzling assortment of jewels caused a small gasp to escape Jane's lips. She sank on her knees beside Meg and ran her fingers through the jumbled collection—the pearl and amber necklace once owned by a

Russian czarina, the blue heart diamond ring originally part of the French crown jewels. Rings, bracelets, earrings—most of which she had never seen before—all made of gold and silver, embedded with precious stones.

"How beautiful," she exclaimed. "I have seen a few individual pieces but never did I realize how stunning the whole collection is."

"What do you think it's worth?" Meg asked in awe.

"It's priceless."

"So what will you do with it, m'lady?"

Jane closed the lid. "What can I do? These belong to the new Earl of Lansdown."

Meg's face fell. "Then I guess you'll be turning them over to Mrs. Elton—or should I call her Lady Lansdown now?" She made a sour face. "I'm only a servant and should keep my mouth shut, but in my opinion it's a shame the jewels have to go to that awful woman and her husband. They are *so* undeserving."

"It's the honorable thing to do, Meg. The only thing to do." The sound of her own words unleashed a deep resentment within her. She envisioned the superior smirk that was sure to appear on Beatrice's face when she turned over the jewels. The thought made her cringe with disgust. How could she let that horrible woman triumph? What a loathsome thought. *But the jewels rightfully belong to the Eltons now.*

Not yet. At the moment, she couldn't bear the thought. Of course she would do the honorable thing, but not right now. "Put them back in their hiding place, Meg. I shall deal with them tomorrow."

"Are you awake, Granny?"

Propped up in bed, Granny looked up from her Bible. "Of course I'm awake, missy. Come in and rest yourself. Judging from that sad look on your face, I wager you have not had a very good day."

"No, I have not." Jane settled herself by her grandmother's bed. Soon she was pouring her heart out. Finding the jewels ... finally giving Beatrice the news she was dying to hear ... quarreling with Douglas Cartland, whom she most definitely would never see again.

Granny laid down her Bible. "*Never* is a long time. What did you quarrel about?"

Jane gave her grandmother a succinct version of her argument with Douglas. No need to mention the time they'd spent making passionate love on the dowager countess' pink bed.

No use. When she finished, the wise old lady remarked, "So you let him bed you and now he's a cad."

Jane had to smile at Granny's shrewd insight. "Something like that, yes. He did say he loved me, but then he put me off." She forced back tears. "It's breaking my heart. My life is over."

"Don't be daft. He must have a good reason."

"But what?"

Granny shrugged. "Who knows what goes on in the depths of the human heart? I suspect Douglas is fighting his demons, whatever they are. Be patient. I have always believed love will find a way, even if it didn't for me. Whatever his problems, give him time to work them out. If he cannot, then you will find other threads of your life to weave into a future. You will move on and forget about Douglas Cartland."

Jane felt strangely comforted by her grandmother's words. She would be patient. Perhaps somehow, some way, she and Douglas could work things out ... perhaps.

❧❧❧❧

Flames from the fireplace in Lord Rennie's library cast a warm, rosy glow as the lord of the manor sat watching his friend pace the room. "For God's sake, Cartland, will you stop that! Why the devil are you pacing up and down that way?"

Douglas muttered an oath and slung himself into one of

Rennie's gilt upholstered chairs. "The minute I finish your canal I shall be off to America."

Rennie observed his friend with curious eyes. "It's the countess, isn't it?"

"Of course." Douglas slumped in his chair, an abject picture of misery and defeat. "It's over between us. Totally, completely over."

"Why? It's obvious you love the woman."

"Must I remind you again of the reason I shall never marry?"

Rennie thought a moment. "If you will forgive an honest opinion—"

"Save your breath." With a weary sigh, Douglas arose and moved to the window, where he gazed moodily out at the rain. "I have lost the only woman I have ever loved or ever shall love, but I'm honor bound to keep my vow."

"That's nonsense. Honor bound to whom?"

"I am a man of honor even to myself, Rennie." For a time Douglas continued to gaze silently at the deluge outside. "It's not good."

"You mean all this rain?"

Douglas returned to his chair. "I mean the chances are, this area is going to be hit with a flood the likes of which we haven't seen since the fourteenth century."

"Are you serious?"

"Absolutely."

"Are you talking about that twenty-foot wall of water again? The one that wiped out Sudberry and everything else in its path?"

"That's the one."

"I find that hard to believe, but then, you're the expert on the weather. Tell me how it could happen."

Douglas nodded gloomily. "Picture, if you will, that fatal summer back in the fourteenth century. The peasants are tilling the fields. The good citizens of Sudberry are going about their business. They had a soggy summer with abnormal amounts of rain, yet everybody's totally unaware that a witch's brew is beginning to develop in the atmosphere.

"One afternoon, a weak flow of moist air begins to develop on the east side of the canyon northeast of here. The moist air rises up the mountain slopes and combines with daytime heat to form a thunderstorm. The thunderstorm lifts over the walls of the canyon and begins to dump heavy rain at about, say, five or six in the evening. Strong winds blow at higher levels, ordinarily strong enough to push a thunderstorm to the east and out of the area. But on this day, the upper winds are extremely weak, not strong enough to push the storm away. Instead, the storm remains virtually stationary for hours. It dumps a foot of rain into the canyon, onto the already water-soaked ground. I'm only guessing here, but I would think at least eight inches of rain fell in a one-hour-long stretch. It's enough to turn the normally placid River Hulm into a raging torrent of water, twenty feet high. So, all of a sudden it breaks loose and heads down the canyon and beyond, sweeping ten-foot boulders in front of it, along with everything else in its path. The wall of water moves so quickly there's no chance for an orderly evacuation. The only avenue of escape is to run like hell for higher ground. Those who are caught have no chance of survival."

A low, amazed whistle escaped Rennie's lips. "So you think it might actually happen again?"

"There's a good chance it might."

"'Pon my word!" Rennie's sense of humor returned. "Well, you needn't worry. With any luck, you will have left for America before that wall of water hits."

Douglas' lips twisted in a cynical smile. "You won't get rid of me so easily. If we're going to be hit by that wall of water, it's going to be soon, very soon. Besides, do you think I would leave now?"

"When the woman you love is in danger?" Rennie asked.

"Of course you wouldn't. What was I thinking? I can only hope you're dead wrong."

Douglas cast a wary gaze out the window toward the leaden sky. "So do I, but this time I have a feeling I'm dead right."

❧❧❧❧

The next morning, in an effort to avoid the Eltons, Jane and her family went down to breakfast early. "We don't have to be 'nice' to them anymore," Jane commented. "We shall continue to avoid them until we leave."

Millicent nodded her head decisively. "That's fine with me. I cannot abide the way Beatrice keeps accusing you of taking the jewels."

Jane answered with a noncommittal "Hmm." Other than Granny, she had not yet told anyone about finding the Lansdown jewels. She knew she must soon turn them over to her sister-in-law, but the moment would be excruciating—one to be put off as long as possible. She glanced out the window at the pouring rain. "I had hoped we could go to the dower house today and start clearing it out. The sooner we move the better."

A series of sighs greeted her in return. Her mother's were the deepest. Amelia Hart had been wrapped in gloom ever since learning the time had come to move.

At least Millicent was trying to make the best of it. "What shall we do with the old countess' stuffed birds?" she asked lightly. "Do you suppose we could sell them?"

"Maybe we could," Jane jokingly replied. "Perhaps there's a huge, untapped market for glass-domed dead birds."

Everyone laughed except Mama, who sat dourly sipping her tea, barely touching her food. Jane was searching for something else cheerful to say when Mrs. Stanhope entered the dining room and approached her.

"May I have a word with you, m'lady?"

"Of course, Mrs. Stanhope."

"It's about Meg Twimby." The housekeeper's brows were

drawn together in a worried frown. "The girl did not come to work this morning, and you know how dependable she is. I suspect it's the river. Last I looked, it was about to break over its banks. When and if it does, the Twimby farm will be right in its path. I was wondering—"

"I shall go at once." Jane quickly arose from her chair.

"Don't you dare," said Mama, suddenly alert. She addressed Mrs. Stanhope. "My daughter is no longer in charge here. From now on, you must take your problems to the new Countess of Lansdown." She regarded Jane with accusing eyes. "Sit down and finish your breakfast. What happens with the servants is no longer any concern of ours."

"Meg Twimby *is* my concern," Jane sharply replied. "We'll discuss this later." She hurried from the room, regretting she'd been abrupt with her mother but knowing she could not have done otherwise. Starting up the stairs, she heard Millicent's voice behind her.

"What are you going to do, Jane? You can't go out in weather like this."

"Indeed I can," Jane called over her shoulder.

"You will get soaking wet. What will you wear?"

"Something that I'm tired of." She raced down the hallway. "My blue riding habit, I guess." It would probably get ruined, but it reminded her of Douglas, so what did she care?

Bruta was nowhere in sight when she reached her bedchamber. In fact, Jane hadn't seen her surly lady's maid all morning. No matter. By now Bruta had probably gone back to Beatrice. No great loss. Beatrice could have her. "Can you get out the blue riding habit for me, Millicent?"

She quickly shed her muslin morning gown and slipped into the riding habit, assisted by her sister. "You will need a warm wrap," Millicent said. She went to the wardrobe and returned with Jane's brown wool redingote, an elaborate affair adorned with multiple, black-banded caplets.

Had Jane not been so worried, she might have laughed.

"That's much too fancy for where I'm going. I would ruin it for sure. Can you get me my plain wool shawl?"

Millicent returned with the shawl, which Jane wrapped around her shoulders and over her head. It made her look like a peasant, but fashion was not her concern right now.

"What *are* you planning?" Millicent asked.

"I'm going to fetch Beauty and ride her over to the Twimby farm. I want to make sure Meg and her family are all right, but I suspect they are not. The very fact that Meg didn't come to work today tells me there's something wrong."

Millicent frowned with concern. "You should not be out on a day like this."

"Who else can help them? I can't ask the servants, and do you think our esteemed new earl would care? Ha! I think not."

"I suppose you're right. The day is young, but I would wager James is foxed already."

"So would I, and I doubt in his condition he could even find the river, let alone cross it." Jane pulled the shawl tight around her and headed for the door. "Meg is my friend. It's up to me to make sure she and her family are all right."

"But what about Douglas Cartland?" Millicent called after her. "Can't he help? Didn't you tell me he's a friend of the Twimbys?"

"Forget him." Jane felt a stab at her heart at the very mention of his name.

The hard rain had let up for the moment. Only a light drizzle was falling when Jane hurried outside and down the path to the river. At the spot where the path curved toward the stables, she got her first close look at the River Hulm. It was over its banks! Not on her side but on the other side. The water was slowly spreading over the fields of the Twimby farm. No question, the Twimbys must leave, if they hadn't already. And how could Meg manage with one little girl and two young boys, one of whom was sick?

She had almost reached the burnt-out stables when she

encountered Timothy and young Hugh. They were leading a string of horses, including Beauty, up the path. "The river's started to overflow," Timothy called in agitation. "I'm taking the horses back up to Lord Rennie's."

"That's a good idea," she called back. "I'll take Beauty." She untied her horse from the line and turned her in the other direction.

"Where are you going, m'lady?" Timothy asked in alarm.

"To the Twimby farm to see how they're doing." She would have to ride bareback. Grasping Beauty's harness, she stuck out her foot. "Can you give me a boost?"

Shaking his head with disapproval, Timothy went to her side. "You can't, m'lady, the river's dangerous and it's going to get worse. You should not—"

"I know I should not, but I'm going to. Please hand me up."

"If you're sure?"

"Positive."

"All right then, but I still don't think ..." Timothy bent forward. She placed a booted foot in his cradled hands. He lifted her to Beauty's back, where she proceeded to sling a leg to the other side. She had never ridden astride before, no saddle or reins either, but she could do it because she had to.

The stableman gazed up at her. "Are you sure you can manage?"

"Positive. Thank you, Timothy. I shall return shortly." She dug her heels into Beauty's flank and off they went along the path, heading toward the wooden bridge upstream. Along the way she noticed another break in the far river bank, worse than the first. With both, the water wasn't gushing through; instead, the flood most closely resembled a silent invasion into the countryside, the water spreading slowly over the fields. When she reached the bridge, she saw firsthand what Timothy meant by "dangerous." The swift flowing current cleared the bottom of the structure by mere inches. Caught in the flow, logs, branches and other debris either raced by or piled against the structure's upper side. As she watched, a large-sized log slammed against the bridge with a noise so shattering Beauty shied away, neighing her fright. When Jane got the jittery animal under control again, she patted her withers and called, "Settle down, girl, let us across." Beauty would not budge. *Damnation!* She would never get to the Twimbys unless she dismounted and walked her frightened horse over the bridge.

She slid from Beauty's back. Holding the lead, she led the animal to the edge of the bridge and examined the wooden planks on which they would cross. Although wet, they seemed sturdy enough, despite the rising water. Surely it couldn't get much higher. She stepped onto the planks and tugged on Beauty's lead. "Come on, it's only a short way across. You've got to make it."

After a couple of false starts, Beauty obliged, although Jane could tell from her widened eyes she was close to panic. Reaching the other side, Jane saw the Twimby cottage in the distance. The sight of it urged her on. The flood had spread a relentless course toward the Twimbys' front door. It was shallow and not yet flowing hard, but a frightening sight, nonetheless. If she hurried, she could skirt around it, get to the Twimbys and offer what assistance she could.

She continued on, leading a reluctant Beauty across a muddy field. Thank heaven, the rain still held off except for a slight drizzle, but the chill in the air made her wish she had chosen the redingote Millicent offered instead of the light wool shawl.

Jane and the creeping water reached the Twimby cottage at about the same time. She entered the muddy yard, now filling with water. Poor Jupiter stood in the lean-to at the side of the house, head down, looking miserable. She pounded on the front door. "Meg, Meg! Are you there? Let me in."

Meg swung open the door. "Countess!" Relief swept over her haggard face. She clutched Jane's arm. "Please come in; I need your help."

Jane stepped inside to the sound of little Molly's frightened wailing. Jonathan, the twelve year old, was stacking the family's meager belongings upon the table. In a corner of the room, Matthew, the seven-year-old, lay upon a straw mattress—listless, pale and drawn.

Meg knelt beside him and tenderly rested a hand on his forehead. "He cannot be moved," she said, desperation in her voice. "He's still too sick and weak from the flu."

Jonathan called, "The water's in the yard. It's almost to the door."

Jane took one look and knew what they must do. "We cannot stay here. We have got to get across the river."

"How can we?" Meg asked. "Matthew is too weak to walk."

Jane thought fast. "Jupiter is outside, isn't he?" Meg nodded. "Then we shall put Matthew on Jupiter. He's strong enough to hang on, isn't he?" Meg nodded again. "Well, then, we won't have a problem at all." Jane went on in her most reassuring tone. "Jonathan can walk. You and Molly shall ride Beauty, and I shall walk beside you and guide the horses. When we get across the river, we shall all go to Chatfield Court to wait for the flood to subside."

I don't think Mrs. Elton will let us in." Meg's voice sounded doubtful.

"You let me worry about that." Jane spoke more confidently than she felt. Who knew what that mean-spirited woman might do?

A trickle of water seeped under the door. Jane scooped Molly into her arms and handed her to Meg. "You take Molly. I'll get Matthew. Hurry, there's no time to lose."

Jane hurried to Matthew's bed, where he lay lethargic on the mattress, covered by one thin blanket. She knelt beside him. "We must leave," she said gently. "If we put you on Jupiter, do you think you can hold on?"

The boy managed a wan smile. "Yes, ma'am, I'll try."

Jane wrapped the blanket around him. He was not much of a burden as she lifted him in her arms. How light he was, not much more than skin and bones. She carried him outside, where she discovered Jonathan had saddled Jupiter and brought the animal around. Between the two of them, they lifted Matthew into the saddle. The pale-faced boy swayed but managed to hang on. "We must hurry," Jane exclaimed, glancing at the several inches of water that now covered the ground.

Meg appeared, Molly in her arms. "I'll walk, m'lady. You ride Beauty."

This was no time for politeness. "Nonsense, Meg. Don't argue. Just get on the horse and I will hand Molly up to you."

Meg did as she was told. The bedraggled procession that left the farmyard formed a dismaying picture, to say the least—a small, sick boy clinging to the back of a swayback horse, Meg atop Beauty, holding tight to her little sister for dear life, Jane and Jonathan walking alongside the horses, slogging through the slowly rising water.

Jane anticipated the bridge with trepidation, recalling the swift current and the debris piled against the upstream side. Was it still safe? How much time did they have before the rising water completely cut them off? "We shall head straight across the fields to the bridge. We must hurry. The sooner we get across, the better."

Halfway there, they were slogging through the flood water when a light rain began to fall. "Do you think we'll make it?" Meg called in a worried voice from atop Beauty. She had brought along a blanket for Molly and wrapped it more tightly around the child.

"Of course we will," Jane replied, but she wasn't so sure. She shivered, getting wetter by the minute, longing for the warmth and comfort of her bedchamber at Chatfield Court.

They reached the bridge. It was still standing, although even more debris had piled against it and the current had risen even higher. Now a thin layer of water flowed over the wooden planks. The bridge shuddered as a large log smashed against it. "We must hurry," she called. "Beauty, don't you dare stop," she whispered to her horse. "You, too, Jupiter." Her heart went out to Matthew, who sat shivering, utterly miserable, atop the old horse. "Hang on, Matthew. It isn't much farther. We'll get there soon." Walking between the two horses, she grasped both leads. Would the horses come willingly? Perhaps being together made a difference because, without a whinny of protest, they moved forward and started across.

When the little procession, all of them wet and bedraggled, reached the middle of the bridge, Jane saw two figures in the distance on the other side. Soon she made out two men on horseback riding at a fast clip toward the bridge ... could they be Douglas and Lord Rennie? Yes! It had to be them. Thank goodness. She needed all the help she could get right now.

The bridge shook again. Beauty shied slightly but remained fairly calm. Even so, Jane sent up a prayer: *Please don't let anything else hit the bridge.* Her prayer was not answered. Something smashed against the bridge, an object so big and hard the overhead beams shuddered, and the wooden planks beneath moved as if they were coming apart.

To Jane's left, on the downstream side, Beauty let out a frightened neigh and reared back, her front legs thrashing the air. "Hold on, Meg!" Jane frantically grasped the lead to try to steady her wild-eyed horse.

"Molly, Molly!" Meg screamed.

Jane watched in horror. The little girl was slipping from her older sister's grasp. "Oh, no, grab her!" Too late. Before Meg could react, the child flew over the railing, into the deadly swift current of the River Hulm.

Chapter 18

Douglas spied Jane and the Twimby family on the bridge. He and Rennie quickened their horses' pace. "What was that?"

"Dear God! The little girl ... she just went off the bridge," Rennie shouted. "There she is." Rennie pointed to a little blonde head bobbing in the water. "See there? She's coming toward us. She ... Douglas, what are you doing?"

In a twinkling, Douglas slid off his horse and ran toward the raging current, shucking his jacket as he went.

"Douglas, for God's sake you cannot," Rennie shouted. "Come back, you fool, you can't survive in that."

Douglas heard Rennie's frantic plea but did not reply. No time. If he could not catch the girl in the next few seconds, it would be too late. He stopped to yank his boots off, then plunged into the icy coldness of the river. Where was she? Ah yes, the little blonde head was coming toward him, sailing along amidst an assortment of debris. *Grab her fast. Do not miss her.* He started to swim. Fast strokes, faster than he had ever swum before. Barely in time, he reached her, grabbing her arm as the current carried her by. By the time he got a firm grip, they were both carried downstream. He tried to swim back to shore, but the strong current held him in its grip and he could not break away. He would be forced to float along ... find a spot where he could reach land. The point! That place where the land jutted out and the river curved around it. Yes, he could make it. He must make it. They wouldn't last long in this icy water. The point was his only chance.

For seconds more, he bobbed along in the debris-clogged river, holding the child tight, making sure her head stayed above the surface. He must get ashore. Quickly. At any moment, they could be struck by a log or other refuse, and that would be the end of them both. Ahead he saw the point. Now! With a powerful thrust, he pushed for the shore, performing a one-armed swim stroke with all his might.

He reached land. Stumbling, fighting for breath, he carried the little girl away from the water and laid her on the ground where she lay limp, her eyes closed. Was she breathing? He pressed his ear to her chest. Yes! She opened her eyes and ... started to cry. "Thank God!" He heard the sound of horses. Rennie arrived, pulling Major up sharply. Thunder followed close behind.

Rennie fairly jumped from his horse. "My word, Douglas, are you all right?"

"We're fine." Douglas picked up Molly and stood. "Give me your coat. She's shivering from the cold."

"You crazy fool." Rennie quickly removed his coat and handed it to Douglas.

"She would have drowned. What else would you have had me do?" Douglas wrapped the coat tightly around the shivering child. "Let's go. I suspect her family is anxious to know if she's still alive."

❧❧❧❧

Jane would never forget those agonizing moments after Molly was flung from the bridge. She had watched, frozen in horror, as the little blonde head was swept down the river.

From a distance, she saw Douglas dive in after her. Then both disappeared. *They must have drowned,* Jane thought with increasing despair. No one could survive long in that deadly current.

In an anguished frenzy, they raced as quickly as they could across the rest of the bridge and down the river path.

"It's my fault," Meg cried in a broken voice. "I should have held her tighter."

"It's not your fault. It just happened." Icy fear twisted around Jane's heart. Molly was gone forever. No way in the world could she be saved.

Then ...

In the distance, they saw Lord Rennie on his horse coming toward them. Douglas rode behind him, and sitting in front of him in the saddle ..."Molly!" Jane cried. "Look, Meg, it's Molly and she's safe."

With a cry of gladness, Meg slid from Beauty's back and ran to Douglas, Jane close behind. She grabbed her little sister from the saddle and cradled the child in her arms. "How can I ever thank you, sir?"

"No need to thank me." Douglas frowned with concern. "We need to get her warm."

"We shall take her to Chatfield Court," Jane said. Words of gratitude rushed to her lips. "Douglas, I—"

"I said, no need to thank me." Hastily Douglas asked Rennie, "Can we take them to Lancaster Hall?"

"Of course."

Douglas turned to Jane. As he began to speak, the rain fell harder from the leaden sky. "A flood is coming. Chatfield Court isn't safe."

Jane shook her head in disbelief. "Whatever do you mean? My home is like a fortress. I can't believe it's not safe."

Douglas swung from his horse and gripped her shoulders. "Listen to me. There's a good chance Chatfield Court is about to be hit by a wall of water such as we haven't seen since the fourteenth century. I hope I'm wrong, but a feeling in my gut says I'm not. Go home. Tell your family, the servants, everyone to get out now. Don't wait."

Rennie spoke up. "I say, old man, are you sure? The countess could be right, you know. Everyone is welcome to come to Lancaster Hall, of course, but is it really necessary?"

"It's necessary." Douglas had not removed his gaze from Jane's face. He spoke again, his voice softened. "Would I lie to you?"

So much had happened. How could she grasp it all? She needed time to catch her breath, think things through. She must gather her wits and do what was right. "Chatfield Court has never been touched by a flood. I cannot imagine that happening when it has managed to survive for centuries. I shall have to think about it, Mister Cartland."

"Think about it?" he repeated, anger in his voice. "Well, you just do that, Countess, but you'd better come to the right decision, and soon."

Amelia Hart gazed at her daughter with incredulous eyes. "I cannot believe you would risk your life for a servant."

Jane had arrived home drenched and shivering from cold. Now, warm and dry, she faced her family in the drawing room. She had related in detail Douglas Cartland's courageous rescue of the little Twimby girl and relayed his forecast concerning the coming wall of water. Although Granny and Millicent had applauded her efforts to save the Twimbys, as expected, her mother was horrified. "Meg needed my help, Mama. My actions had nothing to do with her station in life."

"That was so very brave of you," said Millicent.

"Not really," Jane answered. "Douglas Cartland was the brave one. If he hadn't plunged into the river and rescued little Molly—"

"How magnificent he is!" Millicent gushed. "How brave!

Such a hero! You should marry the man."

In all the excitement of the day, Jane had momentarily forgotten her last quarrel with Douglas and the angry way they had parted. Now that she remembered, her spirits plunged. Millicent was absolutely right. Douglas was all she said he was: magnificent, brave, a hero. Even more, not the kind of conceited London fop Jane detested but a man full of compassion who cared more for others than himself. "I won't be marrying Douglas Cartland, Millicent. There's nothing between us, nor will there ever be." Her heart ached, just hearing her own words.

Granny lifted an eyebrow. "You should never say never, missy."

"It's over, Granny."

"What is this business about some wall of water descending upon us?"

Jane elaborated on Douglas' prediction concerning the impending flood. Before she finished, Mama started shaking her head. "What nonsense! And where, pray, are we supposed to go?"

"To Lancaster Hall. Lord Rennie will take us in."

"There could be no place on earth safer than Chatfield Court," Mama responded. "A wall of water? The whole idea is absolutely ludicrous."

Jane kept her mouth shut. She knew there was no use arguing when Mama crossed her arms and clenched her jaw in defiance.

❧❧❧❧

In Rennie's library, Douglas sat relaxed with his boots stretched out toward the inviting fire in the fireplace.

"Feel better?" Rennie asked.

"Quite." Coming out of that river, he had never been so cold in his life, but with dry clothes and a cup of Mrs. Groton's hot mulled wine at hand, he knew he would survive. "All I have to worry about now is a disastrous flood that will effectively wipe out this valley."

"It won't reach this high up?"

"Lancaster Hall is safe."

"Are you sure, Douglas?" Rennie spoke in a thoughtful tone. "About this disastrous flood, I mean. Not to sound skeptical, but you do sound like the voice of impending doom."

A flash of lightning lit the room, closely followed by a large clap of thunder and the sound of pelting rain. Douglas glanced toward the window. "Do you hear that?"

"It appears a thunderstorm has arrived." Rennie took an uneasy sip of his mulled wine. "So you're saying if it keeps up—?"

"If the downpour continues, we're in trouble. I couldn't be more serious."

"Hmm, then we will have to wait and see, won't we?" Rennie remained silent a moment. "I wonder if you have considered the momentous change in your life that occurred today."

"Change in my life? Other than my saving little Molly—of which I'm proud and grateful, of course—I don't know what you mean."

"Then I shall explain it." Rennie set down his cup and regarded Douglas with thoughtful eyes. "For years you've been a tortured soul, ever since you ran over that little girl."

A half smile crossed Douglas' face. "I never considered myself a tortured soul, but perhaps you're right."

"Of course I'm right. Ever since then, you have not allowed yourself to be happy because of the terrible thing you did."

"That, too."

"Well then, can't you see how what happened today has changed all that?" At Douglas' puzzled frown, Rennie continued, "Today you saved a little girl's life. Does that not make up for the other little girl whose life you took? Tit for tat, to put it lightly. In other words, God gave you a chance to redeem yourself. You took up his challenge—quite heroically, I might add—so as far as I can see, you're even."

A long silence followed, during which Douglas let his friend's words sink in. Could he be right? It had not occurred to him, but yes, he had saved Molly's life at the risk of his own. Yes, the child would surely have drowned if he, Douglas Cartland, former rake and ne'er-do-well, had not dived into the river to save her. Slowly, a joyful realization washed over him. "Rennie, I never thought of that, but I believe you're right. In a way, my saving Molly does make up for the other."

"Of course, it does." Rennie appeared delighted that his friend agreed. "So tell me, what is in the way of your marrying the countess now?"

Another long silence. Douglas was deep in thought. "I agree I have redeemed myself, but it still wouldn't work."

"Why ever not?"

"She's a countess, for God's sake, whereas I am only a lowly fifth son."

"Surely not penniless."

"Not quite penniless, but close. Think about it, Rennie. Jane has lived in luxury for most of her life. The money, the title ... How could I begin to compete?"

"She loves you, Douglas, I know she does."

"It wouldn't work. I'm looking beyond that first bloom of love when she gradually realizes nobody's bowing and scraping to her anymore, waiting on her hand and foot."

"Really?" I don't think she's that kind of woman. She doesn't appear to be shallow and vain at all."

Douglas shut his eyes. "I agree, she's not shallow and vain, it just ... I could never come up to her standards. Now can we change the subject?"

"Of course. We can always talk about the weather."

Douglas' expression remained solemn. "If this rain doesn't let up, that's all we'll be talking about. I'm worried, Rennie."

"I know, but let's not be too hasty."

The deluge continued, accompanied by more thunder and

lightning. Douglas sat listening, his concern growing by the minute.

"One more hour," he told Rennie. "If the storm doesn't let up, it will be time to send out the alarm."

Another hour passed, during which giant streaks of lightning lit the sky and deafening peals of thunder shook the ground. The rain never ceased. Finally, a particularly heavy deluge struck, sounding like rocks hurled against the windows. Douglas sprang from his chair. "That's it. We have waited long enough. It's time to go."

Douglas started for the door, but Rennie cried, "Wait!" and grabbed his arm. "Think what you're doing before you go off half-cocked like this. You could be wrong."

"I'm not wrong."

"How do you know for sure? Telling people to run for their lives? Leave their homes and possessions behind? You are about to cause total panic up and down this valley and you had better think twice. What if you're wrong and there is no flood? There goes your reputation. If you aren't judged insane, at the very least you will be declared a laughingstock."

Douglas gazed at his friend with the utmost calm. "I shall take that risk. Don't you understand? Chatfield Court, the whole valley, are about to be wiped out. I must warn them. I could not live with myself if I didn't."

Hearing the urgency in his friend's voice, Rennie visibly paled. "I'm beginning to believe you, and if what you say is true, then Millicent is in danger."

"Millicent and many other poor souls. Come on, Rennie. Tons of water are about to burst from the canyon. There's no time to lose."

Rennie nodded decisively, as if Douglas' stark words had finally sunk in. "Tell me what to do."

"Grab your coat. You're going to get very wet and very cold."

"I'll order the horses saddled and brought around."

"We don't have time for that. Let's go."

They rushed to the stables, where they found both Thunder and Major in their stalls. "Just slip on a harness," Douglas said. "There's no time for saddles."

"You mean ride bareback?" Rennie asked. "I haven't done that since I was a boy."

Douglas slipped a harness over Thunder's head and thrust a bit in his mouth. "You want to save Millicent, don't you?"

"Confound it! Of course I do."

"Then forget the saddle."

Douglas led his horse outside. With an effortless leap, he mounted Thunder, took up the reins, and peered around. "Well, are you coming?"

Rennie immediately appeared, leading his horse, sans saddle. With a run and leap not nearly as graceful as his friend's, he seated himself on Major's back. "Let's go. I must save Millicent."

And Jane. Douglas touched his heels to Thunder's flank. The horse leaped forward, followed by Rennie on Major. Through the pouring rain they raced down the hill to Chatfield Court. *Thank God, it is still daylight.* Douglas urged Thunder into his fastest gallop. He would hate to think of the chaos if people had to escape in total darkness.

They galloped the whole way down the hill, coming to an abrupt halt only when they reached the front portico at Chatfield Court. Both fairly leapt from their mounts, not bothering to tether them. Both horses were well trained. They would not wander far.

Griggs met them at the front entrance. "Is there something wrong, sir?"

"Order the coach brought around immediately," Douglas replied without preamble. "It's urgent. Then join us inside." He hurried into the entry hall. Over his shoulder he called to Rennie, "All we have to do now is convince everyone to leave."

❧❧❧❧

In the dim light of a rainy late afternoon, Jane, Granny, and

Millicent had gathered in Jane's bedchamber, playing a three-handed game of loo. After the day's ordeal, Jane could almost enjoy the sound of the fierce storm outside, knowing she was safe with her family, warmed by the cozy fire in the fireplace. Douglas' warning hung over her, but each time she thought of it, she convinced herself he must be wrong. She could not imagine a huge wall of water hurtling down the valley, high enough to drown them all.

Griggs interrupted their game. "You have visitors, m'lady. Mister Cartland and Lord Rennie request everyone's presence in the drawing room immediately."

Jane asked, "Do you know what he wants?"

"He did not say, madam. He has ordered the coach brought around, but I do not know why. I must say, whatever the reason, it appears most urgent."

Jane threw down her cards. "We shall be down at once, Griggs. Granny, Millicent, come on. I'll get Mama."

When they reached the drawing room, they discovered Douglas and Rennie soaking wet, warming themselves in front of the cavernous fireplace, water dripping from their clothing onto the hearth. After greeting them, Jane asked Douglas, "Are you here for the reason I think, Mister Cartland?"

"I am. There is not a minute to lose."

The Eltons arrived, James and Percy wearing looks of puzzlement. Beatrice maintained her saintly smile but with an eyebrow raised in amused contempt. Clearly whatever her visitors had to say, she would not take seriously. "Good evening, Lord Rennie, Mister Cartland. To what do we owe the pleasure of this visit?" She exchanged an amused glance with her son. "It must be vastly important to bring you out on a day like this."

"Do you suppose the world is coming to an end?" quipped Percy.

Rennie said, "It's a rather important matter, Mrs. Elton. We—"

"It's *your ladyship*, if you please," Beatrice snapped. "I am the new countess now and I expect to be addressed as such."

"Uh, well, of course, your ladyship, I apologize. I—"

"Don't waste your breath, Rennie." Douglas stood tall and calm, a purposeful ring to his voice. "Listen everyone, and listen carefully." He nodded to the butler who stood by the door. "You, too, Griggs. You must notify the servants at once." Douglas scanned the room, locking eyes with each person in turn. "We have come to warn you that every sign indicates Chatfield Court is about to be hit by a tremendous flood. You must head for higher ground immediately."

A collective sound of gasps filled the room. "Just what do you mean?" asked Beatrice.

"Exactly what I said, madam." Douglas gave a quick explanation of how the thunderstorm over the canyon had stagnated for hours and not blown away. The waters were undoubtedly building in the narrow canyon, ready to break loose at any moment. "The rain has not let up for hours. If my instinct serves, and I know it does, tons of water are collecting above us. At any moment they could crash down upon Chatfield Court, the village of Sudberry, the entire valley."

Beatrice laughed with contempt. "Are we not being a bit overdramatic? Good gracious, even if the water got to our door, these walls are made of stone. I cannot imagine Chatfield Court would ever be in any real danger."

James chimed in. "Quite right, my dear." In his usual glassy-eyed daze, he had listened quietly. Now he addressed Douglas with a petulant edge to his voice. "Not only is her ladyship correct, but I find it quite disagreeable of you to frighten the ladies this way. After all, we have had floods before. I cannot remember the number of times the River Hulm has overflowed its banks. Once, as I recall, it came halfway up the lawn. Do you remember that, my dear?" He glanced at his wife. "Back in eighteen thirteen or so, but we never thought to go running up the hill, as you suggest, Mister Cartland."

Rennie frowned. "Lord Lansdown, let me assure you that my good friend here is an expert on the subject and knows whereof he speaks. You would be wise to listen."

"Just what would you have us do?" Percy's lips twisted into a cynical smile. "Go racing up the hill in our good clothes in this downpour? Good grief, old fellow, come to your senses." He and James shared a laugh.

Ignoring Percy, Douglas addressed James. "Must I go through this again? What we have today is more than 'just another flood.' Can't you understand that at any moment a giant wall of water might come crashing down upon us? If you have half a brain in your head, you will get out now, this instant."

"How dare you," Beatrice exclaimed. "You have insulted his lordship. I demand you leave at once."

Douglas didn't waste a glance at her. "Who's going and who's staying?" He looked toward where the butler had been standing by the door, but he was gone. "I trust Griggs has gone to warn the servants. As for the rest of you ..." He looked Beatrice in the eye. "Are you coming?"

"Certainly not." Beatrice marched to a sofa, sat herself down, and glared defiantly at her unwelcome guest. "If the rest of you want to go scurrying up the hill like frightened rabbits, go ahead, but I shall not be a party to such foolishness."

"I have ordered the coach brought around for the ladies." Douglas directed his gaze at James. "You, sir?"

"I agree with my wife." James sat on the sofa next to Beatrice. "I cannot abide this nonsense. The sooner you leave, the better."

Percy peered haughtily down his nose at Douglas. "I concur with my parents. May I say, I have never seen such outrageous behavior as you have displayed today, Mister Cartland. I personally believe you belong in Bedlam."

Douglas turned to Jane's mother. "I trust you will be coming with us, ma'am."

Amelia Hart sank into a chair and bowed her head as if in

deep thought. A long moment passed. "No, I am staying right here."

Jane took a deep, sharp breath. "Mama, what are you thinking? Of course you're coming. You know we can stay with Lord Rennie. He—"

"I am not coming."

"Why?" Jane fought to keep the panic from her voice.

"Because I'm too old to run. Besides, I, too, think it's the height of foolishness to go running up the hill in all this rain. Leave if you wish, but as for me, I shall go to my room where I shall wait out the storm in comfort, thank you."

"No, you must come!" Jane knelt before her mother and gripped her hands. "Please, I'm begging you. You could die if you stay."

Mama clenched her jaw. "I am not going to budge, so don't waste your breath. Go without me. I insist."

Jane knew her mother well enough to know she would never change her mind. She got off her knees and backed away, not sure what to do.

Millicent's eyes filled with tears. "Mama, are you sure?"

"Positive."

"Then I'm staying, too." Millicent went to stand beside her mother.

"No, Miss Hart," Rennie cried. "There's a flood coming. You are risking your life if you remain here."

She tossed her head. "It's my choice. I appreciate your concern, but if my mother is staying, then so am I."

Jane listened with growing alarm. "Millicent, you know the danger."

In an anguished voice, Rennie pleaded, "Listen to your sister. You cannot stay here. I will not hear of it!"

"Why, Lord Rennie!" Millicent batted her eyelashes. "I am deeply flattered by your concern. However, it isn't only that I don't want to leave my mother. I, too, do not believe any kind of flood could possibly destroy Chatfield Court. Jane, you go ahead. Don't worry. I shall stay right here with Mama and we shall be fine."

Leave both her sister and mother behind? The thought tore at Jane's insides. She opened her mouth to speak, but before she could utter a word, she heard frantic shouts from outside. The door burst open. Griggs rushed in. "The water has broken through on this side of the river! It's coming up faster than I have ever seen"

Meg stepped in and went to Jane. "Griggs is right, m'lady. The water is almost to the door. We should leave at once."

"This is your last chance, everyone," Douglas said.

Beatrice spoke again. "What nonsense. We have had floods like this before and nothing came of it except that the gardeners had a lot of cleaning up to do." From her place on the sofa, Beatrice folded her arms. With a curt nod of her head, she continued, "These stone walls will protect us. I am not going anywhere and that is that."

"Then I shall waste no more time trying to persuade you." Douglas' gaze swept the room. "Whoever is coming, we must leave at once."

Granny had sat quietly, intently listening to every word. "Well, I am not going to sit here and drown. I'm coming with you." Gripping her cane, she struggled to her feet and looked to where James and Beatrice sat on the sofa and Percy stood behind. "If you nincompoops want to stay here and drown, then go ahead." Her sharp eyes skewered her daughter. "Don't be a dunce, Amelia. Come along."

Amelia Hart lifted her chin in defiance. "Go ahead if you like. I shall remain where I am."

"We must get out of here." Douglas headed for the door, followed by Granny hobbling on her cane.

Rennie, frowning with distress, again spoke to Millicent. "Please come with us. I cannot bear the thought of leaving you behind."

"You must, Lord Rennie." Millicent circled her arm around

her mother's shoulders. "We shall be perfectly fine, I assure you."

From a distance came a sharp, ominous crack accompanied by a long, muffled sound of thunder. A hard knot formed in Jane's stomach. It was a strange, ominous sound that seemed to go on and on, as if the gods of the canyon were issuing their final warning.

"Did you hear that, Miss Hart?" Rennie asked.

Millicent shrugged indifferently. "It's only thunder."

"That does it, I've heard enough." Rennie strode to where she was standing. With one fell swoop, he picked her up and slung her over his shoulder.

"Lord Rennie, what are you doing?" Eyes wide with surprise, Millicent kicked her heels and pounded her fists on Rennie's back. "I am not a sack of potatoes, sir. Put me down."

"No, I shall not. If you don't have sense enough to save your own life, then I shall do it for you." He started for the door, carrying his flailing burden as if it were a squirming lapdog. "You, too, Countess. We must leave."

Jane hesitated. How could she leave her mother behind? "Mama, please ..."

Amelia returned a reassuring smile. "Just go, dear. When this storm passes, you'll come back and we'll all have a big laugh together."

No sense arguing. Mama had made up her mind and Jane knew nothing would change it. *I am stubborn, too, and I'm not going to stay here and drown.* "Then I shall see you shortly, Mama. Everything's bound to be all right." With a heavy heart, she turned on her heel and followed the others out the door and into the entry hall where they found the front door open wide to the dimness of the late afternoon light. Servants, some carrying what appeared to be their worldly possessions, were fleeing into the driving rain.

"At least Griggs did his duty," Douglas said to Rennie. "Let's hope the coach is waiting. We need to get these ladies up the hill."

They crowded onto the portico. Jane took a quick look around. "I don't see the coach."

One of the stable boys came jogging by. "There won't be a coach," he called. "Timothy sent all the horses up the hill."

With an oath, Douglas peered into the rain. "Including our horses, Rennie. They must have followed the others."

Rennie, still holding tight to Millicent, replied, "My apologies, Miss Hart, but it appears we're going to have to run for it."

Douglas called, "Quick everyone, let's get up the hill!"

Jane took her grandmother's elbow. The two of them stepped into the driving rain. Never had she seen it come down so hard. It was cold, besides. "We shall need our wraps."

She turned to go back inside, but Granny gripped her arm. "You will do no such thing, missy. We had bloody hell better get up the hill right now." She took a shaky step into the downpour, leaning heavily on her cane.

By the time she took another step, Douglas appeared by her side. "You would never make it, Granny." He scooped her up in his arms, cane and all.

Granny didn't resist. "Just don't drop me, young man." She still hung tightly to her cane.

They had all taken only a few steps when a deafening blast sounded from up the canyon, so loud everyone halted in their tracks to listen. Jane heard terrified cries of, "God save us!" For all she knew, she might have cried out, too. A tremendous roar followed the blast. It was definitely not thunder.

"It's coming," Douglas shouted. "Everybody run!"

Jane picked up her skirt and ran for her life up the road that led to Lancaster Hall. She pushed against the heaviest downpour she had ever experienced; the air was so laden with water she could hardly breathe. Everyone ran together, servants and nobility alike. She saw Griggs streak by, legs churning, his dignity left behind. Mrs. Stanhope passed her, too, wide skirts flapping. She heard the hysterical shrieks of a scullery maid as she raced up the hill, followed by Hugh, the young stable boy. *Where is Timothy?* Jane hoped the old stableman had somehow escaped the deluge.

Directly ahead she saw Rennie set her sister down. Now convinced of the danger, Millicent cast modesty aside as she ran hand-in-hand with Rennie, holding her narrow skirt up around her knees.

Out of the corner of her eye, Jane saw Granny, still in Douglas' arms, hanging on for dear life. Despite his burden, his strides were so swift and sure Jane could hardly keep up with him. He glanced over at her. "All right?"

"Fine," she managed to gasp. She glanced to the north and saw the most terrifying sight she had ever seen. A gigantic wall of water had burst from the canyon. At least thirty feet high, it was crashing down upon them at lightning speed, accompanied by a deafening roar, louder than a thousand cannons exploding at the same time.

They were directly in its path.

"Douglas, look, it's coming," she screamed.

Without slowing down, Douglas took a quick glance. "Keep running. It's our only chance."

She ran on, faster than she'd known possible. Her burning lungs screamed for relief, but the fear of being swept away made her keep up her pace.

The giant wave was almost upon them. Water lapped at her heels, then her knees. Sheer black fright swept through her as it swirled around her waist, dragging her back. "Hold onto me," Douglas yelled. She grabbed the back of his coat and clung tight as he fought his way forward through the swirling water. Terrified screams came from behind. She could hear them clearly above the hideous roar. Then a sudden silence, and she knew someone had just been swept away, hopelessly caught in the deadly current. She fought on, still clinging to

Douglas, with Rennie and Millicent fighting for footing ahead, everyone struggling through the water.

A powerful surge of water hit. She lost her grip. With all her strength, she tried to lunge forward but the relentless force of the water held her tight in its grasp. Once more she struggled against the current. No use. Its overwhelming power kept pulling her backward.

I am going to drown. Nothing can help me. I am done.

A pair of strong hands grabbed her, thrust her forward. Suddenly she was able to grab Douglas' coat again. Who had helped her? She looked back. Bruta!

"Keep going, madam," shouted her lady's maid.

This time she kept a tight hold on Douglas' coat, hanging on for dear life. She continued on, totally exhausted. Finally, when she was certain she could not take one more step, the water swirled away. Everyone stopped. Jane bent forward, clutching her knees, trying to catch her breath. Others did the same, or lay exhausted on the ground, ignoring the cold and wet.

Douglas set Granny down with care. "There you are, ma'am. Looks as if we will survive."

For once, Granny had no sharp answer. Instead, she tried to look back down the hill, but by now darkness had fallen. "Can't see past my nose," she complained in a troubled voice. "What's happened to Amelia?"

"We can't go back now," Douglas told her gently. "It's too dark and the water is still too deep."

"That foolish, foolish daughter of mine." Granny tried to say more but her voice cracked and she began to shiver.

"We must get her to Rennie's," Jane said, putting aside her own fear for her mother.

"Your daughter might be all right," Douglas said to Granny. "I promise we'll find out in the morning."

"At first light," Jane told him. " I hate to wait until morning. What if she's out there somewhere and needs our help?"

"We must wait. There's nothing more we can do tonight."

Douglas took her arm. "Come along to Rennie's. Right now we all need to get warm and dry."

Chapter 19

Jane spent a near-sleepless night worrying over the fate of her mother. Early the next morning, accompanied by Douglas, she started back down the road to Chatfield Court. They left Millicent asleep. Granny wanted to come, but the cold and wet had affected her rheumatism and she could hardly move from her bed.

"Granny, we'll return as soon as we can and let you know if we've found her." She kept reassuring herself that Mama would be found alive, yet dread filled her heart.

Now, making her way back down the road, the farther they walked, the more shocked she became. The morning light disclosed an unbelievable scene of devastation. The whole landscape was changed. Silt, debris, and broken branches lay in tangled heaps everywhere, making the road nearly unrecognizable. Trees were stripped bare. Rocks of all sizes lay scattered where none had been before. "Look at that." Jane pointed to a huge boulder in the middle of the road. "That is amazing. How did it get there?"

Douglas shook his head. "It only goes to show the incredible force of the water."

What about Chatfield Court? What about Mama? The unanswered questions screamed silently inside her.

When they rounded a bend in the road, Jane's heart lifted. In the distance, she saw the walls of Chatfield Court. "Thank God, they're still standing. Mama has to be all right." She quickened her step, rushing ahead, anxious to see her mother, but the closer she came, the more she realized something was wrong.

"Wait up," Douglas called when she drew closer. He came up beside her. "Don't go any farther. Take a close look."

She did not want to look closer but knew she must. When she did, her joy evaporated. The remnants of Chatfield Court stood open to the elements, the roof completely gone. Yes, the walls still stood, most of them. But one wall had completely crumbled, and the ones remaining stood like ghostly symbols surrounding the gutted remains of a great house in ruins. Jane was standing quietly, trying to comprehend the enormity of the destruction when she heard a familiar voice. "M'lady! Praise the Lord, you're still alive." Timothy hobbled up. Despite a bloody gash on his forehead, his face lit in a smile.

"Oh, Timothy, it's so good to see you." Jane gave him a hug. "You survived!"

"Just barely, mum. I spent the night in a tree, hanging on for dear life. But I'm grateful I made it through ..." He looked toward the remains of Chatfield Court and his smile faded. "Not everyone did, I fear."

"Do you know if anyone got out?" Jane asked, half in anticipation, half in dread. "Mister Elton and his wife? Percy? My mother?"

Grim-faced, the old stableman shook his head. "All I know is that water came so fast no one got out if they weren't warned ahead of time and either ran up the hill or spent the night in a tree like I did. They are saying a lot of people just got swept away, so chances are ..." he shook his head dubiously.

"There has been a heavy loss of life, m'lady. Lots of bodies found already, but many of those poor souls will never be found. Some will be buried forever under the tons of rocks and silt that got washed down."

"I see." Jane felt numb inside. Now was not the time to show her grief. With a mighty effort, she gulped and raised her chin. "Thank you, Timothy. You must go up to Lord Rennie's right away. You need food and dry clothes and someone to look after that gash in your forehead."

"Thank you, m'lady." Timothy started away but turned back. "What about Chatfield Court? Will it be rebuilt? I'm thinking about the horses, ma'am, or I wouldn't ask."

His question took her totally by surprise. She had yet to give a thought to the future of Chatfield Court or her dower house, which must be gone, too. "I don't know yet, but I shall keep you informed."

Soon after Jane bid Timothy goodbye, she heard a woman's voice exclaim, "M'lady! You didn't drown."

Jane turned her head to see her former lady's maid standing next to her. The sight of her brought on mixed feelings. On the one hand, Jane hadn't forgotten Bruta's villainous role in acquiring the oil of pennyroyal for Beatrice Elton. On the other, she would never forget last night when Bruta's strong hands helped her escape the flood.

"Well, Bruta, I am happy to see you also survived."

"Just barely. I never had to run so fast in my life."

"Will you be all right? Do you have a place to stay?"

"They took me in at Lancaster Hall, same as you, madam."

Of course, now she remembered. According to Douglas, Bruta had a dalliance going with one of the footmen. Obviously, she was welcomed and treated well.

"I will be fine, m'lady." Bruta's thick brows knitted together in a frown. "Everything is different now that Chatfield Court is gone and Mrs. Elton along with it."

The Eltons are gone.

In all her worry over her mother, she had not given much thought to Beatrice, James, and Percy. Now the realization washed over her that they were dead, no trace of them likely ever to be found. She felt no joy, though, only a sick realization of the extent of this tragedy.

"You're right, Bruta. It appears Mrs. Elton is indeed gone."

"I have something to tell you."

"You do?" Jane could not imagine what this sullen woman she had never liked wanted to tell her.

"I want to apologize," Bruta burst out in her usual abrupt manner.

"Apologize for what?"

"For the oil of pennyroyal. I knew it was wrong, but Mrs. Elton said I would be dismissed without a character if I didn't help her. She was an evil woman, madam, and I'm glad she's gone. She got what was coming to her."

Jane opened her mouth to object, then thought better of it. Why be a hypocrite? Any protest she made would be halfhearted at best. Suddenly, she was seeing her former lady's maid through new eyes. Knowing Beatrice Elton, she could well believe Bruta had been forced to do her bidding. "You're forgiven. I didn't hold you responsible in any case. Besides, any harm you might have done to me, you made up for last night. Remember how you helped me up the hill?"

"I shall never forget. I couldn't let you drown. You're the best mistress I ever had."

That is certainly news to me.

"Do you know yet what you're going to do?"

Bruta didn't hesitate. "I have saved a bit of money. Thank the Lord I put it in the bank, so it didn't get washed away in the flood. I'm going to America, m'lady, to start a new life."

"What will you do there?" Nothing would surprise Jane today.

"I suppose they have maids in America, too."

"Then I wish you the best of luck," Jane replied sincerely. *America.* Papa was there.

Douglas was a great comfort on the way back to Lancaster

Hall. He refrained from uttering false words of encouragement like, "I'm sure we'll find her" when Jane knew in her heart all hope was gone and likely her mother would never be found. Instead, he gave her an arm to lean on and quietly helped her through the muck and debris that clogged the road. Amidst her grief, she recalled how absolutely heroic he'd been. "I want to thank you for what you did yesterday," she said.

"And what was that?" He actually sounded surprised.

"If not for your warning, many more lives would have been lost. If you hadn't carried Granny up the hill, she would never have survived. As for me, if I had not hung onto your coat, I surely would have been swept away. I hate to think of it, but just like Timothy said, my body would have been buried forever under tons of rock and silt."

"I can only wish your mother had listened."

"And the others." Her anger at the Eltons melted away. Awful through they were, even they didn't deserve such a horrible fate. She did not even want to think about their last few moments on this earth.

"Oops, watch your step here." Douglas took her hand and helped her over a rough pile of rocks in the road.

"Thank you." *I love you, Douglas.* She stepped as primly as she could over the rocks, trying not to reveal that her heart had just swelled with such feeling that she wanted to shout her love to the world. What a magnificent man! So heroic, so caring. Such a skilled lover, too. Why had they quarreled? Oh, yes, he was not a marrying man, or so he said. Why not? She knew he loved her, because he'd said so. She could not let him go, at least without trying one more time.

"Douglas?"

"Yes?"

"Tell me again why it's over between us."

He stopped, faced her, and took her hands. "I once told you how I took the life of that little girl. That's when I vowed never to marry."

"Surely—?"

"Yes, I know. Surely I was being foolish to, in essence, to let that incident ruin the rest of my life. Yesterday Rennie set me straight. He pointed out that when I saved little Molly, I made up for the life I took. 'Tit for tat,' he told me in his humorous fashion."

"But it's true. Your heroism has surely made up for any wrongdoing of the past."

"You're right. I can never erase what I did, but at least now I can forgive myself. But there are other reasons why you and I can never be together."

Her heart sunk. "What reasons?"

"We live in two difference worlds. You are a countess, accustomed to wealth and fine living. I am a fifth son, practically penniless."

"I don't care about that."

"Not now, but eventually you would. It isn't just the money. All your life you have been catered to hand and foot."

She bristled. "I am not the least spoiled."

Her response prompted Douglas' hearty peal of laughter. "You are spoiled rotten, Countess, and, I might add, quite imperious. I've seen you giving orders to the servants, your nose in the air."

Only because I was expected to, Jane thought but decided not to say. She had defended herself enough.

Douglas continued, "You have been a countess and treated as such, whereas I have no title to give you and little else. It just wouldn't work, Jane. I'm sorry. More sorry than you will ever know."

She wanted to shout how wrong he was, that she didn't care if he had no money, didn't care about her title. But then, she had her pride, too, and she wasn't going to beg. "I see," she said, her voice flat. "Then there is nothing more to be said."

"Only this." Douglas stood close, gathered her hands in his, and pressed them to his heart. "In my whole life, I have truly loved only one woman and that is you. I love you for your beauty, your spirit, for the way you make me feel when we make love and I know your beautiful body is mine. I shall be leaving for America soon." Gently he touched her face, ran his fingers lovingly over her hair. "I shall carry my sweet memories of you for the rest of my life, my beautiful countess."

He dropped her hands and stepped away. "Shall we continue on? Your family is waiting for your sad news."

"Of course." She swallowed the despair in her voice. She could take no more, had suffered enough pain for one day. Douglas had said it all. There was nothing more to say.

Granny took the news of her daughter's death stoically, just as Jane knew she would. Millicent burst into tears. "Mama so wanted me to be happy," she said between sobs. "Now I am happy and she'll never know."

A while later, when Millicent was feeling better and her tears had dried, Jane asked, "What did you mean when you said you're happy now?"

Despite her grief, Millicent's lips spread into a tiny smile. "I'm in love, Jane. At long last, really, truly in love."

"With whom?" She could easily guess.

"Lord Rennie, of course." Millicent's eyes brimmed with tenderness. "I don't care if he is big and awkward. I don't care if his face is less than handsome. He is truly my knight in shining armor, so strong, so brave, so masterful. I shall never forget how he threw me over his shoulder, even though I protested, and carried me to safety. I would have drowned, just like Mama, if not for him. He's a wonderful man. I just don't know why I didn't see it before."

Jane broke into a delighted smile, her first and only on such a dark day. "That's wonderful, Millicent, especially since I do believe he reciprocates your feelings."

"I hope he does. I haven't had the opportunity to talk to him yet, but I'm going to. Soon."

❧❧❧❧

"Oh, Miss Hart, may I have a word with you?"

"Of course, Lord Rennie." Millicent had just finished her conversation with her sister and had settled in the drawing room. With a grimace she looked down at her borrowed dress. "Forgive me for looking so frumpy. I'm not exactly wearing the height of fashion."

Because the ladies had arrived with nothing but the clothes on their backs, Rennie had offered up the contents of his deceased mother's wardrobe, which he had kept untouched for years. His admiring gaze swept over her full-skirted, pink-flowered gown with the ruffled shawl. "You look lovely."

"This belonged to your mother?"

Rennie nodded. "My dear mother died in 1790. I should have gotten rid of her clothes long ago, but now I am glad I did not. I suppose her gown is rather old-fashioned, but it looks beautiful on you nonetheless."

"That is kind of you to say." Millicent stood to face him. "There is something I want to tell you."

Rennie's face began to flush. "I am all ears."

"First I want to thank you for saving my life yesterday."

His blush deepened. "'Twas nothing."

"It was more than nothing, sir. If you hadn't insisted I come with you," Millicent's voice choked with emotion, "I would surely be dead, along with Mama and the Eltons."

Wanting to comfort her, Rennie started to raise his arms. He thought better of it and lowered them again. "I ... I... was only too glad to be of assistance. You're ... uh, well worth saving, Miss Hart."

Millicent burst into laughter. "Oh, Rennie, you dear, dear man. I shall never forget your bravery."

As her words sunk in, Rennie's face lit in an awakening smile. "Does this mean you could possibly care for me?"

"Yes, it most certainly does. In fact, I would venture to say I have quite fallen in love with you."

"You don't still think of me as a friendly puppy dog?"

"Absolutely not. You are my hero and always will be."

Rennie let out a whoop, picked her up and danced around the room. "Of course, you will marry me." He caught his breath and set her down.

"Most assuredly I will!"

Rennie kissed her then, a long, drawn-out smoldering kiss, the kind he had dreamed of giving her for years.

❧❧❧❧

The next morning, Rennie's butler delivered a note to Jane. Her heart sank when she saw it was sealed with a "C." She could almost guess its contents.

My Dear Countess,

By the time you read this I shall be gone. Know that I love you and will never forget you, but as time goes on, I'm sure you will see it's best we parted.

Considering the vast Lansdown fortune, I have every faith that Chatfield Court, as well as your dower house, will soon be rebuilt, more beautiful than before. I take comfort in knowing soon you will be back in your old life, secure and content again.

—Cartland

First her mother, now Douglas. Jane felt a sense of loss beyond tears—the most terrible of her young life. Long, lonely, dreary years loomed ahead. She would grow old, fat and ugly in the dower house. Maybe she would lose her mind. Maybe she would start collecting stuffed birds in glass domes, just like the crazy old countess.

She would never be happy again.

That afternoon she received a visitor. "Meg Twimby! Do come in." She ushered Meg into Rennie's spacious drawing room, noting with dismay Meg's gaunt appearance: the dark circles under her eyes, the bedraggled clothes she wore, the same ones she wore the day she escaped the flood. "I have worried about you. Do sit down and tell me how you and the family are faring."

Meg settled into a chair and began, "We're doing just fine, m'lady, or as well as we can be after what happened. We're staying with some cousins. Matthew is a little better. Molly is the picture of health despite her ordeal. Oh, ma'am, I will never forget how Mister Cartland rescued her from the river. Such a brave man he is! How is he? One reason I came was to pay my respects and thank him again for what he did."

"He's not here, I'm afraid. I don't know where he's gone." Jane could not bring herself to say more. Her feelings for Douglas were just too raw. "I suppose your farm is gone?"

"We got the livestock up the hill, so the goats and chickens and such survived, but the farm is gone. Our only hope is that the new earl, whoever he is, might want to help his tenants rebuild. Otherwise," Meg shrugged sadly, "it's crowded at my cousin's. Already we're none too welcome, but we will make do."

"I'm so sorry." Jane's heart went out to this proud young woman who had worked so hard, yet faced a future far bleaker than Jane's.

"Don't worry about me." Meg lifted her chin with pride. "I'll find a way, I always do. And how are you doing?"

"As well as can be expected, considering ..." She thought of Mama and fought back tears.

"I am so sorry you lost your mother," Meg said gently.

I must be strong. I am not the only one who suffered a tragedy. "Nothing is easy in this life, is it?"

"No, I'm afraid not." Meg hesitated, as if drawing up her courage. "There's a reason why I came, other than to see how you were faring. I have a confession to make."

"I cannot imagine what it is."

"It is this." Meg had been carrying a large cloth bag, which looked much like a pillow slip with something heavy inside. She had set it beside her on the carpet. Now she picked it up, pulled open the top, and thrust it in front of Jane. "Look inside."

Curious, Jane peered into the bag. What she saw sent a wave of shock up her spine. "I can't believe it. The Lansdown jewels!"

"Yes, m'lady, all here in this bag, down to the smallest diamond."

Meg knelt on the floor and upended the bag. A jumble of sparkling jewels poured out and lay in a dazzling heap on Rennie's carpet. "I took them, m'lady, I couldn't help it. That big wall of water was coming, and there was nobody to rescue them but me. I'm so sorry."

Jane knelt next to Meg and stared in awe at the Lansdown jewels strewn before her in all their gleaming glory. "And to think I had just assumed the jewels were gone forever." With cautious fingers, she selected the pearl and amber necklace from the jumble and held it up to the light. "This was my favorite. Look at it sparkle. Isn't it beautiful? I'm so glad you saved it, Meg, and all the jewels. Why are you apologizing?"

"Because ..." Meg bit her lip and hung her head in shame. "I confess I wanted to keep them, even though I knew it was the same as stealing. The thought of keeping them was just so tempting, you see. We wouldn't be poor anymore. We would always have plenty to eat and we could buy a farm and not have to pay rent to a greedy landlord. Begging your pardon, madam, but the earl cheated us for years and that's the truth."

"So why didn't you keep the jewels?"

"I could not." Meg shook her head with regret. "I knew I was stealing. Lately I haven't slept well because my conscience got the better of me. So here they are, ma'am, and I hope you find it in your heart to forgive me."

"Don't be silly, there's nothing to forgive. Let's see now...who else knows you have the jewels?"

"No one but me."

"Are you aware that everyone thinks the jewels were swept away in the flood?"

"Oh, Madam!" Meg sank back on her haunches. "Are you saying I should keep them?"

Jane remained silent, battling with her conscience. Her head spun with the possibilities. Why shouldn't Meg keep the jewels? She and her family would live in comfort the rest of their lives. They were so much more deserving than the next earl in line now that Percy was gone—whoever he might be. She wasn't sure which of the sons would succeed, but what did it matter? He was an Elton, wasn't he? Therefore, he was bound to be as heartless and greedy as all his predecessors and did not deserve the jewels.

On the other hand ... What am I doing?

Jane had a moment of clarity. *Stealing*, that is what she was doing. She remembered her father's words, spoken to her when she was a little girl: "Do the right thing because it is right. This is the magic key to living your life with integrity."

What was the right thing? The answer was clear as crystal. The Lansdown jewels belonged to the Eltons, despicable though they might be. No one else had a right to them, even though they assumed the jewels were lost forever. "Meg, much as it pains me, I must give them back."

"Of course. I knew you would. I so admire your honesty."

Jane smiled ruefully. "You would be better off if I had a little less of it, I'm afraid."

"No, madam. Rest assured you've done the right thing."

The next day, a somber Sir Archibald arrived at Lancaster Hall. Carrying the bag of jewels, Jane met him in the library, where she seated herself and laid the bag on the floor. She would choose just the right moment to reveal her astounding news.

"My dear, you have my sympathy. What a terrible thing. Why, the loss of life in the village of Sudberry alone is unbelievable. So many farms destroyed, too. Whole families simply washed away."

Jane returned a sober thank you. Despite the solicitor's stuffiness and past indifference, she knew he meant his remarks sincerely.

"You are not to worry. The Lansdown fortune is considerable and will now pass to Ludlow Elton, a fine young man from what I have heard, not like ..." The solicitor caught his indiscretion and cleared his throat. "At any rate, Chatfield Court will be restored. So will your dower house, which, as you doubtless know, was completely destroyed. Also, you can still expect the revenue from the estates in Ireland. They are enough to give you an adequately comfortable life from now on. You will be safe and secure in the knowledge you will have a roof over your head and food on the table for your entire lifetime."

Adequately comfortable. Safe and secure. She might as well be dead already. The very thought made her spirits sink to a new low. Poor Sir Archibald actually thought he was cheering her up, so she put a smile on her face and managed an appropriate, "That is very nice to hear."

The solicitor sighed. "It's unfortunate we lost the family jewels, but I suppose they're buried forever in the muck somewhere."

Ah, the perfect opening. Regrets still assailed her, but she knew what she had to do. "I have something to show you, Sir Archibald." She reached for the cloth bag she'd brought with her and set on the floor. With a touch of the dramatic, she upended the bag and spread the contents on one of the library tables. "Come look, sir. The Lansdown jewels."

The solicitor got to his feet and stared in amazement at the glittering sight before him. "Upon my word! I thought they were lost forever."

"Fortunately, they were rescued by one of our servants, Meg Twimby."

"Astounding!"

"*Rescued*," Jane emphasized. "If not for Meg, the jewels would be buried in the mud forever."

Sir Archibald nodded with satisfaction. "I shall see these are returned to Ludlow Elton. Who knows? He might be amenable to giving your servant a small reward."

"That would be most kind." Jane hid her skepticism. An Elton was an Elton. She doubted Meg would ever see so much as a farthing.

After Sir Archibald's departure, Jane stopped by to visit her grandmother, who had yet to leave her bed since she arrived at Lancaster Hall. Jane described her conversation with the family solicitor. "I hated to do it, but I turned the jewels over to him. He will see they go to Ludlow Elton, who's in line to be the next earl."

Granny nodded her approval. "You did the right thing. Your mother would be proud of you."

The thought of her mother filled her with sorrow. "I miss her so much."

"Amelia would be alive today if she hadn't been so stubborn. There were times that woman was as stupid as a post."

"I suppose." Granny didn't fool her. She might sound uncaring, but Jane detected the tremor in her voice when she spoke of her only daughter. Time to change the subject. "Mister Cartland has left."

"For good?"

"He's going to finish Rennie's canal, and then he's going to America."

"You let him go? I thought you loved him."

"Yes, very much but ..." She could not go on.

"I know he loves you," Granny said.

"I suppose he does, but he said we could never be happy together. It's his pride. He thinks I'm rich, which you know very well I am not. He thinks I love being a countess and living in luxury, and having everybody cater to me."

"Well, do you?"

"No! All I really want in this world are Douglas and my horse." She allowed herself a small smile. "In that order, he would be pleased to hear."

"Well, missy, it appears to me you did not do a very good job of telling him so."

"I guess I didn't." Jane paused to gather her thoughts. "I became so depressed talking to Sir Archibald. He meant to be kind, telling me the dower house will be rebuilt, but all I can think of now is how miserable my life is going to be, living under the thumb of the Eltons. Ludlow Elton will inherit, but it doesn't matter which son, they are all awful. Even if they build me a new dower house, I'll feel trapped and lonely for the rest of my life."

"That's nonsense. You're bound to find someone else."

"Even if I do, he won't be Douglas. He's the love of my life, just as Daniel was to you."

"Then it seems to me you ought not to spend the rest of your life living in a place you don't like with people you don't care for. Life is a gamble at best, so if I were you, I would throw caution to the winds and do what I wanted to do." Granny raised a quizzical eyebrow. "Doesn't that make sense?"

"I suppose," Jane responded with a listless shrug.

"Look at what happened to your mother. She didn't have the courage to take her life in her hands and make the most of it. Instead, at the end, she just sat there like a lump, unable to help herself, waiting to die. And so she did."

For a long time, Jane sat mulling Granny's words. She did *not* want to end up like her mother. She *did* want a life of her own. Was it possible? "Ever since Papa sent us the letter, I have wanted to go to America."

"Then for God's sake, go. They won't call you 'countess' in America, but what do you care? I know you. You won't mind giving up your title and all that folderol."

Her mind raced. Why shouldn't she go? She no longer had her mother to worry about. Millicent was going to marry Lord Rennie and live happily ever after. Granny was welcome to stay right here in Lancaster Hall where she would most certainly be treated like a queen.

Jane leaped to her feet and gave Granny a hug. "Why didn't I see it before? You're right. Why should I stay in a place I don't like, living a life I detest? I'm going to see Papa. I'm going to America!"

"Will you tell Douglas?"

"If I can find him." She thought a moment. "But what if I can't? From what I understand, America is an awfully big place."

"Then you will just have to take your chances. I certainly would, rather than sit in that dower house for the next fifty or so years, waiting to die."

Jane smiled wryly. "You put it so bluntly, but you're right. I am not going to sit here like a lump for the rest of my life."

Jane left her grandmother's bedchamber with a new sense of resolve. Without question, she was going to America. Would she ever see Douglas again? Her heart ached at the thought she might not—probably *would* not. Still, as Granny said, life was a gamble and she would just have to take her chances.

Chapter 20

The next few weeks, Jane busied herself preparing for her journey. So much to do. Booking the passage, writing to her father to meet her ship in New York, acquiring an entirely new wardrobe to replace the one she lost, saying goodbye to old friends, many of whom thought she, a mere woman, was insane to attempt such a perilous journey alone. She had made up her mind, though, and nothing would dissuade her. After all, at the end of her journey her father would be waiting. That fact alone kept her from changing her mind.

As for Douglas, she thought of him constantly and desperately wanted him to know that she, too, was going to America. Where was he? She hadn't heard a word. She decided to write him a letter. What an agonizing task it was. She wanted to tell him he was the only man in the world she could ever love, yet pride told her not to grovel. After many attempts and crumpled pieces of note paper, she wrote:

My Dear Mister Cartland,

    I shall soon be sailing to America, leaving title, my so-called "riches," and just about everything else I own behind, including my beloved Beauty.

If that makes me "spoiled rotten" as you put it, as well as "quite imperious," then there is nothing more I can say.

If fate decrees we meet again someday, I can only hope you will look past your nose and see the woman who gave her heart to you without reservation. You still have it. What more can I say?

So it's farewell! I wish you good fortune and hope that someday, somehow, we will meet again upon those far distant shores.

With utmost kind regards,
—*Jane Lansdown*

Having no address, she asked Rennie about Douglas' whereabouts.

"You might try sending it to the Blue Bull Inn. I believe he's there, but then again, I'm not sure. They're building a new canal farther north, so maybe that's where he is."

"Could he already have gone to America?"

Rennie shrugged. "Who knows? I suppose he could be halfway across the Atlantic by now."

With an aching heart, she sent the letter to the Blue Bull Inn. Douglas might not ever receive it, but what else could she do?

One day Bruta came to see her. Jane greeted her cordially. "Are you still planning on going to America?"

Her former lady's maid nodded briskly. "Yes, I am, madam. I've heard you are, too."

"You heard correctly."

"Then I shall be your lady's maid."

"But ... but ..." Jane launched into an explanation as to why such an arrangement would not be a good idea. She planned to go alone and could manage quite well, thank you. She was giving up her title and had no need of a lady's maid or any kind of servant whatsoever.

Bruta listened with arms folded across her chest, her chin set with determination. After Jane finished, she declared, "I don't care if you won't be a countess anymore. You still must dress properly, and from what I have observed of your careless habits, you certainly cannot cope on your own."

Jane continued to argue, but somewhere along the way she realized she had lost the battle. But had she really lost? She had not looked forward to making the journey alone. Bruta could actually be of great help. Not only that, her attitude toward Bruta had done a turnaround since the lady's maid confessed her unwilling part in procuring the oil of pennyroyal. Through new eyes, Jane perceived Bruta as a hardworking, loyal servant. She might lack many of the social graces, but Jane would be lucky to have her. "Very well, you're hired for the passage. As to what will happen when we reach our destination, I'm not sure. I can't promise a thing."

Bruta broke into a satisfied smile. "We shall worry about that when we get there, m'lady."

Jane started to protest she would not be called m'lady anymore, then changed her mind. She would be wasting her breath. As always, Bruta would do as she pleased.

On the day before Jane was to begin her journey, Meg Twimby came visiting again. The former servant wore a new dress and new shoes. Her face shone with excitement. "Wait until you hear my news, m'lady,"

"Well, do sit down and tell me."

"Sir Archibald came to see me. You would never guess who came with him."

"Tell me."

"It was Ludlow Elton, the new Earl of Lansdown. He wanted to express his gratitude that I saved the Lansdown jewels. Can you imagine? The earl himself came to my cousin's cottage. He was ever so kind, and I must say, downright humble when he said he was aware I didn't have to give the jewels back, that I easily could have kept them for myself with no one the wiser."

"I'm glad, Meg. I know we did the right thing."

"I haven't got to the best part. Listen to this, m'lady. He gave me a reward of five hundred pounds! Think of it!" Meg beamed with happiness. "I keep wanting to pinch myself. I was so worried, but now, thanks to his lordship, we shall have plenty of money for food and clothing, and we can buy another farm."

Words failed her. Jane threw her arms around her former servant and gave her a hug. "You have no idea how relieved I am. Now I can go to America without a care in the world." Well, almost. She remembered Douglas.

"What about Beauty?" Meg asked.

"I must leave her behind." Jane felt an acute sense of loss, thinking she was about to lose her beautiful horse. "When I booked passage on the *Columbia*, the captain refused to take Beauty. The ship is too small, you see ..." Her voice broke and she could not go on.

"Oh, madam, I am so sorry."

"I keep telling myself she'll be in good hands. With Timothy around, she'll always receive the best of care and, hopefully, when I arrive in America, I shall buy a new horse." She smiled. "I will never find another Beauty, but they do have horses over there."

When the visit was over, Meg departed with a grin on her face. "Thank you for all your help, Lady Lansdown."

"No, don't call me that anymore." Jane shook her head decisively. "I most definitely will not bring my title to America. As of today, you have seen the last of Lady Lansdown."

Dressed in her new brown wool redingote with matching hat and muff, Jane caught a sniff of salty sea air as she and Bruta stepped from Lord Rennie's coach onto the dock at Liverpool. With eager eyes, she took in the sights of one of the busiest ports in England: docks teeming with activity, a forest of masts stretching as far as the eye could see. Directly ahead, workers were loading the *Columbia*, a small ship of two hundred eighty-two tons, which would carry her from Liverpool to New York. The sight of the graceful ship caused excitement to course through her veins, tinged with an indelible sadness. She was leaving England forever. Only yesterday she had bid Granny and Millicent a tearful goodbye, given Beauty her last carrot and kiss on her nose. She missed them already. When, if ever, would she see them again? How hard this was—uprooting her whole life, leaving family behind, plus every friend she ever had, perhaps forever. *And Douglas.* She felt a wretched sense of loss whenever she thought of him, which was most of the time. He had never answered her letter.

A crazy thought popped into her head. Perhaps he was here! Her pulse quickened in anticipation. Perhaps he *had* received her letter. Perhaps Rennie had told him the name of the ship and he had hastened to Liverpool to meet her. Eagerly, her gaze swept the docks. Nothing. *You fool.* Her luck could never be that good. She might have known.

Soon after the *Columbia* sailed from Liverpool, the pitch and roll of the small ship caused an increasing queasiness in Jane's stomach. At first she ignored it, but when a wretched wave of nausea struck, she was forced to rush to the railing where, in decidedly unladylike fashion, she lost her breakfast. By this time, she felt so terrible that she did not care for her dignity and could only groan in misery as Bruta helped her below to her cabin. She spent the next five days lying prone on her bed, so sick from constant nausea that she feared at first she would die, later fearing she would not.

What would it matter if she died? She lay in a state of utter misery, picturing how they would sew her poor, ravaged body into a canvas bag and dump it into the sea. Who would care? Certainly not Douglas. He wouldn't even know she was dead, and wouldn't care if he did know. Of course, she looked forward to seeing her father again—if, by some remote chance, she happened to survive—but still, she knew in her heart she would mourn her lost love forever and never be truly happy again.

At least she had Bruta. Thank God for Bruta, who suffered not a trace of a queasy stomach and devoted herself to giving her suffering mistress the utmost of tender care. "You must eat," Bruta admonished. "I shall bring you a bowl of broth."

"Oh, God, no!" Jane moaned and declared, "If you mention food again, I shall die."

"You are not going to die, madam." Bruta laid a cool compress across Jane's forehead. "You will soon start feeling better."

"No, I won't. I shall never be well again."

Bruta was right. After a few days, the nausea disappeared. Though weak as a kitten, Jane felt well enough to climb to the deck and clutch the railing. She breathed deeply of the fresh salt air, thinking nothing had ever smelled so good. Even so, she could not shake her feeling of sadness. She leaned over the railing to watch a school of dolphins leaping alongside the ship. They appeared to be smiling. She wished she could smile like the dolphins, but how could she? She was haunted by the constant remembrance that Douglas was gone forever. She would never see him again.

Even the thought of seeing her father could not lift her from her doldrums.

One bright morning, after weeks at sea, the *Columbia* sailed into the sparkling waters of New York harbor. Despite the seasickness she'd suffered and her heartache over Douglas, Jane stood on the deck and watched with high anticipation as her ship approached the South Street docks. America at last! She would see her father again. She would get a new start. Someday, perhaps, she would forget Douglas Cartland ever existed.

But not now, she thought, hating herself for having such dreary thoughts on what was supposed to be a glorious day.

A sparse crowd stood waiting on the dock. Was her father among them? She hoped word had spread quickly that a ship had arrived. She searched for a tall, stoop-shouldered figure with white hair. No, she didn't see him. Again her gaze skimmed over the crowd, this time catching a glimpse of a man with dark hair, holding the reins of his horse. She could not see his face clearly, but something about him ... the way he was standing—at ease, yet confident and alert. That horse ... it looked like Beauty. In fact, exactly like Beauty.

It cannot be ...

The ship edged close to the dock. Crew members tossed thick ropes ashore, to be tied to the stanchions. Closer now, with disbelieving eyes, Jane looked at the man again.

It was Douglas Cartland, and the horse whose reins he held was Beauty.

Why was he here? *How* did he get here? Jane waited in stunned disbelief and an agony of impatience until the gangplank was lowered and she could leave the ship.

By the time she stepped ashore, Douglas had tethered Beauty at a distance and stood waiting beside the gangplank, amusement twinkling in the depths of his warm brown eyes. "Good morning, Countess. Did you have a pleasant journey?"

"I am stunned."

Douglas took her arm and led her away from the gangplank where Bruta, burdened with luggage, was about to disembark. He turned to her. "I received your letter and returned to Lancaster Hall the very day you left. Rennie told me what ship you were on."

"How could you be here ahead of me?" She was still trying to pull her spinning thoughts together.

"It's not so impossible. I hastened to catch up with you. Rennie suggested I take Beauty along. Somehow we would get her on the ship. I was too late. By the time I reached Liverpool, the *Columbia* had already sailed."

"Then how—?"

"To my good fortune, I found another ship leaving for New York the very next day. I sailed on the *Belfast*. At four hundred ninety-one tons, she is twice the size of the *Columbia* and nearly twice as fast. Captain Bunker gladly allowed me to bring Beauty along. Thunder, too."

She managed a casual, "Oh, really? But why would you want to join a spoiled rotten woman like me who's been catered to hand and foot all her life?"

With a crooked smile, he replied, "I read every word of your letter. You convinced me." The smile disappeared. Suddenly serious, he cupped her chin tenderly in his warm hand. In a voice shaking with emotion, he continued, "I thought I could put you out of my mind, but I could not. That's because I love you with all my heart and I want you to be my wife. What I said was wrong. Remain a countess if you like. I don't care what you're called as long as I have you by my side."

Her heart swelled with unprecedented feeling. "You're sure?"

"Positive. Be aware that I don't have a fortune, nor is it likely I shall ever have one. I shall do my best, though. We will never be poor. Surely there are canals to be built in America, and I'm the one to build them. So there you have it. Will you marry me?"

"Yes, yes, yes!" She gave him a joyful smile and threw her arms around his neck.

The sound of appreciative shouts, whistles, and foot stomps rose up from the dock workers busy unloading the *Columbia*. The man and woman standing on the dock seemed to be engaged in more than a simple welcome embrace. In fact, the way he was devouring her with kisses left no doubt as to what would happen once the two of them were finally alone.

Epilogue

New York City, 1825

From the day it was built by renowned canal engineer, Douglas Cartland, the two-story Georgian style mansion that overlooked a bend in the East River perfectly suited the needs of the happy, growing family that lived there. Now, on a warm summer's night, the sounds of a toast rang out from the elegant dining room. Wineglasses were raised. "To you!" came a chorus of voices. "Happy thirty-fifth birthday!"

Mistress Jane Cartland stood to acknowledge the toast in her honor. "This is the best birthday of my life." She raised her glass and gave a nod to the distinguished, white-haired gentleman who sat to her left. "I raise my glass to you, Papa. I am so proud of your success." Her father had expanded his business. Five stores already and more to come.

"Here is to my two sweet children." She held her glass toward three-year-old Georgina, her blonde, cherub-faced daughter who sat next to her grandfather; then to Nicholas, her bright-eyed son who was seven and much resembled his father. They had both been given special permission to stay up late to celebrate their mother's birthday.

"Millicent and Rennie." Jane nodded toward her radiant sister and dear Rennie who recently arrived from England on a much-awaited visit. "After ten years, you two still look like newlyweds. Imagine! Six children!"

"We're not done yet." Millicent gave a loving glance at her husband.

Jane raised her glass high and looked upward. "A toast to you, Granny. How I wish you could be here, but in a way you are." Jane would never forget her grandmother's sage advice which she now was passing on to her own children.

"To my dear husband." Jane nodded at Douglas, who sat to her right, her heart filling with love and pride. He was still as handsome as ever and over the years had acquired a polished veneer. Not only was he considered an expert in his field, his work on the Erie Canal, as well as others, now earned him a substantial income.

Just then, Bruta entered the dining room. She had not changed a bit. Now the children's nanny, she firmly announced, "They have stayed up late enough. I am putting them to bed."

"Of course, Bruta." It seemed so long ago that Jane wanted to get rid of her brusque, sullen lady's maid. Now she couldn't do without her and treasured Bruta's loyalty and dedication to her work.

When the children were gone, Jane turned again to her husband, but before she could speak, Douglas stood. He held a velvet case in his hand and extended it to Jane. "A little something for your birthday."

Jane took the case and opened it, wondering what sort of trinket lay inside. When she saw the contents, she gasped. "I cannot believe it!" She reached for the pearl and amber necklace she had always loved and held it up by its gleaming gold chain for all to see. "Douglas, how did you get this? How did you know?"

"Meg Twimby told me how much you loved the necklace."

Douglas placed a warm kiss on her cheek. "So, on my last trip to England, I went to see Ludlow Elton, the Earl of Lansdown, who is not a bad fellow, by the way. After a certain amount of negotiation, he agreed to sell me the necklace. He did make clear he would sell a part of the Lansdown jewels only for you, Jane. 'You deserved it,' he said."

"How can I thank you?" She was quite overwhelmed.

"We will discuss that later, Countess," he whispered in her ear, then aloud, "Let's see what it looks like around that lovely throat." He stood behind her, slipped the necklace around her neck and clasped it. The light touch of his fingers sent little tingles along her spine, reminding her once again what a wise decision she made when she took Granny's advice and said goodbye forever to her title and all that other folderol.

Shirley Kennedy has published Regency romances for both Ballantine and Signet. Born and raised in Fresno, California, she has lived in Colorado, Texas, California, Bogota (Colombia) and Calgary (Alberta, Canada), where she earned a BS in Computer Sciences. Before returning to her first love, writing, she worked as a computer programmer/systems analyst for several years. Shirley currently resides in Las Vegas, Nevada where she belongs to The Romance Writers of America, Sisters in Crime, and Las Vegas Writers Group. Her historical romance *Heartbreak Trail* was published by Camel Press in 2011.

You can find Shirley online at www.shirleykennedy.com.